Crimson Kashmir

The Devotion

This novel is dedicated to my father Kunwar Rajendra Singh whose simple tenets of honesty make me a very proud son. More importantly, I as a soldier am totally indebted to numerous nameless brave soldiers of the Indian Army, whose valour in adversities is unknown to the Indian public at large, the resolve to pen this story would otherwise have been difficult. It's a unique privilege to command them. White men who had the God's fate to do so, almost a century back, would'nt be so melancholy in their yearnings for them. The Indian soldier's faith in the goodness of the Indian part of the sub-continent, its vibrant culture, freedom to opine and absorb the goodness of varied faiths, gives him a unique unidentifiable profile in courage to meet the unknown enemy, motivated by an alien thought, as summed up in the poem below:

Beware you enemies across the Wells of Badr,
Beware of the fury of the Southern Wind.
From the fury of Southern Wind - beware,
Will emerge Gabriel's horse - victorious.

– Old Arabic Saying

Crimson Kashmir

Col. M.S. Jaswal

Manas Publications
New Delhi-110002 (INDIA)

Manas Publications
(Publishers, Distributors, Importers & Exporters)
4858, Prahlad Street,
24, Ansari Road, Darya Ganj,
New Delhi - 110 002 (INDIA)
Ph.: 23260783, 23265523:, 23842660 (R)
Fax: 011-23272766
E-mail: manaspublications@vsnl.com

ISBN 81-7049-300-5
Rs. 495/-

Typeset at
Manas Publications

Printed in India at
Nice Printing Press, Delhi
and Published by Mrs Suman Lata for
Manas Publications, 4858, Prahlad Street,
24, Ansari Road, Darya Ganj,
New Delhi - 110 002 (INDIA)

Author's Note

From my bored wooden table
Was born this crazy fable.

The parts are near to our hearts,
For the memoirs they kick start.

Flashes come out jumbled,
The brain agrees and mumbles.

It's a slammer,
Nail bang on hammer.

But alas, no living, perceived or dead,
Has actually broken the bread.

It's only a foggy old tale,
For you all to regale.

Dear shrew,
The brew is definitely not true.

Author

Contents

List of Maps

Glossary/Abbreviations

Abbu	-	Father
Adam Khor	-	Man-eater
Age	-	Ahead
Ali Baba aur challis chor	-	Ali Baba and forty thieves
Allah Tala	-	Merciful God
Alu/Aloo	-	Potatos
Angrezi	-	English language
Ammi/Amma	-	Mother
Ammi jan	-	Dear mother
Apne	-	Our
Ayo re Gorkhali	-	Gorkha's are coming, war cry
Azadi	-	Freedom
Baba	-	Old man
Babu	-	Gentlemen, clerk
Babugiri	-	Officialdom
Badhai	-	Congratulations
Badshah	-	Emperor
Bakarwal	-	Indian Gypsy, goat herder
Bai	-	Attendant woman
Baje	-	Grandfather (Nepalese)
Baniya	-	A miser or money lender
Barat	-	Wedding procession

Barati's	-	People attending the wedding procession
Bayen	-	Left
Begum	-	Married woman, stately address
Bhag	-	Run
Bhai	-	Brother
Bhainchod	-	Sister-fucker
Bhangra	-	A rhythmic Punjabi dance
Bharna	-	Increase, advance
Bihari	-	A man from Indian State of Bihar
Bindi	-	Dot, on forehead of a woman
Biryani	-	Mutton and rice baked dish
Bukhari	-	A room heating stove
Burqa	-	Veil
Chacha/Chachu	-	Father's younger brother
Chaddar	-	A cotton sheet
Chamar	-	A low caste man, derogatory remark
Chunni	-	A fine muslin scarf
Chappati	-	A flat Indian bread, roti
Char	-	Four
Chavvis	-	Twenty-six
Chowkidar	-	A guard
Dar-ul-Islam	-	Land of believers
Dar-ul-harb	-	Land of non- believers
Dera	-	House, a place to stay
Deobandi	-	Follower of deoband Muslim philosophy.

Dharma	-	Religion, moral code
Dhoti	-	A cotton garb
Diwali	-	Indian festival of lights
Do	-	Two, let, give
Durga Mata	-	Hindu Goddess
Dusheri	-	A variety of mango
Dushman	-	Enemy
Elam	-	Free country (Tamil)
Falus	-	Underhand money
Fariad	-	Request
Fatwa	-	Edict
Fauji	-	Soldier
Fidayeen	-	Suicide attack
Firan	-	Long overcoat (Kashmir, India)
Garam	-	Hot
Gora	-	White
Gosht	-	Meat
Gudiya	-	Doll
Gujjar	-	An animal herder
Guruji ab kya hoga	-	Teacher what will happen now
Gya dul	-	Gone fallen
Halal	-	A method of slaughtering animals
Hajoor	-	Sir
Havaldar	-	Rank in Indian Army
Hari bibi	-	Low-caste woman in Pakistan
Hasina man Jayegi	-	Idiom, "The lady will agree"
Hijra	-	Eunuch

Hum to chutia nikle	-	Idiom, Stating that I was a fool
Hukum	-	Order
Id-ul-Zuha	-	A Muslim festival
Inpa (New Word)	-	State of suspicion between India and Pakistan
Izzat	-	Honour
Jan	-	Life, dear
Janam Kundli	-	Horoscope
Janbaz	-	Fearless
Jaldi	-	Quickly
Jamaiti	-	Political arm, propagator of Islam
Jawan	-	Young, soldier
Jhannum	-	Hell
Jihadis	-	Participants of Jihad
Jihad	-	A holy war
Ji hazoor	-	Yes sir
Junglee	-	One living in jungles, not well bred
Kafir	-	Non-believers of Muslim faith
Kaftan	-	A dress
Kala	-	Black
Kali	-	Hindu Goddess of destruction
Kameez	-	Shirt
Kamina	-	Scoundrel, Cheat
Karna/karo	-	To do
Kashmiriat	-	A way of life of Kashmiri people

Kawa	-	Kashmiri herbal tea
Khakhi	-	Earthly, yellow colour
Khalsa	-	A devout Sikh
Khate	-	Eat food
Khudda	-	God
Khukri	-	A curved Gurkha knife
Khuni	-	Murderer, Bloody
Kitne	-	How many
Kuch	-	Some
Kulcha	-	Fried bread
Kurta	-	A half shirt
Kutta	-	Dog
Lagao	-	Put on
Laga rehe	-	Keep on
Ladkon	-	Men
Maaf	-	Pardon, Excuse
Madad	-	Help
Madarasa	-	A Muslim school
Madarchod	-	Mother-fucker
Magar Kya	-	Then what
Mannat	-	Wish, idol of pre-muslim Arabia
Manus	-	Men/human beings
Maulvi	-	Teacher of Quran
Maulana	-	A title of Muslim clerics
Maut	-	Death
Mein	-	Inside
Mukti Bahini	-	A Bangladeshi Freedom Fighter Force in 1971
Mujahidin	-	A God's warrior

Mujra	-	Nautch dance
Mullah	-	A Muslim preacher
Mukhbir	-	An informer
Mussalman	-	Of Muslim faith
Nallah	-	A small rivulet
Namak	-	Salt
Namaz	-	Time for reading Quran
Nan (or Naan)	-	Baked flat bread
Naswar	-	Narcotic, generally opium
Namak haram	-	Traitor
Nunchai	-	Salt tea
Pahar	-	Mountain
Paki	-	Acronym for a Pakistani
Pandit	-	Hindu priest, a caste class
Pansari	-	Seller of utility items
Par	-	On
Pathani	-	A Pathan
Peeth	-	One's back, above buttocks
Purėe/Puri	-	Fried Indian flat bead
Purohit	-	Hindu priest
Pyaz Sabji	-	Onion vegetable
Randi	-	A whore
Rogan Josh	-	Coloured mutton
Roti	-	Indian flat bread, chappati
Safed chamri	-	White skin, women (derogatory)
Saheed	-	Martyred
Sahib	-	Sir
Salwar Kameez	-	A women's dress

Sardarji	-	A Sikh gentleman
Sarhad par	-	Across the border
Saris	-	Indian women dress
Sahayak	-	Helper, officer's battle-mate
Shabash	-	Good, felicitation
Shahadat	-	Martyrdom
Shariat	-	Muslim religious codes
Subedar	-	A rank in Indian military
Tanzeem	-	Organisation
Tandav	-	Dance
Tir/ Teer	-	Arrow
Tongas	-	Horse drawn carts
Toosh	-	Wool of mountain deer/goat
Unka	-	Their
Wazwan	-	Kashmiri feast, food preparation
Yagna	-	A fire ceremony
Ya Ali	-	Muslim battle cry
Zannat	-	Heaven

Abbreviations

BN	-	Battalion
BSF	-	Border Security Force
DET	-	Detachment
GR	-	Gurkha Rifles, Grid Reference
GOC	-	General Officer Commanding
HQ	-	Headquarter
H	-	Hour
HMG	-	Heavy Machine Gun

MMG	-	Medium Machine Gun
Km	-	Kilometre
ISI	-	Inter Services Intelligence
ICS	-	Indian Civil Service
LMG	-	Light Machine Gun
LoC	-	Line of Control
OC	-	Officer Commanding
RAJRIF	-	Rajputana Rifles
RL	-	Rocket Launcher
2IC	-	Second-in-Command

Main Characters

God's Men

Asif Gul*	-	Commander El Jihadi Special Force Group, chief coordinator

Kashmir Valley

Doctor Mehboob Shah*	-	Terrorist Sympathiser
Khushbu	-	Sympathiser of Tahir
Nazir Lone	-	Battalion Commander, *Hizbul Mujahidin,* Lolab Valley
Rasool Bhat*	-	Commander *Freedom Fighters,* Kashmir Valley
Reshab Mehmood	-	Terrorist master guide
Risal Mehmood	-	Terrorist guide, Reshab's cousin brother
Tahir	-	Commander *Muslim Janbaz Force,* Srinagar
Usman	-	Tahir's lieutenant

Pakistani

Brigadier Altaf Ghaur*	-	Chief Field Coordinator, Kashmir Desk
Maulana Amjad Ali	-	Deepcover ISI agent in Kashmir Valley
Jalal Omar	-	District Commander *Harkut-Ul-Ansar*

Captain Ahmed Khan	-	Third Special Services Group, Pakistan Army
General Ibrahim Lodhi	-	Officer on Special Duty, Kashmir Desk
Major Irfan	-	Jihadi launch group coordinator, in charge Pakistan Post Kabul
Rani Sahida	-	Pakistan International Airlines employee, Thailand
Subedar Mastan Gilani	-	Post Commander, Pakistani Post Kabul on LoC

Indian

Captain Imran Khan	-	Officer in Indian Army
Colonel Mushtaq	-	OC 762 Army HQ Liaison Unit, Srinagar
Colonel PP Singh	-	Commanding Officer, 14 Rajputana Rifles
Colonel VS Thapa	-	Commanding Officer, 1/9 GR
Grover	-	Indian Intelligence Officer, Sri Lanka
Havaldar Pun	-	Commander, Number Four ambush, 1/9 GR
Inspector Pathania	-	Intelligence Officer, J&K police
Lieutenant General Rocky Dass	-	GOC 15 Corps
Major Jesse*	-	Company Commander, 14 Rajputana Rifles
Major Shamsher Singh	-	Post Commander Post Khukri on LoC, 1/9 GR
Major Sunil Yadav	-	Company Commander in Rashtriya Rifles
Nafisa*	-	Bakarwal Girl, in Srinagar University

* Profiled in the chapter 'Grandpa Stories'.

Naib Subedar Gurung Bahadur	-	Overall commander of ambushes of 1/9 GR
Nurie	-	Nafisa's uneducated younger sister in village Nusur
Rifleman Gobar Singh	-	Number Two of LMG Det, Number Four ambush, 1/9 GR
Sardar Ranjit Singh	-	Public call office owner
Sibal Kumar	-	Indian Intelligence officer, Thailand

Others

Rashmi Srivastava	-	Investigative journalist, Sri Lanka

1
Grandpa Stories

"In the weave of past, we live our present.
The present weave is a peep into past."

— **Jesse**

Bangladesh/ Pakistan

The Indians wanted him to play the role of a quintessential ape-man.

He had been tied to a termite-infested pole for the last seventy-two hours.

Tied to that yellow teak stake, totally nude, for the last three days, he felt like a quintessential ape-man.

The captors had removed everything. He adorned nothing. Only his hobnailed army leather boots provided some succour to his stark naked body. Around him were his half-naked men, the men he had commanded. All were looking down in shame.

His remaining forty-six odd men surrounded twenty-two Bangladeshi females. Aping him in ape-like faith they also were without a stitch, totally nude, their lush ripe bodies shimmering in the fierce sun. More importantly, they were dead and he alive, tied to a teak stake amidst them.

These lovely creatures had been dead for over three days, sadly including his favourite 18-year-old Amina Haq, hacked to pieces.

It was a gory sight and his nostrils quantified the degree of stench. It was awesome, ten at scale of ten.

Their rotting bloated bodies gushed out stinking gases, which hung in the still air around them. Humid conditions, despite the winter-cold had advanced the decomposition. Their pyrolytic putrid flesh was melting out of their bodies. White shining maggots, big, medium and small, all were having a field day, oozing out of their noses, mouths and their vaginas, enlarged by his troops repeated use. Those now dead but once such handpicked handsome living ladies had been their most effective shields against *Mukti Bahini* attacks and they had slowly become a gateway to vent their frustrations with fiery semen and other warlike juices.

In the earlier surprise attack, Indians had killed 82 of his men. Twenty-two of these women had also died.

God only knew by whose fire!

He had not chopped his Amina. But who had perpetuated this dastardly act? His English college educated Amina, haute girl of Dacca, cute, demure Amina, the eldest daughter of the richest traitorous local landlord. She was a girl of big O's, O smile, O buttocks and O bust and only if her father had not been a traitor, a *Mukti Bahini* cockroach, he would have sanctified that big beautiful O to his life. He had loved the big 'O' of her cute round face when he had punctured her the first time. The same 'O' now mocked him, fixed, immobile, resting on a small rock, just below his earlier instrument of terror, less her luscious body, God knows dumped where.

The previous shameless stomach crawling *Bengali* ants wanted them dead.

Local villagers had surrounded the tiny hillock in millions. Brothers and sisters of ants and larvae in sheer numbers. They had come like swarm of flies, immediately after the last shot had been fired and he had surrendered.

What the hell could he do without any orders to the contrary?

The relief forces had run into a sickening *Mukti Bahini* ambush about five kilometres to his rear. The event had quickened his resolve to lay down arms. A few men had run out in sheer panic, only to be chopped into pieces by endless civilians. His rifle company had watched helplessly as the deserters screamed for mercy and his intervention. However, he was helpless. He had only adequate ammunition for self-defence, approximately hundred rounds per man. Not adequate for a rescue foray but enough to save his precious body being shamelessly dismembered and displayed as a shopping mall carcass. Therefore, they had stuck to their defenses to be rescued.

The Scheduled Caste regiment of the Indians had saved them from certain butchery by frenzied locals but those sly Indians had also ensured his constant humiliation.

For three days, he had cried, naked, tied to the pole. His tears fell on his Captain's epaulettes lying on his feet. His sacred epaulettes lay soiled on his feet, in puddle of his urine and excreta; just ahead the open grinning fixated mouth of his once lovely Amina. Till, all his men had fainted due to hunger, thirst, putrid smell of nausea and death, and then only did the *chamar* Indians remove them from the scene.

This was no way to treat soldiers.

So what if his troops had indulged in some pillage.

All was fair in war.

Only few Bengali women of traitorous locals had been interned. What was a big deal if few had been raped. In any case most had willingly compromised. They had fattened on their company's lavish food where none existed in the countryside. Why the hell that black skinny Indian Hindu Major had made such a hue and cry over it? He knew why. Only to humiliate the glorious Pakistan Army and belittle the Muslim warriors. Fuckers will pay. He had studied law and knew the rights of soldiers and citizens in full measure. He will raise it as violation of Geneva Conventions.

The Indians will be made to pay.

Despite his rising newfound blind hatred for his captors, that ever-invasive offensive smell of his earlier dead captives never left him. It became the lavender of the balance of his miserable life.

The rotting odour of human flesh clung to him in his depressed awakening, sleep and dreams in equal proportion. He even embraced pure vegetarianism, much against the tenets of his family ethos but that smell of rotting human flesh never left him. One day after an agonizing sleepless night, at a family reunion, someone accidentally served him muttonchops. He screamed at the sight of perceived human parts. He screamed at fleshy lumps of Amina. He screamed and screamed till his throat bled.

He screamed everyday, till he died five years later.

His wife could never console her teenaged son after that. She watched in alarm her once bubbly Punjabi male family mascot; withdraw inwards, gulping his shame and anger. How it happened, why it happened, was not acceptable to the young man who had lived each day just to catch a fleeting glimpse of his father. He lost hope in any miraculous positive intervention by his Gods as his countless daily prayers were left unattended. He was shattered in faith. He reduced his tortured fatherly pangs, by clutching and staring endlessly at the photo frame of his once handsome father, in full Army uniform, whenever he could.

He would never forgive those who had reduced his father into that pathetic state.

He dreamt and sought revenge, hour by hour, twenty-four times a day.

Kashmir, India

At that precise instant she learnt that she was unkempt, dirty and ugly.

One of the most beautiful girls she had ever espied upon of her own age was playing along the bed of a small freshwater stream. She had adorned a pink lace frock and held an even cuter doll in her hands.

That fairy's parents were lounging on chairs a little distance away and her *abbu* was serving them sumptuous meat. She had never smelled the likes of them before and a small morsel she had slyly tasted when no one was looking by dipping her dirty fingers was out of heaven. Her father had angrily shooed her off.

But beyond all that, what she wanted the most was that *gudiya* in that girl's hand.

Bravely she went up to her. Conscious of her tattered clothes, she pointed towards the doll and said, "Give me that." She stared at that godly girl, to will her into submission.

The girl in the pink frock glanced at her and struck her tongue out, "Go away, you beggar. You have to study to get a doll. Papa presented it to me when I came first in my class."

Disappointed, but not in the least shedding her resolve to possess the captivating doll, the little beggar girl lunged and a howling fight started. A stunning slap resounded on her soft cheeks, as her *abbu* pulled her off the lovely girl, who was desperately clinging to her favourite doll.

She howled and cried, "I want that *gudiya*."

Her father cringed, apologized and lay on the feet of the master when he came running to investigate. The master on hearing the story, supported a curious smile on his face and entreated, "Baby, give her the doll, I will get you a bigger and a better one."

"No," she screamed in protest. "I got it because I came first in my class." She was vehement in her reaction.

"No baby, no," cooed her father. He whispered something into her cute little lobes. She was nodding silently to the tune of each soothing word being fed to her unsoothing ears. She loved her papa too much to refuse him, despite desperate yearning for the doll clutched tightly in her hands. She looked back towards the defiant beggar girl, tried to smile but failed miserably. Then she did what a child of her age could do best without a parental prompt. With a look of disgust and pure hatred, she threw her doll at the beggar girl.

The astounded beggar girl whooped in surprised joy and picked the deserted doll up in one swoop and before her *abbu* could react, she was running up the slopes, with her prize. At each step, she resolved, "I will study, I will study so I will get more such dolls".

Later, in her mud thatched house she told her *abbu* of her dreams. The illiterate old man broke down and cried.

Uttaranchal, India

Atop the world, atop the mystic and sacred mountains.

They were nestled in the Himalayas.

His father dressed in his scarlet white *dhoti* with his big hairy naked chest bounded by the sacred black thread, sat cross-legged on a big black stone. He sat similarly attired, minus the sacred thread and the hairy chest. The holy *yagna* was in its last gasps of formal completion and with each Sanskrit incantation, both threw mixtures of aphrodite-blessed foods in the holy fire to appease the plethora of unrelenting Indic Gods.

Through the haze and blur of leaping crimson flames, he could see from top of their hillock the plains of mother Ganges. The vast vestige of an ancient civilization, the focal point of his motherland, lay before him. This was his mother's womb, the womb that had nurtured and bred millions like him before. He was very proud of his culture, his religion and the land, which had fed likes of his generation for five thousand years before him. To have similar beliefs for five millennia, good or bad, withstand the fissures and pressures of gentle Buddha or even gentler Mahavira or survive the cruel sword of Islam and the monetary subversion of the suave and smooth talking children of Christ, calm the influences of ten gurus, something fundamentally had to be good in his religion. He was sure that it was not based on collective fear, paranoid hysteria for *kafirs* or heathens or divine salvation or retribution from an unknown evil.

Who could question a way of life?

It was the way of nature.

It was the way of their beliefs.

When his religious contemporaries were eating uncooked savage foods, wrapped in animal skins indicative of their level of development, his patron saints were churning scientific treatises, one a day, still stumping now these advanced societies.

How come they had stolen a march over them? To survive them was still very remarkable.

He belonged to the original religion if not the race, of the only earliest recorded religion in the world, the oldest surviving one. This was his land, the mother of existence. He was a proud, staunch, *Sanatan Dharmi.*

His father turned to him and with trembling fingers put the sacred thread around his shoulders, across his back. From the middle of it hung a small flat silver amulet with three golden lines running across its horizontal plane. He kissed it and bowed his forehead to embrace its holiness.

His little empty head nodded vigorously as if he understood all the actions of his ancient father. "This is your first step into manhood. This is the first step to your religion. Do no evil. Do good to others. Do good to the Mother Nature, which feeds you. Guard your *dharma*. To guard your *dharma* you have to guard your beliefs, for what you live for, for what you desire for, for what you love for," stated his father in a gentle tone that his father wanted him to understand.

In fact, at that point, he understood almost nothing.

When they came down from the mountaintop after four days of holy hibernation, their world was devastated.

The village had been razed to the ground. His family temple dedicated to Lord Shiva, their six hundred-year-old sanctum of prayers lay desecrated and destroyed. His mother and his elder sister were missing. Grim faces of state armed police personnel could never tell him actually of what had happened to his dear ones. Those were very sad days of religious riots. His smiling, vibrant, happy father aged overnight and a few days later died of shock. The proud village *Brahmin* had died a pitiable old broken man. He then painfully understood the meaning of each word his father had wanted him to understand.

He only remembered that before leaving for hills to north, a *mullah* had visited the village from Pakistan.

Kashmir, India

"Coward, coward," chanted the children, as he could not muster enough courage to jump across a three-feet-wide water channel.

"Coward, coward," chanted the girls, as he shrieked while running away, escaping the dread of a caterpillar thrown at him by his classmates.

"Coward, coward," chanted Sikander, as he fainted dissecting a frog in his High School biology class.

Yes, he was a shameless coward and the truth was not painful.

He was afraid of all evil, all pain, all misgivings and all ridicules.

He was a confirmed coward.

He loved being a coward.

It was safe being a coward.

Why should anyone take a decision that could bring about a torment in otherwise peaceful life? Who had told his crazy father to just get up and charge across the expanse of the battlefield and land up dead? Why take such stupid decisions? Let others do that dreadful work for you. It was nice to be a coward. Cowards don't have to decide. They live.

Crying unashamedly, he had told the sum of his agonies to his loving *ammi*. But his *ammi*, lovely soft, crooning beautiful *ammi* told him to ignore all those fools and only concentrate on his studies. She had promises to fulfill to her dead husband.

Ignore the fools, his intelligent brain had reasoned.

But his heart reasoned otherwise. It pumped up an alien desire. He wanted to emulate Sikander, the brave Sikander, and the heart-throb of all known Muslim girls in school.

Sikander the brave had thrown stones at Indian patrols, ever since he was 13. He was expelled from school when he slipped his hand up the skirt of a Hindu girl who had defied the *Islamic* dress code. Though out of school, he was his hero, his idol.

Chants of *azadi* had shaken his beliefs. Muslim brotherhood from Turkey to Kashmir was his vision. The government repression, when it came, created many incidents, which made him spit at anything Indian.

At the Srinagar Medical College, he became a slave of his High School fail zealot, Sikander. Mother constantly scolded him and pleaded with him to avoid *jihadis.* "This bloody bread you eat comes from India. The money, which I get, is Indian. Your brave father had died fighting Pakistanis in the 1971 war in this valley. He was honoured," she had screamed, raved and shouted.

He remained deaf. Deaf as a dead dodo, he chose to remain emotionally mute to his mother's pleadings. She was too much an Indian lover for his liking. But because of her immense love and sacrifices, which he saw and appreciated, he did not brand her a traitor outright.

They had burnt the Indian flag at the stadium during an Indo-Pak cricket match. What a glorious day it had been. He felt like a conquering emperor, just the way Babur must have felt on snatching the throne of Delhi. Even Aisha, the neighbour's sickly daughter, had smiled at him for the first time. His chest had bloated in macho pride.

They came like swarms of bees. They stung worse than a swarm of bees.

When the Indian troops were dragging Sikander out of his house, he as a bystander eyewitness suddenly felt scared, so scared that the earlier gratifying sensation was reduced to scrotum pulverizing pain. Pomp and splendour of earlier elation vanished in thin air.

Their eyes met. Sikander's legs up in the air, head dangling down. Their eyes met. He was begging for help. But what could he do? Fear had locked his feet, totally immobile.

"Coward, you meek coward," shouted the eyes of Sikander. He looked down avoiding the accusing gaze of his best friend.

He had not dared to look up for the next four years, till *Allah* had given him deliverance from his sin, by treating an injured *mujahidin*, accidentally.

Despite all his underground help, that fixed accusing gaze of Sikander, never wavered off him. He did not have the courage to attend the funeral of his revered idol, Sikander, who died after four days of constant torture. Code-named "angel" because of his deeds to the injured, he had been an evil source of death for his friend. They had homed on to them courtesy the video footage of that wretched cricket match. That awful black ugly man, sniggering interrogator, his muscular pain giving goons, his beseeching, pleading mother, all played on his fragile nerves to accept his guilt without any protest. It was he who had broken down in the first basic questioning, blurting out Sikander's name.

His willing cooperation had saved his body but not that of his friend.

There was a shuffling of feet across the screen. He looked up. A big man in a loose brown *salwar kameez* looked at him. He shivered involuntarily.

"I need you angel," the man said.

Kabul

They were the bravest band of five brothers. He, the youngest, felt as such.

The little boy tottered behind his elder brothers. He worshipped the soil they ran on. Oodles of courage fell from each step they took. Splendent images of that courage were etched deeply in his nascent mind.

They were simply fantastic, God like and God gifted.

Alone they could climb trees, milch cows and pluck apples. They could trek alone, raiding and stealing others' fruits, vegetables and occasionally a few chickens. They always were laughing, content and happy. They all clamoured for his mother's attention. That was the time when he felt a little annoyed. All would fight to be fed their favourite mutton *biryani.* All would not eat by themselves, for all would fight for morsels fed into their mouths by their loving mother.

But somehow before he could comprehend factually anything more pleasurable, the good life changed dramatically.

Strange-looking alien men changed their lives. The white men came. They looked pale and sick. The white pale looking sick men came with their even stranger looking machines. Those monstrous machines looked satanically evil.

Alarmed at the sight of witnessing the evil, he rushed to his mother, bravely covering himself under the safety of her *dupatta.*

He was petrified of those thundering steel boxes that moved and spat vicious fire. But his brave brothers as usual set the matters right for him in a jiffy. They were the bravest of the brave, weren't they? They ran up from the rear or the sides and mocked the iron monsters by pelting them with stones.

They laughed, threw stones and laughed again.

Apprehensive at first, but seeing his brave brothers in action, he left his mother's side and laughed. Clapping with his frail hands, throwing stones, he laughed. His brothers were really too brave. It made him proud, even fearless, to the extent of allowing his tiny self to pick up fights with his bigger friends.

"Bloody white shit-head Ruskie", shouted his brothers. "Bloody white shit-head Ruskie", he shouted, aping his brothers. "Pig-eating cunts", shouted his brave elder brothers. "Pig-eating cunts", he shouted mimicking his brave elder brothers. He fought with his big brothers when they refused to tell him what was a cunt. Less that cunt-spoiling instance, he loved his brothers.

His *abbu* always looked the other way when those pale sickly men passed on in their big machines. He had that strange animated look which had hallmark of pure unadulterated hatred.

"Fucking traitors, bloody communists", his father would retort at a few like him of his own clan, riding those big monstrous machines. "Fucking traitors, bloody communists", he would shout animatedly shaking his fists at them. "Fucking traitors, bloody communists", his elder brothers would shout shaking their plucky genitals animatedly after them. "Fucking traitors, bloody communists, ", they all would gleefully shout aping the bravest of the brave, their father, the only person his brave brothers feared.

Late in the morning one day, one big machine blew in front of his house. All his brave brothers cheered at the sight of an overturned dead iron monster.

By late afternoon, bullets started screaming and dancing around their house. The iron monsters made a frightening entry. They came back spitting fire.

By late evening, three of his brothers lay dead amongst piercing wails of his mother. He learnt a very important lesson that day that bravery doesn't stop bullets nor his father was the bravest of the brave.

By night, his father bundled up all they possessed and started walking in the darkness of night.

Four days later, tired and hungry, they were in Peshawar, Pakistan. His father knelt down and kissed the holy earth. *Allah* the merciful had saved their family from further decimation.

A week later, the little boy clutching his *abbu's* hand, walked past a big granite building. Entering by the main gate, he saw hundreds of his age sitting in neat rows, chanting strange verses. He looked up questioningly at his father. The old man had tears in his eyes. He wailed and thrashed on his father's chest, as he was bodily lifted into the arms of a strange man with a long white beard.

"He is your father, mother and home from now. Take care of yourself, my son. Oh *Allah,* please forgive me," he cried and ran away.

That was the last he saw of his not-so-brave father for the next three years.

Not that it mattered after a week of separation. He found unbridled love, peace, stomach-filling sumptuous meals and, more importantly, a strange old man who loved him more than his biological father.

He rarely missed home in his new home.

Punjab, India

He was born under the wrong phase of the moon.

The astronomical angels drawn by plethora of heavenly stars were also ominously awry. Even the *Purohit* did not make the *Janam Kundli* for the first two weeks.

However, this did not deter his anxious father from bulldozing his way into the domain of protesting nurses in the labour room and assure himself with authenticity of his own eyes that the child in question supported the important thing between his wobbly legs.

He liked what he saw.

The overjoyed father then ran around distributing sweets.

In a bout of raving generosity, he also presented pure silk *saris* to all *bais'* who had brought about this happy event. He gave his grateful wife a diamond solitaire and his sulking widowed childless half sisters gold marriage sets while the real surviving one got something undisclosed. After only four months, he packed his heart-throb daughter away to an obscure village life as she displayed life-threatening sibling rivalry.

But as a son, the son didn't for a long time give his thankful father an opportunity to elate.

His son battled against four hernia operations, a rarest of full-moon bronchitis asthma, two shoulder dislocations, twice cracking his right hand from the wrist and the elbow, tear his knee ligaments, have one of those twisted and a chipped lumbar spine digits and burdened with lesser issues of countless broken finger bones or sewed skin patches, presenting a perfect cocktail of living life on an edge.

It didn't at all please his alarmed father who ran from one soothsayer to another to kill the evil spell of the murderous moon. If the physical pain was an acceptable justifiable norm in dealing with his son's existence, the dusts of Venus added another dimension to his son's woes–women. Four/five girls down including his basic language teacher and a school housemistress and such simple philanderings enabled an easy rustication from his prestigious private boarding school. The dramatic rustication drama repeated in college only six months later, thankfully not women related, but for giving seventeen stitches to his classmate, was not fun to his self-made, self-educated engineer father.

And all this misery he bestowed on his family before he crossed his teens.

He was eleven years old in 1971 and proceeding on a holiday trip on the Pathankot-Jammu road when enemy planes straffed hapless military and civilian vehicles.

It was war; the first impressions of which he captured peering out of the big windows of their old trusted Ambassador car of 1958 model. He witnessed a soldier firing a long gun at the fearsome, crisscrossing and shrieking enemy aircraft and then jump up in joy, as the plane above him caught fire. He witnessed the war in a ride of his life, through the window of their rusty car. His otherwise calm father was driving in a rare fury to perhaps overtake the events being perpetuated around him from evil Gods above.

At that moment, he knew what he wanted to be.

Latter's disillusionment was complete when he, obese and pampered, surprised everyone by joining the military academy at Kadakwasla, Pune.

All this, well before his innocent teens.

GENERAL MAP OF KASHMIR

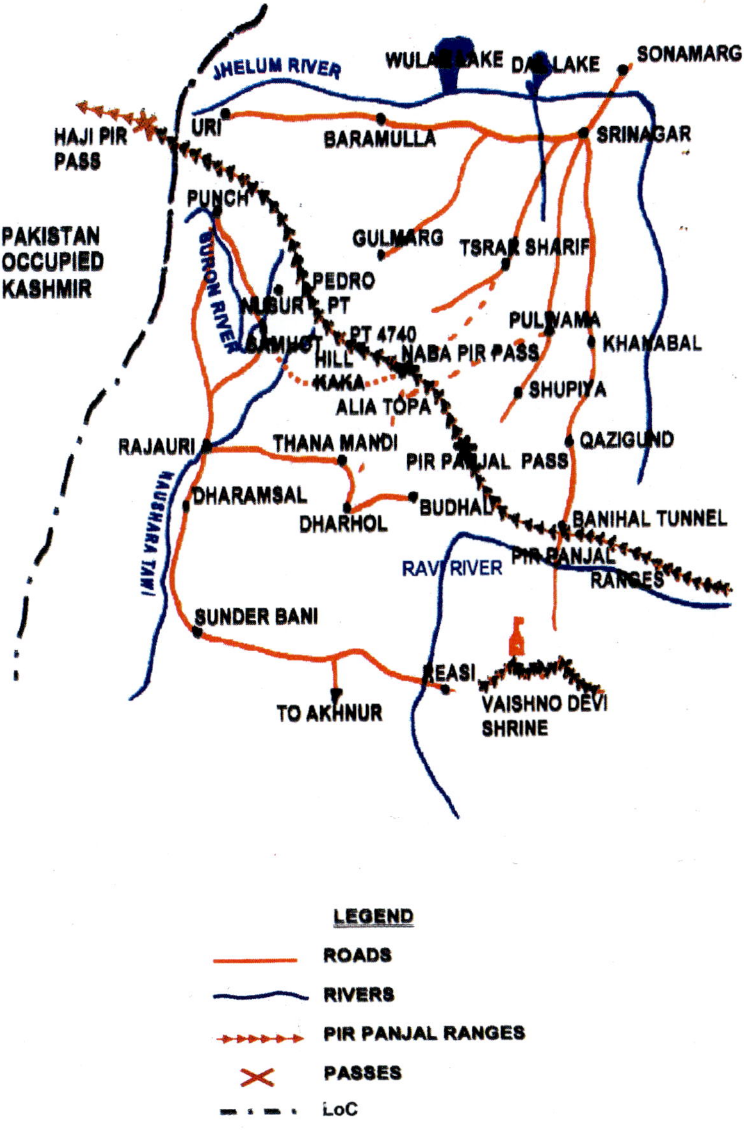

Map not to scale

2

Fuel and Fire

"More explosive in content is the hate-laced intent."

— **Jesse**

Dardpura, Lolab Valley, Kashmir

The game was being played repeatedly since October 1989, with different characters and at various locales. For now, the time was 1200 hours, February 15, 1997.

For the sought and the seeker, trust was an unfathomable element. It had not been sowed in this land since popular people's uprising. Nor did the winds carry its sweet scent anymore.

The meeting was not innocent.

It was fraught with peril.

The danger of betrayal, lack of trust and above all, death.

Major Sunil Yadav, Sena Medal (Gallantry) recipient, sitting camouflaged atop a 400-year-old Chinar tree, was aware of it intimately. It was his second tenure in the Valley and he was not taking any stupid chances based on trust.

Nazir Lone, alias Gazi, Battalion Commander of *Hizbul Mujahidin*, Lolab Valley, also knew of it in ample measure. He had not survived the last eight years in this business based on trust.

Certain feelers had been sent. Positive feelers had been returned. A meeting without a profit in Kashmir was unthinkable.

Yadav spotted them first, clearly from his vantage point. He wouldn't have chosen the site otherwise. The terrorist's father appeared first, then at regular intervals his mother, wife and lastly the endless line of his *islamia* educated kids. They had come to sanitize the area, to preclude any betrayal. Finding the place innocent, calm and serene they left suspicion-free. Good trustworthy fellow, a man of his words, that Major *sahib,* they smiled at each other and opined.

They were at least half a mile wrong.

Sahib's Quick Reaction Team was very skillfully concealed, a mere hundred metres away, tucked inside muck, grime and humus of plentiful green vegetation. Handpicked by the officer, they were the best of the best and had ample terrorist headhunting trophies to prove their calibre. They won't let *apne* Major *sahib* down. They had been in that invisible state since the first light at 0430 hours. None had moved, none wanted to move; they had been trained not to move.

From above, Yadav watched Nazir below hesitatingly totter in, looking around nervously. He sat unobtrusively under him, at the stump of pious Chinar for next half an hour. That major had duped him. He will not come, reasoned the fear-shivering terrorist. As he got up, maybe to leave, a voice beckoned him from the heavens above.

Nazir Lone looked up incredulously. Major Yadav, aping and shaming the Tarzan, suddenly appeared below.

"Don't worry, I am unarmed," the major hurriedly said after ensuring that two of his snipers had Nazir firmly fixed in their telescopic sights.

"Me too," replied the terrorist, adjusting his *kurta* concealing a cocked 7.62mm Chinese pistol.

"We have lot to discuss," said the Major. They discussed something for the next five minutes or so.

Murree, Pakistan
(2045h, 02 Mar)

It was a pitch-dark night.

One could barely see the back of one's hand. Harsh winter draft was screaming down from the lofty peaks of Hindukush Mountains. But the gusts of wind had a different character from the ones that had blown six months earlier, chilling the mountain passes to deep depths of un-negotiable snow. The present winds brought down with themselves massive amounts of latent heat trapped in the upper stratosphere above Afghanistan, furiously melting the snow-trapped gullies and passes, the military significance of which was not an unknown quality to the top brass of both countries of India and Pakistan.

In a nondescript, two-storey old British-era building, located in a remote corner of Pakistan's 12 Infantry Division Cantonment, a few incandescent lights were illuminating the long mosaic floored corridor, through an open oak door. Surprisingly, no sentries seemed to be around to guard such a significant office complex and the rear of the building adjoining massive birch tree forests was protected by a mere strand of barbed wire.

Two American 'Land Rover' jeeps, one flying the pendant of a three-star general from General HQ Islamabad, drove in along the mud gravelled driveway and screeched to a halt under the small bougainvillea adorned porch. The co-driver, a young smart ADC, jumped out acrobatically even before the vehicle could properly halt and opened the rear left door with a slight consenting bow.

"We are at the field coordination office sir," informed Captain Zaheer in his crisp military voice.

General Ibrahim Lodhi, the Officer on Special Duty of Kashmir Desk, stepped out of the vehicle. He slowly gazed around taking stock of his immediate surroundings and did not like whatever he could see up to the extremities of illumination. The place, lacked military tone, the likes he was accustomed to. It was an essential quality, which he had mastered as a young cadet. This had caught the eye of dashing artillery major, an instructor in Pakistan's officers' military academy at Quetta. Later, the major had manipulated the young cadet's posting to his regiment and made him his adjutant when he commanded the regiment. Such flirtations, cultivated over the years had brought him to a position envied by all, except the Chief Executive Officer of Pakistan who had chosen him ignoring many senior generals. He had proved his trustworthiness by commanding the troops to ensure the safe landing of his beloved boss at Karachi airport and the rest was history, known to the entire world.

Before the general could take three unsteady steps after an arduous six-hour journey, a bald man in civilian dress greeted him. To any bystander, he looked like a clown dancing around the general and after animatedly shaking an ice-cold hand; he guided the esteemed visitor inside the building.

After crossing three small dimly lit anterooms with sparse furniture, the guests reached the main hall, which was dazzling with a number of tube-lights hanging from the walls. Each glow focused below on various maps and enlargements, all pertaining to India. The various annotations, markings, pinups and overlays reflected numerous hues of information to whet the appetite of any seeker.

Brigadier Altaf Ghaur, the chief field coordinator, was half bent over a colossal map of Kashmir with transparent plastic sheet rolled over it. A cheap Chinese mini tube-light emitting an equally poor quality of illumination provided a strange aureate halo around his round head. The vigour with which he was munching the end of the china graph pencil, demonstrated the degree of concentration with which the Brigadier was studying the map. He was about to mark something on the mass of confusing contour lines when the noise of visitors being ushered in made him look back. As he saw them, his face broke into a big smile.

"Good evening General, welcome to Murree," said Brigadier Altaf beaming and at same time extending forward his soft hand, "I hope you will have a comfortable stay here and the outcome of your visit will be fruitful."

General Lodhi, after casually shaking the hands without being offered a seat, pulled a chair, sat down slowly and faced the speaker.

He saw a slightly built man, with lines of determination crisscrossing his forehead, staring back at him. He knew the power this puny man enjoyed. The military intelligence folder reflected his absolute control over various *mujahidin* groups engaged in Kashmir. This man was an enigma; those holy warriors swore by him and at the same time feared and hated his guts. Despite Inter Service Intelligence group man's massive reputation, he was this little man's de-facto boss and this man better understand that. Moreover, he had serious allegations to investigate.

"It better be for everyone's sake Altaf," replied the General very deliberately and signalled his ADC and the civilian to leave the room. He further added, "Our targets are going haywire, projections have been cockeyed and results are a big zero till date. Special operations financial directorate is hopping mad. They gave directly to Kashmir field desk, that is your office, rupees 213 crores last year and are twiddling their thumbs now. They want complete audited accounts and are asking for each penny spent, co-related with what has been achieved by our magnificent organization."

"What do you expect sir, that in those measly 200 odd crores India will give you Kashmir on a platter," shot back Altaf in a tone bordering dissent. "The money the grateful people have provided is only peanuts. Hope those army auditors can visualize the task we have set ourselves to achieve. We are hurting India where it hurts the most. The sly Indians are on a defensive for the first time in decades. Their military hollowness and fighting capabilities have been exposed to the whole world. The government of India is in a quandary on what to do. They are crying like little babies. You give me some more money and I will put their whole army, no let me phrase it better, their whole nation out of business. Those *babus* want to know what we have done with the morsel full of money. It is disgusting even talking about it. We have inflicted a thousand cuts on the rotting bloating body of Indian elephant in this decade, something our nation as a whole could not do since independence. And with the kind of other novel plans we now have in place, the Indian elephant can be executed within a year," he finished in a rush, visibly irritated.

"Despite your bravado with words my dear Altaf, your accounting procedures are atrocious. As per the financial expenditure details forwarded by your esteemed office, purchases of arms, recruitment, training, incentives and money pumped across do not tally at least in the first glance and god forbid, what will happen on a detailed scrutiny," quipped back the General in a very impersonal tone. "We all will be hung by the nearest tree if we cannot explain the spending of government money correctly to those *babus."* He deliberately added we, just to throw an idea of collective accountability.

"Sir, I am in total consonance with you on this matter and comprehend the significance of correctly accounting for the public money," the Brigadier spoke this time a little softly but still unable to suppress a note of insolence in his voice. "You must understand that normal sources of funding are just not adequate to cover the costs of our covert operations and other sources, being so sensitive in manner of procurement, cannot be reflected in normal accounts. We had obtained permission in principle to that effect from the last government once it was made clear to us that adequate funds will not be forthcoming and alternative avenues of funding should be explored. As both normal and other income heads are same and interrelated to a specific task being executed, asking for audited expenditure is not feasible or possible to audit under normal circumstances," he added forcefully.

"My dear Altaf, the ground reality on the home-front has changed hundred per cent if you are not aware of it already. The Chief is visibly annoyed that despite ten years of focus, nothing concrete is visible. Kashmir is where it was a decade ago – with slimy Indians, a situation not acceptable to our supreme commander at any cost. Even bloody civilians have started smirking behind the curtains at our ability to handle the conflict anymore. I am sure it will make you a nervous wreck only answering their chirpy wives, 'General what has gone wrong in Kashmir'," replied the General and thumping the table with good measure for effect, wherever he felt necessary.

Brigadier Altaf had a vague suspicion of the nature of the General's visit earlier when he came to know of the immediate secret visit bypassing the normal channels of military protocol. His own faithful and well-wishers had forewarned of certain bewailing in the service headquarters at Islamabad. As the General's diatribe began, his temples started throbbing in sheer anger. What does this old faggot of an ass-licker know of the situation on the ground, thought Altaf. Little coddle nut that the General was throughout his service. Moreover, back at the service headquarters sitting in an air-conditioned office, these creatures could never comprehend how he single-handedly had achieved in making the *jihadi's* turn to him. Yes, he had moved a mountain and these rascals better appreciate that fact. If they annoyed him a bit more, the shit he could throw, could drown thousands like this General but his insatiable love for his country made him think rationally. Cool down please, he reasoned sanely with himself.

"We never had such a stupid situation before where years of hard work is being belied by lack of trust. Why the sudden interest in how the money is being spent now after a decade of our relentless efforts? When we initially started, directions were to carry on regardless of the cost and I have written orders to that effect. It was the last civilian government, which came under immense coercion from the United States to freeze the funding to these *mujahidin* groups. It was then our proposals of alternative funding were accepted," he added, little assertively.

"I know the advantages accrued from the profits of white gold. However, do you know how much we had to invest in setting up the network in India and abroad? Before we could reap the benefits of unaccountable money, we, as a nation have been branded as dope-dust economic power. Worse still, our people in uniform have been apprehended in America, smuggling heroin. To top it all, our alternative-funding department did not know of this good little side-business everyone had started. So do not even talk about it and, in any case, we have to wind up this scheme, as money is being siphoned and ploughed back into our economy at a rate you will feel it's just funny. Whole Afghanistan, our NW provinces, Karachi and now, Azad Kashmir are in total grip of drugs. Have you seen people in the villages? We are a shame to any civilized society. In any case, this is no quorum to voice virtues of morality and we better stick to the old British system of clean accounting. We are fighting a just war with an enemy and we should plan for it openly," said the General rubbing his palms to fight the cold seeping in through the corridors.

"But what you are giving us officially, I repeat again, is too meager. I implore upon you, sir, to please increase our funding to a minimum of three times of present levels without disturbing my external sources of revenue. You would agree that despite your personal morale conflict, this is the only motivating factor – infinite money. *Jihad* be damned for the majority of essential players concerned if money, more importantly, unaccounted money is not made available. How do they drag the youth in the conflict – lure of money when none exists at their homes? If no more powder-money is made available, then majority of my operations would just die, as the one I have planned for tonight, the magnitude of which will surely astound you and my esteemed Chief, if I succeed, *Allah* willingly," replied the Brigadier triumphantly.

The General leaned back on his chair and then staring into the eyes of the man opposite said, "We are looking into your requests and for your information you will be getting Indian rupees 500 as asked. Don't ask me their source but they are definitely not tainted with heroin." He paused for the effect and added, "But other sources you are banking upon are definitely out and that authority ceases as of now. Your office will shortly be getting a copy of the executive order signed by the Chief within a day or so. And as for the operational requirements of money, you need not bother and I will ensure that none of the line operations are affected for want of crisp hard money. These *mullahs* better know and acknowledge that the begging bowl is filled due to our magnanimity and logically directed towards us. Though we showed them the way, we do not want independent sources of revenue to get into their heads so that they can start dictating terms to us. In fact some are already acting like governments-in-power. This ridiculous situation better be nipped in the bud or we will have hell to pay at a later stage. Now brief me about the little coup you are planning."

Brigadier Altaf looked a little pale, as the news was hard to digest so quickly. With all funds channeled through Islamabad, his empire would shrink drastically, including his influence over the people. Damn, he thought, it was better dealing with buffoon civilians than the idiotic men in uniform. At least the civilians could be manipulated into doing what one wanted. With pyrosis-stung chest, he vacantly stared at his falling fortunes.

"I will, sir, firstly, I must request you to join us for dinner. Please excuse transgression on my part for having invited some key *jihadi* elements without your approval. It's a public relations exercise and an opportunity for you to get acquainted with these people of whom one is a dying octogenarian but essential to meet. You will be dealing with them for a long time as destiny of our nation, our offensive capabilities, our strategic depth in the West and other issues to keep India tamed depends upon them," he said throwing a no-win situation at his boss for instant compliance.

Lodhi solemnly got up, to be led and was sure to be lavishly fed.

Colombo
(2055h, 02 Mar 2000)

She was the most lascivious woman of her country. This was a confirmed fact and authenticated by an independent survey conducted by the BBC office at Colombo.

All lusted for her.

She lusted for none, except her daughter.

Rashmi Srivastava was putting her eight-year-old girl child to bed. She was a bit tired singing lullabies for the last one hour, but Nana was not satisfied or amused by her mother's ministrations.

Nana pulled Rashmi's hair and sweetly cooed in a rebellious tone, "Ma, I want to hear the story of Frog Prince and I don't want to sleep. Mama, you better give up singing those boring sleeping songs. You are a terrible singer and now I think I can hear cows collecting outside my window."

"You rotten spoilt princess," said Rashmi bending down and tickling Nana's tummy with her nose. "I sing on TV and if it is good enough for people then it better be good for you."

"Boo, I want a story and nothing else," lamented Nana sticking her tongue out.

"All right," sighed Rashmi and started narrating the story of the Frog Princess, each word of it she was sure that her spoilt and overly indulged daughter knew by heart.

By the time she came to the point where the beautiful princess was kissing the frog, she found Nana fast asleep. Rashmi cuddled her daughter into her arms and stared at her innocent face. Nana was her life and the only reason for her existence. The vagabond professor, Nana's biological father, had run away on the first instance when she as an awe struck teenager, had told him that she was pregnant with his baby. Her father, a high ranking officer in the Sri Lankan Army, had instantly disowned her and thrown her on to the streets than to face the ignominy of the disgrace of his pure Singhalese bloodline impaired by a Tamilian rogue.

It was on the streets of Colombo that she had learned to survive and do what she loved the most – investigative journalism. She had survived catcalls, lewd remarks, snide remarks, obscene suggestive gestures, outrageous money for a glimpse and services of her body, birth of Nana, poverty, slums, one room shanty and soon became a buzzword on live on-the-scene reporting.

The second shock in her life came two years after Nana's birth when the doctors diagnosed a defective valve in her tiny heart. Her Nana was dying, unable to breath.

She had died the second time in her life that day.

Rashmi ran from pillar to post, her parents, her relatives, the lanky handsome former lover, but alas, all had mercilessly turned her down. In sheer desperation, she met the Indian Ambassador to Sri Lanka, who was totally taken aback on hearing the cosy relationship between the Sri Lankan government and the Tamil guerrillas in the early eighties to rout the Indian Peace Keeping Force. It had been a relationship of convenience since then and Rashmi had never regretted it.

The ring in her special cell phone, a gift from her newly acquired friends disturbed her chain of thoughts. She extended her slim hands to pick up the telephone.

"Hello, how's our beautiful lady tonight," crackled the voice. "The vast ocean hungers for your touch," continued the speaker in a suggestive tone.

"Emerald always shines bright," replied Rashmi.

"How much does she shine tonight," asked the voice?

"Enough to blind the crown of your heart. Our esteemed Foreign Minister is going to soft-peddle Kashmir in the next SAARC meet and thereafter at UN," she seductively whispered into the phone.

"What! has the idiot gone mad? He seems to be propagating quicker birth of *Elam* than his pregnant girlfriend can deliver the child," shot back the voice.

"No need to get vulgar, dear friend," she scolded. "Nevertheless, the relationship runs deeper and is not an eyewash. Check out Attapattu naval base. I believe ships of your friendly neighbour have been enjoying our uninterrupted hospitality since the last few weeks. Believe in addition to some heavy machinery, a few very macho men have impressed the young wives of several officers in bed and out of it.

"Thanks and how's our esteemed princess, Nana," boomed the voice.

"Fine and as lively a brat as I knew her an hour ago. She is due for her last operation in June," she said.

"Do not worry, everything will be arranged as usual," said Grover and then dropping the telephone, he disappeared into the night, thanking his boss for the first time in providing the scrambler version of mobile to Rashmi, thus doing away with the ever dangerous exercise of a physical meeting.

Murree, Pakistan
(Same night)

The dinner had been a social coup.

The high-rank officer from Islamabad had wriggled his fat bums to the dance of mystic Zaida churning out Bollywood songs at a furious pace. Zaida, adequately dressed in revealing clothes, showed more intentionally than hide her sumptuous curves in mock modesty. The *Jihadi* types had been fixated to their seats, confused, agitated, but never letting that 'evil woman' out of their shamed sights. The more she wriggled her buttocks and gyrated her boobs, the more they sank into the cushions except his boss who, like those mystic seers, seemed to float in the air. Not given to miss anything he quickly concocted an extended recreation plan.

These *mujra* performing girls were good and convincing Zaida to give an exclusive private performance to the lusty-eyed General had been easy, a mere some thousand rupees later. Zaida with big poetic lips stared expectantly at the big patron, willing on the massive man with smiling eyes. His boss's ruby red eyes had sparkled, and he silently nodded his consent to the wild suggestion thrown. One more mighty had fallen to a lowly woman. Not at all odd, these creatures were such; he reflected being himself the victim of a few. More than that, he was satisfied with the boss in mixing with those slimy civilians, as such pretenses mattered in the long run. They had hugged and chirped all confounding words about the holy work being undertaken in Kashmir. It had also pleased the General somewhat. Rather reluctantly, both called the end to the festivities.

They had serious business to conclude, the business of fine-tuning Indian destruction.

Back at the operational room, with the General sitting opposite him, not so nice earlier observations, came rushing back, to spoil the sumptuous taste of venison, the fondness of it he had acquired as a young Captain while serving in Drass sector.

The Brigadier collected the sheaf of papers and started tapping them on the table to get all loose sheets in order. He hated at not being in command of any situation and the old goat had outmanoeuvred him at least till now. Looking back, he replied in a soft voice. "Well sir, as for operations this week, seven minor and one major intrusion have been planned. In fact the major one is on tonight and if we succeed, it will be the most daring infiltration in history. Forty-six *jihadis* led by a tiger of a man are crossing over to the Indian-Administered Kashmir to start an operation, which just might initiate events to sound the first death knell to India. Operation '*Ghaznavi Tir*' has been launched and has all the right ingredients for an unprecedented success."

"I am not sure of the death-knell part, for we or at least I have become skeptical about hearing that word so many times for the last ten years," the General replied tapping his manicured nails on the table. "But a forty-six people group is definitely big, in fact very big. How come I have not been informed of such a magnitude of operation before," asked the General.

"Sir, we certainly cannot slip on such a major operation. The detailed planning was finalised three months earlier and a summary of daily operations has been forwarded directly to the Chief's directorate. I am sure the events of the last few months overtook the normal daily briefings at the Service Headquarters," Altaf added and could not restrain himself in not taking a dig at the General. 'I will ensure personally to wake up the concerned staff to keep you adequately briefed," he further said.

"No, you need not do that, for I am sure that your hands are already full. The concerned person will surely get a big boot, provided your information is right. As it is too late to do anything about it right now. I am sure the basic nitty-gritty of the operation would have been worked out by your staff," said the General. "Who is leading them," he inquired.

"Asif Gul sir, and with him are six Afghanis, basically his junior commanders, to keep an eye on the local rabble being inducted for their administrative support," Altaf informed.

"Why induct Kashmiri locals when we are not sure of their capabilities? Wouldn't it have been better to keep one homogeneous group," the General quipped.

"Well sir, all pros and cons were considered. It was deemed essential to give an indigenous colour to the whole operation and at the same time keep the control in our hands. It is basically an ISI operation, may be that's why the regular briefings did not pass through your desk," explained Altaf.

General Lodhi did not like what he heard. He hated these ISI types trying to run their own shitty rotten empire. Most of them were officers from the Pakistan Army on deputation and they behaved as if they were the only saviours of this nation. Had those idiots given correct advice to Yahiya Khan and accurately assessed the Bengali opposition, this country would have remained united and they would not have been so desperate to destroy India. And Americans have given them a *jihadi* feather in their cap, which they will only take off if this country splits again. Idiots think they control the *Jihadis'* or *Taliban* for that matter. The way they are going, his progressive Pakistan will be a quagmire of mad *mullahs'* in a short time. He was ashamed of ideology being imposed in Afghanistan despite himself being an ardent Muslim. Even today those ISI types smirk and dictate national policies. Sad, very sad, indeed.

"Don't worry, this situation of bypassing any issue concerning Kashmir will also change very fast whether ISI or even a private agency is involved," shot back the General, irritated by this recent development. "Now give me the whole profile and scope of the operation," he added after a brief pause and a little later noted something on his writing pad.

Brigadier Altaf, scanning a sheet of paper replied, "Sir, Asif Gul is a very interesting man. Aged 32 years, six feet tall, brown haired, muscular Pathan. Recruited into *mujahidin* in 1982 at the tender age of fourteen, in Peshawar. His parents were Afghani refugees who lost their three children while escaping from Kabul. Thus natural hatred for anyone connected with previous communist regime in Afghanistan exists. By the age of twenty, he had completed thirty-two missions inside Afghanistan. His bosses, including the CIA controlling staff, were so impressed that they allowed him to raise an independent group, a suicide squad of sixteen people when he was himself only twenty-two. In fact, he did the first trial firing of TOW missiles over the Khyber Pass. He also led the famous raid on Jalalabad air base and destroyed five Russian MIGs on ground. He was the inspiration to initiate a handful of freedom fighters when all seemed in the enemy's favour."

"How come such a daredevil never came into public limelight before?" asked the General.

"Our fortune, on number of accounts," said Altaf "Firstly, he is media shy and secondly, he gives all the credit to *Allah* for success. Lastly, the major factor was that his senior leaders wanted to grab all the doles themselves to consolidate their relative power base inside Afghanistan, thus sidelining him. However, Gul did not object. But that is not all about the brave lion. His speciality lies in brokering alliances. He was instrumental in forging a joint front at Kandahar against Maqsood and his Indian cohorts, once the Russians left and bringing that tract of territory under control of Taliban for the first time. It is for this unique capability, that he is being sent across so heavily armed, as in coming months he has a key role to play for us."

"Why?" asked General Lodi with his eyes sparkling and showing interest for the first time.

"Sir, you know how fragmented the various groups operating inside Kashmir are. Each one is fighting another for the turf of territory and Indians are exploiting this issue to the hilt in keeping the rebellion under check. These buggers are so vain that they see no reason in joining hands to fight a common enemy and are actually vying with each other, in dropping information of their rivals, at the doorsteps of the Indian security forces camps. The lazy Indians do not need to step out, to get any information. We give them money but on this issue, cooperation is not forthcoming. You can imagine the situation across inside India, when they refuse to train together here, inside Azad Kashmir," the Brigadier explained.

"So how does that lion help us when our own house is not in order. You have just reinforced our observation that it's the money and its unlimited supply which govern their hearts and not the holy cause in kicking the Indians out," the General pointed out.

"Maybe you have a point here sir, but if Gul can even achieve half of what we expect of him, then under one umbrella you can imagine how easy it will be for us to control the operations. The joint synergy of the groups will definitely break India's back," said the Brigadier.

"How come we keep on churning out such *jihadi* elements?" inquired the General further.

"Well sir, on this let me quote an Indian officer. He says that the number of freedom fighters/terrorists does not depend on any ideology or perceived wrongs, but is directly proportional to idle youth multiplied by quantum of heretics you can throw at them. On this, I am in total agreement as Pakistan has both in great numbers," Altaf replied, smilingly.

"Now I see why you are so smug about the operation. You have unlimited supply of raw material and an achievable target. You have the right to be, if it has been conceived and being implemented by your office. Pray to *Allah* for its success, but for against Indians, count on what has been achieved and not what you can," the General retorted and simultaneously confirming his observation of *mullah*-mechanism spawning his land. He must bring this to the notice of his Chief Executive who had once hinted in a similar direction.

The Brigadier smiled broad for the second time and continued, "Sir, I have bèen able to persuade with great difficulty the various groups here engaged in *jihad* to agree to this proposal in principle. The whole exercise took over a year in hard talk and negotiations. It was Gul who tilted the balance in our favour. The leaders on this side of the divide were of the opinion that only a man like Gul could effectively achieve what we wanted, so they literally begged him to take control of the operation. Again this was a master stroke for we managed to dump our man on them."

General Lodi digested the news.

Conceptually, it was a brilliant plan.

Similar to the one this man as a half colonel had been able to achieve when he had paralyzed the Indian city of Bombay with the help of one smuggler in the summer of 1993. In that too, it is believed, he had made a considerable personal profit on the sly and only with great difficulty could he explain the ownership of two shops in that smuggler's commercial building in downtown posh Karachi metropolis. But above all that, what a glorious magnitude of chaos he had been able to bestow upon India. Their pants were blown apart and there dirty asses had gleamed stark naked for the first time in so many years. We need young blood like him to infuse energetic strategic concepts, but they need to be directed, he thought. No wonder that such a junior person had been promoted to the post of the Brigadier and was directly responsible for feeding the turmoil in Kashmir for the last four years. Let's hope this plan succeeds. At least it will dim his chronic nightmare of being a one month old commissioned wounded POW at the mercy of Indians at Khulna in the shameful war in East Pakistan. He himself had a soft corner for anyone who would spit on the Indians and this man at least was trying to hurt them. The allegations levelled against this man were serious. He was sure that the magnitude of siphoning off funds, as reported, was not going on without Altaf's knowledge. But for now, he will put the inquiry, on hold. The operation had very grave implications for any loser and it would not be right on his part to sidetrack any effort due to an inquiry.

For his own bloody sake, the Brigadier better come up with an ace, mused the General as he got up to keep the promised date with the utopian dancer, Zaida.

3
The Divide

"True love in union of souls.
Purity of hate, severed in faith.
Fearless, pure innocent breeze,
bound by the goodness of earth.
Nations, far apart, across a thin line,
in surreal world."

— Jesse

The Line of Control (1948-65-71-till date)

It was the most asinine line cut across the map anywhere in the world.

The asininity ran 813 km long.

The genesis of the line defied mundane thinking. It was not meant for knowledge of mathematically inclined meek. The line defied the laws of linearity and stumped Newton's gravity business conceptually.

One had to be a very near relative of an ox to understand it.

It had no logic. In fact, it logically defied any logic.

It did not separate any geographical features. It did not divide on the basis of population, religion, ethnicity, tribal affiliations or culture for one. It did not demarcate any communications, lifelines or natural resources. It did not differentiate between flora, fauna or climate. It was not based on mountain ranges, highest definable ridges, rivers, the natural watershed principle or any other conceivable internationally accepted issue, which demarcated boundaries between sensible nations. It started from the sea level in Jammu region to soar into invisible peaks of Ladakh. Of few known tangibles, it definitely had uprooted families, separated families and severed the scenic wonders of this magnificent land. However, one thing it failed miserably was in its inability, to diminish the majestic aura of the ever dominating Himalayas and its various subsidiaries.

The line cut haphazardly across desolate mountaintops, ridges, forests, glens, vales, pasturelands, rivers, lakes, ponds and villages, and in one interesting case, bisected a house. Poor, confused and terrified owner, Mohamad Yakoob, bathed in India and defecated in Pakistan. His sons studied alternatively in Indian-Administered Kashmir or Pakistan-occupied part, depending on the quality of education or the chances of passing the grade on either side, but his daughters definitely attended the Indian school.

This great divide was the outcome of death, blood, sweat, and countless charges across its desolate wastes. Many a youth of their country had breathed their last on it sealing this line's fate. Madness was sublime, tactless with impunity, confounding and never ending, but so were the extreme national passions attached to it. Where human blood was shed, reasons became immaterial, logic lost in aimless wind. Both the armies propelled by sheer sacrifice and some stupid blunders by eminent politicians on the Indian side and despots across had ensured the creation of this majestic invisible line.

Most of the uniformed men, on this or that side of this ludicrous line, owed their soul to it.

One could be labelled a traitor, insensate, punch-drunk goon outright if you did not pay your witless, trivial, daily dose of obeisance for it being so omnipresent, as real as the majestic land it stood on.

Behind this line and sometimes on top of it, lay two most hostile armies in the world, eternally sizing up each other. Distrust was downright acceptable and so was the unfathomable hate.

No quarter was given or asked.

An eye for an eye, a tooth for a tooth, was its anguished tale.

Having studied the symptoms of its occupants for the last five decades, the social scientists were on the verge of coining a new word called '**Inpa**'. 'Inpa', the new word, will find usage in *English Oxford Dictionary* and be defined as the complete breakdown of mutual trust between two societies, total incompatibility, and existing only to harm each other (origin, **Indo-Pak** mutual distrust over ages). Genetic biologists going a step further, were investigating the manifestation of mutant gene in the form of a tail or a wart on right side of the brain. God only knew what it would be referred to scientifically.

All this stemmed from unidentifiable hate.

It was also the most heavily guarded line in the entire planet. It could shame the famous dividing lines of Korean thirty-eight parallel or earlier Sinai or the German iron curtain ones.

The line had witnessed three wars, each bigger and more ferocious in death than the last. Seers had it predicting a nuclear war now if its sanctity was further breached or if it courted another conflagration. It had pukka minefields of 1948, 1965 and 1971 vintage, including some intermittently laid in-between. All exploded with equal ferocity, killing in equal measure. In reality, the older ones were meaner. No authentic records existed of their actual deployment. You only discovered them when you were negative in a limb or a life.

Multi-layer defence systems and almost all the arms listed in the 'Jane's Defence Weekly' were very tastefully deployed. The well-known arms factories in the world of some substance had made a killing here, fuelling mutual fears. Legend had it increasing western countries GDP by a mere per cent. They were ever too thankful for it remaining disputed, with assured yearly remunerations so obtained, to fatten and spruce companies' account books. They would move governments, overthrow dictators, and sow more distrust to ensure that no tranquillity returned to this good profitable line. It was their oil strike in this otherwise miserable area.

Along it, on both sides lay thousands of bunkers, gun positions, mortar pits, automatic weapon pits, observation posts, listening posts, medical bunkers, tactical operation bunkers, ammunition bunkers, rest shelters, cookhouses and all a mind could comprehend. They were over-ground, under-ground, cut in side slopes, over the trees, under the trees, on front slopes, on rear slopes, in tunnel form, etc. They were made of brick, cement, iron, sandbags, cut logs, rocks and in few cases, soiled wheat/rice bags or jerricans. Wherever, however they were, the aim was very clear. Each had to have the best visibility towards the enemy, with maximum killing zone or impact and be secure from enemies' observation and fire. Any commander could go insane meeting all the above requisites. May be, they deserved the line more than their soldiers manning it. The atmosphere would have been surely less tense had brilliant strategists, unit pride or desire to do that bit extra, had not made a straight line on a map so complicated that sometimes one could not comprehend who was in the front, flank or the rear. Desire to nibble at other's folly still persisted and was exploited to the hilt by any mentally robust leader.

Such commanders breathed in abundance on both sides of the famous divide.

On these defences lived human beings. Same in anatomy, blood, vital parts, but definitely different in thoughts.

On the Indian side, Hindus, Sikhs, Muslims, Buddhists, Jains, Parsees and Christians of various hues—from North to South or from East to West, representing the entire mass of Indian Sub Continent, manned the defences.

On the Pak side, Muslims and only more faithful Muslims shouldered each other to stem a more numerical superior army.

Despite olive green or khaki one wore across it, men on both sides of the line, laughed, aped, mimicked, cried, sulked, backslapped, cracked bawdy sleazy jokes, and fantasized avidly. When bullets were not being exchanged as a daily bread and butter routine, they showered choicest expletives at each other with full fervour and gusto. Sometimes when loneliness got the better of post-commanders, much against vehement advice of their men, they sauntered up to that line and exchanged pleasantries, sweets, food and sometimes much in demand, Indian manufactured liquor. Few moments later, they would personally be throwing grenades, firing weapons, to draw enemy's blood, across that demeaning line.

They lived, slept, ate, woke-up and existed because of that famous line.

It was called, the Line of Control, LoC in short.

And on that line, the state of 'Inpa' was complete.

Khuni Nallah
(2030h, 03 Mar)

It was also a very dark night that blanketed the entire Haji Pir sector. Its black effect was accentuated; more so, in the narrow defile leading to the LoC. The dark surrounding became bleaker because of the early moon hiding behind the thin layer of clouds. Man-high, thick foliage of bushes and Fir trees compounded the problem of light even further. Winds were steadily picking up their tempo howling their way up the slope. Dull shapes of ragged crest-line bordered the distant canvas in black timeless overhang.

They had been walking for over an hour, but to be precise, they had been actually crawling crablike on all fours. Both men were sweating profusely, more due to fear, than the actual fatigue. Reshab Mehmood slowly parted the branches of a thick hibiscus bush behind which they had taken temporary rest and peered cautiously down the slope. He easily picked up the silvery snake like bed of the river flowing diagonally across his position. It was shining in splendor in spite of the darkness of the night. Its roar of watery flow also rumbled on to his ears clearly. He scanned the area carefully, first with the naked eye, then through the night vision goggles hanging on his chest with the help of a thick nylon strap.

He registered nothing suspicious.

Caressing his new goggles, he felt pride seeping into his anxious brain. Out of all the trainees and known guides, in all thirty-six different *Jihadi* camps, he and his younger first cousin had been chosen for this special mission. They had proved their worth earlier and had passed the stringent test organized by Pakistan's Special Services Group and the ISI with flying colours. However, despite the capabilities of this new gizmo, he still preferred his animal instincts to lead him, as they were your very own in usage and trust. Trust no one except your instincts had been the family and his community's motto, and he be damned to put his life into danger in the hands of this toy.

Getting the group across was a major responsibility bestowed on his shoulders and he had serious differences on the timing and planning of infiltration. The group and that ISI bigwig preferred a dark night while like all guides he wanted a full moon night for the basic advantage of good visibility. Those fools can never visualize that undergrowth adjoining the de-facto border for miles in depth provided adequate cover. If one knew the jungle pathways, one could move in a tunnel of bushes, right through the LoC.

Afghani's paranoia against moonlit night stemmed from the fear of better Russian hit capability during full moon days. Moreover, the basic terrain they operated upon in Afghanistan was stark naked in vegetation. The bloody Indians had no matching capability to look so deep or engage them effectively at night. The need of those crucial hours, when you were effecting infiltration, was your ability to see reasonably the path you were treading upon and undertake effective evasive action on being detected. On these treacherous slopes, one false step meant certain death and God forbid if one had to run in dark.

He had agreed to this plan, as he could not refute the logic of that potbellied ISI officer. He had reasoned that the Indians did not chase the infiltrators and fought from static temporary pickets at night. That too hitting one, the probability was one in twenty. It was only in the morning that even on a small suspicion they launched massive rear area searches. The dark night will preclude that possibility also and as for night navigation, he was given this wonder toy.

He slowly slithered forward from his hide. The lower portion of his elbows had become raw due to continuous crawling. The leather and cotton cushioned elbow pads were good for an hour, but definitely not more. With a shake of his head, he willed the pain away, trying to concentrate on the job at hand. The rustle of bushes behind, being trampled by his half-brother Risal Mehmood, was a reassuring sound to his chilled ears.

This was an excellent place to infiltrate.

All they had to do was roll down the slopes. It did not require negotiating steep mountains initially. Knowing the area before like the back of his hand was a definite advantage. The spine along which they were climbing down was steep and narrow enabling keeping an easy direction. The problem would start only once they hit a small fast flowing stream. It had been nicknamed *Khuni Nallah* by both sides due to the heavy toll in human blood this stream had extracted during the 1971 conflict. Above the opposite slope of that stream lay a dominating Indian post, which provided effective observation on both sides of the Pir Panjal mountain range.

His father had witnessed many fights in these lofty mountains since 1947 as an Indian fighting porter, lugging ammunition up these blood soaked slopes. Toothless, old, tottering *abbu* had regaled countless children of his family narrating the tales of distant battles. The most fascinating and his favourite one had been fought at this *Nallah,* in which scores of Sikhs had died trying to capture the right eastern hump from the hands of Pakistani Rangers. The battle had raged for two days, with Indian troops stuck at the base of the massive rock, held back by accurate Pakistani machine gun fire. The fierce Indian Commanding Officer had charged along with few men at that accusing gun holding back his victory and died leading the third assault. Those mad *khalsa's* had carried the body of their beloved Commanding Officer into the attack, strapped behind a *jawan's* back and charged the summit like deranged dogs, to win the day for their dead Commanding Officer. The area has been in the Indian hands ever since and at present was occupied by some *Nepali* troops. He could never understand these strange slit-eyed people. Why the hell leave your land and fight for another country. Fight under and whose loyalty. But of what little he had heard of them, they fought well and fought hard, hard enough to send shivers down few Baluchis he had met. Crazy people they were, he reasoned.

Despite the obsession of both those sides to man an invisible line, his community regarded all this as a big farce.

His clan had never recognised this illegal boundary between the armies of Pakistan and India. It had no local standing in his community. For generations, their grandfathers had moved along the majestic mountain slopes and used these tracks. The green pastures, vales and crystal clear mountain rivulets were their property gifted by God to them. This was nature's bounty and it helped them to sustain their livestock, a holy work passed down from the times of the Prophet.

Who were these silly people to deny them their natural rights?

As for the actual boundary, it was a belly aching joke amongst his tribe. Especially in his earlier formative years he had soiled its sanctity at every opportunity offered. It had been a secret initiation into manhood. The communities cabal conducted such organized hops once every two years. Few oldies gloated in training them to slither, crawl, observe the movements, and live in cold till the time they were confident that the young wards will not balk at the first sight of danger. The fear of crossing the world's most densely manned, heavily mined and fortified line had disappeared by the time he had attained his sperm ejaculating manhood.

His own half cousin's beloved wife, Bijli was from Kalakot, twenty kilometres across the LoC, inside Azad Kashmir. Ah! what a time it had been. The whole *barat* of thirty-one men had fooled the Indian post bang on the LoC and bribed the post commander of Pakistan Rangers to get across safely. Three days later the whole party had returned but this time with a bride, to their make shift *bakarwal* camp, right under the nose of the Indian Battalion Headquarters. The very next day, he had presented his precious shepherd dog to the Commanding Officer and had gleefully obtained a jerrican of even more precious kerosene for being so generous to the gullible *Bihari* troops. But, those were good and easy times, about eight years back.

The LoC was not manned so heavily then, as now. In his middle years, the anxiety of repeated crossings had given rise to fear and worry. Ayesha, his husky wife, hated his sudden trips across, but this was the only honourable means left to support his clan. *Jihad* had been a God sent opportunity. Only the *bakarwals* had the ingenuity, aptitude, adequate sense, intelligence and the guts to exploit the God's cause. For each crossing, he was paid rupees 10,000 by Colonel Iqbal of the ISI, including a free AK-47 to boot. This time he had hit a jackpot. For the same work that fool was giving 50,000. Well it was their money and who was he to comment on someone's generosity. But whatever the case be, he wanted any one side to win the conflict. At least the whole *Pir Panjal* range will be free to roam and exploit. They had given the Indians last fifty years to do so, but they had not delivered the goods. They lacked will. They were a weak nation; for by which logic did they return the captured areas back to Pakistan after each victory.

A victor being so generous?

No wonder the grave of India's bravest Rajput was in Afghanistan and not the other way round despite the plunderer losing seventeen times. One has to grab the one, the only one chance, for the God does not bestow largesse each and every time.

What part of brain did the Indian leaders use?

Not the saner one, surely. He was certain, at least leaders of his clan would never make such a gross folly. The only problem was that his like-minded religious leaders or the nation based on such pure ideals had never won of late. Where had the bellyful fire of the earlier Muslims disappeared? He was not sure on whose side the all-merciful *Allah* was.

His father had rejoiced the famous Indian victory at *Haji Pir* in 1965 only to cry at their stupidity, later. The legendary tale of it was well known even to a nincompoop child on both sides of these sacred ranges. Few brave men had encrypted that legend in golden letters by driving out a horde of panicked Punjabi Muslim soldiers from a mountain fortress without firing more than a few rounds.

But who wants legends if one can't nurture them.

This was another famous Indian problem and weakness. They do not bind on sacrifices of their soldiers or dwell with pride to make brave legends. Where a soldier is not respected that nation was sure to die repeatedly. It had been Indian history since ages and fools never seem to learn from the past. He had seen how the Pakistani soldiers were respected. It was an eye opener and they sure will win. Now for the next fifty years, they will support Pakistan and give them the chance to unify their divided lands.

It had taken them the better part of an hour to come down three hundred metres to *Khuni Nallah's* edge. Reshab had been scanning the opposite sky line, patch by patch, through his night vision goggles to pick any presence of Indian ambushes, which he was certain will be placed with regular monotony. The only major issue was where they would be located? In this guessing game, fruits generally fell on the lap of a man who displayed more patience. So many times he had sensed presence of Indian troops by their nervous movements, small sounds of hushed whispers, loud farting and even a whistle like snore once. It had been tragic to that snoring idiot, as he had slit the person's throat, escaping in the wake of confusion he had left behind. Aren't those idiots taught that noise travels far at night?

However, today no sound except the shrill shriek of the screaming wind pierced his immediate surroundings. He hated this. Though this would help in muffling the sound of a large body of men walking through the bush, but it took away the advantage of his acute sense of hearing. Again, the time was at premium, as it was not a crossing of five or six men this time. Head to tail in single file formation, it will take at least an hour for those forty-six odd *jihadis* to cross the *Khuni Nallah* only, not discounting the time required for crossing the ambushes in depth.

He peered a last time into the oblivion ahead with the faintest hope to catch something. He was disappointed again. He touched Risal's shoulder and gently tapped it twice. This innocent, silent, signal had been practised many times in the past and mastered at one of the *Tanzeems,* but ISI run, training academy at *Kala Pahar* in Kel sector of Pakistan-Administered Kashmir.

Risal took out his Japanese torch and pointed it towards Pakistani post Kabul. He blinked it repeatedly twice in quick succession of three flashes into the void of darkness above. At the same time, Reshab took out his walky-talky and whispered, "*Tir Allah Tir,*" twice.

Post 113, Pakistan
(2045h, 03 Mar)

"Who are you?" whispered the devilish old man discreetly.

"A devout Muslim."

"Who is the maker of this world?" inquired the white-haired man quietly.

"*Allah.*"

"What are you?" the old man crooned into his ears softly.

"A messenger of *Allah.*"

"What is your role in life?" interjected the old fool quickly.

"Do as *Allah* wills."

"What is *Allah's* desire?" questioned the old sage.

"Make people see the righteous path."

"What is your desire?" quizzed the tottering half-bent man.

"I have no desire except to work for *Allah's* cause."

"What is *Allah's* cause in these times?" the red lips thundered.

"Show the infidels the light of *Allah.*"

"How will you show the light to the infidels"? shrieked the old fraying *maulvi.*

"By simplicity, love, logic, persuasion, coercion, terror and death," he calmly replied.

Gul opened his eyes to the sound of running shoes.

There was a sudden alarm in his mind. The body lying on the bed tensed. His hand automatically crept towards the AK-47, for reassuring safety. The weapon was not far, and resting on the crook of his left arm. He was drenched in sweat and breathing hard. Head still, his grey eyeballs quietly rotated on their axis and confirmed the absence of any hidden dangers inside the confines of the concrete pillbox. Mad *mullah* will never let him rest in peace, he thought. God bless his soul for showing an insignificant man like him, a glorious path to *zannat.*

"Gul, Gul the message has come," shouted panting Mosul excitedly as he galloped inside the bunker. "They have confirmed it by the right code on the radio and I myself saw the correct light signal."

"*Allah* be with them," he said getting up. Putting on his shoes, he walked outside.

Group of forty-six *jihadis* were expectantly waiting for their beloved leader to make an appearance. Six feet tall this Afghani did not disappoint them in the manner of his entry. Gul knew the importance of impact on his freedom fighters. As was the custom amongst tribes of *Hindukush,* it was who they feared the most, was always the undisputed king. He approached them like a lion on the prowl, with eyes fixed straight ahead, mesmerizing the void in front to his personal command. He purposely let the shawl covering his shoulders slip sideways, revealing a sleek AK-47 reflecting against the dim light. Four grenades casually clipped in two rows and a side holster holding a reminiscent relic, a .38 Webly Scot police special of 1928 fame, a fantastic steal of his grandfather, of a killed, famous, rich, white-trader of those times, made up the part of the armament on body display. The crown piece was a rocket- launcher strapped on to his back.

"The day has come to fulfill our childhood dreams and keep the promises made to the almighty *Allah.* On the other side of that divide lie armies of *Dar-ur-harb* who have suppressed the right of free worship of our Islam. Those infidels believe they can deny that right when people dedicated to righteous path like you, exist in abundance. If we could make the mighty communists run away like dogs, with their dirty tails shamefully tucked in between their legs, then who are these half-cast *kafirs.* They don't even have half the army or weapons, the likes we faced in Afghanistan. It is adequate time in history of the millennium of our religious calendar that the sword of Islam beheads idolators of *Hindustan*. The fight has been going on for a little over a thousand years. It's time we finished it. You all will finish it. They are the same kith and kin of defilers of our sacred land, booted out by merciful Mohammed and avenge them we shall, even in hell," he thundered pointing his hands above. "You are my tigers and we have tasted blood, death, dangers and victory together before. *Zannat* does not come by visiting *Mecca* or *Medina,* but by dying for a true cause. Death, glory, wealth and women are yours to plunder in the vale of Kashmir. Remember Gazni, Sher Shah and the great Mughals who conquered these weak people, on a whim of an idea. We have that faith, strength and resolve to achieve the impossible. On your shoulders, rests the fate of a nation and eyes of the Muslim fraternity, from Istanbul to Islamabad, are fixed on you. You are their deliverance. Be rest assured that I will never let you down and I expect nothing less from you," he exalted the stunned audience of ardent Muslims.

Blood began boiling amongst the group. Passion aroused, team began sizzling. It was hard not to be seduced by Gul's fiery bantering. He had the conniving knack of stirring life into a dead man. Few started cheering and clapping wildly forgetting for a moment the sensitivity of the place.

Subedar Mastan Gillani, post-commander of Pakistani post Kabul, (called post 113 by the Indians) ran up to the open compound shouting, "Shut up you fools. Have you left your small pecker thinking brain at home?" Grabbing the nearest *jihadi* who was about to let a burst from his Klashnikov in the air, Frontier style, he screamed in chaste Punjabi. "*Bhainchod,* are you strolling on the streets of Lahore with a *randi* by your side? Keep shut and stop making this ridiculous comic drama," he thundered even more forcefully and concurrently scratching his massive buttock in not-so-subtle manner. The big flat nose implanted on him also flared, deep crimson red.

Momentarily, Gul was taken aback. Comprehending the situation quickly he gestured his fellow warriors to calm down and dismissing three inch taller Mastan with the shake of his hand he carried on, "Tarik and Mosul you will be the scouts. Ahmed's group will lead from the front. I will be in the middle followed by Kasim's group. Fazal will bring up the rear. Remember we have rehearsed this movement many times. Fire back immediately on being fired upon. Indians love to hide behind boulders and bullets will keep them fixed there. Remember that dead men cannot fire back. Safety after detection lies in arms held in your hands and so use them well."

Irritated, Subedar Mastan sulking in a corner grabbed the first opportunity of break in Gul's dialogue and interjected now scratching his big nose in sheer nervousness, "You all must leave now. Do not make noise while leaving the post. *Bhainchod* Indians are very trigger-happy but don't worry I will provide all fire support, if your move is detected. I have two machine guns covering you. *Allah* is praised on your brave efforts. Whole Muslim community is indebted to your sacrifice. Move, hurry-hurry, I saw an all clear signal ten minutes back." He waved his M-16 rifle around in animated jerks to goad them to move.

Annoyed, Gul shot back a threatening stare at Mastan and let the man feel his annoyance. He sat on the ground pensively. He mouthed powerfully "Allah-o-Akbar" and started his prayers. Without a murmur, all sank into the floor in prostration.

Five minutes of prayers followed. Mastan, with his head bent down at an acute angle from the neck, frustratingly walked around in circles. His hands darted in quick draw towards his bums or the nose or the hanging balls to soothe the equally mysterious itchy eruptions.

He hated this rabble.

No person in right frame of mind could or should trust them to do anything meaningful. They create only problems for his post, whenever they cross. Last month in Indian retaliatory firing, he had lost two good boys hardly in their teens. They in sheer childish enthusiasm had creeped out in the open to see infiltration being carried out. Their bodies had been torn in two equal halves, as they caught an accidental heavy machine gun burst right in their torsos. His own life had been made miserable by the Commanding Officer on failure of command and control at his piquet. He had begged his Major *sahib* to use some other post this time, but the rascal had turned down his request. But his superior officer had given him more visible nose-bound ulcers and few hidden ones inside his underwear when he had forced him to accompany the guides and the key men of this unruly bunch down to the *nallah* for a dry rehearsal for area-familiarization and confidence building. His own confidence had been shattered in leaving the safe confines of the post. He had even mumbled some excuses but the smiling assassin, his Major Irfan had turned it down even before he had blurted in his request. He had reluctantly gone down with *Allah's* name on his lips and had returned uttering the same Almighty's name uninterrupted for minimum five hours. He was last to leave and first to enter back to the safety of his bunker. His waning faith in God had taken a sudden upswing after that death-defying walk down to the naked LoC.

All seemed to be creating deliberate trouble for him, he belched to his own thoughts. It was time he checked through the person of his native village, employed as a batman to Colonel *sahib,* of any pressure being applied by someone in the unit to have him replaced. He liked the independence enjoyed here. S*ahibs* only made appearances before a major visit or during an induction operation. His immediate boss regularly skipped that part too, often to be in warm bed of a low cast *kafir Hari bibi,* in the rear. Believe that those low caste *Hindu* woman made a very enthusiastic bed. Such a major operation and all the directions he had got were on a telephone through the Battalion Adjutant, whose face he had yet to see in person. Company Commander had made a brief stopover in the morning and had left everything on him. If any fuckup takes place his head was sure to be hanged. To top it all, these idiots were making merry and dancing before crossing the LoC.

Indians were just across.

The Russians, who only operated from Kabul or other secure bases in depth, allowed everyone to dance their way, straight into the war. However, Indians, like flies could be found in every imaginable nook and corner. Safety lay in silence. Unlike the chicken hearted Indian troops he had served on this LoC, a decade earlier, these queers fired even at the noise of a silent fart, that too done under a quilt. Earlier, it was a standing joke that their orders of fire, would come from *dhoti-clad* masters, in Delhi. Now it was pure and simple, a tooth for a tooth and an eye for an eye. You fire one burst they fire back two, send one bomb, receive two and the game continues. Life was reduced to showering the choicest abuses, as boys also shied away from firing back.

Gul caressed his beard thrice with the cup of his hands and with religious gyration of his head he got up silently, at the same time beckoning others to follow him. He paused at the entrance of the crawl trench and shook hands with his men as they disappeared into the next bend. It was good to have experienced war-hardened section commanders. Without his active involvement, he was confident that they would keep the flock together. With an expert eye, he made out everyone file out in right order of march.

It was also good to be a leader. It also felt good just being one.

With it came the automatic right to direct troops from the centre.

His youth had passed courting death for his leaders and now it is their time to do it for him. In any case as an Afghani, he could not be sacrificed for these, feminine Kashmiris. We had never asked for their help fighting the Russians. We all fought alone. Only later did the Americans came and fawning Pakistanis entered when victory was almost in their grasp. At the first opportunity, these Indian ass-licking Kashmiris came begging to us for help. Where were they when we were at war? Hiding beneath *firans* of their women and warming their hands in those small fire-lit earthen pots they carry even to shit, I am sure. How could these Muslims live with Hindu heathens in the first place?

Weak earlier-Hindu genes, may be.

He briskly went over the issues at hand. Mental arithmetic reflected an awesome firepower he was lugging. Twelve rocket launchers, eight under barrel grenade launchers, two hundred fragmentation grenades, few silencer pistols, one hundred and twenty kilograms of RDX, seventy pencil timer detonators, thirty-six AK-47, ten sniper rifles, five 62mm mortars, seven hundred rounds per weapon and the first American Stinger missile of the war in this theatre was an impressive booty indeed. He was more than prepared for Indian border patrols and will get a surprise of their lives if they barge into his brave *jihadis*. When these weapons will bark in vale of Kashmir, then its misguided inhabitants will listen to one voice of mighty *Allah*, through him.

If *Allah Tala* loved him, he will definitely succeed.

Wasn't it the *maulvi* at Peshawar who had prophesied to his father that he, Gul, had bigger missions in life to achieve? Rehman Gul, his father, had not even batted an eyelid in giving his sixth son in charge of the *maulvi*. Blessed be the soul of his father and that of Islam Mohammed for showing him the true path. Days in *madarasa* had element of fun, caring, carefree attitude and passion for all that stood for almighty *Allah*. *Maulvi* had loved him like his own child, goading at each step to develop qualities of leadership, which he displayed in abundance. A tap on the shoulder by Fazal rudely shattered his thoughts. "Your turn to go," he said.

Subedar Mastan bear-hugged the loving-departing brother Gul and escorted him up to the strands of barbed wire enclosing the post. Waving him off, he walked over to his field office situated inside a bunker. He opened a wooden shelf. Profusion of various knobs on the console stared back rudely at him. He hastily connected the mains to a 12-volt battery and the console now lit up like a Christmas tree. A young engineer from Islamabad had specially installed this radio set a few months back. He fiddled with the knobs and the harsh static clutter disappeared when he pressed on a flat switch highlighting on green neon background, 'Transmit'.

"*Akbar* to *Badshah*. *Tir* launched. I repeat again *Tir* launched," Mastan shouted into the microphone.

Without waiting for the message confirmation, he turned off the power supply. That young engineer had told him that any message reception at the receiving end was automatic and taped. Good, his nation had made such stupendous leaps in technology, but he still had one mundane report to give. He picked up his field telephone and on cranking the shaft vigorously got connected to his Company Commander.

He gave detailed account of the days proceedings. "*Ji hazoor,* the whole post is on stand to. All men are operating the automatics. We will give them a befitting reply," heard his runner Attar who was waiting outside the door, with mess tiffin filled with special mutton curry and piping hot *nans.*

It was the time for sepoy Attar Sayeds' commander to eat good and rest long.

Kannaur
143 Experimental Unit
(2057h, 03 Mar)

Atop the Kannauri Peak, overlooking the famous Indian Goddess shrine, housed in a dugout, Naik Bhonsle of 143 Experimental Unit, was totally bored. It was a six-hour shift and it had not even crossed his half time duty mark. He was dividing his attention equally between two-month-old *Bollywood* film magazine and stealing frequent glances on the screen ahead. *Pakis* seemed to be recuperating from yesterday's *Id-Ul-Zuha* celebrations. At this time of the night, the set in all probability should be busy enough to leave him dazed. The squeaky short rattling snores of his number two, cuddled near the warmth of an oil *bukhari,* told the sorry tale.

The latest state-of-the-art Siemens ATM 2500 set, with number of small boxes with 'Bharat Electronics Limited' written across their face, mounted co-axially on to the latter, filled half the space of the room and was an awsome sight. Capabilities of this re-engineered equipment were tremendous. It could acquire a whisper, on any HF, VHF or UHF radio set, up to fifty-five mills error, from the plains of Punjab to the crest of the *Pir Panjal* ranges, with an in-built computer chip to monitor five hundred known frequencies. Its fabricators boasted of automatic decoding sequence, performing million operations per second, to break almost any known code in the world. It was best of the best that Indian technology could deliver. It had not disappointed the manufacturers or the users alike till date except for a few glitches here and there. With deployment of four such sets in a grid, they virtually covered the entire Northern Indian sub-continent.

Green flicker of lights on the control panel combined with the sound of whirl of winding tape, he re-focussed his attention to his dominion of specialization. He hastily put on his microphone headset and rewound the tape, which had stilled after completing its pre-programmed operation. "*Akbar* to *Badshah*. *Tir* launched. I repeat again, *Tir* launched," the message filled his ears. He leaned closer and carefully noted the angle of message reception.

"Wake up you lazy Bhogal," giving a light kick on the makeshift wooden box bed on which he was snoring.

Bhogal got up with a start and stared stupidly at Bhonsle. "Call the duty officer immediately," and Bhogal slowly lumbered out, to the adjoining room, where the duty officer was busy watching the highlights of the cricket match between India and South Africa.

Lieutenant NP Singh, an officer on temporary attachment, listened to the taped transcript and dialled on direct hot line, one by one, other stations on the grid. He then busied himself noting something on his drafting pad.

"Get me the quarter metre map first," he said without looking up, obstructing the mouth of the telephone momentarily with his palm and replied "thank you" before putting the handset on the cradle. He spread the map and started marking long lines across it. He then walked over to the metre scale map, pasted on the sidewall, which occupied its area in its entirety. Consulting the earlier map repeatedly, he started feverishly plotting the line all over, the second time. Three lines originating from various units like this one bisected each other, east of Haji Pir Pass, in 311 Mountain Brigade defended sector.

Lieutenant NP, with twenty-six days of Army service under his belt and entrusted the important job of manning the 'mad house' for the first time was at quandary on deciding as to what to do with the intercept. His boss was on a sneaky pilgrimage to the *Vaishno Devi* shrine with his relatives, who had dropped at the base, today morning. Resolve to do something sparked when he saw the Naik expectantly looking at him.

With mock authority, he called the operator. "Get me 311 Mountain Brigade," he ordered. At 'who in the brigade?' on operators query, he got a bit flustered on not knowing designation of appointments and then hesitatingly said, "Anyone." After a considerable time and number of army exchanges later someone replied, "BM, three double one."

"Sir, I am officiating OC 143 Experimental Unit. We have just intercepted a transmission from your area." He pressed his ears to the handset and again repeated the same details but this time added his rank and name to it.

"Lieutenant NP, our sector is 76 kilometre wide along the LoC. How can you precisely help?"

"Well sir, at one hundred and ten kilometre distance that we are from you, I can give an accuracy of two kilometres and the grid reference we have recorded is 789456," NP proclaimed knowledgeably.

"Ahem, that's something positive. By the way, do you guys exist? This is the first time in my two years here that I have heard from your setup. Hope it's no military buck passing of a goof up on your end," Brigade Major, Major Zusti echoed his sentiments.

NP was taken aback, immediately going on defensive and wondering had he made any blunder, blustered without thinking, "No sir, we were established in 1982 and our reporting is regular, twice a day, to Command Headquarters. In fact, you can hear the taped version of the intercepted message," running the taped version, fed directly into the telephone. "Hope that has satisfied you sir that we are not lying," he added without much ado.

"Thanks, keep in touch." Brigade Major put down the phone and dragged the small talc covered map lying on the side table of his bed. It depicted the deployment of the forces down to the last man of 311 Mountain Brigade. He carried the map even to his toilet and it had virtually become an extension of his body. He knew the grid references of the entire length and width of the Brigade Defended Sector by rote. Though he always discounted all the contact-intelligence provided by higher agencies by factor 6 out of 10, he willed himself to inform 1/9 Gurkha Rifles of eminent danger, only because of the fact that he had never interacted with experimental unit earlier. Only intelligence worth reacting was the one provided by the units on ground. For more than once, they had footslogged the jungles and beaten around the bushes, on some vague information, some vague person, in a vague location in the rear had obtained from a vague informer.

The indispensable problem was that everyone wanted to play a cowboy without coming in front, where the tangible dangers lay.

THE LoC: AREA OF KHUNI NALLAH

N

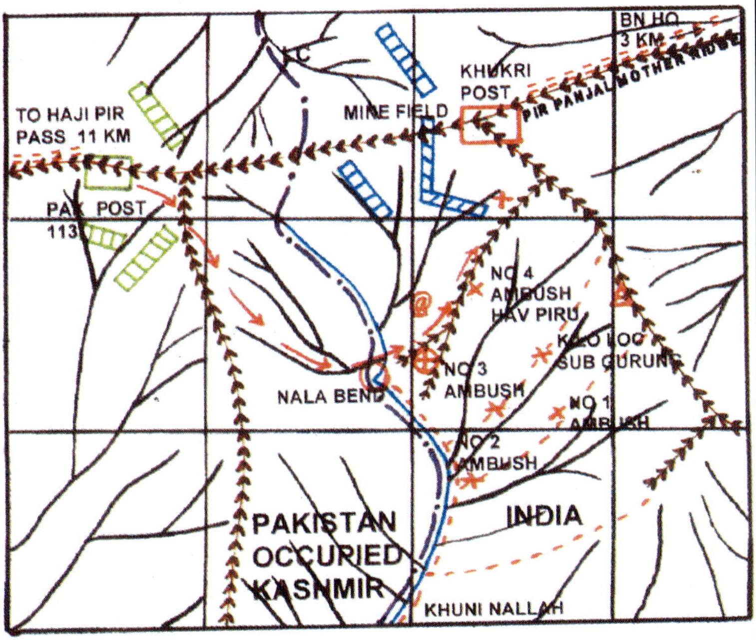

LEGEND

LOCATION WHERE GUL FELL	@
LOCATION WHERE GOBAR FOUND	⊕
LOCATION RESHAB SHOT	+
AMBUSH LOCATIONS OF 1/9 GR	×
ARTILLERY OBSERVATION POST	△
THAPAR CONTACTS PAKI MAJ	○
ROUTE OF INFILTRATION	→

Scale: One Square: One Km

Map not to scale

4

Dark Night

"Revel, rejoice and shine bright,
You wicked creature of the night.
In deep sinister bosom of dark,
Evil in black, say you lark.
With humanity fearless asleep,
Valiant men on dutiful keep.
Man – the evil creature of night?"

— Jesse

The LoC (2139h, 03 Mar)

Naib Subedar Gurung Bahadur, deployed with his four ambushes, 1875 metres southeast of Pakistani Post 113, put down his headset, after hearing the latest instructions from his Company Commander. He looked at his luminous watch. It read 2139 hours.

From intercept to warning troops in forward locations, it had taken exactly forty-two minutes.

Four men each, in four ambushes approximately three hundred metres apart, the basic gap was too much amongst them, thought Gurung. Intimate mutual support was not possible as basic military sense dictated. His Infantry School instructor, who had adjudged him the third best student in Tactics, would be appalled at the deployment if he saw it on ground.

These were pressing times and menial niceties of sound tactics could not be implemented in true spirit.

Not that they would not plan for it, but most of the times, pressure on manpower left crucial voids. Men had to avail their leave, go on courses, do temporary duties, execute fatigue tasks and most importantly rest adequately. Shamsher *sahib* was a stickler for rules and would personally detail men on ambushes and guard duties after ensuring that each man had one complete day off the previous day, including compulsory sleep, for eight hours. *Sahib* had promised immediate fire support from medium machine guns, rocket launchers, automatic grenade launchers and 51 millimetre mortars in case he ran into trouble. He had himself registered almost all conceivable targets in front and both the flanks of his company post. The best part was that they had fired and registered the targets during normal daily exchange of fire with the Pak Post 113, right across on the next crest-line. It had been a good cover for the stated intention. Whatever be the assurance from the Company Commander, men on ground were less and in battle, as always, faith and confidence came with numbers.

But that was the classical military quandary.

You take more men, the likelihood of detection increased proportionally and chances of a contact reduced in that magnitude. Lesser the numbers, it inversely increased the likely contact ratio due to reduced detection.

It had been a third continuous day since the ambushes had crept forward up to the near edge of the *Khuni Nallah*, from their locations on the ridge in rear, which came right down from the company post.

Major Shamsher had led the ambushes on first two nights consecutively. Major *sahib* had reasoned that the positions in depth on the ridge though very defensible, could be bypassed by a number of lateral tracks running along the *Khuni Nallah*. These jungle tracks looked no good to us but could take the infiltrators across with the help of local guides, who were operating in plenty. If one could control these trails, they could control any movement on them, thus checking infiltration, he had explained it to the whole company. *Sahib's* right and convincing reasoning apart, they were right under the noses of death. That Pak post hung like a fairy tale monstrous castle, in the air above them, ominously.

Havaldar Pun, the commander of number four ambush, under the deployment command of Gurung, was peering down towards the *Khuni Nallah* through his passive night vision binoculars. He had been on a continuous watch since his party commander had informed him of possible intrusion that night. Fierce cold wind was biting through his coat parka and jute cap balaclava, which clung to his round head, making him shudder in the cold now and then. These bloody army clothes were no good and wind passed through the woollen leggings as if an air-conditioner was blowing merrily inside one's underwear, he icily reasoned. His buddy rifleman Bhopal Gurung was watching his left flank and his light machine gun detachment was covering a small spur coming up from the river below.

Observation by night vision binoculars was a stressful business.

His eyes said so.

Water droplets finding the origins in his cornea were streaming down his cheeks due to the strain of continuous peering drill. In the sea of whiteness, pale yellow bushes danced in the wind and the rivulet resembled the flow of molten lava. At only 250 metres from the LoC, he had his night vision binoculars focussed at the optimum, range though nothing comprehensible was visible beyond the *nallah*. Those technical goons from Dehradun claimed 600 metres of effective range, but parametres of ideal conditions they always loved to sing, will only be available on the full moon, he thought. Ambient moonlight, my left foot, he cussed. It required more than two million photons of light to function as per its stated capabilities. He felt there were less than two light photons available at present. Who will produce moonlight when infiltrators will infiltrate on a dark night like this one? By the time the area gets illuminated by flares all the rats would have hidden in their burrows.

At first he thought it was an illusion.

Two dots appeared on extremities of the vision field of his night vision binoculars, almost camouflaged with numerous electronic dots running crazily across the screen. It was only when the dark shapes firmed in and moved defying the static of the still background, did Pun remove the binoculars and re-focussed them hurriedly. Yes, at the edge of the *Khuni Nallah,* he made out two distinct humanoid shapes slowly making their way across the stones in the riverbed, half bent. Bingo, he thought. For first time he was seeing something, which he had heard his friends, boast off. Fascinated, he followed their movements till they turned towards the spur on which his ambush was sighted.

On reality check, few seconds later he immediately patted Piru's back and harshly whispered, *"Do dushman, nallah bend par. Jaldi night sight lagao. Fire mere hukum par."*(Two enemy at nallah bend. Quickly put on the night sight. Fire on my orders)

Like a drilled mechanic, Piru put on the night sight atop his barrel and brought the light machine gun at the designated point of fire by resting the barrel on a wooden peg aligned towards the target. They had placed such pegs facing various directions; covering expected avenues of infiltration. Primitive, but effective method in aligning towards the enemy and more importantly giving more stability by nullifying the effects of horizontal azimuth accentuated due to burst fire mode.

Pun on turning 180 degrees, frantically flashed his torch towards his Platoon Commanders expected position and at the same time pulling the woollen blanket over his head to reduce his voice signatures, he whispered into his VPS radio set, "Kilo four for kilo, kilo four for kilo, message over."

"Kilo four pass over."

"Kilo four for kilo, two infiltrators sighted at *nallah* bend. Repeat, two infiltrators sighted at *nallah* bend. Moving between kilo three and kilo four location, over," reported Piru starting to sweat inside the thin blanket.

"Kilo for four roger. Kilo four do not open fire, I repeat do not open fire. *Dushman ko age bharne do.* (Let the enemy move forward) Out to you. All stations kilo come to stand to, I repeat come to stand to," Gurung was shouting into the radio set. In any case all bloody men were always on 'stand to' in the ambushes, lest they wanted to die sleeping, like what had happened in one such ambush in the neighbouring battalion, seven months back, he reflected.

He was passing the message to his Company Commander on his unreliable hand-held VM-mark three radio set, when the night lookout man, his ambush buddy, barged in and in heavy rasping breathless manner, stammered, "Danger indication received from direction of number four ambush," and vanished as quickly as he had appeared.

Not Far
(Little Later)

The ice cold howling wind, cut into his eyes, despite him hugging the rugged surface. His eyes were watering due to the harshness of the cold and his ear lobes felt as if they had been dipped into liquid nitrogen. His senses were chilled into submission, but the brain spoke otherwise.

Use me or die.

He peered from the side of a tree stump and tried to comprehend the confusing mass of ridges above. This was the trickiest and the most dangerous part of this exercise, which was breaking through the crust of the first line of Indian ambushes. Those bloody Indian ambushes had to be deployed somewhere on the crest of those craggy rocks above. They must avoid gullies, re-entrants or tracks near any prominent landmark, the most favoured places of Indian security forces. Rough edged stones were jabbing into his knees but he dare not even murmur in relief. All was going well, till now. Risal was close on his heels and he was confident that Gul's group was thirty to forty minutes or three hundred metres upslope. They had practised this part, live, with Special Services Group so many times that it was now a predictable routine to move and guide even a blind man.

"Risal which way today," Reshab casually inquired.

"Let's take the route which passes below the Indian post," Risal confidently replied.

"But that could be bloody dangerous," Reshab alarmed shot back.

"That's why it's safe. Indians send most of their troops in ambushes and the posts are scantily manned. You know that ambushes are deployed a little down slope but always on the dominating crest-line, leaving the post on top under-manned and vulnerable. Last place they will expect any one of us to cross is through that pathetic 1965 vintage mine field, next to the post. I know a safe route through it over the rocks. Don't you remember how shitless scared they are of stepping into it. We must exploit this, as we have a larger group to infiltrate this time," Risal explained.

Reshab could not search for an equivalent counter argument.

They, as per their own evolved and time-tested drill, both did not agree to a known, pre-discussed, set-route for infiltration. It had irritated that fat ISI army man, trying to disguise as a civilian even further. They had very strong reasons for the same. They had suffered earlier as their whole party of JKLF cadres had walked into an Indian trap, two years ago. It conspired later that one of their members, was an Indian informer who had passed the precise route including the halts to the enemy a month earlier.

The cunning and he was sure 'grinning' Indians had a month to plan for their bloody reception.

No wonder only five had survived out of twenty-five. By divine intervention, they both were in those lucky five. Both had backtracked, discovered the un-Islamic betraying man and later killed the informer's whole family, but only after savagely raping his two lovely teenaged virgin daughters trussed like animals for an entire week. It had sent ripples of shock in the area but now none dared to double cross. Since then, both had vowed not to discuss the infiltration route earlier and to refine the security even further, decide it only on crossing the LoC. They had various gadgets to guide even blind men. Yes, Risal always spoke sense. In-fact his half brother was intelligent and proving himself beyond his shallow age every time a mission was entrusted in his hands. Though he had joined the cause five years earlier than Risal, the bugger already knew more tactics and more routes than him. He had handed over the charge of daily dealing of weapons, delivery schedules, intelligence gathering, eliminating informers and most importantly, financial transactions to him. He loved his half-brother, admired his loyalty towards the family of which he was the titular head and in turn always listened to Risal's sound advice.

"OK, blink back the signal and place the LED fluorescent marker facing upwards but away from the infidels post direction. Hope Mosul and Tarik will not goof up the turning," Reshab whispered.

Risal immediately did as instructed. He crawled up the slope and took out a small roll from his right pocket. He unwrapped the tape and put it on the ground. He quietly got down to work, practised so many times earlier and it took just fifty-six seconds, eleven more than his usual time.

Moments later, snail-paced, both lumbered up the spur leading to the Indian post Khukri. Reshab stole a look behind, from twenty metres up, at their guiding contraption assembled below. No trace of light towards Indian side was visible except the faint reflections of the LED blinker, which blinked once after ten seconds each time. He was sure that a little further up the slope that those homing in reflections too would get hidden, due to the folds in the ground. Hope the God's men coming behind would react as drilled and not miss the marker.

Number Four Ambush (More Later)

Pun's eyes were glued on the two figures like a hawk ever since he had acquired them in his night vision goggles. Fascinated, he watched their movements.

"Kilo four, kilo four, they are headed towards our spur, over," said a shaken voice.

"Kilo for four, do not open fire, I repeat do not open fire, out," instructed Gurung.

"Kilo four, wilco," Pun replied heavily and turning back towards no one in particular hastily whispered, "Don't make any noise. No firing unless in self-defence, that too, on my explicit orders. We have to let them pass. Subedar *sahib's* orders."

What stupidity, thought Rifleman Gobar Singh, the number two of the light machine gun detachment. One never lets the enemy pass. That was the logic his *baje* had drilled into his simple head when imparting endless tips on fighting recounted out of his participation in the Second Great War. That is pure sacrilege, but orders are orders. Do not know what these *sahibs* keep on planning after reading maps and books. If the enemy is in the front as he is now, then shoot and kill him was the best option. It is better to kill a cobra while he is facing you, than to tackle him, with your back towards him. However, mother-fucking orders are orders and that is what he will do. He or others for that matter could not see beyond twenty metres in the darkness. Moon was still struggling to peep out of the black sky. Excited whispers along with animated gestures of his commander created more fear and apprehension than confidence.

He adjusted his fibreglass helmet and touched the silver handle of his *khukri* for assurance.

It gave him confidence.

It was his revered family heirloom. It was his grandfather's *khukri*, a present from an ever-grateful British officer, whose ebbing life *baje* had saved in World War II, by chopping the head of the fanatical Japanese imperial soldier, who was about to bayonet the hapless wounded *Gora sahib,* the second time. His *baje* had nursed his injured *sahib,* poked only once in the stomach by a Japanese bayonet, like a little baby, for two nights in the Kohima Town District Court complex and was awarded a Military Cross, for bringing him back to safety, two miles back, right under the nose of the enemy, guarding the ridges above.

Baje had told him of his war stories ever since he could remember.

Papa had broken the old man's heart by taking premature discharge. He could not cope up with the rigors of the army in the wake of 1962 Indo-Chinese war where he had somehow survived in a wounded state and that too as a prisoner of the Chinese, having been captured at some place called Lumpo, in Arunachal Pradesh. When he, as a youngster, had shown an iota of interest in joining the regiment, his grandfather had jumped up from his proclaimed deathbed and gleefully assumed command over his life, thankfully for three months only. He was a hard wily old instructor and had taught him all the field-craft and drill even before he could join his regimental recruits training centre, at Shillong. The problem he encountered later was that the drill and much of his tactics he had acquired from the old goat were totally British, of pre-Independence era, and he had to slog double, in first unlearning what he had mastered and then learning the right Indian way. He could never forget those tears of happiness when he joined *baje's* own 1/9 Gurkha Rifles. The toothless old goat had got totally drunk and danced throughout the night, with one of the local *didis*.

"Kilo for kilo four, message over."

"Kilo four, pass over."

"Kilo four do not fire at guides. Let them pass your location, out to you. All stations kilo, do you see *nallah* bend over."

"Kilo one, negative over."

"Kilo two, partially over."

"Kilo three, negative over."

"Kilo for kilo two re-site for better engagement, kilo three move two hundred metres right to engage *nallah* bend. Kilo two and three out. Kilo one, fall back to kilo location, over."

"Kilo one, wilco."

"Kilo two, wilco"

"Kilo three, wilco."

If silence was death, then all four men deployed in the number four ambush were definitely, quiet dead. They were lying so still that even the normal breathing of each other was resounding like a deafening roar. Heartbeats ticked like megaphones on full blast in their ears. The ticking was eardrum shattering. After a few minutes, they could hear the laboured breaths of the two infiltrators including the unmistakable sound of feet scrapping against the undergrowth. Pun brought his night vision binoculars down lest the infiltrators identify his position due to the ambient glow his binoculars emitted and had also switched off his radio set also as a precautionary measure. He watched them with acute apprehension from his vantage point. They passed, ten metres below their location. Their round turbans and cross-slung AK-47s were clearly visible. He waited for about seven minutes, after he could hear them no more, before he could muster enough confidence to pass back the report.

Khukri Post
(Same Time)

Pulling back the talc sheet lying on the table Major Shamsher Singh peered over his map, perhaps for the twentieth time, in the last so many minutes. If one looked closely at the sheet staring back at him, one could only marvel at what he was studying, for it was more than an ordinary map. Ridges and various spurs stood out due to light pencil shadings and red markings of all known routes of infiltration glared back, almost giving a panoramic overview of the entire area up to fifteen km radius. Notations on sides of known sympathisers, guides, militants, demographic profile, move timings to different places by varied sizes of groups, obstacles, difficult no-go areas, own patrolling schedule and ambush sites for the day, all read like a fairy tale story book.

Sick of getting no worthwhile catches, despite his sources giving him bi-weekly news of various militant movements through his Area of Responsibility, he had reappraised the situation alone, last week. Though he was convinced himself of the efficacy and soundness of his decision, he was sure that if the Commanding Officer was ever consulted he would be back in the rear base for trying to be a 'Napoleon in his nappies', a phrase he always used to restrain young officers. He personally would hate it, as he hated counting onions and potatoes for provisioning of the soldiers. It was not the reason that he had joined this unit or the army for that matter. Some of his friends and course-mates revelled doing this silly logistic business. He could never reason why. They should open a *pansari ki dukan,* earn more moneyed-respect and then why serve in the army. He felt comfortable with a rifle in his hands and commanding the respect of his troops in situations beget with danger.

Well, two men had been sighted by number four ambush in charge of his company's ace footballer Havaldar Pun. They were traversing this ridge, he reflected deftly tracing it on his panoramic map with a pencil. How odd, a further up they will hit his post. He was sure they were the advance route reconnaissance guides employed by the militants. It had taken a considerable argument in convincing the men, not to open fire, at first sight of the enemy. They had been vehement in disagreement initially till he managed to convince one of the youngest Rifleman and ashamed seniors then followed suit, though without much ado. Policy in general was to allow the initial guides pass through in hope to catch the larger group, invariably following. This was what he planned to do for now and not let his Commanding Officer spoil his show. First, he should warn his post to throw one more ambush ahead on the edge of the perimetre minefield, as those two men were headed this way.

Khuni Nallah, On The LoC (30 Minutes Later)

Mosul saw the LED first. "Tarik stop," he whispered.

"Yes, what for," came back an equally hushed voice.

"Look, route guide marker is right ahead. We must head for it."

Both crawled slowly towards the LED marker and on examining it, Tarik cursed, "Stupid *bakarwals* have changed the plan. They are going by the uphill route. We must warn everyone of this change in the route. The idiots have taken the least desired route option number four, of all routes earlier discussed. Mindless idiots."

Gul was feeling confident tonight.

The *bakarwal* guides seemed to have got clean through. Either Indians were sleeping or ambushes were not placed ahead as anticipated. In any case, Colonel Iqbal had told them of paucity of men and material in Indian ranks in the frontline, due to the havoc caused by the *jihadis* in the rear areas. He stumbled into two of his men kneeling down and irritably shouted, "Why have you stopped, you fools?" The unknown kneeling Kashmiri, pointed ahead.

"Change in plans," answered Tarik when he married up with him a little later and then explained the problem.

Gul's, otherwise calm disposition gave way to fitful bout of irritation. Unworthy local rascals, he thought. How can you trust someone when he does not trust your plan? What was that famous saying amongst the Pakistan Punjabis; you can trust a snake but never a local of this area. In any case, these weak-kneed people had betrayed the true cause thrice earlier in 1947, 1965 and 1971. Imagine they betrayed their own tribal Muslim brothers. He was the second of his family to be in Kashmir. His father's twice removed cousin had died in 1947 at some place called Pattan fighting the Indians. His family was destined to make a name in this vale. But if these shit-holes had woken up then, this muddle wouldn't have been there. Besides cursing them avidly he also could not do anything. He gestured Tarik to hurry on.

The group quickly crossed the *nallah*. One of the *mujahid* in Kasim's group fell on the slippery rocks with his rifle making a sharp metallic clang, as it fell on the stones.

"Hush you idiot. Noise travels far at night," retorted Kasim.

Number Four Ambush (2205h, 03 Mar)

The noise did not travel as far as feared that night.

The wind from Indian positions was blowing away, but the fall was definitely registered by Pun who was glued to his night goggles. His hands were drenched in cold, apprehensive, sticky perspiration. Holy-shit, an endless line of people had crossed the *nallah*, like ants. He with a determined resolve again convinced his disbelieving brain that what he had witnessed was not an allusion. He had counted about thirty after the first shock had worn off. He tried looking upwards, but an overhang clouded his vision. He could not see two people who had crossed earlier.

"Kilo four for kilo," he rasped into the microphone, "thirty to forty men are crossing the *nallah* bend now, over." His three other ambush-mates scampered for more effective cover on just hearing this shocking report. They stared at him in dark, daring him to speak with saner mind and sight the second time.

"Kilo four, reconfirm figures again, over."

"Kilo four for kilo. I said thirty to forty and am passing after counting twice," Pun half-screamed into the handset, in total frustration of not being believed in first place, "and accord permission to open fire, over," he later begged.

Pun's battle-mates were shocked and had full reason to rebel. Four against forty was not even worth discussing and wasting your money to place any reasonable odds on.

"Kilo four, negative, I repeat, negative. Fire only when infiltrators within forty to twenty metres range. Fifty-one millimetre mortar will provide illumination within five seconds of your opening fire, out to you. All stations kilo, provide fire support to kilo four if enemy visible or bring down speculative fire at *nallah* bend. All stations kilo, out."

All kilos rogered almost in unison. Apprehension breathed out of Gurung's handset at each reply.

"*Guru ji ab kya hoga,*" (Reverend teacher what will happen now) asked the youngest Gobar.

"*Diwali aur maut,*" (Diwali and death) echoed mind-dead Pun. All the battle-mates heard the resolve laced with the fait accompli. None had the courage to rebel.

Srinagar
(2210h, 03 Mar)

The place had witnessed much better times.

Now it was a dead city. It became deadlier at night.

It was the price of *jihad* and its ungrateful citizens refused to acknowledge it.

The fact was actually too shameful to admit and admit failure, never. Like anything bad it could be passed to as an Indian conspiracy or better still to repressive security forces, but never ever to the price of *Jihad.*

Except for the stray dogs that guarded their packs territories, the streets were totally deserted. Their occasional barks pierced through, in otherwise silent night. Heavy fog, descending from the mountain ranges all around had engulfed the city and was making a slow progress along the river Jhelum.

The city halted after 1800 hours, well before the dusk-to-dawn curfew imposed by the Indian authorities.

Another price of *Jihad.*

All thanked their plethora of Gods, as dear ones were cattle-counted and safely tucked in for the night. None whispered or spoke or sang or entertained or opened doors to anyone, if possible. In the dead of night people covered their anxieties in fitful bouts of sleep. Nevertheless, few men like him engaged in the business of warfare were awake, only daring to operate in the safety of the night. They were too well known to move in the candour of daylight. Indians had numerous spotters mingling with crowds to home in to known or suspected militants. Like him, fellow bandsmen in various parts of the city kept night vigil, peering through secret places on the movement of Indian patrols and cordon parties. Thanks to his efficient organization and civil telephone department that all sectors got adequate warning of impending danger.

The figure in black moved down the deserted back streets, in Lal Chowk commercial-cum-residential area. He, as always, had deliberately chosen black, to blend with the darkness. He desperately vied for that magical half second of delay and confusion in spotting him. It had saved his life from the Indian bullets many a time and he struck to his dress code as a religion.

The man in black peered cautiously from the side of the building into the open square lit by a lone electric street lamp. Finding it deserted, he quickly darted across and started moving in the shadows of the triple storey edifices, guarding the flanks of the street. On crossing the shop named Zahir Silk Factory, he slid along the compound wall, into three feet wide, side alley. On its fifth window, an innocent white paper sticking out of the joinery, indicated all clear. He thanked God for safe transportation and tapped the small wooden door adjacent it twice in succession.

Almost immediately, the door opened in anticipation. It made no noise for it was freshly oiled at the hinges. Nothing could be left to chance. He smiled at the eye for detail and efficiency of his host. He entered a small square room.

"Why did you call me here. It's forbidden," said the man in black.

"Importance of events," replied a calm voice. "Time has come for deliverance and the destiny of Kashmir now lies in our hands."

"What do you mean," he asked and through the slit in the black layers of wrapped clothes, eyes darted across the face of *Maulana* Amjad Ali and searched for an answer.

"Collect all your able men. Initially handpick the best five and give them to me. Ensure that they are well armed and are available within a week. I will seek for twenty more at a later date," instructed the *Maulana.*

"What for," inquired the man in black.

"Do not seek reasons. You possibly cannot fight the *jihad* alone. It is a fact and you are intelligent enough to digest this issue. We have to come under one banner. United we have a better chance at the war being won quicker. It is basic commonsense. Our friends in foreign countries are exhorting us to do so or all that has been achieved till now will vanish as fast as the dipping evening sun. In half an hour from now, Tarik, Jilani and Lone will be here to pledge similar support."

"I will do as you seek. To obey you is my life. If bigger birds are flying, then, how can a small fly on the same pedestal sit idle? But remember you will be giving your best-kept secret to others," the man in black said. Later at not getting any reply, bowing his head, the figure in black disappeared as silently into the night as he had come.

It took him more than two hours and two near brushes with Border Security Forces patrols to reach his two-storey house in the prestigious Raj Bagh area of the city. Jumping over the shoulder high wooden green coloured gate, he quietly slid into already unlocked ajar door. Moving inside the house with aid of pencil torch, he threw down his black turban on the floor and lay on the bed. Staring at the darkness above Rasool Bhatt said, "shit" and closed his eyes.

Four kilometres southwest of Rasool's house, in the sprawling Kashmir University complex, Nafisa was sobbing in her bed. Sleep had eluded her all the night. Her best friend Khushbu was fast asleep in the next bed oblivious to her troubles.

Indian Post, Khukri
(2215h, 03 Mar)

Major Shamsher was biting his nails in sheer nervousness. The contents of the latest situation-report from the ambush-sites had him gulping for precious air for a few seconds.

The report from Kilo four was painfully disturbing.

Had the Pakistanis gone mad?

Dammit thirty to forty men were attempting infiltration.

Bloody Pun must be having multiple parallax problems. He was expecting six to eight terrorists at best, to attempt infiltration, a manageable number, but never ever could he dream of forty. Pakistanis were assuredly going mad. A mad-failed nation and what could one expect from them with their ideology that if we can't progress then how the neighbour can? The information was good enough to give a minor heart attack to the old man and more than adequate to create a major riot, in all those headquarters, up the chain.

Bloody hell, his whole appreciation of placing the commanders at more vulnerable ambushes had gone wrong.

Wish by some magic wand he could change that buffoon of Gurung with dynamic Lieutenant Thapar. Gurung, though a good JCO, had not been tested under fire and was slow to comprehend any fast fluid situation, while Thapar had single-handedly killed two militants last month. Out of eight ambushes out of his company post tonight, four had been deployed on the Southern slopes at *Khuni nallah* under Gurung and the balance covered the Northern slopes under Thapar. He was sure that infiltration would be attempted from the North of the *Pir Panjal* ranges.

The mother-spine on which his company post was located, peeped into valleys both in the North and the South, in equal measures but Northern slopes occupied his focus, as the militants could descend directly into Srinagar valley, the hotbed of fundamentalism and local support. The valleys to the South of these sacred ranges were inhabited with *Rajput –Mohammedan* or *Moslem - Mohammedan* which changed the demographic profile to India's favour. They considered themselves the true and purer Muslims than those Kashmiris, as their forefathers coming along with conquering Mughal hordes had converted these infidels of the valley into Moslem fraternity, only a few centuries back. Mostly from *Gujjar* and *Bakarwal* communities their mutual dislike for supposedly snootier Kashmiri brethren ran deep. Leave aside inter-marriages, they refused to sit and eat together. Historic subjugation apart, their physical and mental attributes also fueled the rivalry. The Southern men were dark, taller, and rugged and their muscles gave them the animalistic swagger, while their counterparts in the North were fair, mild, feminine and let their upper story do the talking. No wonder he had persisted with an officer-led ambushes in the Northern slopes.

Major Shamsher picked up his field telephone contemplating to speak to the old man, but before he could speak into it, he threw it down, as if it weighed a ton. He had to organize the few men around him first, before he dared to speak to his Commanding Officer.

"Company Havaldar Major (CHM)," he shouted on top of his voice and like genie in comics the CHM appeared, before his Company Commander's reverberating voice could die down.

"Mine field ambush mein kitne manush gaye." (How many men are deployed in the minefield ambush)

"Char hazoor."

"Post to Stand par hai."

"Ji hazoor."

"Reserve."

"Chavvis hazoor."

"AGL and MMG targets."

"Post 113, hazoor."

"Good, line tor," replied Shamsher.

After ensuring the perceived correctness of his undertaken actions he picked up the field telephone and asked for his Commanding Officer, Colonel VS Thapa. A few seconds later, he was put through to his boss. Animated grunts and crisp resounding of yes and no sir filled the room for the next five minutes, giving enough indication even to Rifleman Bijoy Thapa, his beloved *sahayak*, that *sahib* was having a grueling time with the Commanding Officer.

Three Km Behind Mother Ridge (2225h, 03 Mar)

Fucking shit, fucking shit, he screamed to his disbelieving ears.

Soothing heady intoxication, ensured by five large whiskeys he loved to enjoy almost daily to kill monotonous routine, receded magically by the time Colonel VS Thapa, Commanding Officer 1/9 Gurkha Rifles, put down his phone. His heartbeat had drastically dimmed and his cute little ass was literally "on fire" as per the army parlance.

That mother-fucker tells me now, of all he has done, he grumbled to himself. It was too late to retrieve the situation or to intervene effectively. Family histories in this unit ran deep and he had seen that toddler turn into a fine man, but at present if someone asked for a second opinion, he will shout and shout loud that the idiot is a mentally ill military lunatic.

Shamsher was a second generation officer whose father had died bravely defending this battalion headquarters at slopes of Tsandhar in Namkachu area in Chinese war of 1962, similar to his own father's last heroic stand, a mere hundred metre away at the units three inch mortar position.

Both had audaciously died defending the honour of the unit.

In any case the positions they had been told to defend were not tactically honourable and honourable soldiers had no business to do unhonourable biddlngs. But they were Indian soldiers in heart and mind. Your safety, honour comes last every time. The honour of their country defied mundane thinking and came before self everytime.

Multitude of well-armed Chinese hordes did not aver their resolve.

So they had fought, a little distance apart, shouting, goading each other till they ran out of their given hundred rounds of ammunition, which an educated Prime Minister and his academically brilliant Defence Minister had provided and thought was adequate to fight the largest Army in the world.

Then they ran as fast as their laboured lungs could support their suicidal rush.

They ran with their *Khukris* held high, its polished steel glimmering in full brightness of the burning sun.

They ran straight towards the hordes of gloating Chinese and chopped a few heads.

Later, the astounded Chinese remembered to mow them down with automatic fire and plentiful ammunition, which had been provided by their uneducated peasant born leader. The tale narrated by a wounded survivor had been very dear to his heart and to both families. Shamsher was revered by his troops, was precise and wholly professional but it was his daredevil approach and hell for leather attitude which worried him the most. The guy was also impulsive, always up to something and worst still he informs you after he has executed his plan. Left to him, Shamsher's half cock-and-bull schemes would never see the light of the day. Holy cow! He had changed the deployment pattern without his knowledge and now admits that ambushes as per him were a bit exposed. He was damn sure that they would be hundred per cent exposed to the enemy fire.

Once his finger-holding toddler had jerked his arm across and jack-knifed it up his anus. It was too painful even to scream coherently.

He was also racked with conscience, whether to report the matter to his superior officer or not. Knowing the jumping jack above him and associated problems of managing him at his forward company base, which his boss would surely reach tonight, he reasoned against it. It was my battle at least for now and he would wait to see how it develops, he thought. Colonel Thapa then quickly summoned his file browsing Adjutant and issued instructions to lay his battalion Mortars on India Mikes 17 and 48 (Nallah bend and Pak post 113 respectively) and turn in his Quick Reaction Team for immediate move.

Rather than to punch the air in desperation and stare at the barren wall ahead for the moment, he walked up and prayed to the idol of fiery '*Durga Mata*' installed in the corner of his room, to bless his battalion and protect his men.

On the LoC
(2255h, 03 Mar)

The darkness was total and frightening.

One could not see beyond the fifth or the sixth man.

The big rucksacks they were carrying slowed their pace and each step became an exaggerated affair. But there was no choice, thought Gul. These rucksacks contained grenades, RDX, timer detonators, light activated detonators, ammunition, walkie-talkies and many other arms to further the cause of *jihad* in the subjugated Kashmir valley. Indians will never leave vale of Kashmir. They were too powerful to be driven out by conventional war. Pakistan had tried it thrice earlier, and each attempt had resulted in a miserable failure. They even had lost half of their country trying to do this.

Thank the shitty Ruskis for showing Muslim brotherhood the way. Why thank Russians. They just gave us an opportunity. We must thank those *gora* Americans for organizing them and showing them the true-lighted path to heaven. The true light of *jihad,* ironically has been shown by his religion's biggest enemy; the Satan infidel state of U.S.A.

God bless America, he murmured. Actually he hated that vulgar satanic country.

How can you live in a society where women walk half-naked? Do they have no shame? Their women nude and drunk all the time. What morales do they teach their children? Do they actually have any religion as labeled by his mentor? Women holding hands of men in public, kissing in public, men kissing women or men kissing men or women kissing women, free pornographic photographs pasted on walls, such movies even freely available to see. It was beyond him to think anything more ugly or repulsive than that.

Those people were uncivilized.

Thousand cuts.

Yes, this was the only solution to defeat a superior army. Kill them slowly, by thousand cuts. Bleed them like a *halal* goat. Yes, let the blood ooze out in small droplets simultaneously ebbing its life. Ah, there were dedicated Muslim militants from Europe, Sudan, Checheniya and Afghanistan to pick up arms for their cause. Once India lost Kashmir, its famous neck, it will disintegrate like a house of cards, just as U.S.S.R. Then we will rule the jewel of the crown. The only bastion of non-believers in South Asia. What Changez Khan, Timur Lane and Ghazni, could not achieve, we shall achieve.

Putting his head down, Gul started trudging up the slope, slowly.

"Kilo four, message over."

"Kilo, pass over."

"Kilo four, minimum forty men, in my killing zone. On my fire, illumination out."

"Kilo, for kilo four roger, kilo two and kilo three, situation over."

"Kilo two, enemy sighted, at maximum range, over."

"Kilo three, enemy seen, in range, over."

"Kilo, to all stations kilo, join with all fire power. Good luck, out."

As always, the bullets arrived earlier.

They arrived in great numbers much before their shocking sound could explode in Kasim's ears.

Mosul's face erupted like a burst watermelon, as the first burst of 7.62 mm Light Machine Gun (LMG) caught him squarely. He dropped to the mother earth, faceless.

Piru had aimed at the centre of the body, but down slope firing had affected the trajectory of bullets. Through his crew served weapon night sight, he could see streaks of bullets flying over. He quickly adjusted the aim and fired in small controlled bursts much lower this time. The bullets raced, grazing the ground and hitting true.

He saw three more men tumble.

Pun in good military anticipation had also kept his hand grenades ready and primed. He, in quick succession, lobbed three of them. They uncannily fell smack in centre of Kasim's group, blasting with an identifiable low crunch four seconds later.

More men tumbled.

Then the rest of his battle-mates joined with their guns blazing. They had no willing reason to hold back anything in terms of ammunition delivery. It was they or themselves.

More men tumbled.

Then a couple of fractions later, devastating fire from other like-minded and similar intentioned ambushes reached the focal point.

Then more men tumbled.

It was a simple tumbling game. It was an Army's favourite game. It required no deft reasoning or better comprehension. It was the game of simple mathematics, addition and subtraction, which the biggest army dodo could also compete in. Any side which ensured the tumbling of his opponents more, more quickly than his, more importantly won.

Before Kasim's shocked brain could comprehend anything acceptable, bright flashes caused his lower limbs go numb. Unsupported by his fragmented legs he fell heavily on the inclined earth. Wounded, in excruciating discomfort he whimpered for help. None moved towards him to provide any solace. In a trance, he saw a dance of death unfolding in front of his eyes. He tried to shout, trying to summon help but could only croak, "*Allah, Allah,* please save me." After uttering that lamentation, he died.

Light Machine Guns of all the ambushes were simultaneously, in unison, racking the exposed flanks of the intruders. Red bullets tracers lazily flew in the air. Volley after volley of fire echoed along the mountain slopes. Volley after volley of automatic fire ripped into infiltrators. Volley after volley of lethal bullets burst their guts, liberally soiling the slopes with blood. At each dying retort of a volley, more men tumbled.

Gul thought the world had slipped under his feet. "Ambush, ambush. Go to ground, go to ground," he thundered taking control of his emotions. His long years of battle inoculation against the Russians, came back instinctively, "Fire back Ahmed. Get up you fools fire back. Kasim hold the right flank. Yusuf get mortars in action. All *jihadis* fire back," Gul screamed, hidden luckily below a boulder.

Suddenly, the sky above him illuminated. Two shooting stars lighted his left flank and the wind blew them towards his position, where he hugged the ground. Sharp crunch of bombs and steady bursts of fire created a maddening noise. Some idiotic fragmentary ones fell smack in middle. A few more men tumbled.

Gul hurriedly scanned around. Limbs of Kasim's men were scattered all over and hardly anyone was visible. Suddenly a bullet slammed at a man next to him, lifting him clean off his feet. When that man fell back to ground his body tumbled to one side, revealing his bloody face. Blood oozed out of his neighbour's mouth. Blood, oh my God, blood was everywhere. Few were whimpering in agony. Gul then felt a sharp sting on his right shoulder, they have got me, he thought. The pain was sharp and acute. The bloody Indians have got me. Those white Russian pigs could not even scratch his body in so many encounters and these lowbred Indians had shot him.

Within him a blinding fury of hate rose choking his throat. The pain, the stinging fire like pain, drowned in his pure anger.

He lifted his AK-47 and fired a wild burst towards the nearest position, which he could discern from the trajectory of the tracers. "Charge, charge, follow me," he hoarsely shouted as he let off three grenades from the Under Barrel Grenade Launcher, attached with the weapon.

In the madness and melee all around, six fanatics rose as one, from God knows where and joined him shouting, *"Allah ho Akbar, ya Ali, ya Ali,"* charging the Indian positions, simultaneously firing their guns and grenades.

Ahmed and Qurban were mowed to death before they could cover four yards.

Havaldar Pun, Lance Naik Piru and Rifleman Bhopal, did not feel the blindness, which overtook them as the grenades burst all around their ambush position.

Gobar, who had crawled to a small cleft of stones to get extra LMG magazine, felt the earth shake around him. He quickly recovered his wits and urged, "Piru left, fire left, Piru fire the stupid LMG."

He stared at Piru. It seemed million seconds before he realized that Piru was lying on the LMG, unmoving. Oh my God, Piru is dead.

"Pun, Bhupi help me. Piru is wounded, come to the LMG, help me," Gobar shouted.

He quickly scanned around. The twisted shapes of all his comrades momentarily visible in pyrotechnic light told him the grim story. Oh my God I am alone, thought Gobar.

"Kali Ma give me courage," he muttered under his breath.

He grabbed the LMG and cocked the bolt while taking aim at the advancing enemy shouting, *"Ya Ali, Ya Ali.*

He carefully aimed at the centre of the chest of the fanatic goading other men.

He pressed the trigger in rising panic. Noise of an empty click was all he could hear.

No, not at this time, his weapon could not misfire. Not at this crucial juncture. *Kali Ma* don't desert me now, he prayed. Shit, no time to reload. He watched death in numbers charging at him. '*Diwali aur maut,*' his inert Havaldars retort filtered into his ears. His hand automatically slipped to his right waist. It was better to die fighting than be mowed down like a rat.

Baje, I will make you proud today.

Brandishing his *khukri* high above his head, he jumped out of his position and charged the enemy crying, *"Ayo re Gorkhali, ayo re Gorkhali."*

Animal instincts overtook him. He was a tiger fighting for his survival. There was no fear. His mind, his hands were in complete union with his *Baje's* jewel; the eighteen-inch long *khukri.* Suddenly he found himself surrounded by bunch of hostile men. They momentarily withheld fire, to avoid fratricide amongst them. Gobar was not in mood to give them a second stupid chance. Kill the cobra when you are facing him, his body talked.

The first arc of downward stroke bisected a neck. The cut was clean and clear. Abdul didn't even feel the prick.

The fountain of blood hit Bhogal's face. It sprayed on to his face as an intoxicating perfumed deodorant. Like barbers aerosol, phush-phush, it hit his hot face. He felt better, the warm blood cooling his boiling head.

Gul saw in fascination the head fall off Abdul's shoulders, bounce like a rubber football and tumble onto his feet.

The backstroke split the abdomen of the second *jihadi.* His guts burst, intestines slowly slithering out, spilling on the ground.

Like a beast possessed Gobar charged at the remaining three.

In the semi-darkness of the night, Gul spied on a strange glow emanating from this advancing madman. Due to an illumination flare bursting directly overhead, he saw an eerie looking, slit-eyed man, face covered in blood, his tongue darting out to savor its taste, advance menacingly. A feary man eating cannibal. The Indians had employed cannibals. The advancing one seemed to be enjoying the taste of body fluids sprayed on his face and oh God what will he do to his body. To be eaten and not buried. Surely there would be more such animals behind him. Simple dread of an *adam khor* overtook his steely nerves, "Run, run, turn back, run," he mumbled, scared for the first time in his life.

Mehmood, about to press the trigger at his AK-47 at the advancing devil, hesitated for a fraction of a second on hearing Gul's voice. It cost him his life.

Gobar's *khukri* flew like a missile, impacted with a thud and then bisected his ribs into two. In the same running stride, Gobar plucked out his weapon protruding out from half kneeling man and started running after the remaining two enemies.

"Run, run, run," screamed Gul.

In the darkness, Gul ran. His life depended on how fast his legs churned the ground beneath his feet and he ran very fast in the darkness of night. He ran fast not knowing where he ran. He ran fast over the dead bodies of his fallen comrades. He ran fast over an overhang. His body flew very fast in the air. He shrieked in agony and fear as no ground came to meet him and when it did after about five seconds, he had blissfully fainted.

"Ayo re Gorkhali," Gobar let out a blood curling war cry as he covered the last five yards with a long leap from a small platform of rocks above and crashed into the last visible *jihadi*.

Blinded by fear, the *jihadi* got up and turned towards Gobar. In the red paleness of the bursting para illuminating bombs above, he could see the glint reflect off the steel of the *khukri* as it raced towards his head. Instinctively he raised his hands above his head in protection. The steel blade sliced through his left ulna just ricocheting enough to miss his neck.

"Oh *Allah*, have mercy. Please, please don't kill me," he howled in pain and slumped to the ground, one hand less.

Gobar quickly grabbed the AK-47 fallen from the hands of the whimpering man and with contempt granted him his life wish. Slowly he surveyed the scene below. In semi-lit night he could register some persons running back into the *nallah*. Back into the vaginal hole from where they had emerged the first time. In a jubilant cry he again shouted, *"Ayo re Gorkhali,"* and led out a wild burst from the captured weapon, in no direction in particular.

For Gurung, about three hundred metres distant, the events flashed in sonic speed, too fast for his brain to register all the intricacies of the firefight. Initially he could discern the firing from all the ambush sites. Noises of grenades bursting and wild chatter of guns and anguished cries filtered back to his position, three hundred metres back, clearly.

"Good, keep the illumination on," he excitedly shouted to his fifty-one millimetre mortar detachment commander. "Keep the area illuminated every thirty seconds. Yes, keep the point of burst much to the left and short. Strong wind is blowing away from us and don't forget to fire HE in between," in addition he instructed.

Suddenly unmistakable cries of, *"Allah O Akbar, ya Ali,"* filled the semi-lit surroundings. Shrieks, cries of pain, of hollering mercies, of whimpered defeat, of pungent prayers, of goading, of excitement, of battle whoops and also wails of despair followed. Intermingled, overlapping, the riot of noise defied decipherable acoustics. After a few seconds later, ominous silence whiplashed his soul.

"Oh my God," he muttered. "The firing had stopped from No. 4 ambush. The enemy seems to have overrun the boys," he fearfully intuited.

"Sahib, no firing is heard from No. 4 ambush. Yes, just some shouts, yes. Seems enemy has overrun the ambush. *Kuch aur madad karo,"* (Provide some more help) he shouted in sheer panic and helplessness into his radio set.

Unit HQ, Mother Ridge (Few Seconds Later)

"Mortar action," the magnetic voice boomed out of the megaphone. "Direction; 233°, height 56° and 30 minutes. Charge four, three rounds, quick mortar fire," the megaphone croaked again.

The 4.5 kg Mortar High Explosive bomb, slipped 61 inches down the length of the barrel. As its tail fin hit the base plate, the static firing pin struck the igniter cap. Heat and friction due impact initiated a small spark side, igniting the primary cartridge. The small crescendo of a resultant bigger fire and flash reduced to ash the retaining cardboard that held them. The fire then raced through the steel transmitting tube where it was evenly distributed to further ignite 30 grams of Xenon explosive. The slipped on secondary charges burnt furiously exalted by Xenon, producing pressures up to 400 tonnes per square inch, inside the confines of the mortars steel tube chamber.

Gases finding no escape route, hurled the mortar bomb back, upwards the barrel at a velocity of 372 metres per second, enough to cover 4000 yards distance to the target. The sudden upward jerk allowed a small steel ball inside the head of the bomb unhinge from its groove, freeing a striking pin. Under the tension of a helical spring, the striking pin came out of its encasement. Simultaneously the detonator cap rotating on its axis rested when it came just below the striking pin. All these chemical and mechanical forces executed in microseconds armed the bomb, as it was just about 15 metres from the mouth of the mortar tube.

The oval shaped 379mm long low-grade metallic body, gracefully flew up in the air. The tail fins quivered and rotated the bombs to give it stability in the flight. At 1300 metres above the ground, almost half way up to the target, all sixteen of them, one by one, came momentarily to stand still as gravitational forces conquered the chemical counter parts. The nose dipped down and with increasing speed each second they raced down to meet the mother earth. On impacting with the ground, the brass nose body buckled and the striking pin crumbled into the detonator, which initiated 705 grams of the main filling of TNT, into a blast of fire and death.

On The LoC (Thirty-Two Seconds Later)

They generally arrive without a warning, despite what all foggy old soldiers say.

Gobar did not hear the expected distinctive shrill whine of overhead passing bombs as they exploded hundred yards ahead of him. The earth suddenly seemed to spew up smoke and fire from its bowls. The distinctive accompanying crunch of simultaneously bursting bombs was deafening.

The belt of mortar fire caught the remaining infiltrators as they were running down the slope.

They were plain unlucky. God was not in a mood to bestow any largesse upon them.

The target registered earlier was the river they had crossed, at least three hundred metres more distant. Due to the process of silent registration of the targets (i.e., not active firing) the first shock of bomb discharge bedded the mortars by additional two inches into the soft ground, reducing the elevation by a degree, just enough for the bombs to fall two hundred metres short, smack in their middle.

"Mortars again, three rounds, rapid fire," boomed a voice three thousand yards in their rear.

Thud, thud, thud, replied mortars in largo musical harmony.

Many mangled men had managed to reach the rivulet line.

The bad luck persisted.

Fate was anti them. God had chosen to abandon them.

Bombs now following the true trajectory due to the corrected bearings, fell in an area of hundred yards square. Each bomb with a killing radius of about nine metres, it completely saturated the crossing over the mountain rivulet. Few who had reached it were riddled by millions of bursting steel shrapnel.

Human blood mingled with icy cold water of the *Khuni Nallah,* flowed merrily down the mountain slope. Nothing disturbed its magical crystalline flow.

Its water had tasted similar blood in 1965, 1971 and at a few occasions, of late. The silent river smiled. It had lived up to its name in totality.

Strangely the taste was all too familiar. Strangely, the taste was not religion or army differentiating. Strangely, despite men of different armies falling, its colour remained same – deep crimson red.

Gobar was flush with childlike excitement. These had been the most fascinating minutes of his life. His hands were quivering as adrenaline pumped into his veins. In fascination he kept on walking slowly down the slope. Oblivious of the friendly fire raking the ground around him, he jumped with joy, when the second salvo fell smack in centre of running shapes.

"Don't ever come back this way, you swines," he shouted, waving the captured gun and his *khukri* in equal measure, with both hands.

Naik Deb Magar in number three ambush, observed a man wave hands, trying to rally the running men. He quickly brought his sniper rifle to his shoulder and aimed in the hue of his weapons night-sight. The maniac's silhouette was clearly visible against the silvery background. It had to be a side shot, the issue he had no control over, except the dire necessity to kill that terrorist herder. The crossbar in the telescope aligned with the shoulder of the man. It would be a difficult shot at that range and an impossible one at night.

The agitated figure stilled for a second.

But that was the reason that he had been an Army sniper champion for last three years in running.

With weightless finger he then pressed the sensitive trigger.

The bullet traversed four hundred metres in less than $1/5^{th}$ of a second.

Gobar felt as if a mule had kicked him.

Before he lost consciousness, he saw the proud face of his *Baje* smiling from the heavens above.

Pak Post Kabul
(2256h, 03 Mar)

Subedar Mastan Gillani, the commander of the Pakistani Post Kabul, after a very gratifying meal, was about to open his second shoe, when he heard the first stucco of fire. Instantly, his fat nose flared again much to his discomfort. He ran barefoot outside his bunker and shouted, "Khan man the MMG, Gul seems to be in trouble."

Three kilometres behind, Major Irfan picked up the telephone after five rings. Who could it be at 10.57 PM, he thought, picking up the telephone? He was getting late for his date with that infidel low caste woman. Subedar Mastan's agitated voice came through the handset irritating his impatient mind.

"Sir, I think *Tirs* group has been detected. I can hear a lot of firing ahead."

"Why the hell are you speaking to me, you fool. Go out and fire back. Extricate the group. Move, move," shouted back Irfan.

Mastan dropped the telephone like a hot potato. He hobnobbed with one shoe outside his living bunker.

"Khan, you fool, open fire," he screamed. Getting no response, he rushed to the MMG bunker and saw Khan with his crew of three getting the MMG belts out.

"Fire you *bhainchod,* fire, target the Indian post quickly," he thundered.

"But sir," quipped in Khan.

"Magar kya, can't you hear me, fire," thundered Mastan in total madness. Then he looked around. The men had started coming out of their living shelters, curious to witness the sounds of battle raging below. Oh God! They were not protected.

"Stop, stop Khan, wait. Everyone get back into your concrete bunkers first. Those tin sheets don't stop bullets," he screamed running along the crawl trench connecting various living huts and using choicest expletives in urging everyone inside the bunkers.

"Get inside, we have to help *jihadis,* but get back inside the bunkers first," Mastan pleaded.

"Sentry, can you see where the firing is coming from," he remembered to ask and he went running past the post lookout man. He was perspiring badly. His forehead was shining with sweat. His two eyes were darting left and right in uncertainty, as he craned his neck forward to look in the direction of his woes.

"It's below and to my right, see those Para flares are illuminating the area," the sentry replied pointing with his extended arm.

"Khan now what are you waiting for, fire, fire," thundered Mastan, heading towards the MMG post, about fifteen metres behind.

"Sir, the MMG will not dip down to that elevation. This position is unsuitable," quivered Khan, totally confused.

"Then change the bloody location," he screamed, slapping his forehead with his right hand repeatedly in sheer frustration and ran puffing and panting to speed up the whole issue by his personal intervention.

Khan and his bullied men had almost fed the belt of first MMG clip into the MMG feed tray at the alternative firing position, when he heard the unmistakable sounds of heavy mortars being fired. The resounding echo was ominous.

"Wait, Khan wait," he whispered, putting his arm on Khan's shoulder.

He stared into the darkness ahead. The salvos of mortar bombs falling thirty-two seconds later dimmed his resolution further to fire back.

He had a very sudden urge to pee. No, he wanted to crap first, he thought.

These Indians, will give him ulcers. Since when have they begun to retaliate so ferociously, thought Mastan? Earlier, they never used to fire back, and now a days, at the slightest opportunity, they shower down heavy volume of fire. Shit, he reminisced, his whole planning to serve calmly on the LoC, in front of scared shitless Indians, based on his previous experience, had badly misfired.

"Wait, don't fire, don't fire. Indians are firing mortars. I am sure they will target us if we open fire. Remember what happened last time. Major *sahib* does not know of the conditions in the front," he added irritably.

Near Post Khukri
(2330h, 03 Mar)

Havaldar Tirath Nath, lying behind the bushes, on the flank of 1965 vintage minefield, let loose a burst of AK-47 in the direction of the sound. In fact he emptied his whole magazine in one single press of the trigger. The crescendo of fire and bullets caught Risal simultaneously. His thighs fragmented. Risal had catapulted back and fell into Reshab's hands, even before he could utter a stifled scream.

For Tirath, it was a very lucky shot.

He had not seen any target as such. He had fired in the approximate direction of the scraping suspicious sound and on seeing some movement in the bushes. It was against his Company Commanders' personal orders to open fire only when you can see the grey of enemy's eyes. He was proceeding on pension in the next two days and he be damned if he took any stupid chances.

Islamabad, Pakistan
(0315h, 04 Mar)

"Hello, good morning, Malik here."

"Yes, it's Lieutenant General Tarik Mohammed," replied a sleepy voice.

"You might be interested in collecting some body-bags near Haji Pir Sector, today."

"What are you talking about," wide-awake now, General Tarik thundered.

"As if you don't know," came a quiet retort. " If you don't," the voice continued, "You can check with your Brigadier Mustaq, Commander of 209 Brigade at Haji Pir."

"Listen, General Malik, don't beat about the bush. First you wake me up at 0315h in the morning and then you talk nonsense," Tarik berated. He was annoyed at his counterpart giving the name of his Brigade Commander. So much for confidentiality.

"Well, for your information there was an infiltration attempt from your post 113, South West of Haji Pir at Grid Reference 789456 and if you are interested in collecting a few remains please do let us know," replied Malik quietly.

"Mister Malik, we do not violate international boundaries or for that matter any disputed lines. Nor do we infiltrate anyone across, for what happens in your country is your business. I am sure they must have been ingenious *Kashmiri* brethren, who would have attacked your post, to repel an offending and obnoxious occupation forces. For freedom, people do fight. I claim no responsibility for innocent people you may have butchered," he paused to take breath and continued, "Moreover, we are sure that perpetuated massacre of innocent *Kashmiris* is in your territory. You want us to react so India can sing to the entire world of our involvement.

"A good speech General," Malik interjected and continued, "But what about the body-bags. I am sure you would want a few families of your service personnel and may be ISI to see their near ones, even if dead."

"Well, in the name of humanity, I will instruct my post to observe cease fire till 1200 Noon with effect from 0530AM today. You can search for your dead soldiers or you wouldn't have rung me up like this," rasped visibly offended General Tarik.

"OK, 0530 AM to 12 Noon today. Do instruct your post to fly a white flag. Ours will do the same," reconfirmed his Indian counterpart.

Lieutenant General Malik, quietly put down the phone, disconnecting the hot line established between the Director General Military Operations of both intransigent neighbours. He closed his eyes and pressed his palms on them to relieve that throbbing pain and irritation in his eyes due to lack of sleep. Picking up the fourth black phone from array of seven adorning his desk, he quickly passed stream of instructions into it.

By count of hundred many were scurrying around like mad bitten rabid dogs to meet the deadline.

Indian Post Khukri (0500h, 04 Mar)

The dawn broke majestically over the *Pir Panjal* ranges.

Redolence of beauty was stunning, winds aromatic.

The sunrays caught and illuminated the lofty Himalayan peaks to the North, in rich golden colours, first. The *Kargil* ranges to the North West stood tall, stubborn and uncompromising in its cavalier arrogance, scoffing the lowly human minnows below. Famous sacred lofts of *Vaishno Devi* to the South East emitted their holy radiance from a halo formed by the sun's reflection. The Jhelum River in the centre of the vale, was winding down the *Uri* gorge, like a silver strand, as it had been doing since ages, fed by thousands of silent steams from above.

Beauty awed hypnotic trance, engulfed uncomplicated greys in dermatitis infected cranium, affixed not very ceremoniously atop Colonel Thapa's lumbering body.

My God, what a beautiful sight, bewitching, he introspected. Beautiful enough to behold any man and captivating enough to nurture brazen lust for it. This was the nearest one could come to heaven on earth. Yes, this was what we are fighting for. Any fool would fight for it with blood. This was an ancient land where basis of his religion were tempered in soul searching, by *rishi's* and *munni's.* The vale was magical in its purest omnipotent form. It was breathtaking in its various manifestations. So why blame *Pakistanis* for indulging in such a wishful dream. It would disrepute any part of a society not willing to spilling blood over it. The wind had died down to a slow gentle breeze and it did carry the sting of its chill along. The snows had not melted fully. The soft patches of creamy flakes constructed designs of gigantic white marble buildings in the foreground.

Colonel Thapa had rushed to the *Khukri* post at night when the battle in *Khuni Nallah* was enjoined and was sitting cross-legged on a shivering wooden bench at the OP location of his post. He looked down and to the left, across his shoulder, towards Major Shamsher and asked, "Are all arrangements in place?"

"Yes sir," Shamsher nodded.

Colonel Thapa then turned his torso right and shifted his gaze on a small dominating knoll within the company perimetre fence. Atop it flew a white flag tied to a bamboo pole. The makeshift bed sheet of required size replicating as a peace flag, was fluttering lazily in the wind.

"Are the battalion mortars on stand to?" He inquired further scratching his dandruff-ridden baldhead.

"Yes sir," shot back Shamsher.

"What about artillery effort?" he further quizzed scratching the peppered red flesh even more furiously.

"Sir, the Brigade Major Zusti confirmed that 113 Medium Battery and 86 Heavy Mortar Battery have been instructed to provide support to us. In fact, their OP officers have reached the ridgeline overlooking *Khuni Nallah*. They were in position by 0445 hours," said Shamsher in one breath.

"Good," muttered Thapa leaving the itchy bald dome alone to the mercy of fate and lifting his binoculars he peered toward the enemy post. He could spy a similar white flag against the pale blue-sky line.

"You can move now, but remember be alert. Don't approach any dead body directly. Cover each body with two men each, and then one person should approach from one side. Remove the weapons and grenades first," he paused to shift his legs, which were getting cramped in the cold and before he could look up or kill more erupting itch, Shamsher intervened.

"Yes sir, all the boys have been instructed accordingly. Two officers, two JCOs and fifty-two men are ready to move out sir," replied a crisp military voice with an equally crisp salute and then Shamsher turned back to vamoose towards his standing comrades. That's the best way to disengage from the old man, mused Shamsher or his instructions will never end. The old goat still treated him like a toddler he cuddled with a few generations back. I know how to deal with an unclaimed body. Shoot a round into that dead corpse to confirm his total inertness. Balls if one or two men will approach them without firing. Hadn't one presumably twenty hour old dead terrorist got up and shot one Lieutenant Colonel, in another sector, only recently. Yes, he should use silencer carbines as not to create ruckus near the LoC.

"In single file, move forward," he shouted further instructions to his men, gathered in three rows deep, in a hollow square formation.

Each file, turned left and in its order of march, headed out of the company post. The leading man was carrying another white flag as a precautionary measure. One by one the soldiers crossed the company perimetre gate and dipped their heads in abeyance to *"Goddess Kali"* whose small idol had been placed in a small wooden structure, at the exit. The leading man turned to his right away from the gravelled road into a well-beaten foot track going down to *Khuni Nallah*. As Shamsher crossed the gate, he glanced at his Rolex watch, a present from his sister settled in the U.S. It read 05:29 AM.

All staff officers, holding any worthwhile portfolio, had already started eating his and his adjutant's head. They all wanted the complete story, exactly as it had happened, even before it had been concluded and were aghast, when he shut them up by saying, "Wish I knew." They were already rumbling at the inefficiency of reporting after seven hours of the incident. Only if they could pass their silly slips of papers, in pitch dark night, from one desk to another, without using their massive generators, expeditiously, he would tell them how information flows at night, from ambushes facing the real enemy, specially when one is totally wiped out, reflected Thapa irritably. Staff officers were the bane of this not-so-bad army. Their efficiency was proportional to production of information where none existed.

The ambushes had come back at 0400 hours just before the first light.

It was remarkable that Subedar Gurung had brought back all men safely, without an incident, when he had made an impromptu rendezvous at night and even had searched non-responding ambush party site to discover unconscious and wounded three soldiers. All men alive or wounded had been accounted for except one Rifleman Gobar Singh. The thought had millions of ants sprinting across his sensitive top hide. He only prayed that he had not been captured by those barbarous *Afghanis* who constituted the bulk of *Kashmiri* militants. He was sure they would send back his body minus all his vital parts. Those barbarians loved mutilating bodies, an apt reflection of their rich culture and religious beliefs. Very intriguing was the fact that *Pak* post had not opened up as on earlier occasions. No fire support to infiltrating columns? What was their game plan now? Were they infiltrators or their regulars coming to attack his post? In this madness, Pak was capable of doing anything. Only the search will reveal the complete truth.

More interestingly, he had seen company boys dragging an unconscious man, when he had entered the post yesterday night. According to Havaldar Tirath there were two of them, but one had managed to escape. The unconscious terrorist had been dutifully disrobed and each nook on him was checked. From his combat pouch, they had recovered a coded signal matrix and crisp Indian five hundred rupee notes, whose counting had stopped at one thousand and thirty. He also had the latest Japanese Kenwood radio set, like he had not seen earlier.

He must be an important person, an organizer, and provider or otherwise so much cash on the person was unexplainable.

He would love to interrogate him, but first, he had to survive.

Khuni Nallah (0530h to 1200h, 04 Mar)

Lieutenant Thapar had been searching continuously for over five hours.

He had not slept for the last thirty-six hours, being out for night ambushes first and then being quickly inducted for search. Well, fatigue disappears when actions are live, he reasoned. He had slowly enlarged the area of the search, fanning out tactically, but the tale of violence had been confined to a small quadrant. Till now, they had discovered twenty-six dead and initial few interesting ones had their bodies cleaved. Finally, more evidence of severed limbs, led them to where Rifleman Gobar Singh lay. His left shoulder was a bloody mess, but surprisingly there was life in him. Gobar along with two other wounded but unconscious *mujahids,* had been evacuated, half an hour back. Now he was almost at the tip of *Khuni Nallah*'s famous bend from where the whole nightmare had begun. As he topped a small rise before the embankment, he saw another macabre sight.

In the riverbed lay sixteen corpses. The water in their immediate surroundings was still deep crimson red which slowly retained its natural blue tinge further down the stream.

"Bayen dushman, position," warned his section commander and all quickly dived for any available cover.

Thapar cautiously peered over a stump of a tree, and assessing the void of any perceivable threat, slowly brought up his binoculars to scan the hazardous zone right ahead. Across, he made out a kneeling person in *Khaki's,* almost aping his actions. From his opponents position to the right and above from a rock face vertically thirty metres up, a bipod and the barrel of a light machine gun was protruding out, menacingly. Bravado apart, none ventured without their pet henchmen.

Their binoculars, locked on each other simultaneously, trying to fathom any hidden threats. There seemed none.

Instantaneously the hands of both went up in air, lingered for a few seconds, then waving in exaggerated manner for an assured sighting. Recognizing the unique officer clan, the forty-metre divide between them disappeared suddenly.

Tall, well-built Major Irfan, with unmistakable *Pathani* built, nursing a pistol in his left hand, shook hands with Thapar, who had slung his INSAS rifle across his shoulders casually, in a cocked position.

"Well it seems your chaps had a terrible night," said Irfan, disengaging his hands and casually looking over Thapa's shoulder to discern any unpleasant observations. You could never trust these Indians.

Thapar eyed him squarely and replied, "Well the misery is all yours to reap." He simultaneously adjusted the slant of his beret; an innocent gesture picked up immediately by his section commander, indicating all was fine up to now. You could never trust a *Pakistani*.

"You will be picking up the bodies now," inquired Irfan smiling but a bit peeved at counter-part's flamboyant answer.

"Yes immediately, but technically those two are in your territory," he replied, pointing to two mangled masses on the further edge of the stream.

"Well you can dump them anywhere as far as I am concerned. These are not our people. By the way how many casualties did you suffer," Irfan inquired, staring expectantly at Thapar.

"Sir, definitely less than what you lost last month at your post. By the way including them, it will be forty-two dead infiltrators," Thapar quickly added ten more, just for an effect.

And the effect was clearly visible.

"What? You must be fibbing," paling Irfan countered in typical Queen's English. Holy shit, he thought. The whole group had been wiped out. Only three badly injured *jihadis* had limped back till now to tell the shocking tale of the gory ambush.

"Major, we do not lie. It's not in our military ethics," shot back Thapar.

"Then you better work fast. Only an hour is left, before the guns boom again my friend," said Irfan cockily and then turned back.

It was exactly four minutes to twelve when the parties trudged back over the crest line. Shamsher turned left for the company post. It had been a very tiring and a cumbersome task, lugging the dead bodies and recovered equipment. He had reprimanded Thapar for so impulsively walking over to meet the Pak Major, but what Thapar had narrated was worth writing in the Battalion War Book. As he had covered about hundred paces up the rocky path he looked towards the *Pakistani* Post. The white flag was coming down and red one had temporarily been installed. A similar gesture was being reciprocated by the Indian post *Khukri.*

The temporary man-imposed truce was over, and the war zone was declared red, redder, hot red and deep red once again. One could also coin hot, hotter, hottest, piping hot, burning hot, scorching hot, seething hot, steaming hot, sizzling hot, scalding hot or any other wishful hot and jumble them in any haphazard manner and be right in intention all the time. Shoot to kill; live to shoot, shoot at sight, kill at will, the madness was back in business, in its full gusto.

Back in his ten feet deep and ten feet thick bunker, tucked inside his warm cozy down feather-quilted bed, Shamsher amusedly went over his dear ex-academy pal Jesse's letter. He incidentally would be relieving him at the same location in a few months. What caught his fancy was his friend's one of the famous quips, which he had noted as one of his universal laws. It read; that a successful ambush is equal to the total sum of, the hand of god, lots and lots of luck, abundance of careless and overconfident enemy multiplied by and to the power cube to the total number of brainless dodos you can muster to go where the enemy actually treads.

He had a hearty laugh.

Assuredly they had not been very intelligent.

Khukri Post
(1700 h, 04 Mar)

General Rocky Dass was going over the line of dead bodies. "Who did that?" he inquired about the headless corpse.

"Sir, I believe when our ambush ran out of ammunition, Rifleman Gobar Singh charged the enemy with his *khukri*," replied Colonel Thapa.

"How come did the ambush run out of ammunition? Weren't they carrying adequate in the first place? What scale did they carry?" inquired the General staring at Thapa.

Thapar quickly bit his tongue for stupidly blabbering more information than required. This chap pounces on you like a hawk hardly giving you a breather to recover the lost ground. "Well sir the ammunition is as per on the weapon scale, but it seems that due to infiltrators retaliation our party got neutralized and only Rifleman Gobar was fit enough to carry on the battle. The use of under barrel grenades came as a surprise," muttered Thapar, a little incoherently.

"Ahm, I see," reflected the General nodding. "What else," he again asked.

"Sir, we have killed thirty-two infiltrators, captured two in wounded state and as regards arms and ammunition, there are twenty-six AK-56 of Chinese origin, six 51mm mortars, three rocket launchers, eight sniper rifles, ninety-nine kg of RDX, fifty-six detonators, seventy-eight grenades, fifteen Kenwood radio sets and approximately five thousand rounds of assorted ammunition," said Thapa, consulting a little notebook off and on, "Worst is this launcher. I believe it's a Stinger anti-aircraft missile," he further stuttered, pointing at it, accusingly. His brain fidgeted whether to report about the cash recovered. His heart was not in tune with this moralistic blurting all the facts. He was already lagging behind in the payment schedule to his sources and more dough was not visible in the horizon. If army trusted him with lives of about eight hundred souls, then a lakh of cash will not corrupt his mind. Report, the money will go into the government treasury to be misused by corrupt contractors and other palm greasers. He had better intended use for it to fight the terrorists.

"What there to believe colonel. It is an anti-aircraft launcher. Enough arms to start a bloody war," observed General Dass examining perhaps the first catch of such a missile tube and its assortments. He then searched visually for his staff officer who was busy scribbling something in his notebook, as usual. "Tell Colonel Intelligence to give me an update the moment I reach the headquarters and also call Mushtaq of Liaison Unit along with him," he instructed. Turning back to Colonel Thapa, he added, "Ensure all boys are properly recommended and where's Shamsher. Ah, there you are. Come here my son," clasping his hands he continued, "that was an excellent show. Keep up the good work. I want his name too," nodding towards now beaming Thapa.

"Subedar Major shabash, ladkon ko meri badhai dena. Morale up rakho," (Subdar Major congratulations, give the boys my fecilitations. Keep the morale high) : he said before moving out.

"Yes sir," in a blur of movement, Subedar Major saluted the General, stiff as a rock.

5

Rendezvous

"In meeting, we meet friends and foe.
In meeting, we conquer our fears."

— Jesse

Near Khuni Nallah
(1000h, 05 Mar)

The chase was endless. He was running non-stop since his birth. That tireless cur, the executioner from hell, seemed to be gaining on him continuously.

He was running through the fires of *jahannum*. His soles were on fire. A big fire, emanating from his feet upwards was engulfing his whole torso. He could smell the damnatory odour of his charred skin and it was revolting. How much he tried, jumped, acrobatically danced, twisted, turned or hid in coolness of water, the confounding fire never left his side. Demons on the side alleys were jabbing their red-hot tongs at him, laughing maniacally. *Kafirs* were enjoying his acute misery. Shitless, inhuman rascals. Oh, *ammi jan* help me, he had to escape. But escape from which side? Holes in the ground were gushing out dancing flames. They were blocking all conceivable escape paths.

That slit-eyed mad monkey was just a few steps away.

He quickened his pace but it seemed to be a losing battle. His feet were refusing to obey his screaming commands. Run, run, run, he shouted to his feet but terror-stricken idiots did not move.

He was also being weighed down by tonnes of rock mysteriously tied to his back by those demons.

That ferocious, scheming, evil-intent *jinn* wanted him dead.

He looked back in abject terror.

Ablaze monkey-eyes focussed on the back of his head, the piercing gaze burnt, as the monkey-man raised his big hooked knife, to strike. His jitterbug constitution allowed his jittery bowels to open and he heard himself scream into oblivion.

Gul woke up with a jerk.

The hot rays of the sun basking him were awful and were hurting his eyes.

He was totally drenched in sweat.

His morbid, wildly pulsating heart burst instantaneously with joy on perceiving the falsehood of his earlier situation. There was no death like chase. That monkey-man was an illusion. Thank God, it was only a silly but scary dream. He felt relieved of his phantasmagoric state.

He tried getting up but doubled back in pain. Oh God, he was hurt. Much later he willed himself to move his hands slowly, feeling goodness of each good part of his body. Everything seemed fine except his right shoulder and the chest. Oh shit, he had also urinated in his *salwar*. His thighs were wet from inside, but worst his right shoulder. It hurt very badly. The aching throb was sharp and acute.

It seemed a million seconds before he could turnover to his better and less painful left side and slowly unshackle the heavy rucksack off from his back. He looked up and saw the straight face of the cliff from where he had slipped. It was a clean twenty-metre rock face. The thick bushes had broken his fall. He was just plain lucky, he thought. *Allah* was with him, as always. He turned his wrist to see the time. It read 10 AM, March 12. Dear God, he had been lying here for more than twenty-four hours.

His shoulder stung as if it was on fire. He slowly turned his face to examine his area of discomfort. The sleeve of his shirt was full of clotted blood. With effort he tore his shirt's sleeve to expose his wound. It was a bloody mess. He again praised *Allah* for small mercies. The bullet had grazed through the biceps muscles, missing the bone, thus causing superficial tissue damage. With bone being gone he wouldn't have been able to move his arm or the shoulders. The shoulder rotated without much pain in its socket. The fact that he was lying unconscious on this very shoulder for a long time had helped in ebbing the blood flow. Small dark brown crusts were visible on the sides of the deep gnash.

He dug into his rucksack and rummaged through the contents till he hit upon a small plastic bag. Gingerly going through various coloured pills, he palmed four red ones. Yes, he remembered the doctor telling him that that the red ones were for pain and it was the excruciating pain he wanted to kill. He opened his dry mouth and popped up four painkillers. He looked around for his water bottle, but not finding it nearby, he quickly worked up some saliva and swallowed them. The pungent bitterness of the medicine was insignificant in relation to the agony of pain he was experiencing. He then opened up the bottle of antiseptic powder and emptied almost half of it on the wound's gaping mouth. He clenched his teeth, as it hurt more and suppressed a scream moving up his throat, while he simultaneously pressed the powdered wound, with his other palm. The blood seeped through the white powder making big crimson spots. Somehow he managed to dress his wound shoddily with a bandage.

The efforts had drained him totally. He felt very tired. Suddenly his vision dimmed. Before he could comprehend what was happening, he slumped back into a fitful slumber.

Next time, when he woke up, the sun had disappeared behind the *Pir Panjal* ranges. Slowly he managed to sit up. He was definitely feeling better. The pain was less acute; demons had not reappeared and he was breathing easier. A happy situation given the circumstances but he could experience a vague unidentifiable discomfort throughout his body. May be it was the general stiffness, he reasoned. He again opened the rucksack and took out his emergency rations. He satiated his hunger, relishing a piece of jaggery and numerous monkey-nuts. Suddenly, he sighted his green plastic water bottle, about ten yards to his right. With tremendous effort he crawled up to it and gleefully took large sips to drench his parched throat. Much later, after finishing half his supply of precious water and food, he unsteadily got up and took few unsure steps back towards the place he had fallen. Removing the plastic lid of the medicine container, he again mouthed four more magical red pills. It's better to kill the pain till he recovered fully, he thought.

After changing his urine stained *salwar*, he overturned his rucksack and started discarding the non-essentials. One must travel light, if you want to survive, he again reasoned with himself. In any case he was not in a physical state to lug his full equipment. Equipping himself with one AK-47, two magazines, two grenades, his family heirloom .38 police special revolver, the medicine box and dry emergency food packet, he got up to survey the scene. On second thought, he quickly hid the other weapons and extra military items in the bushes, lest the Indians lay their hands on them and this pile further becomes a cause for another death-chase.

Gul looked up the cliff face.

It had a small narrow cleft covered by clump of bushes. No wonder, the Indians could not locate him. He was more than sure that they would have searched the encounter site in great details. On parting the thick bushes, he saw a small animal trail disappearing around the bend in rocks, jutting out from the side of the cliff. Slowly he placed the rucksack onto the good side of his body and started moving up, labouring step-by-step, in spasmodic pain.

It took him twenty minutes less to an hour to bypass the approximate place of the previous encounter site.

Initially, as he trudged the very death-evoking path, he was awed and at the same time moved by the innocence of the locale. Bodies of his men were missing. He saw the body drag marks going upslope. So the Indians had come and searched the place. His men had died; many of them had died. It was a haunting experience. He half-shut his eyes as he made his way through the mounds of blood-soaked slopes. This temple of death was brutal in appearance, too savage to look straight in the eye and move.

By now his vitals had heated to a pleasant circulation of warm blood considerably diminishing aches, sores and stiffness in general including senseless fear. Gul paused to look up and observed the slopes above, this time very deliberately. He could not detect any abnormality in bushy spur-line just ahead despite repeated scans. He knew the Indians would be back within an hour. The daylight was still out in good measure but the shadows of the trees were elongating every minute. It was now or never, to cross that much-hated spur, into the safety of Indian-occupied hinterland. But the earlier haunting memories came rushing back. That madman had almost got him and it was God's providence that he was still alive.

He had been a fool to be taken in by that idiotic guide's assessment.

The Indians had not deployed their ambushes on the crest line as appreciated by those moronic goons. They had surprised his whole group by coming more than halfway down to the forward slopes of *Khuni Nallah.* Idiot like, he too had violated the basic tenet of war, to never underestimate the enemy.

In his preliminary fact finding talks with other *jihadis,* who had operated in Indian Kashmir, they had confirmed that most of their troops were *junglee* cannibals. Unlike white pig eating Russians, these soldiers chased you on foot. Helicopters were easy to fool and evade, but not foot soldiers on a hot chase. They will home on like ants on to a drop of honey, bemoaned one legless veteran. Firefights in an encounter could go on for days and days.

It was his over-confidence that had made him disregard their advice. He had been naïve.

If he had chilled the Russians into fear, so who were these feminine Indians. He had boasted. It was a mistake, a mistake he had paid dearly in terms of his men and almost his life. He resolved not to underestimate these dhoti-clad heathens again and moved a few steps forward.

It was precisely on the fourth step that the twin imps, yin and yang rushed to greet him.

His heart punctured, a fear tipped arrow slammed straight into his heart. The stomach magically rumbled painful sensation laden warnings. The mind went numb. Unknown dread danced a Tango with his incompliant body. Terror returned from nowhere. His feet faltered and body shivered in dread. He was alone and was being brutally hunted, that too without the safety of his faithfuls. His third eye did a double take, brain sensing out an exact replica of frightening acoustics witnessed not so behind in time. He captured the chatter of automatic fire and screaming hail of whining bombs coming straight at him.

Fear had no bindings. It had flown, found him alone, exposed on this desolate slope.

I should go back, the yin in Gul reasoned.

He was wounded, alone and tired.

The reason was adequate enough to accommodate any misdeeds. Yin, was a reasonable pal, yin listened. It understood the needs of a man, like the perfect woman in him he saw the reason of his pain, but above all yin understood. Good mistress yin.

But then go back with what face. Why, any cowardly face would do.

He, the most feared and successful commander of *mujahidin* special task force, was running away from fear of Indians. The wound was just but a mere scratch. Faithfuls were dead, so what. All died for a cause and then why was he alive with a belief similar to that of his friends.

Running from the battlefield. It would be a good, wholesome, body-saving run.

It would be blasphemy. Pure un-Islamic.

The entire *mujahid* community will laugh at him. His standing in the council of chiefs would be ridiculed. His family for generations dishonoured, eyes never to leave the sight of peoples' soiled feet. No, it was not acceptable. His ass would literally be the butt of all known cowardly jokes. Then the mocking darling yang melodiously sang, "*Gul gya dul,*" (Gul has fallen).

Yang with guile, won the fear induced immobilizing debate, hands down.

Mustering all the courage he could, he slid through the tall wild grass, upslope, directly eastwards, towards the Indian administered Kashmir, muttering *Allah, Allah*, at each step.

Srinagar
(0800h, 05 Mar)

The girls' hostel in the university campus as always was a hotbed of sundry activity.

Chatter, music, love-hymns, discotheque drums, soft laughter and more mindless chatter, permeated along the long white marble chipped corridor. The musical din was pouring out from plush rooms that adjoined the corridor, housing some very beautiful girls. They were heartbreak models for most egoistic goons who had elevated their infallible male human status on the campus. Whole communities of teenaged, little above teenagers, young adults, middle aged adults, old adults, found reasons enough to sniff this hostel's surroundings, if not the actual women residing inside. Only spying on this famed building rushed their oxygen starved brain and delicate hearts. They skipped, they hopped, they jogged, in vain hope of some black magic attaching them to the famed beauties inside. Even sweepers had a strict rooster to avail the privilege of rummaging through its discarded trash.

Khushbu was sitting in front of the dressing table, eyeing herself very critically in the mirror across. Her face definitely required a beautician's sitting. The dullness of her skin was disheartening. Few frustrating hairs on her upper lip would also definitely go by the time the sun goes down. Only problem was that she could not do it openly, as it was against her religious upbringing and Islamic atmosphere, created of late. Then through the mirror her eyes suddenly fell on her friend Nafisa, lying on her bed.

"Nafisa *begum*, do you plan to rest your tender buttocks throughout the day?" she inquired casually.

"Yes, I think so," Khushbu heard a faint mumbled reply.

"Why?"

"I am in no mood to go out. Firstly, the first two classes are of Mrs. Fatima, and I hate that flat-chested crone. Secondly, she squeaks like a crow and I hate her voice," Nafisa said half-rising up slowly, with her slender back gently supported by a cotton pillow.

"What's your problem enlightened one. You have not been in your elements lately. I see you fighting with everyone. Ahm, tell your beloved friend. Tell me what's eating you up," crooned Khushbu softly.

"You have your *jihad*, but I may lose my life, my dreams, my hopes, my happiness all together," sobbed Nafisa. *"Chachu jan* wants me to get married to an uneducated fool," she sobbed further in more short gasps, with tears running down and wetting her rosy red cheeks.

"Ahm, that's a big problem. I understand. Keep your head up," Khushbu walked over and ruffled Nafisa's long tassels. Caressing her soft cheeks she added, "What does your prince charming do," she asked smiling.

"An idiotic goat-herder," Nafisa wailed more loudly this time. "What's this education for? To produce endless kids," she cried shamelessly into the pillow.

"Shut up you lovely fool. You know that's blasphemy. We are what we are. Wasn't your *abbu* a goat-herder or your mother a daughter of one for that matter? We should do what our elders wish us to do," quipped in Khushbu sternly.

Nafisa was momentarily taken aback by the hostility in Khushbu's voice.

"You didn't listen to your *abbu* or your mother, when you jumped into *jihadi* bandwagon," Nafisa accused.

"Because, it is *jihad*. That's what our *Allah* wills us to do. That's what my countrymen will want me to do," Khushbu literally shouted getting up adjusting her parrot green *kaftan* and walked out of the room.

Khushbu was a bit peeved at Nafisa. Though her best friend, her total disregard for Islamic way of life perturbed her immensely.

Not that she agreed totally with what *Islam* taught personally. For example, she hated most in this whole Muslim awakening, was this stupid *fatwa* on the dress code, no cosmetics, no jewellery, no fashionable clothes, no skin baring ones and *burqa* for every occasion. The clerics screamed it not being sanctioned in *shariat.* Who will tell those learned men that the holy book was written a thousand years back and its relevance now had to be re-worked. Thank *Allah* that at least the *burqa* was not required inside the university campus. No jeans, no tops or jewellery was infuriating. But she reasoned that by unity, Kashmir's cause was being projected by women's solidarity. She felt sad about her little trite with Nafisa. I will make up with her, when I come back from this vital mission, she said to herself. Nafisa was always forgiving and very loving.

Khushbu had discovered the thrill of senseless power, when she on a whim had joined a sit-in demonstration, demanding a human right probe into firing and killing of a student inside the boys' hostel. She watched helpless security forces, big gun trotting macho men; make a fool of themselves in trying to remove a few determined girls. Police said, an AK-47 had been recovered, from the dead boy.

"All rubbish," Tahir had animatedly shouted. "We are the students of tomorrow and we fight without arms, at an intellectual level." There was magic in his forceful sweet voice. When he spoke from a makeshift pedestal, all girls had swooned. They listened to him in rapt attention. Each word made sense. Each spoken sentence told them of their useless existence. The black verbal magic had ripped her emotions apart and had pulled her to him.

"I want to help you, ask of me of what you want," she had said boldly. Boldly enough with her eyes speaking of a lusty surrender. "I will, when the right time comes," he had replied, dismissing her with a wave of hand. As the demonstrators were being physically removed, with her in the middle, the international media had a field day. Anything to capture Indian brutality and the shocking stories which emerged through clandestine Pakistani grapevine.

She became a local queen overnight.

Then came respect, awe and fear. She loved every second of it, a socialite holding a centrestage. She got the best dollops in the canteen, people ran to attend on her, students did her silly class assignments and she was happy. Even teachers called her lovingly in a soft respectful voice and ignored her disappearances from their classes, when she was toiling for her *jihad*. It was a lovely feeling.

Tahir had said that it was extremely urgent, when he called her last evening, to the university cafeteria. She was to deliver a small letter to some silk factory in downtown Lal Chowk residential area. She smiled with pride. Her already ripe breasts ballooned egoistically. She was amongst the trustworthiest.

Khushbu purposefully walked out of the big cast-iron gates of the university compound. Outside, seeing the teeming bustle of humanity, she hesitated and then pulled a *burqa* from her handbag. One could never be sure of some old heretic spraying her face with acid. Sadly a few girls, of late, had become victims of such an enforcement. Adorning it on her head, she walked towards the auto-rickshaw stand, a few yards away. We are in twenty-first century and she had to cover her face. This was definitely not *kashmiriyat*, but positively *Islamic*. How senseless she thought, almost climbing into a three-wheeler taxi but then suddenly changed her mind. It was a nice cool morning for a walk. At least she will see people she so dearly missed inside the quiet confines of the university campus. Life cannot go on in this backward manner. But things would certainly improve for better, she was sure.

A small unassuming boy of twelve, employed by the canteen contractor, stepped out of the shadows of big Chinar trees lining the main road and started stalking a striking figure clad in green *kaftan*.

It was not very difficult to miss Miss Khushbu in the crowd.

Back in her room, Nafisa was sobbing silently going over a few spreads of littered paper. Imran, my sweet Imran, why is God testing our love. Imran was the only secret in her life that she had kept from Khushbu. Her only likely saviour, a saviour of her shattered dreams. And if the events went the way they were written, he too will disappear. She also knew that Khushbu would never ever understand this unyielding desire.

Indian Hinterland (0430h, 08 Mar)

He had been walking through the night for the last three days.

He was tired, in fact very tired.

The discomfort had returned as his supply of pain reducing red pills had finished. The blood had started oozing out from his biceps and the wound had turned nasty blue. Fever had hit him for the first time, this morning. Yesterday, his last morsel too had vanished into his ever-eager mouth. His stomach protested with painful hunger-laden pangs. Thank God that there was water in abundance in the mountain streams, unlike dry and arid Afghanistan.

The pain had slowed down his pace considerably. The tortured breaths were coming out with great effort, in short gasps. His lungs protested at their sheer fatigued misuse. The distance he was to cover in one night had taken over two and he was still not sure where he was. Without those *bakarwal* guides, moving cross-country in an alien terrain was maddening. Forced to move only at night and hide during the day had further impeded his progress. He had navigated by keeping *Pir Panjal* to his left and was sure that *Poonch* town was generally behind towards his right and rear. On the midnight of the third day, he had started climbing directly up slope to the North, from where on the crest line he hoped to see more area around. The vegetation on the slopes obscured his vision to arrive at any reasonable assessment of his location.

The day was about to break as darkness had started giving away to pale light. From the break in the trees, for the first time he could make out a big feature in front of him. Oh! praise *Allah*, he seemed to be near the top. With sweat pouring out from all orifices of his body, he quietly trudged on in sheer agony. He then stopped. Oh! he had to find a shelter before the day broke in full honesty.

He desperately looked around and saw a big uprooted tree. Where it had fallen, its branches had rested on a raised rock, creating a natural shelter. He moved tenderly through the thicket and sat under the tree trunk.

Gul threw his pack on the ground and using it like a pillow, slowly eased into it. Lying face up he could not see the sky above. Excellent he thought. He would be hidden from air. At least, one worry less. He had also seen those small moth-shaped Indian helicopters, crisscrossing the jungle slopes for the first two days. He was safe from them, for now. Before he could reason further, his heavy feverish eyelids closed, momentarily. Before Gul could comprehend what was happening, he was snoring in cool black comfort.

His badly beaten and ravaged body did not protest against such a blissful luxury.

It was not only collective, but also sharp and ferocious barks, which woke him. In alarm he jumped straight up. On his haunches he reasoned with the logic of the noise. Shit, Indians were using dogs to track him. How stupid of him not to have planned for that. His defensive reasoning was diminishing and he reprimanded himself for that.

He was in no condition to run. He was sick and tired of running.

Brave men do not run, he reasoned. Cowards do and he was not a coward.

He will fight.

God willing he will make a glorious stand here. Yes, he will make a stand. Yes, a last great memorable stand. He will take out many Indian bastards today. Let there be lamentation in Delhi, squealing hordes of breast beating Hindu women.

He quickly took out and placed his two remaining grenades on his left side and laid his one remaining magazine on to the other, for easy loading. He patted his grandfathers' British revolver for assurance. That would be his last line of defence. The barks were just around the corner, and soldiers surely a few feet behind.

He smiled to thank his almighty God.

He brought his weapon to aim, resting confidently on his right shoulder. This is it, he thought.

Two black majestic beasts broke cover, along the spur he had climbed. They were growling excitedly as they advanced sniffing the ground in front. Strangely no uniformed targets appeared to avenge back his place in heaven. Suspicion laden, he maintained his unwavering aim.

The dogs stopped about twenty metres short from where Gul hid. The blood trail was further infuriating their nubile senses. The blood was fresh and the prey wounded, their odour sensitive brain registered. The movement of the prey was also laboured, well; it will make the task of killing that much easier, the dog brain further reasoned. Thick white froth dribbled in savory anticipation from their lower jaws. The leader-dog gave an excited whine, as he went down on his front paws. He then looked around for his mate. She was approaching those bushes from a different direction. Good sensible bitch, he growled in appreciation and then yelped to pass his latest tactical instructions. The she dogs gave him a knowing bark of complete understanding and turned towards the meat-laden bush. He will attack when she charges from the flank. He looked confused as the bitch momentarily stopped. She gave a menacing threatened growl and looked expectantly at her mates' direction for support. As he saw a man emerge from the bush, he knew what was the reason of her discontent. He joined her fearlessly in a full throated yelping stand.

It's better to kill them, than die a terrible death, Gul bravely whined. Their killing abilities were legendary. These *bakarwali* shepherd dogs in a pair could butcher a leopard alone into gulp-able shreds in seconds. And he was a mere man, not a tiger and nothing, a complete zero without his weapons.

Confused, his mind refused to accept such a pitiable unsoldierly death.

Where were the *bhainchod* Indians.

Sending dogs ahead to kill.

Cowards, as always lurking behind the safety of petticoats of their women.

Come and fight Gul face-to-face you cowards, he silently screamed. He, the brave Afghani will not give them that ejaculatory satisfaction of seeing him dead, killed by these rabid dogs. Kill the dogs and let the cowards come ahead to kill me, he reasoned.

He took a careful aim at the centre of the growling head and was about to pull the trigger when a female in red flashed through the lips of his foresight.

"Shera, Bibi, Shera come back you fools," sang the *houri* from hell in melodious voice. "Come back Shera to your a*mma*. You stupid Bibi, where are you," *houri* continued to sing the devilish song from hell.

The death, fatigue and fear forgotten, Gul lowered his AK-47 and stared unblinkingly at the graceful gait of the *houri* from hell.

Nurie screamed at the sight of the devil. Her two companions tore their throats in appreciative barking, nodding vehemently in agreement of the unknown man-danger. Her hands flew to her mouth and eyes registered a faint curious shock. Sure indeed, a man devil stood in front of her.

The devil in black smiled. His eyes bored into *houri* from hell. His eyes mesmerized the shocked women into submission. He felt the vibrations of her naked flesh, beneath her *firan*.

The devil seemed pale and tired. Sweat was pouring onto his stubbed goatee beard. He smelled like an animal full of dung. Strangely the aroma seemed sweet. She looked down at her feet, feeling uncomfortable. The devil's eyes were burning. They were emitting eerie red laser beam. It was scalding her soft skin. Shera and Bibi having climbed down from their earlier intransigent stand were as confused as their mistress and ran around in circles on her heels, growling in low screechy whines.

The initial three seconds of mutual assessment seemed to go on for ages. Time stood still, staring at infinity. When the two sided staring became uncomfortable, Nurie then mustered up some courage. "Who are you?" she asked, throwing her chin up initially but a little later, turned her head sideways to avoid the devils blood-red unblinking gaze.

"Asif Gul, commander of El Jihadi Special Force Group," the voice of the devil echoed slowly in the mountains, "And I am an Afghani," he added on an after thought. He was totally fascinated by her voice, and she, equally by his.

"Oh! *Allah,*" she sang bringing the black *burqa* down to cover her face. "Bibi keep quiet," she caressed the foreheads of her beasts, calming their frayed nerves.

"Which place is this?" asked the devil.

"Upper Nusur," the *houri* sang further. .

A wave of relief rippled through his body, "And Pedro point," the devil further inquired.

The *houri* from hell pointed towards a cliff face to the North.

"Seen any army, Indian Army," Gul added. *Houri's* head danced, implying no.

"Take me to Reshab Mehmood's stead," the devil instructed forcefully. His red eyes did not move and locked to her breasts like a hawk. Eyeballs moved up and down with each rise and fall of her excited chest.

Without a word, the graceful doe-eyed *houri* turned her back and started walking along the path of *zannat.* After a few steps she looked back and beckoned him on. *Houri's* hips were swaying as beholding Chinar trees, dancing to the gentle cool breeze.

Like a child entranced, brain-dead, he followed.

Never before had he seen so much beauty in one moment. It jammed his senses. In any case, in his native country, beauty had vanished decades back. Only cold, brutal, dead countryside, with even more defeated dead-faced people, littered the landscape. Never before had his heart stopped seeing a woman, devil's own creation. Never before had his loins stirred as badly as they were doing today. He was thankful that she was walking ahead of him, oblivious of the obvious bulge, in front of his *salwar.*

He put his rifle lower to cover his decency.

Yes, yes, no wonder Kashmir was heaven on earth. No wonder, all his friends queued and fought to come here and die in this land. No wonder, this was the den of non-believers. No wonder, people of this land required people from his land, to come here, to fight for their *jihad.* No wonder he was here to drum sense into those idolaters.

She took him around the edge of forests full of fir trees, along a small mud track. Despite her bewitching gait, her strides were purposeful and almost running. Never did she look back again, as much as his heart desired. Her two beasts stuck to her heels, occasionally glancing back baring their white fangs, if he came a bit closer.

Suddenly he felt good, pain and exhaustion forgotten, he was a free fearless man. There was love and happiness in life, and there was that bouncy spring in his walk. The *houri* stopped. Lifting her hand, she pointed through a clearing in the trees, to a massive stone brick house, tucked inside a small culvert, surrounded by black rocks from three directions. Smoke was lazily spiraling upwards through one of its chimneys.

The fence on the western side of the house housed numerous goats. Their animalistic putrid smell, flavoured with their dung and urine filled the air. He turned back to face his lovely *houri.* She had vanished as silently as she had enchanted him earlier. Carefully picking his steps through the boulder-ridden path, he started moving down towards the house.

He had hidden his AK-47 under the folds of his loose *kurta* when he knocked on the door. The noise of shuffling feet across the other side of the door, made him curl his finger on the trigger of his gun.

The door opened.

He saw the bewildered face of Reshab Mehmood. Gul fainted.

Lalpura, Lolab Valley (1630h, 09 Mar)

The earlier sought, now sought the seeker. Their roles had reversed.

A second meeting was arranged.

The time and the location had changed. Other elements remained same. No faith, no trust, a betrayal, surely yes.

Few issues needed to be ironed out. The price earlier offered was unacceptable. Not rupees six thousand per head but twenty. They haggled like unscrupulous traders and ultimately settled for twelve.

A meeting without profit, definitely not in Kashmir.

They parted silently, as silently as they had come.

Upper Nusur (2030h, 12 Mar)

The body lying on the makeshift bed had been racked by unabated fever, continuously for the last four days.

It was the body of his famous commander and he could not let such a situation persist for long.

It was only when the bluish green pus began oozing through the bandages on Gul's right shoulder, did Reshab start getting worried. The concoction of local herbs and village medical attendants antiseptic powder had failed. It was time for modern satanic medicines.

Gul would have died had it not been for his younger niece Nurie, the daughter of his eldest late brother Karim, who had been instrumental in getting their, very poor family, into money, prestige and power they enjoyed today.

May God bless his eldest brother Karim.

Had big brother Karim not landed in a government job of a peon with that big merciful large-hearted Hindu Minister, their life would have been one of an undignified bonded labourer. God bless his late brother's soul for helping their clan and having a dutiful daughter like Nurie, unlike her spoilt elder sister. Nurie had helped initially in placing cold press on Gul's forehead. She had sat hours at night without complaining, changing one wet cloth strip with another. During the day she worked as if she had slept throughout the night. Together, both had managed to clean Gul's grime infested body thrice by sponging, but only under the stern eye of his old senile mother.

Even in delirium, Gul was a difficult man to control.

He had to call in other woman of the house, to hold him down, when he was thrashing about in pain. Gul must have revered his *abbu* and *Maulvi Islam,* for he repeatedly begged for their mercy, for failing them on this sacred mission.

By the evening of the fourth day, Reshab resolved to go to Surankot. He, during his stay in Azad Kashmir *freedom fighters* camps, had come to know of a great Islamic missionary, who could revive almost a dead man. He was loved and revered by all *mujahids* of various *tanzeems,* with equal respect. For that, he would have to speak with a few elders, in Srinagar. For that, he needed a telephone and they did not exist in his isolated village. For that, he would have to go to the nearest town, which was a minimum eight hour trek. To save Gul, he would have to leave immediately. He quickly opened his diary hidden under his room's wooden plank and turned few pages. As he started walking down from his rusty sleepy village at night, he precisely knew whom to seek.

Surankot
(1030h, 14 Mar)

"I need you angel," a voice boomed.

Doctor Mehboob Shah, MD, resident doctor of Surankot's 30-bedded civil hospital, looked up in fear at the big man in a brown *salwar kameez,* who had uttered his magical code name.

He did not recognize the face.

Fear returned instantaneously, his stomach spewed juices straight to his anal passage and in sweaty desperation he stared across.

Who was he?

How did he know his code word?

Should he respond immediately? Was he an Indian plant? Was he a renegade, working for Indian Security Forces? All unimaginable dark thoughts lurked simultaneously in his mind. Screaming face of Sikander and his inability to stand two minutes of interrogation by that mother-fucking jet black South Indian, Indian Army Major, nine years earlier, came haunting back with vengeance. That ruthless Major had rubbed his black cheeks with his pure white ones and had very suggestively asked ' what will happen when...' and he had shamefully begged forgiveness. That black rub still burnt. He avoided looking at the present questioner's eyes and looked the other way as if he had not heard anything.

"I need your help," repeated Reshab and added 'angel' in a whisper to complete the sentence.

"Who are you? What is your medical problem?" stuttered back Doctor Mehboob Shah. "Why are you calling me that?" he further added, still avoiding a direct eye contact. His hands were trembling. He quickly took them below the table and tucked them under the warm confines of his thighs. The fear flogged fingers clasped other nervous protruding comfort zones.

"Doctor Mehboob, I am sorry. I spoke to *maulana* in Srinagar. We have a grave emergency. He told me to immediately contact you," Reshab spoke in a hushed tone.

"Which *Maulana* are you referring to? There are so many of them floating around uselessly in Srinagar," angel questioned quietly.

"*Maulana* Amjad Ali of Lal Chowk area. He told me to tell you that *Sikander* lives in heaven," Reshab answered.

"Oh, it's OK, state the problem." Blood rushed back to his veins, in a gush of relief. "You should have stated the last portion first. There are many enemies around to pounce on us. I cannot take chances with so many Indian spies floating around," he said.

The operative line was right. *Maulana* and his few handful of men knew the exact code.

They huddled in for about ten minutes and spoke in animated whispers.

Angel quickly grabbed his leather medical bag, stuffed up to the brim, with free samples of medicines provided by numerous medical sales representatives and stood up to leave. He quickly grabbed the telephone and spoke to his boss, "Sir, I want two days of leave. Emergency in the family. My mother is not well. Oh no, she has an exaggerated case of acute angina. Sir, I will try my level best to be back by twenty-seventh morning but I hope you will cover for me if I am late due to the exigencies at home. Yes, yes, I will definitely keep you posted. Thank you sir," dropping the phone, he walked out into a bright sunny day, with Reshab tagging behind.

Reshab thanked his stars and was amazed at *Allah's* providence that one "angel" he was seeking throughout Jammu and Kashmir was available at his back door. *Allah* had strange ways to repay and reward his beloveds.

Gul certainly was a star amongst them.

Upper Nusur (0100h, 16 Mar)

Mercifully short, but a stiff climb of an hour and fifteen minutes, got them to Nusur village, from the road junction below.

The first sight of the wound had sickened him.

It had hastened angel's actions immediately.

The wound was badly infected and the situation was precarious. It was a classical case of wet gangrene. The affected area was deep blue and emitting foul flesh rotting odour. High body temperature reflected the intensity of spread of infection. He was glad that the girl was giving the hydrotherapy correctly. He felt the pulse and it echoed back on his stethoscope, faintly. He then quickly broke one-gram penicillin ampoule and deftly filled the injection. Without much remorse, he sank it on the left buttock of the naked body, covered only with a dirty woolen shawl. No time for niceties of his profession, like cleaning to sterilize the area of proposed prick with antiseptic, he reflected. Why this, there was no time to check the rudimentary fundamentals of penicillin reaction before hand. If anything happened, he had the antidote ready. He now broke another ampoule, 2cc of paracetamol and sucked its dose into the syringe. This time he poked it with even more apathy into the neighbouring buttock.

Nurie wincing, watched the show, in agape fascination.

"Get me boiling water and the stove to heat my implements," he ordered without referring to anyone in particular. He quickly unwrapped the dirty, makeshift bandages. What he saw sickened him further. Dark bluish tinge had spread to almost two palm lengths. At worst, he would have to amputate the arm, and would certainly do it, if by next two days nothing improved. He quickly placed cotton wads below Gul's shoulder and gently started pressing the inflamed areas of biceps around the mouth of the wound hole. The pus erupted as if it was stored behind a big dam. The bluish green and later yellow discharge intermingled with blood collected on the cotton wad below, after travelling the whole length of the shoulder. He dabbed at the molten mass repeatedly and started cleaning the area delicately.

The girl offered him the boiling water. He quickly emptied the whole Dettol antiseptic bottle into it and started squeezing hot mixture at the gaping mouth in the biceps, with the help of a cotton sponge.

"Heat this scalpel till it is red hot," he again instructed and restarted examining the wound to see the precise area of incision and likely infected flesh to be surgically removed, to stop the spread of gangrene.

The red-hot scalpel was offered.

"Hold the body down tightly," the angel instructed. "No not from here, but here and here," he said again pointing at the body parts, which had to be held down. Satisfied, he dipped the scalpel in the white antiseptic water bowl and then purposefully cut into the soft flesh. He made a diagonal cut across the earlier wound configuration.

Nurie shrieked as if the scalpel had attacked her. The devil's pain was totally, hers.

The doctor looked up at Nurie. The inquisitive face of doctor could not register the reason why she had shrieked. Weak-hearted woman, he reflected. The thought made him quickly bite his tongue. Was he any stronger than she, he reasoned, as he dug deeper into the patient's flesh, ruthlessly?

Without displaying an iota of any remorse, Mehboob Shah then quickly snipped the hanging flesh on the sides to expose the wound further. Reshab closed his eyes at the gruesome sight of blood. Having made three more incisions, the doctor started pressing the sides again. Various hues of coloured pus flew out instantly. Only when bright red blood started oozing without interruption did he stop.

Gul's body writhed in pain.

Oh, the demons had returned back from hell. He screamed and arched his straining back upwards. He was to die surely. Terrified, Gul opened his eyes. The demons were desperately clinging on to him. They wouldn't let him move. That bloody madman was back and plunging his knife deep into him. This time it was not a scary dream, he was awake and that slit-eyed phantom had a knife. He shrieked and shrieked in abject terror. He wanted to retaliate but strangely his body again refused to obey his commands. Then there was this smell, which confused him.

Subconsciously, he tasted an aroma of a woman. The same familiar aroma of that *houri.*

His eyelids lowered. He felt breasts pressing against his chest. The feeling was pleasing. Oh! yes, Oh! God yes. The heavenly *houri* was clinging to him. She was a good woman. She will surely ward off the devils. Despite unbearable pain, he smiled and slumped back again into oblivion.

The commotion allowed the woollen cover to fall exposing Gul fully.

Nurie fascinated, watched the black monster between the devils leg with unblinking resolve. Were they always so big, she blushed to think, having spied at thumb like ones of her young male cousins only? The scary snake was shaking in consonance with Gul's spasms. She wanted to look somewhere else, but her eyeballs were impaled to the sight. The black snake, the brinjal, with its light pink round head, glowed. Oh! my God, what a size, she groaned. "Oh *Allah,*" she sighed as a strange wet sensation overtook her own shaking lower body. Is this desire? Was this love her other friends so excitedly spoke off in giggled whispers? She was virginally unsure. If it was love, then she was surely in love.

She had foolishly fallen in love with this unconscious man.

Rajouri
(1200h, 01 Apr)

The bus ride was uneventful and except tiredness it had imparted nothing.

Reshab got down from a rickety old Jammu and Kashmir State transport bus, which had definitely seen better days, a quarter of a century back. The journey had taken over four hours, to reach from Samhot. He had changed the buses twice. He had dared not to make a call from Samhot, where almost everyone knew everyone. The mixed populace of Rajouri town offered safety in anonymity of numbers. As he emerged out from the bus station, he started loitering around lazily in the bazaar, thronged by small shops, rising in terrace, along its inclined pot-holed road.

Gul had made a remarkable recovery. *Allah Tala's* hand was surely instrumental in his welfare. Within two days, his fever had subsided and on third, he was, pacing the room up and down, like a caged tiger. He had never met anyone as remarkable as him before. Not that Gul was mountain like, but his six feet of frame seemed always to burst with energy. His voice was firm, deep, resonating and pleasant. It came to you from behind your lobes and hit you like a whiplash.

His eyes, oh yes, his eyes.

At initial glance they looked like a simple pair of small grey-tinged eyes. If you had the courage to dwell deeper, it would send a chilled shudder down your spine. They followed you around and registered all infinite movements, with each blink having a specific purpose. They never moved illogically. His ice-cold expressionless stare was good enough to out-blink a poisonous king cobra. Only his smile was a bit awkward, sneer-dipped, and unsmiling. He had roared like a wounded animal on learning that none of his faithfuls had made it across the LoC. "By *Allah*. I will kill these Indians," he had ranted again and again.

Running around like a rabbit at Gul's commands and nursing him to his feet earlier, had left him no time even to mourn the loss of his cousin brother. The women like always, like all brave *bakarwal* women, had taken the news well. They had dutifully shrieked, wailed, breast thumped in agony. What more could they do. Moreover, what choice did they have in not taking it well? Any more lamentation for more than two days was not acceptable and he would have kicked their round bottoms himself into inducing positive movement. Who the hell will prepare food, graze goats, get firewood, wean cows, dump manure, tend to the vegetable garden and do other womanly works. Not him assuredly. His personal loss was immense. Risal had urged him to run, as he fell into his arms that day. Wild, inaccurate firing had helped him to roll down the slope and hide in a small gully. Later, he had heard a single shot and a chilling scream of Risal. Absolute silence later convinced him that merciless Indians had killed him, at point blank range.

Savage rascals.

Risal's wife was barren.

That made the matters a bit easier. He would have to get her married off again. It was his responsibility being the eldest male member and more importantly as the head of his clan, he reasoned.

He had only lumbered a few steps down the street when he suddenly froze on his feet. *Allah*, what will happen to six thousand goat-heads of Risal. If Bijli, Risal's wife remarried, he would have to give more than half in dowry. Loss was not recoverable or acceptable. She might fight to have it all quoting those confounding city laws and he will be helpless in compliance.

It then struck him like a mule-kick.

Why can't I marry her and keep the wealth in the family. Yes, he was allowed to have four wives and at present had only one. Yes, it was a good idea. More he thought of it, more he patted himself, with his original brilliant thinking. He could easily pressurize Aisha to see reason and manipulate his grandmother accordingly. Aisha would sulk for a few months but what else could she do. Bijli talked too much, but on the other hand she was young and beautiful. He will throw the *chaddar* on her and settle this issue within the clan. He had the right, didn't he?

It was getting late, he thought. He quickly zeroed on two public call offices, running side by side. Seeing one deserted, he rushed in.

"Private call *sardarji.* Can you leave me alone? I have to speak to my wife," he politely requested.

The pale lanky *sardar* nodded, got up and left the small cubicle. From outside he glanced back through the transparent glass frame and noted in amusement at the *bakarwal* push telephone buttons deftly. Not strange, but definitely unusual. The buggers were becoming educated and suave.

After two beeps, Rani Sahida, at Pakistan International Airlines Front Office at Bangkok, Thailand, picked up the phone and crisply replied, "Rani from PIA counter, how can I help you sir." She looked up at the electronic clock on the wall. It was 1245 PM.

"I am Mr Badshah from Multan. I wanted reservations for a flight to Dubai. Can I get one?" asked a faint echo. Reshab congratulated himself for speaking good passable English. His eldest uncle's determination that all the clan children were to study at an English school for two years in Jammu had paid off.

He had hated each and every day of it.

That stupid alien education was not for him. Anyone, who could tell by the colour of goat-shit, of what illness she was having or by smell of air, if it's going to rain or by one look at the ground know how many had trodden the path and when, was educated enough and his tribe needed that education only. But English was good time pass to impress village belle's, in his native place. He chuckled at the thought how many virginal legs he had magically parted by a simple, "I love you." But it was for this English speaking ability, that he had been specially hand-picked for working with Gul and ISI spymasters.

Rani, without batting an eyelid and maintaining a sweet smile at the customer in front of her desk, pressed a black button beneath the counter. The tape silently twirled as an electronic circuit got connected.

"Can you repeat your requirements once again sir. Yes, thank you, Rani can certainly help you, Mr Badshah. Can you fill me up with more details of your travel plans," she inquired sweetly.

"Please book me on economy class on PIA flight 112, from Dubai to Bangkok, on 12 April. By the way do you still give free presents for children on the flight," the voice across, inquired.

"Yes sir, we still do," replied Rani.

"Well, last time you gave me a plastic bow and an arrow. I regret, the quality was so rotten that within a day the bow broke. My son still carries the arrow around, with a mournful look. Please re-supply a sturdier one this time," said Reshab. He glanced back and saw the tall Sikh loitering outside the closed cubical door. "Good, I will pay cash, on arrival," he further added.

"Sir, consider the arrangements complete in all respects. Please report, two hours earlier. The ETD is 0130 hours on 27th April. Yes sir, want a return flight? Yes, seats are available. Yes, you will be booked on return southern bound flight to Karachi on 27th April. Please reconfirm your return bookings on 25th April. Thank you sir, have a good day," crooned Rani replacing the handset on the cradle and simultaneously removed the tape from the miniature tape recorder.

"Excuse me for a moment please," she said to the customer in front and trotted to the ladies powder room at the rear of the building.

Inside the privacy of the smelly toilet cabin, she took out a brown envelope and sealed it after putting the tape inside and hurriedly scribbled with her lipstick, Badshah in brackets Multan. She put the envelope in her carry bag and came back to her desk. Without looking up, but still maintaining a toothy smile, she dialed a number. After considerable time someone picked up the phone. Irritated at the delay she snapped, "This is PIA front clerk. Please send one chicken pizza by home-delivery to Rani," and banged the phone down without waiting for any confirmation.

When she looked up, she saw an impatient lady drumming her fingers on the isle of her counter. "I am sorry madam to have kept you waiting," she said. Then she attentively listened to her customer and within seconds was buried into the sheaf of papers in front, to keep up with their unending requirements. In any case, her work was a bore and not as exciting as the one she loved to do for her country cousins. More importantly they paid.

The pizza delivery-boy came, when the rush hour had ebbed. to twiddling thumbs, work-wise, and her counter was deserted. He quickly placed the flat pizza box in front of her and slowly asked for payment.

The brown envelope was handed over even more quietly.

Pizzas were fun, she mused smiling at her efficiency.

She quickly opened the box and lifted the pizza bread dripping with hot molten cheese. The aroma was definitely hunger enhancing but more invigorating than the savoury aroma was that red envelope beneath the crispy roasted brown bread. It would be a fruitful weekend ahead, she gloated. Another two thousand Bahts to indulge in perfumes, clothes and jewellery.

These silly games were a load of fun.

6

God's Men

"From heavens they came, evil to slay.
From heavens came the God's men."

— Jesse

Sopore
(1323h, 05 Apr)

The life was good.

For a former convict, who had only slain his brother's daughter in Baluchistan, Pakistan, in a justifiable honour killing, the life until now had been excellent. That prostitute, his shameless niece, had held that boy's hand in public. Imagine, that clan-honour-soiling-bitch. He would have killed that boy too had he dutifully not run off to seek protection of the *mullah* in the village *masjid.*

He laughed at his fate. *Jihad* was pious, self-cleansing and he liked it.

Thirty-year-old Jalal Omar, the District Commander of his *tanzeem* of Sopore area, was licking his fingers greedily and his jaws were simultaneously working noisily on the tender lamb-flesh, placed in front of him, in form of *"rogan josh."* He had an AK-47 slung across his back. Never part with it, echoed the cautionary remark of his instructor at *Harkut-ul-Ansar* camp, on the outskirts of Peshawar. He was proud that he had never parted with it, even while screwing women here. The *gosht* was tasty, but these idiots laced their food with too much of chillies and oil and above all, he hated rice, never ever having eaten a morsel of it in Baluchistan. *"Roti,"* he shouted, blowing his nose into his sleeves. A woman appeared and tried to place one in the basket in front of him. Even before the *roti* could be put down, Jalal grabbed at it and began dipping it in his sumptuous, red-hot curry.

Frail, grey-haired, Abdul Malik, sitting on the floor opposite was slowly playing with his rice. His sane reasoning had left him nude, a long time back. He watched in sheer disgust as Jalal let out a loud belch. Cannibals, he thought. Sheer muck, cultureless bastards. But what could he do. He and all others around were partly to blame. They had burst crackers, danced like silly monkeys, thinking that *azadi* was around the corner and Pakistan, the land of pure, will deliver them from yoke of slavery. He had donated money to innumerable outfits. He even had forgotten the names of half of them, which had mushroomed overnight. He had hugged initial Kashmiri youth returning from training camps across, he had seen their true passion. His friends, his family, all had out-vied others to invite foreign returned guests to their houses. All had caressed the *mujahid* beards to honour them.

Why did the same hands seem so sullied now?

His heart knew the answer.

He had gauged his passion, a diehard "*jamaiti*" and his coterie of friends had galvanized the whole village, in driving out Kashmiri Hindu *Pandits* and making everything Indian not work, or at best be a broken past for them. But much later, the truth hurt, when locals gave away to foreign brand of *jihad*, their unfamiliar *Deobandi* Islamic ideology, brutalism, mistrust, contempt for valley's youth, rapine lust for our beautiful women, blood of innocent Kashmiris used as cannon fodder, betrayal by so-called puritans across, pilferage of money to build palaces at Jammu, Delhi and even Dubai, had broken his heart. Worst was that public conveniences had disappeared. No lady doctors, no schools, no electricity, no water, no industry, no investment and he a graduate of economics from Aligarh Muslim University, was convinced that they were moving slowly back into the quagmire of under-development, reflecting seventeenth century social development index. Afghanistan had stepped back into Stone Age, with their pure and successful bandwagon of *jihad.* They had fine tuned ochlocratic oligarchy to perfection and will ensure that his prosperous Kashmir also meets the same fate. There was still happiness, available in abundance, in this magical vale for these God's men to comprehend logically and ration their loot. But this glorious *Jihad,* being run from across Pakistan, on shoulders of petty criminals, who will infuse sanity or reason?

Jalal slyly smiled at Karina, baring his yellow *naswar* stained teeth, as she hurried around serving food. What a luxury, he thought. This was the land of plenty. Back home, four *rotis* with tea in the whole day was considered a good gratifying meal. War-ravaged fields grew almost nothing with people having forgotten how to plough the fields. *Gosht* was restricted to a few festive days. He had better make the best of his stay here.

"*Gosht,*" he almost shouted.

Karina, avoiding any eye contact, poured him more red-hot meat. Jalal stared at the outline of her small, ah yes, firm breasts he saw through the neckline of Karina's *firan.* She felt Jalal's blatant stare burning her chest. She quickly adjusted her *chunni* around her neck.

Jalal giggled softly.

Jalal liked what he saw: the obedient and compliant women of this sissy valley. They have so much and still they crib. One look at the barren landscape of his native Baluchistan, these buggers will realize how lucky they were due to the quirk of geographical bonanza. Still they cannot fight their war by themselves. Women – all of them.

He giggled again at the thought of spineless clan-members around. It was worth fighting *jihad* here. White, spotless white women like Karina, all to be taken at his will. This was a warriors' land. The land for brave and courageous people like him, who defied death, who wanted *shahadat* for God's cause, who had the will to crush opponents of Islam. He was fighting for these people, it was their war, they had invited him here and they bloody well look after him nicely. He had no remorse of his earlier pickings and those planned in the future. In the last eleven months, it was his ninth house and he had refused the services of two families, which had only old ugly hags to serve him.

Wiping the steel plate clean of any traces of mutton gravy with the last morsel of his *roti,* he barked his orders directly staring at Karina. "I will take tea in my room, after fifteen minutes," and walked out of the room.

Abdul Malik, an economics honours student, sole owner of sixty- eight acres of prime apple orchards, on the banks of river Jhelum near village Acham, sat quietly, without touching his food-laden plate.

He could not meet the accusing gaze of his eldest daughter Karina.

Back in his room, Jalal dragged a wooden box from underneath the bed and opened it to examine its booty. Four AK-47's and one rocket launcher would be adequate for the mission. He had clarified from Gilani, his superior commander that the basic ammunition for training and operation would be provided by the *Maulana.* They all had to march to the South somewhere. The exact location would be disclosed later. He did not like it and had let his reservation known, in working under some other umbrella organization, he had never heard of. Gilani, his mentor, had said it was for Kashmir's cause and he had been instructed not to raise any question. His boss had been very adamant at his participation. "Cause," he had said. Bloody hell, what did they think he was doing here, without a cause. Stupid, mindless idiots, all his senior bosses of *Harkut-ul-Ansar.* Someone was hijacking their fight and all these eunuchs were clapping for someone else's success.

A soft tap on the door diverted his attention.

Karina stood there holding a glass of brown coloured broth in her marble white nimble hands. He grabbed her shoulders and pushed her roughly inside the door and a light kick by his right foot closed the privacy-granting door. He guided her to the bed and sat facing her. Her hands were shivering in fear or excitement, he could not fathom. Whatever be it, he did not care. Bending his torso, he slid his coarse hands slowly up her long slim legs. He liked what he felt. Hairless, creamy, soft touch. She was not wearing any underclothes as usual. This was another thing he liked about women of this valley. As he roughly pulled her to him, the tea spilt on the carpet. "Bitch," he muttered, as he got busy undressing Karina. Head bowed down in shame, her small budding breasts quivered as Jalal mouthed them to taste another lump of his favourite food; raw flesh. This sure was a good *jihad.* This sure was heaven on earth or that bloody Mughal emperor would not have uttered those famous words.

Abdul Malik heard the door slam shut.

He was still sitting cross-legged in the dining room. Intricate designs, on his very precious Kashmiri silk carpet, did not evoke any pride-sprouting 'look it's mine' interest.

He also heard stifled muted screams of Karina.

Sometime later, his youngest seven year old Zarina came to her *abbu.* Seeing him sit so solemnly, she quietly lay down and rolling over the carpet, placed her head on the comfort zone of her father's lap.

She was puzzled and could not understand why the tears were slowly trickling down from her *abbu's* cheeks. In spite of her desperate loving hug they would not stop.

She also could not comprehend his senseless mutterings, "*Khudda maaf karna, khudda maaf karna.*" (God please forgive me)

Diwar, Lolab
(1200h, 06 Apr)

Both had been seeking each other. The seeker and the sought. Actors had exchanged places. Need was same. Mutual profit. A meeting without a profit was never heard of late in Kashmir.

They exchanged notes not for more than three minutes. Beyond that duration there was no trust.

Three hours later, Major Yadav leading his battalion and other operational teams, surrounded and killed two Lashkar terrorists, holed inside a hideout in the basement of a house. They had been quartered there since the last two months. Not many knew of this secret house address.

Six hours later, in the middle of the night, Nazir's wife received Rs. 30,000. Out of that Rs. 24,000 for two heads and an additional six, as a future investment in trust.

Rajauri
(1056h, 07 Apr)

The bill took Sardar Ranjit Singh aback.

The *bakarwal* had paid Rs. 882/- in cash and had taken the receipt. After he left, he switched on his computer machine and noted the number through the recall facility.

Strange, absolutely strange, indeed.

A *bakarwal* making an international call to Thailand was strange and then paying more than fifty bucks was mind-boggling. Till, Delhi or Bombay a call would not have aroused any interest, but this was certainly suspicious. He had mused over what to do for more than a day. Exposing oneself now-a-days was fraught with danger and the terrorists displayed no remorse in killing informers. But his inner-self did not agree to his cowardly inaction. A coward S*ikh,* no never. He recalled the community security-coordinating meeting in which inspector Narinder Singh Pathania had asked them to report anything unusual. Even a dog not strolling along its usual path was unusual and should be reported, he had reiterated. This call was quiet unusual. He scanned his diary and dialed the inspector's number.

Srinagar
(Same Day, Afternoon)

As usual, it had been a busy day.

Rasool Bhat had been on his routine morning ramble. His army of little monkeys, as he had nicknamed them, had passed good information. Border Security Force and Special Operations Group of Jammu and Kashmir Police had conducted a pre-dawn raid at Batmalu locality, but had found nothing. The anonymous tip off had reached camped *Harkat-ul-Ansar* cadres just in the nick of time, to affect a panicky flight. Three injured *Hizbul* men had been admitted to a private hospital in Lal Chowk. The latest on security forces pickets was also known and marked on his city map. It would help him plan the route for his nightly sojourns. While walking he picked up a local paper. It was the good old 'Greater Kashmir' an excellent expression of all things anti-Indian and recourse of all *Jihadi* views. Of late, there was nothing in it, which eulogized its greater name, covering only the distorted news of the valley and its longing love for Pakistan. It was also a medium for passing secure terrorist messages right under the Indian noses.

The headlines screamed "LIFE IMPRISONMENT NOT ACCEPTABLE. DEATH FOR ARMY RAPISTS."

Why can't these army guys keep their dicks in place, he thought. Maybe their virility stemmed from the barrel of the gun. Shameful incident. These buggers should be hanged and local sentiments were not far misplaced.

He scanned around.

The city had started bustling to its peak activity.

Shouts, screams, haggling, vendors, shopkeepers, were all hustling for space and scheming for quick profits during available time. God only knew for how many days the town would close, on some stupid organization's call. Make hay while the sun shines, had become a subconscious ethics of this society. He entered a tea kiosk and told the proprietor "phone." He was well known and respected for needing any basic introductions. The bespectacled, beggarly looking owner moved to the rear room of his tea stall swarming with flies and removed the telephone hidden in a cupboard. Rasool dismissed the tea maker, before he started punching the numbers. Continuous faint rings echoed back into his ears. Thank God, the lines were through. Even a fainter click confirmed the connection. He spoke rapidly, "Baba here, send five freedom fighters from Alpha Squad by tomorrow. You know the place." Not waiting for any reply, he replaced the handset. He liked this private arrangement and avoided public call offices, as most of them were monitored. Bills could lead you to actual owners and locations. He had talked the old tea stall man into installing the phone. Obviously, he had agreed when he had offered to pay all the bills, with his calls included, but only with a rider that the original bills were handed over to him instantaneously.

Bangkok
(1630h, 08 Apr)

He had been sweating since a long time.

About hundred metres across the Pakistan International Airlines office, Mr Sibal Kumar, the third secretary of Indian Embassy, Thailand, sat behind a spotless white console, housed inside a specially constructed graphite steel dome. "Grave," the nickname given lovingly by the embassy staff, to this steel structure, housed all electronic and signal devices used by them. Most importantly, it was the make-shift branch office of the Research and Analysis Wing, India's premier foreign intelligence agency, in Thailand. Sibal headed the outfit.

He was sweating despite central air-conditioning, as he laboriously worked on the monitored transcript. The duty communication operator had ticked him of a coded message and had placed the hard copy of it yesterday. He studied the whole message again, reproduced on a white bond paper. So the beautiful Rani was on her routine masterly performance again. He would love to crack her skull to dwell into the secrets of her mind. Computer analysis had given him a faint direction to look into. Previous data bank, in fact all earlier Pakistan generated messages had drawn a blank. No link to anything previous. Codes were being used for the first time. Must be a big, deep secret? Something sinister was assuredly on and like all intelligence staff all over the world, even premier agencies like CIA etc, he would have to start from scratch, to make any reasonable guess-estimates out of it.

Dabbing at the liberal production of sweat, housed on his forehead, with his spotless white handkerchief, he pulled out a blank sheet and rearranged the intercepted data with his assessments.

BADSHAH FROM MULTAN	- Activation code.
FREE PRESENTS FOR CHILDREN	- Requirement?
BOW AND ARROW	- Specific equipment dispatched.

BROKEN BOW, ARROW FINE	- Few items received.
SOUTHERN BOUND, 17 APR	- New route and schedule.

The more he pondered over what he had deduced, more irritated he became.

Something was happening, but he could not place his finger on it. Wish he had the ability to trace the incoming call, but the telephone line maintainer, Ratna Buddhir Rama could not help more in this regard. Whatever little coup he had generated, he had to be thankful to his good detective work and Ratna.

Seven months ago, when Pakistan International Airlines had acquired the office complex in the second storey commercial building, just overlooking and opposite the Indian embassy, he had been very worried. He knew it would be used for surveillance, both covert and electronic.

The "Grave" was the consequence of it.

He had discreetly visited the office site when the interiors were being reconstructed. It had been a quagmire of unlaid electric and telephone wires. He, by sheer luck had stumbled upon Ratna working on the telephone distribution panel, outside the building, when an idea struck him. After that, he had followed Ratna for more than a month, and was sure that he knew more of him, than his poor, pale-looking, and plain simple wife. Ratna stayed in a two-room ramshackle cardboard house in downtown city. Maybe it was the dank smell of that crowded place which forced Ratna to the open beaches, very regularly. Whatever be it, Ratna loved to roam alone.

On the third weekend, when he had tailed Ratna to Pattaya beach, did he get an opportunity to intervene? The telephone man loved drinks, sleazy dances, cheap girls, and obviously all vices above his meager pay packet. He was having an argument with the owner of the "Dragon Ladies" club who was using his hired muscle to throw Ratna out, due to non-payment of earlier dues, when Sibal had thrown innumerable Bahts on the counter saying, "My friend, look after him and the whole show is on me."

Groggy, incoherent Ratna was suspicious and confused at first but polite, shy, backslapping; innocent-smiling stranger quickly submerged his apprehensions with more scotch. A bottle of Vat 69 later, both had humped hussies of Ratna's choice. They had become weekly drinking and whoring pals.

The request had been innocent two months later.

Ratna had surprised him with vigour and energy to repay a trusted friend. By the time Pakistan International Airlines front office opened to public, he had managed to monitor the first congratulatory call from Pakistan International Airlines headquarters from Islamabad.

Ratna received his monthly retainers for whoring and drinking, but all alone after that.

But what to do with this half-baked knowledge, thought Sibal, staring at the paper in front of him. It was best if he let the spooks at Delhi reduce a bit of fat from their heads worrying over the problem. He quickly made a brief along with his assessment and fed the hand-written paper in the fax machine. He started breathing easier only after he had pressed the transmit button.

Srinagar
(1200h, 15 Apr)

It was the peak-trading hour of Srinagar's Lal Chowk commercial market.

Everyone wanted to complete their chores within those compressed 14 hours from 5 AM till 7 PM, before the curfew was imposed again. People had crawled out of their depressed homes like ants. Mad-rush disease had infected all. Old men trotted, the middle-year ones cantered and young surely galloped. One could not waste time walking.

In one remote corner of the bazaar, a fortified bunker, with four men sticking out their Self-Loading Rifles, indicated that not all was as calm, as reflected by the daily hustle and bustle of the bazaar.

Their nervous eyes were darting at everyone who moved.

Tension in their eyes lasered out and could be felt by all who crossed them from minimum twenty metres away, a line inside which, they will shoot anyone, without an iota of remorse.

The town folk had seen many such bunkers crop up in all corners of the city, over the years. They had seen many bunkers go down and men behind them turn into bloody goo, due to some sneak grenade attack. Both, the men in *khakhi* uniform and the city folk protected their drawn-lines, fanatically.

The noise, the din, the babble of voices, click-tic-click of *tongas,* shouts, fights and haggling, all rose into a crescendo, that carried to a room in the left extreme corner of Zahir Silk Factory.

Maulana Amjad Ali sat on a raised divan, dressed in white silk *kurta-pyajama,* with an equally striking white *toosh* shawl draped around his shoulders. His eyes were closed. The face reflected flushed red concentration. Facial muscles were taut and rigid. Nothing on his face moved except the mouth in repeated intervals.

"*Lashkar-e-Toiba*"

"Yes"

"*Tarique-e-Jihad*"

"Yes"

"*Jammat-e-Islami*"

"Yes"

"*Al Badar*"

"Yes"

"*Hizbul Mujahidin*"

"Yes"

"*Muslim Janbez Force*"

"Yes".

"*Harkat-ul-Ansar*"

"Yes"

"*Jammat-ul-Mujahidin*"

"Yes".

"*Freedom Fighters*"

"Yes"

All eyes turned towards Rasool Bhat. Various commanders stared at him for they had never ever heard of this group.

"*Allah* be praised," said *Maulana* opening his big buffalo eyes. He stared at the gathering in front of him and felt elated at his own achievement. Something impossible a few weeks back was unfolding like a dream in front of his eyes.

"We have all gathered here to achieve the ultimate objective of our cause. I know, that all of you brave honourable men tread different paths, but, if you peep into your hearts, all of you have only one aim. The liberation of Kashmir from the shackles of India. You are the true believers. You are *Allah's* chosen ones. God has given you power to see reason. Your reason for participating in this holy war was initially to fight infidels. You came to this *Dar-ul-Harb* to propagate our Muslim brotherhood. Our enemies have been defeated in Iran, Afghanistan, Chechnya, and Bosnia. How were they defeated?" *Maulana* paused for effect. He liked the rapt attention encountered.

"They were defeated by the loyal and combined participation of believers from Sudan, England, Egypt, Syria, Lebanon, Afghanistan, Malaysia and Bangladesh. Name a country in the world from where they did not come," Maulana thundered, with his fingers jabbing at each man in front of him, he continued, "You, you and you are all here for *Mohammed* so wills. Without his grace, would we all be sitting here? You all combined have the strength in you to throw the violators of true faith. This pure land is being raped by these *kafirs* from Hindustan. Our women are in danger. We cannot protect their dignity. We must liberate its oppressed people. Once this beautiful vale falls into our hands, the coveted crown of India will fall on its feet. India will whither and die like a headless corpse. Then the armies from *Dar-ul-Islam* will sweep the only bastion of non-believers in South Asia. From shores of Atlantic to Indian Ocean, we will have a land worth living for, for centuries. To see that our children beget heaven on earth, your cooperation is necessary. We must fight Indians like a single clenched fist. *Shahadat,* if it comes to you, will take you to heavens," *Maulana* paused to palm his long white beard and then added, "Before we proceed further, I want to know, who all are with me for this righteous cause." He looked around. A general murmur of consent rose from all sitting. The *Maulana* had crooned the right words, which played straight with your heart.

"Good. You will all head south. Details have been worked out. Initial trail by fire is in your hands. If we succeed in this one mission, then we can participate in bigger events and engulf our enemies. Remember, when the might of the combined hurricanes hit the enemy, it will sweep away all the non-believers from its path."

"Who will control the operation?" asked the *Al Badar* representative.

"A tiger like yourself," answered the *Maulana.*

"How can we trust these smaller groups? Their capabilities are peanuts in front of us," the Hizbul man boasted.

"All are equal in the eyes of the God," *Maulana* held his voice expressionless.

"But, all of us have connived against each other, one time or another. Without faith, we cannot fight together," the Lashkar man thundered.

"When blood flows from the wounds inflicted by a common enemy, your blood will bind you together in faith," replied *Maulana* calmly staring at the eyes of Lashkar commander.

"But who is that man and his group? We have never heard of him or his *tanzeem,*" asked Jalal the representative of Harkat, pointing at Rasool Bhat. He had observed all the commanders assembled. This person was different. His steady cool demeanour disturbed him. All others had met, passed glances, smiles, and nods of acceptance, except that man in the black turban.

Before *Maulana* could reply, Rasool got up shrugged his shoulders and spoke softly, "I am nobody. A man without an army, but few dedicated men who believe in Kashmir and all it stands for. Had it not been for me," he pointed to Jalal, "your five men would have been shot like dogs yesterday night in Batmalu. My timely information saved their miserable lives. At present three of your men injured at Gandarbal, in army encounter are taking treatment not more than four blocks from here," he looked squarely at the Hizbul leader. "We might be nobody, but nothing moves in Srinagar without my knowledge and those are my credentials," he sat down amongst open stares.

Maulana smiled openly perhaps for the first time. "I agree and am indebted to such patriots of Kashmir. Now go out and work for God's cause," he goaded others.

"Like a clenched fist," he shouted again as all got up to leave.

Same City
(1400h, 16 Apr)

Within the confines of now evil-dread city, this place was Shangri-La.

Hotel Cecil was one of the few left in Srinagar, which still attracted locals during the day.

The hotel had been a hallmark in hospitality for the last 80 years of its existence. The old grandeur and ambience permeated from its furnishings. Mr Nusrat Ali, the present proprietor, prided in the fact, that despite uncertain political climate, the Cecil was still open to public. Trade conferences, entertainment of friends and families were organized in this heavily guarded hotel. Constructed on illegal land adjoining Dal Lake, it provided a scenic backdrop, which awe-struck many people. Serenity was a welcome contrast to the madness of violence prevalent outside. The waiters in their light blue uniforms were scurrying to meet the demands of a few, old and many, new rich Muslims.

They had struck gold, on driving away even a richer band of Hindus, almost a decade ago. Sipping on wines, the fat money belts, gold-laden females justified the Hindu massacre. They had become rich, hadn't they?

Nafisa walked into the white Italian marble-floored lobby, anxiously scanning the strange faces. Imran, after a gap of one month, had contacted her last week through a letter. It had shattered her fairytale love story. The straight round precise words had shaken the foundation of her existence. Imran's parents, a known Muslim ICS family, were contemplating his marriage this year and Imran like a true gentleman had come to her asking for a commitment. How could she, a *bakarwal* girl and against the wishes of her family, take such a bold step. All alone and marry? It would be sacrilege, enough to start a generation of bloody family feuds.

She remembered with lump in her throat, the day she had accidentally bumped into him at Delhi's Palika Bazaar, as she was rushing out, after arguing with the Kashmiri-artifacts shop manager for charging such unearthly prices. She had wanted to pick up presents for her younger sister and *amma* when her three-month-old teacher's contact program was coming to an end.

Delhi had rocked her life and evoked feelings of which dreams were made of. Hesitating and apprehensive, the unsure *bakarwal* girl saw the open world, through the eyes of a life-imprisoned convict on a parole. Freedom, laughter, casualness, openness, clothes, oh God, what clothes, beautiful women, their uncaring attitude and zest for life, was too much to take in one outing from Kashmir. She had thought herself to be cat whiskers, coming to Srinagar from an obscure village, in the Pir Panjal ranges. Delhi had stoned her soul to think and live. What savages we were, she thought. This will continue till education did not reach all, but who the hell will be educated in *Madrasas*. They teach nothing except religion and of late, only hate. Modern education was needed, and *Allah* permitting, she would provide it.

Imran lying on his bums, blue jeans, and legs apart, with his books scattered all around had been a comical sight. Despite two second old acquaintance, she had instantaneously leaned down and helped and Imran hesitatingly hobbled to life, collecting his books. Apology, a few smatterings of continuous sorry had given Imran the courage to safely escort her to the bus stand, before she toppled more people around, he had remarked jokingly. Later they found themselves sipping coffee in the Indian Coffee House and discussing their lives. God had his hand in their union and she had always maintained that belief. A lone Muslim girl, to meet in Delhi, a smart Muslim boy, out of millions of people, had to be God's intervention.

Now Imran had only two months left. His parents were getting him married. He had bared his child-like soggy heart to her in his letter and thus this sudden meeting. The girl in question was the only daughter of a very rich Muslim businessman. Despite his firm no, his parents were unrelenting. In a standoff, he had taken leave to come and meet her at Srinagar.

Imran's profession initially had come as a rude shock. He shockingly was a captain in the Indian Army. But seeing his love for his uniform, his die-hard spirit for his country, she was a little confused and later softened her views. She had loathed anyone in olive greens and the Indian Army in particular, as many hair-raising tales of their brutality against their Muslim brothers, had fed her developing intellectual beliefs.

Her community, of late, had dreamed of Pakistan as the saviours.

Everyone's sacrifice had been supreme and they were so ready to welcome the *Khaki* coloured marching Muslim armies in 1990. But their hopes had been belied in 1990. Then they hoped of it in 1991 and then every subsequent year till 1996. By then they knew they would never come. It was then, many tongues started wagging that Pakistan did not have the guts to throw out the infidels and their army was full of useless heretics, who farted loud and did nothing.

Kashmiris were being used shamelessly.

Her people were an excuse to die and keep the pot boiling. If she, a woman with no interest in politics could understand it, she was sure others had comprehended the situation much earlier. The problem was that too much of power and prestige was involved for anyone to dither now. Many in Hurriyat had gulped in too much of Pak-financed rupees to be allowed to back out.

Imran was sitting in one corner of the coffee shop. His face lit up like a small boy presented with a chocolate, when he saw her.

His innocence in love was what she would die for, a thousand times over. He ran up to her and held her firmly. The only place in Srinagar, less inside the four walls of one's home, where a boy could do so, thought Nafisa. In their animated state of words and reassurances which lasted over 45 minutes, just sipping cold coffee, they did not notice the waiter on the neighbouring table, give them ugly stares, since long.

Bloody hell, thought Abdullah. That's no way a decent Muslim woman should meet a man in public. The man himself looked odd. No, not a local, not a rare tourist or a journalist either? He was too smartly dressed for them. Suddenly his cropped hair caught his attention. Oh! my God, he looked like a defence personnel. Well, very brave of him to come out alone. He must alert his local commander of *Muslim Janbaz Force* immediately.

A good soft target, for some good crisp easy money.

Abdullah hurriedly narrated the whole incident to Mehmood Usman, his information liaison man. "I think he is a *fauji,*" he added further, "Alone and unarmed."

Almost an hour later, when Usman reached the gates of Cecil with his two executioners, he saw Abdullah waiting outside the parking lot. He ran over and hurriedly said, "The man caught the tempo which just went out and the girl is walking down the avenue. She is wearing a red *salwar* under a brown *firan.*

Usman quickly reorganized his men and instructed one of his boyish looking henchmen, "You follow the girl. See where she goes. Do not alert her. We will follow the tempo. Quickly to Badami Bagh main entrance, you Bengali," he said pointing to the driver. Black, of a small stature, Aminul Rehman was shaking with fear. These *freedom fighters* will get him into trouble. After two years of wandering all over Pakistan and crossing the border twice he had managed this job. If caught and deported, how will he feed his family of nine children in Chittagong, Bangladesh. These people will surely get him into trouble. He quickly kick-started his auto-rickshaw and headed towards the instructed destination. He will disappear after this. These puritans of faith will not even give petrol fare, he fearfully reasoned.

By the time they reached the main gate, Usman saw a very smart man dressed in black trousers and cream coloured shirt with red silken scarf, show his Identity Card and go inside the security of man-made, wire fortress. Sensing the uselessness of the situation he punched Rehman in the back and whispered, "Go man go." Shit a golden opportunity missed to earn rupees one lakh and twenty thousand, a price for an Indian officer killed. Bloody hell, he had also missed the *maulana's* invitation, but he was sure that his immediate boss would attend it. The stupid woman had passed the wrong dates to him, which he was sure was done very intentionally. That bitch slaved on his boss and envied his closeness to him. He had apologized over the phone and now he had to organize five men to move at short notice when ordered. He had looked at this as a golden opportunity, thrown at his feet by God that would have restored some confidence in him and made him look better in the eyes of other commanders. He clenched his fists in sheer frustration.

Altaf had no trouble in tracking the girl in red to the university and subsequently to its girl's hostel. In fact, he was surprised. A traitor, in the tiger's den. In his own backyard. He had taken a good look at her from various angles. She was stunningly beautiful and too pre-occupied to notice him following her. What could such a heavenly girl be doing with security forces man? Must be a *mukhbir*. Our own women, stabbing our backs was bad, very bad indeed. She will get her reward in due course, he reflected as he turned away from the hostel gate confronting a massive black cow of a woman, the *chowkidar*.

Engrossed, he did not notice a small boy, watering the plants outside the hostel, staring at him.

Murree, Pakistan
(1000h, 18 Apr)

It had stunned them all to silence. At such situations silence was like a loaded pregnant pause. He had mastered to control silence.

The initial reports of the fiasco, at *Khuni Nallah* near the Kabul post, had put everyone in a pall of gloom.

It was not a fiasco, but a bloody disaster.

They had chosen the sector very carefully. Only one infiltration, out of eleven, had been detected in that sector, earlier. He knew the Gurkhas, who were manning that part of the line of control, were finishing their tenure next month and by nature of all accumulated military psychology, troops would naturally be lax. It was basic human nature, not to rake up trouble before leaving and better to move back intact as a unit, without losing men in stupid bravados. They had planned the exact slopes for infiltration keeping in view the nature of ground and accessibility of locals in the vicinity. He was sure that the Indians would have done their homework in detail and guarded the approaches more in strength, where the villages were nearer the LoC and accessible. On the Southern slopes of Pir Panjal, they were adequately behind. Then how come such a mess, mused the stunned Brigadier.

His boss's earlier caution mocked at him repeatedly, "Against Indians count on what you have achieved and not what can be done."

General Ibrahim Lodhi had ordered the after-action review. It was to be conducted by his feet-touching lackey, Colonel Imtiaz Ahmed, who had flown in especially from the capital. They had given their depositions. Major Irfan had explained all the precautions he had taken to ensure success, including leading the *jihadis* personally up to *Khuni Nallah* twice on dry runs, just to build up their confidence. Thank God that idiot Subedar Mastan had goofed up the issue of fire support and the blame was put entirely on him. In fact, he was facing a court martial, for not exercising proper command and control and cowardice in the face of the enemy. At least, the blame was not on him. Good, at least 36 *jihadis* were confirmed killed, despite that Indian Lieutenant bragging of 42 dead. Good, that gave him a cool profit of Rs. 36 Lakhs. He, as always, had persuaded the men to leave half of their given cash with him, though all had dutifully signed for the full amount of rupees two lakh per head. Let the holy *tanzeems,* swindling the money blatantly from people, pay for their dead.

The news of Arrows safety had been a blessing in disguise. It enabled him to send Colonel Imtiaz Ahmad packing back to

Islamabad and keep that stupid interfering Lodhi in check. Organizing the Bow had been a problem at such short notice.

The infiltration of seven faithfuls, on special leave from Third Special Services Group, the elitist commando force in the Arab world, scheduled to be inducted via Khasghar on 15th March, had to be stopped. The operation was cancelled, as no news of Gul was forthcoming.

The southern-bound route took frantic calls and threatening language to Pakistan International Airlines and director, passport and immigrations. To put the operation back on track in six days had sapped his energy. He slumped back on his fat cushioned chair and relaxed as he glanced at the time. In another two hours, the Bow would be airborne. Rest all as always, will be in *Allah's* hands. He picked up the phone and dialed an Islamabad number. It's better to satisfy that General's ego, he thought.

Channadaji, Bandipore (1353h, 24 Apr)

He was offered a sweet cup of tea.

Thank God, he had graduated to better things in life than to gulp down that miserable salted version of it. Good life, why not yes. The sexiest woman in the village, his wife, was also the part of good life. Twenty prime rice-producing acres of land, two hundred apple-producing trees, thirty almond-bearing trees, a plot of land in Sopore, a bus plying to Srinagar, two local taxis in his name, the life was on an upswing. The only crib he had against the Almighty was that he had no children. Only three feeble girls from five years of marriage was not manliness in any form. Even his sulking wife showed no desire to have a male child. Bloody BA educated pampered daughter of local contractor in Bandipore. Whatever I do for her is inadequate.

Ungrateful bitch.

Ashraf Khan mused over his tidings of fate.

From a poor, landless, uneducated lout, seven years back the fate was certainly smiling. This *Jihad* had been also good for his family. He had returned all his family dues with compound interest. The land where his father used to work as a daily labourer was his. The owner and his family were dead for exploiting the village poor. His inhuman previous employer, minus a throat-slit only son, was now his compliant father-in-law.

The role of an executioner for his *tanzeem, Lashkar-e-Toiba* was respect generating.

The whole village, which had mocked the Khans earlier, was at his mercy. These vermins referred to him as *sahib* now and they better, if they didn't want to land up dead. Respect was good but it was the smell of money, which came along with it that invigorated his soul. Money came in organizing reception of the infiltrating groups and motivating young boys to go across. In addition, as the launch commander for entire valley including areas of Drass in North, he was filthy rich. He had been instructed to go to Khasgar to receive a group but before he could put his machinery in motion the orders had been countermanded. Strange and not to his liking, as missing money-making forays was not palatable.

As unpalatable, as this sweet tea offered by his wife.

It had a lousy bitter after-taste, which lingered. The right profanity to rectify his wife's' digression was on his lips, when suddenly, his jaws locked. He could not understand his good fate, nor why foamy bubbles were emerging out of his mouth or why his beautiful wife was speaking into his radio set. His chest suddenly heaved and his eyes closed.

A few minutes later, an officer leading a bunch of Garhwali troops entered the house and took the dead body away into the nearby jungles. He fired many shots into the inert body of Ashraf Khan to claim an encounter, to eliminate the traces of poison and most importantly, to stage a drama to protect the innocence of a women being raped non-stop for the last five years.

All this, in name of the Almighty God.

Bangkok
(1200h, 26 Apr)

Sibal had an equally frustrating week.

He had puzzled over the puzzle and it had left him stoned.

He hoped against hope that Delhi would come up with some breakthrough where he had failed. To ensure that some nincompoop analyst did not file his report in an obscure corner, he kept on pestering the desk officer. They remained as much in the dark as he was. They were pouring over all ship and air movements from Islamabad to Bangkok and Dubai to Bangkok. They had leads but nothing definite was emerging. He had gone all over the tabulated flight plans of Pakistan International Airlines. No flight returned back from Dubai on 27 Apr. He had also tabulated all the flight plans. The only flight from Karachi, which flew South, was Pakistan International Airlines 402A, directly to Colombo.

He pressed the taped transcripts on once again. Beautiful Rani's voice filled his cabin, "Yes Mr Badshah, we confirm your return south-bound flight non-stop to Bangkok." This had come in yesterday.

The only south-bound flight was to Colombo and none to Bangkok. He mused over this information with nothing worthwhile to do; he dialed his counterpart, in Colombo.

Srinagar (1800h, 26 Apr)

"How's my forlorn Chinar," quipped Khushbu as she ruffled her hands through Nafisa's long hair. She loved this wild *bakarwal* girl.

"OK," shot back Nafisa.

"How's your mood. Seeing you smiling after a bloody week," her friend observed.

"I am fine," she replied.

"Well gossips are galore. I believe someone was asking for you at the hostel gates. Bibi just told me so," crooned Khushbu.

"Must be some stupid love-struck man following me," replied Nafisa quiet agitated by this fact. She must speak to Bibi. Bibi, in fact was a massive black woman, God's genetic defect, six feet tall and weighing over hundred kilos. Nothing could get pass her gate, which could harm her lovely girls. She was the gate-keeper, a friend, sex expert, advisory board, match-maker, all rolled into one. For one's happiness, Bibi had to be kept happy and it was a very rational decision for anyone to be on her right side.

"Well, we all are going on a picnic, this Sunday to Tsrare Sharif. Tahir has organized a bus exclusively for the girl's hostel. He has even managed the security passes," said Khushbu.

"If it is Tahir's doing, then sure, something is amiss. How come such a largesse is being bestowed on us lesser mortals? How come now-a-days you blush like a bride taking Tahir's name," Nafisa spoke staring at Khushbu fixedly.

"You devil, I love Tahir, I love his voice, I love his reasoning, I love his love for Kashmir, I love his killer looks, I love his patriotism, I love his energy, but more than that he has shown me the way. He has shown us the reason for existence. Don't worry; he cannot get girls into trouble. We are his eyes, ears and subtle hands. In any case, you are coming," she said with finality that left no room to say, No.

Colombo
(0800h, 27 Apr)

Even hurry takes time, he agitatedly mused.

Bloody Sibal had just given them nine hours notice. Not that they had less work here, keeping tab on various militant groups and eavesdropping on the numerous political parties and their leaders for their views on India.

This place was fast turning into a quagmire of quick sand.

Tamil groups were emerging stronger day-by-day and Government resolution was weakening, proportionally. Violence perpetuated more violence and the solution had to come from within the country. At best, what he could do was to faithfully record acts of violence. At best India could mediate. Since the IPKF imbroglio and betrayal later by the invitees themselves, the nature of conflict had reached very scary proportions. He was not sure who was helping whom and all including ISI, Mossad and CIA, had jumped into the fray. Good pickings for any enterprising mercenary on this island, he thought.

"Fernandez, have you placed your man inside the terminal," asked Grover, peering into the terminal, from the car park.

"Yes sir," he replied.

"I want everyone photographed as they alight from the plane," instructed Grover, as he nervously glanced around. You could never be sure who could be watching you in this bloody hellhole.

"It will be done the way you want it, sir. Rashmi Srivastava will be doing an article on airport security and they have allowed her to photograph the whole setup," answered Fernandez. "It was difficult persuading her and then even worse organizing the event. It will coincide with the Pakistan International Airlines 402A landing here," he whispered further, avoiding looking at agitated Grover.

Information had been vague. The way Sibal had described the events, it had become clear that something was definitely on and had strangely coincided with his own meager inputs. When the Pakistani ambassador's car was detailed to go to the airport, his curiosity had been more than aroused.

He was grateful for small bits of information, he could pick via their carpool. Bloody shit, it was the highest level of RAW infiltration inside the Pak embassy. His bosses were constantly pestering him, to do something more worthwhile. Goddamn it, he was not a Superman. Before that, the highest informant was a mere vendor, selling flowers, outside their green-domed embassy gate. More, more, more – how much could he do with his four men and five deep cover agents, who operated in the city? Worst still, he could control only one of them and that too a woman. He would be glad to be back. The safety of his wife and two lovely kids always irked him into anger.

"Announcing the arrival of Pakistan International Airlines flight 402A, non-stop from Karachi. All de-boarding will leave from terminal No. 3. Thank you," a melodious voice announced on the public address system.

As the passengers moved in their queue, about 15 minutes later from terminal number three, one by one, De Silva caught a clear angle in her video clip.

"The security of the airport is tight, in fact watertight. They even checked my video camera as I entered the main entrance," she spoke into the microphone. "Professionalism is appreciated and good to see. Own inconveniences are forgotten when you see smart men and women in their blue uniforms thoroughly combing all the people and the area," she further added into her recording chip.

She moved ahead, for a closer shot.

"In this era of terrorism, bombings and mundane violence, the public will appreciate the security measures, incorporated here." As she moved near the head of the line, two men quickly turned back and started walking to the rear. Before she could refocus on them, the security lady tapped her shoulder and said, "Madam, your time is up now. Hope you will produce a good clipping. It will do a lot good for our morale." Rashmi thanked the security officer of the airport and walked out.

Grover saw Rashmi climb into the cab lugging her video equipment.

After a few minutes, three big holdalls were loaded with great difficulty into the Pakistani ambassador's Korean car. "Corps Diplomatic Bags" was boldly splashed on them. Too big for normal mail, observed Grover, or unless, they were the detailed plans for an invasion of South East Asia. With break-up of erstwhile Pakistan, the paranoia of its establishment and its abundant military rulers, they desperately wanted to do the same honours to India. So the fatness of anything emerging out of Pakistan had ceased to surprise him anymore.

"Fernandez you move out, we will meet at 1600 hours at Hotel Pearl," Grover said. Lot of debriefing had to be done to know what was happening. "Check with men. Tail any suspect to its destination. Split into twos if you have to, but then take care," he said starting his white nameless Pagero.

7
Spider's Web

"A million weak strands make one strong web"
— Jesse

Point 4714, Pir Panjal (Intervening Period)

He had liked the site, the moment he set his eyes on it.

The immediate terrain and the hideout in particular was an ideal military feast.

On the three sides were sheer unassailable cliffs. On the remaining side there was a massive peak, a steep jagged black dagger, jutting out of the broken rock crest-line.

The rising rocks resembled the minarets of Mecca.

Yes, this was a holy place.

Allah's blessings were necessary to wage a holy war. It had a small crater at centre of its base, allowing the snow to melt into a small scenic pond. The sides of the crater had a number of huge wide cracks, aged by erosion, creating deep crevasses onto its sides. He had explored these small caves. Good, they could house people, in fact much more than he had envisaged. The best part was that it was difficult to see the bowl, in the base of massive peak, from air. Billets inside the rocks could never be seen. He had tried going along both the side-shoulders of the rock from East and West. He had explored with Risal's help, but could not proceed further as there was a sheer drop, whose bottom he could not see, in the swirling mist below. The cliffs were just too steep. Good, an excellent fortress. Not negotiable from North, East and West. The only route to it was along a narrow spine, which innocently bifurcated from across Pir Panjal Pass along old Mughal caravan route, from Punch Gabbar to Hirpur in the Valley.

It took Gul a good part of three days, to trek back to Nusur, straight into the arms of his caring Nurie. He had recovered from his wounds, all thanks to the doctor's medicines and Nurie's ministrations. The shoulder had healed well including the minor fracture in the ribs. The pain had long since gone. A dole of mutton, vegetables, milk and pure butter, ensured his strength was back to normal. He was raring to kill.

Reshab had resisted the affection bestowed by Nurie on him, and had threatened to bring the girl in line with his rigid thinking. A talk, a very mild talk had smoothened matters, but not before Reshab in his typical *bakarwal* sense of making a quick buck had managed to squeeze fifty thousand rupees from him, to protect the family honour, as Nurie was not to be legally wed to him.

Bloody family honour, thought Gul.

The sly man was himself planning to marry the widow of his cousin Risal, who had died not even two months earlier. There had been a lot of wailing and breast-beating, but Risal had become charmingly adamant, after the financial deal had been sealed and he alone thrust this *houri* from heaven, into his panting laps. He was even ready to part rupees two lakhs to obtain Nurie. She had mesmerized him totally. What was money for? In any case, he did not care about the expenses, as the Government of Pakistan would foot the bill, for his sexual escapades, no, better phrased as his spiritual upliftment, he reasoned.

Nurie stalked him like a slave. Ready to obey even before he could utter a command. Ready to please. She had found a good reason for her existence in him. He would definitely take her to the camp. It would add to his stature. As it is, men-folk of Nurie's clan, even children held him in awe. He was the chosen one, the one who would give them deliverance from this Indian misery.

Wasn't it that he was the only one to escape from the Indian massacre? His time would come to avenge that painful loss. His blood and passion had been aroused. He felt young again and he will repeat his daring sagas of Afghanistan. They had not called him *"janbaz"* for any miniscule reason. Earth and winds of Afghanistan bore mute testimony of his bravery and incredible band of forty men. *"Ali baba and chalis chor,"* was another nickname Ruskis had given him. Yes, he was a thief. He had stolen back his country's freedom from the yokes of white pigs and infidels. He was again ready to steal the freedom, for his Kashmiri brethren, the second time.

Warmth of the small campfire above Reshab's house, in the side brook, away from direct observation, bathed his shoulders. He played with a stick, fiddling the fire embers and charcoal. Reshab was sitting opposite and his face glowed in sudden flickers of the fire embers.

"Reshab, the camp site is good, we have water and shelter, and now we need to stock it with food," spoke Gul.

Reshab nodded silently.

"I don't want any locals or any known *tanzeems* helping us. All have been hopelessly infiltrated. Indians come to know the moment they belch. Colonel Iqbal did not choose you and Risal without a reason. You both were good. No, in fact, the best. I know you breath and smell money in everything you do. You won't be disappointed. Important thing is how to organize the camp, at such a scale, without being found out," Gul spoke, scratching his madly itching wound, vigorously and further inquired, "And what happened to the list of persons to contact. They are our sources for money channelled through their business deals."

"Well almost all of them have been contacted. Fund flow has started. I have already collected rupees ten lakhs for this purpose and more money is coming. It's in your account. You don't worry. The summer is on us. I will shift my herd to the mountaintop. It's one routine yearly migration. I will get adequate security passes too. Though it is a bit early, I will stake the claim for that area. In the movement to establish one's *dera* on mountain top, we will carry rations," replied Reshab.

"OK, then plan to move within the next three weeks. Ok yes, this is important, no other women or children," interjected Gul.

"Are you mad, how will we cook, who will look after the goats or milk the cows," cried Reshab raising his hands in despair.

"No woman, I repeat no woman, except Nurie who comes with me." He hesitated then added, "OK, take male children over 12 years of age and as for milking and caring for goats I will teach you all, like little children. All men, all *jihadis* will work in the camp and in any case, you can't fight the war, with women."

Reshab stared at Gul in dark silence. "Well then, we have much to do. Can you lend me an advance of rupees eighty thousand to buy the mere essentials," he asked, without mincing any word.

The genetic fleecier would want more for main essentials. Reshab had made his intentions clear and it was time to make his clearer too, mused Gul.

"Take the money immediately from our account. I warn you, do not, I repeat do not cheat on it. I will be very harsh if I found out otherwise. Spend it wisely. First, within this week, you have to go to Jammu and then again to Srinagar. We have to tie up a few details. I plan the initial orientation not at the main camp, but much lower of Pir Panjal Pass near the forests of Hirpur. It is going to be small affair for three days. If we succeed, then a full-fledged operation will be conducted from '*Allah's* Rock'. Yes, *Allah's* Rock is the name I have just conceived for my camp," Gul rasped in total concentration.

Reshab groaned on money restrictions imposed. But what the hell could a foreigner do in his land. If he can't be trusted for purchases they were welcome to organize it themselves. Whatever little side cuts he had planned and will certainly do were for covering the cost of dangers he was engaged in. It was legitimate and not cheating. The boss himself had misappropriated half a lakh to hump his sister. Was that a true cause? But to keep the cow milking he had to be cautious and keep Gul amused at his money accounting honesty. He smiled a big toothy picture to Gul and said, "I work for the task of God. How can I even think of making profit from that holy enterprise? To cheat would be to burn in hell."

Gul stared back at the innocence of intentions displayed. He didn't believe the man opposite a bit. Their blood was devoid of that haemoglobin, a defect passed down from the times of *Allah*. A known minor pilferage was acceptable and necessary to keep this excellent organizer in good morale. Check he must, to stall the operation from being converted into an organized money loot programme.

Aroma of herbs, brewed with tea, filtered in before his majestic Nurie made an appearance. Staring at her visible shape of nipples protuding out of her *kameez*, he quietly took the steel cup and noisily sipped on the sugary broth.

"I am presently helpless, like a toothless tiger, my fighting claws have been severed. Little more time, say within ten days, we will have 'God's own Army' to give me the sword to chop Indian heads with. What a glorious day it would be," Gul said but not before intentionally brushing his hands with Nurie's, small round tight buttocks.

"Yes, Badshah of Murree has confirmed. The operation is under way," whispered Reshab. "I have arranged few Kenwood Radio Sets from my underground channels. I will guide and receive them well," he further added, staring at the face of Gul, who in turn was staring at blushing Nurie. Bloody immoral woman, he thought. She was bringing shame to the family by flaunting herself about, but then what's shame to the money she brought, he reasoned.

Colombo
(1315h, 01 May)

The game was full of uncertainties.

Minuses fell on your lap like popping packet of popcorns. Pluses were rare and rarely made an announcement. He had not seen them of late.

Grover was perplexed.

Seven men from hotel "Emerald Isle," attending Pak-Ceylon business promotion meet had disappeared. The front lobby, under constant observation, had yielded nothing. No one had passed and yet the front office had confirmed room vacation, at 6 AM.

Fruitcake Fernandez. Why couldn't he use his peahen brain? All earlier good work had come to a naught. But what could his four-man army, do. Twiddle their big thumbs more furiously at each other. His repeated requests for more manpower and money were always turned down. His last off-duty personnel had to be rushed back, to track Pakistan's second secretary's impromptu holiday drive, along the western highway to Jaffna. His merciful, famous carpool had provided a timely tip. He must shower that man with more money. Mr Rafiq Raza, alone with his petite, nervous-looking wife, with four big suitcases, had gone along the coastal highway. Own trailing idiot ran out of petrol 145 km North of Colombo and had lost further track.

Grover peered over the map.

The chase was sixteen hours old.

The fool had taken eight hours, in just heading back to Colombo, to speak from the nearest telephone. The road passed through many villages abundant with fishermen. His fingers slowly traced the villages, name by name. He suddenly stopped and circled a cluster of five villages, North of a town called Paltalun, where river Kala Oya met the Indian Ocean. They were the only pure Muslim villages in the whole western province.

An hour later, after bumping along the gravelled roads, they came on a small clearing, atop a bald hillock. The stunning blue expanse ahead dazed both of them for a few seconds. They treated their eyes to the deep blue of the Indian Ocean. It was deceptively calm and beautiful. Below them, lay the biggest village of Shahpulai. Numerous boats danced in the waves, penned to the makeshift wooden piers, along the white stretch of the beach. They stopped their car and walked the remaining hundred metres, posing like mad tourists in Bermuda shorts and big straw hats.

After two hours of making half-hearted purchases and persuasive haggling on smuggled Indian goods, Grover could find out that a fast boat had left supposedly for Maldives, early in the morning.

"Yes, a *sahib* from Colombo had seen them off. He came in a big car, with a very smart woman. About seven very muscular college boys, may be more, boarded the boat. They were working on some project about oceanic studies, on fish movements, in the Indian Ocean," muttered the old crone, selling coconuts, on the beachfront. Grover was three thousand Sri Lankan rupees down, for this small tidbit and was ready to be ten times that amount down, if he only could get the exact destination of those stated fishy studies.

My bloody left foot, he thought. *Pakis* studying Sri Lankan fish movements and that too muscular ones.

It was very laughable.

Even the dear God seemed to be running out of any more interesting brainy hypotheses. It did not gel as an acceptable idea, not even in his wildest figment of imagination.

With top speed of thirty nautical miles per hour, the bloody *dhow* could be anywhere in twenty-five thousand square km area, most likely near the Indian coast by now. Twelve hours of lead was too much to catch up immediately. He glum-faced peered into the vastness of the blue haze, helplessly.

At least, he still had some time, to warn the concerned people.

Tsrare Sharif/ Srinagar (1130h, 07 May)

It had been nonstop gaiety and fun. She was glad that she had come despite her earlier inhibitions.

They had all been singing for the last two hours. In tune or out of it, in melody or without it. They had sung movie songs, Kashmiri songs, patriotic songs, and militant songs, all known ones, minimum thrice over. The most comical was that when the Indian Security pickets stopped them, they all sang old Indian melodies and just beyond their hearing distance, Khushbu would lead the pack with pro-militant, pro-*azadi* singlets. Singing and munching on soft baked *kulcha* and *nans* was child-like merriment. Nafisa was already dreading the remorse when this pleasurable day would end. It was too good to be true. For the first time, in so many days she had giggled like a silly teenager. There was love and happiness in the air. But she was a bit peeved at a strange man sitting with Tahir. That idiotic, short, feminine, pansy looking, man would stare at her, at repeated intervals. His eyes bled lust and curiously enough, hate.

The boys were sitting in the front seats along with the driver, with Tahir, making a throne over the bus bonnet, sat facing them.

A flirt thought Nafisa, as his eyes darted from one girl to another.

He wore that thin crooked smile when looking or speaking to them. In any case, more than half were ready to run into his arms, legs apart, if he wanted. If rumour mill was to be believed then he had bedded almost all of them present now, including her dear friend Khushbu, who just did not want tc hear anything negative about her secret lover. She had guessed Khushbu's situation nearly three months back, when she had paled and howled on missing the first three days of her periods. Happiness, crazy thankfulness had overcome her friend on seeing her spotless white bed-sheet stained crimson red, one fine morning, but only after popping a few clandestinely obtained menstruation inducing medicines, from an equally shady character, who lived off from income generated in rectifying such poor girls.

Suddenly, just five km short of their destination of the exalted sacred shrine of Tsrare Sharif, the bus was pulled over into an apple orchard, obscured from the main road. All the boys jumped down and started unloading their suitcases piled on top. God, why carry suitcases for picnic, Nafisa thought. Suddenly only half of them were left. Only then she noticed that more masculine looking amongst the boys had disappeared with Tahir.

Somehow the planned picnic finished in the orchard.

The bus did not show any sign of moving back to the main road, onward to its stated destination. Rather than just sit, Khushbu again bossed over everyone to move down to stretch their legs.

She somehow knew that Khushbu knew that the journey was terminated. But of what happened subsequently, she was sure that Khushbu had no prior inkling. All the girls eagerly skipped off the bus chattering profusely. As she alighted, suddenly that feminine looking man singled her out and shouted, "Yes, it was her, she is the one who met that Indian Army officer at Hotel Cecil, a week back. She is a bloody *mukhbir,*" he shouted more agitatedly.

She agape, stunned, stared at the frightening accusing voice.

Her head whirled with accusation. She wanted to shout, to protect her love, to bray her innocence but no words came from her shocked sealed mouth. Khushbu's eyebrows were riding her forehead in mock horror. Her face was fury red. Someone roughly grabbed her from behind and suddenly the whole world around her collapsed as she fainted.

She woke up with a start to a stifled silence. Strangely the eerie silence was painfully loud and frightening.

It was pitch dark and she was also shivering cold. The onset of summers had not thawed the cold beset in her bones. Soreness tore through her slender back. Uncut stones were jabbing into her soft flesh. She very slowly, in dreaded apprehension stretched out till her nimble hands met a wall. She felt her way around, in huge laboured breaths. Yes, she was alone in a small room, maybe eight feet by six feet. Alone in a small dark room was not comforting. Suddenly, she was very frightened. She opened her mouth and screamed. Her muted sobbed screams continued till the wee hours of another glorious dawn. Not that anyone noticed or heard of her plight, beyond those desolate walls.

She was a golden sparrow in an unknown sorcerer's cage.

Jammu
(1830h, 14 May)

Jammu Tawi-Kanyakumari Himgiri Express lazily rolled into platform number three at 1830h.

The train was only four hours late. Not bad considering 2289 km of distance travelled over two nights from Coimbatore to Jammu, reflected Captain Ahmad Khan alias Mr Ashok Gupta of Third Special Force Battalion of Pakistan Army.

It had been a hectic and an eventful journey. Karachi to Colombo in style by air, in comfort of a fishing boat to a deserted beach near Kanyakumari, and lastly by a spacious taxi to their first safe house in Chennai. He admired his country's premier intelligence agency for having such an effective and wide dragnet in and around India. That ISI operator, running a two-star hotel in Saidapet locality, bang on Usman Road, in the black-human metropolis, was a masterstroke in luxury and pampering. A good ten bloody days of orientation to the Indian ways of life had invigorated his earlier tense demeanour. The man Friday had provided new sets of identities, which all had practised to master in twenty-four hours, though he hated his Hindu *baniya* one. He was a very proud Punjabi *Mussalman* and to be equated with such unscrupulous people, whose tales of even robbing their dead, were legendary in their clan. It was personally, very demeaning.

The journey further fragmented out to other small towns in garb of sightseeing. He was impressed with diversity of the intriguing culture.

Prosperity was even more disturbing.

What they had embarked upon was the only solution to drag India down to their level of economic growth. Given equal opportunities, Indians will gallop away and his country's elite wont be able to explain that why the land of pure was in the quagmire of poverty.

It was ultimately that from Coimbatore they had boarded his first class air-conditioned coupe. The trip bisecting the heart of his enemy-country's territory had been very comfortable. He could not travel with his dear fellow conspirators, who were lugging it out, in an ordinary second-class compartment. Even in hostile territory, he had to maintain his separate officer's status.

This was his second infiltration into India.

First had been in the valley last year, to protect and induct three valley chiefs of various organizations and key ISI coordinators into the town of Kupwara. It had been via the land route. That had been a very tough assignment, infiltrating through Indian defensive positions on the LoC. They had lost two men going in and further three while exfiltrating. He had been very lucky on both the occasions to miss the main ambush by ten to twenty metres in the pitch-dark night. That was the general safety distance, from a certain death to safety, always.

The most interesting part of this second journey inside India was that three girls accompanied them. All decent local Muslim girls, provided by their operator in Chennai. They were a fantastic cover up. He hugged Ayesha alias Sita as he alighted to find a taxi to take them to Hotel Asia at Katra. Amongst the chaotic crowds and throng of teeming humanity, he and his acquired bride moved out of the railway station. They were devout Hindu tourists on their way to pay homage, in that famous infidel's shrine. Others would also reach by bus or taxi as it suited them. Further coordination would be done from Katra itself.

Bangkok
(0930h, 15 May)

"I am Mr Badshah from Karachi," said a gruffly voice.

"This is Rani from Pakistan International Airlines, what can I do for you sir," she replied sweetly as ever.

"I wanted to thank you for our reservations earlier. We had a good flight and have reached our homes comfortably, all thanks to your excellent service. I was told for onward destination to contact you," the male voice spoke again authoritatively.

"Yes sir, please note down. Your cousin from Multan will be available at 146.750. Thank you sir, nice to hear from you," she said, putting the phone down.

Few minutes later Sibal was pulling his hair down.

Voice amplification signatures showed a totally different voice. The piece of equipment had reached its destination. Where? Again it was a big question. Contact number did not tally with any known telephone codes, so it must be a radio frequency. He must sound alert for a general monitoring of it. He himself was not convinced of his intelligence tomfoolery but warn he must. All the elements seemed to be in place and they had no clue of what it was, except maybe, an infiltration of some key personnel as confirmed by Grover in Colombo.

What was it for?

He was in total dark and fearful.

It would be worthless to discover their intent when the event was over.

Katra
(1430h, 16 May)

Multan had confirmed his arrival half an hour ago.

Relief was instantaneous, when visual contact was established, at the congested bus stand of Katra. No one paid attention to a *bakarwal* hugging a masculine young Punjabi-looking Hindu, accompanied by his *sari* clad, little darkish, typical South Indian-featured wife.

The hotel staff was perplexed.

The visitors wanted immediate clearance. They had not even gone up the shrine for the visit. However, the smart young man after collecting the *Vaishno Devi* shrine visit passes explained that they, after the visit, would not return and go back straight to Jammu. Why should I worry, thought Mr Narendera Jamwal, the manager of Hotel Asia, if his visitors had paid the full amount including the day of their visit to the shrine.

Two hours later, three taxis left for Poonch via Riasi, carrying a marriage party. The bride was being taken home. Ayesha was decked up accordingly and played her role perfectly. She even took out real sobbing tears at each security checkpost on the road axis. Even sternest of military personnel all over the world, melt, drool, tears drop, display a queer sense of caring, when confronted with teary brides. Manifestation of their pathetic family life must be so, the Special Forces officer calmly reasoned. Malleable gullible buffoons, laughed Captain Ahmad Khan hugging his voluptuous wife referred to as Ayesha and her firm tits in good measure.

The taxis were flagged through and went unchecked, through three checkposts, till the road head, just short and below the village of Nusur.

Delhi
(1030h, 24 May)

Chaos was his working hallmark. He believed in its ideology in full measure and thrived in it.

Mr Mukand Sharma, Director, Intelligence Coordination and Analysis Desk of RAW, had a busy schedule, as usual. Appointments had eaten into each other and even his cute smart secretary was not sure who was late or ahead in time but her boss still huffed and puffed in and out of his office at a breakneck speed to keep all amused. His desk lay cluttered with reports, analyses and numerous inputs from abroad and sister agencies at home. Two computer screens on his desk were churning over some data at a furious pace. It further added to the chaotic display on his desk. Only Sharma, with one blink of an eyelid could focus and decipher the shifting data on screen in front of him. His stubby chin and bloodshot red tired eyes did not deter him to do what he dwelt on passionately, knowing about what others were doing around him, at all times.

He had read reports of Sibal and Grover. Isolated inputs far apart in geographic context but co-joined in intent. The separate events were beginning to make some sense. But why such an exercise? Something very dear to Pakistan was being executed. For what, what purpose? What could be the aim?

It was like a boil in the ass. Pus accumulating, but not bursting.

What had happened in the last two months, which had miserably, backfired for Pakistan and made them run around like panicked colts on a death chase? He jotted down a few major events, which had occurred recently.

- Cancellation of US orders for F-16 aircraft.
- Putting 'persona non grata' their ambassador in Nepal on the charges of distributing fake currency.
- Disclosure of arms shipments to Sri Lanka.
- Killing of their deep-cover mastermind ISI Muslim MLA, again in Nepal.

- Interdiction of forty odd *jihadis* at the border – the biggest catch ever, on the troubled LoC, in Kashmir.

Of all above, the first three issues did not require shifting of men and material, at any stage. They were dead issues and best politically motivated. It required Foreign office intervention and not his. The last two were promising. But replacing something like their Nepalese MLA would require only a one-man changeover and to his best of knowledge their basic machinery had not been affected. He was sure they were very firmly entrenched in the Himalayan kingdom. Poor Nepalese, they did not know what shit they were getting into, in wooing Pakistan or for that matter China, as a counterbalance to India. They were welcome to free flow of *jihadi* ideas and communist subversion.

You always reap what you sow.

We had bitterly learnt it in Sri Lanka. When he had tried explaining it to his Nepalese counterpart and an old Saint Paul school friend, he had grinned and just shrugged his shoulders. But what he had uttered later had amused him.

"If there is no difference between India and Nepal then how will the elite rulers, big, small or petty ones, survive. How will we get and sanctify our minor privileges otherwise? We have to ensure that the differences exist. If none exists then we will create some to exist. That's how we can justify a separate Hindu state, away from mainland Hindu subcontinent," he had explained. But to him it still did not make any sense despite his friend's smugness. They were willingly and knowingly stepping into anti-India quagmire.

Best of luck, long lost pals. You will definitely need it in years to come.

His young, slim stiletto-healed secretary, walked in with his favourite coffee and chicken mayonnaise sandwiches. She prepared them to his exact taste, much to the annoyance of his wife, if he ever compared the finery of art of his secretary's cooking. Thanking her without looking up, now to the utter annoyance of his doting secretary who loved being pampered, he opened up a detailed report passed through Army Intelligence, on the incident near

Haji Pir Pass. Only two pages into the twenty page thick file, he knew he had hit the jackpot.

Poshiana Forests
(2030h, 30 May)

Their grim faces were shining intermittently.

Pale long faces with equally iong unkempt beards were shimmering in reflection of kindled flames, leaping out from the pine logs placed in a two feet deep pit, slightly ahead of them. All were sitting in a hollow square, on a green opening, sloping downwards. Across the fire-lit pit, sat three men on a little higher ground pedestal, supposedly the new commanders of these *jihadi* forces. By the evening, all *jihadis* knew them, at least by face, if not by name. They had been instrumental in welcoming all to this place and organizing their short stay. *Jihadis* of various *tanzeems* had poured in one by one from various directions at different times.

For the last one day of their forced march through these jungles they had only one aim. To reach the massive thirty feet in diametre, the magical Chinar tree on the Northern periphery of the village of Poshiana. They were received with due courtsey, escorted nicely and looked after well, at least till now. Apprehension still remained as none trusted the security arrangements of another and was evident in the nervous looks, which frequently darted across. Feared Indian Army could come in from anywhere, anytime. Who was sure that they had not been betrayed? However the trio of men had been firm. The camp security was theirs.

It was visible and looked good.

Rasool Bhat's generally very steady eyes had been roving around, and sizing up the men loitering, on the perimetre duty. He had been the one to take up the issue of security.

The men looked different.

Their weapons were lazily brushing their side hips as they walked casually. Their gait was definitely not *jihadi.*

It was crisp, comfortable and very deliberately relaxed.

Body profile also looked too athletic. Biceps and muscles gleamed and wanted to burst out of their cotton fabrics. It was very unlike the cute paunches he had seen most God's men support.

No stained yellow teeth.

No habit of living on the high, generated by narcotic *naswar.* He remembered his old Kashmiri *jihadi* joking about Afghani mercenaries he had encountered, "They can dump *jihad* but not *naswar.*" Unlike any other war waging blokes he had earlier known. Rough hands but clean. No dirty animalistic smell, typical of months of accumulated sweat, emanating from their clothes. Beards yes, but trimmed neatly. Before they all sat down together, he had observed one of the cleaner version of the God's men stiffen as one small but muscular one approached him to supervise the overall security of the makeshift camp.

Then it struck him like a brick falling over his genitals.

Not that any pain reflected on his otherwise calm face. His breath deepened and eyes fractionally narrowed in concentration.

He knew what he was looking for. He knew what he wanted to see. He was sure now that he knew of what he had been suspicious of, so instantly. His worst fears had come true.

They were men in uniform, in *jihadi* fatigues.

They were *Paki* Special Forces Commandos.

Srinagar (1000h, 06 Jun)

As usual he had nothing concrete to go by.

Reports filtering in for the last two months had been vague at first, however, later they had stabilised to something plausible. But in intelligence, no information was true, unless proven by facts. Everyone worked on hearsay or verbal communication. No one ever gave you written detailed notes of any terrorist intention or plans, unless of course, you picked ISI funding/operational plan dossiers. They came, but at best once in two years, if you were extremely lucky. You deduced, the best you could, from tidbit of information, filtering from various sources, intercepts, police, robbers, pimps, moles, spies, captured terrorists, turncoats and plain gossip uttered from scotch stinking mouths of politicians, businessmen, doctors, lovers and the best and most authentic, from the jilted lovers.

Life was lackluster, holed up in one corner of Badami Bagh cantonment.

After Fort Knox, which housed America's wealth, the most heavily guarded place on earth.

Warming his lean buttocks in the workplace one could not obtain intelligence.

His job meant meeting hundreds of people a day. At best, he could interact with ten personally and about twenty through telephone. Somehow he still pulled on. He deputed his deputies to give him secondhand knowledge, where, by all logic, he should have got it, first-hand. The corruption due to different perceptions soiled the purity of his information. Still he invested in them, as he had deadlines to keep, some bosses to please, who could read his reports without any mind tease. The problem did not finish here. He was a Army HQ unit, located at Badami Bagh. A copy of all his reports was endorsed to the local formation where he was stationed. To make matters worse the local Corps Commander treated him like his own staff and he had to be present at his will, to decipher nuances of his projections and to clear the old man's foggy views but a very sharp analytical mind. For the last ten minutes, he had been standing at ease, opposite Lieutenant General Rocky Dass who was scrutinising his latest inputs.

"This last summation is interesting. But what is the actual possibility on the ground," asked the Corps Commander gently.

Colonel Mushtaq, Officer Commanding 762 Army HQ Liaison Unit, stiffened and replied, "Sir, I believe such an operation is already underway. All ground inputs have confirmed terrorists of different *tanzeems* moving out for an ultimate mission. Having corroborated all the inputs including the neighbouring 16 Corps, I feel the camp will be established somewhere in *Pir Panjal* ranges. It has its advantages. It's central to the valley, Poonch and Doda districts. Moreover, it's in the interior and it is a very difficult terrain. Army deployment too is meager and grossly inadequate. Even the RAW-alert has confirmed that a major group for the same has infiltrated via Sri Lanka, when its initial attempt was foiled at Haji Pir sector last March. They are up to something very big, sir."

"Any inputs from those captured terrorists. I am sure, it was part of the same plan," told the General.

"Nothing sir. They were minor Kashmiri boys, who knew nothing of any bigger operation," replied the Colonel and then further added, "We have identified their commander. One called Gul. He is an Afghan. With RAW's help we have got his dossier. His capabilities are remarkable and if he is being inducted for the reasons he specialises in we do have a problem in our hands."

"I foresee major operational problems if only ten per cent of what you say, comes true," said the General and beckoning the Colonel closer, he continued almost in a whisper, "Let me share a secret with you. The Chief the other day, told me to bring up the subject with you only in an emergency. I feel this is an emergency. I will not question you again or you mention the subject ever, except that one more person that is I am in knowledge-trap. What about Black Falcon?"

Colonel Mushtaq took a sharp intake of air-conditioned air, to keep his composure, unbreakable. He stared back and replied, "Black Falcon has disappeared. No communication since the last two weeks. I am myself worried too."

"OK, I am sure you are working on the problem. Keep me posted on specifics. Let me see if we can refocus our attention on to some suspected areas. Oh, leave that dossier of that terrorist. One more thing, no need to alarm everyone, at least not till now. See you later," said the General, dismissing him.

Each stride out of the General's office rattled his sanity.

The Colonel cursed all and sundry.

His only ace was becoming a public knowledge.

If this sharing of the secret business kept going on, then his ace will surely become a two of spades and a dead dodo, within a few months.

"Yes Ranvir, that's what I mean. Please come tomorrow with refined concept of keeping those areas under surveillance," said 15 Corps Commander. After listening for a few seconds again, he replied, "Ranvir, I know you are very thin on ground. Surveillance by other means is being reassigned. Yes, at worst pull out two battalions from the present Counter-Insurgency grid. No, you do it and present the plans. Sorry, I can't give you any additional troops. See you tomorrow."

Maj Gen RV Singh, GOC 9 Mountain Division located about forty km away from his boss, bit his knuckles in frustration. He had just stabilised his deployment of troops a few months back, when suddenly additional 311 Mountain Brigade sector was given to his division. It had made no sense. By all refutable logic, that Brigade sector should be with the Rajouri division. He had no access by road, except pony tracks. The sector was maintained ex-Poonch falling under different formations.

Now again a reshuffle.

He was not sure of Corps Commander's intentions, but he had an inkling of suspicion. Very garbled intelligence inputs after the March incident were filtering in. Despite his vehement disagreement of inclusion of the disputed sector into his area of responsibility, he had loved the glory, which came with that successful operation of 1/9 GR.

Back in his office a little later, Colonel Mushtaq tore open a letter and read its contents. Shit another one of those circulating chain letters. How come the postal authorities don't get to the bottom of such muck? Exemplary punishments across the board will immediately set the malaise right. As he got to throw it in its rightful place in the dustbin, he spied on an interesting quote, a universal law of some idiot Jesse stating that the clarity of intelligence is directly proportional to the number of intelligence agencies involved divided by a constant; the constant being that singular source in avid employment of all known Indian intelligence agencies.

On that score he could not fault that stupid man's observation.

Bn HQ 1/9 GR, Pir Panjal (0930h, 07 Jun)

It had been burning his innards for last so many months. Now the pain was too acute, to let it fester in that state and a balm, a human balm was needed to lessen it.

A great risk had been taken and was enough in nature to sack him, if found out. A gambler's dice was wedged at the rim of abyss, ready to fall off and reveal its magical numbers. He knew that the dice was loaded against him. But then you can't command military units without taking risks. The secret was safe in the battalion but he could no longer hide it. He had not reported capturing the guide, in a wounded but unconscious state, hoping to discover more information about terrorists later. One day merged into another and the thing got postponed inordinately. Though the Regimental Medical Officer had done his best to ensure that the chap did not die, he had failed to revive him back to consciousness. There was no medicine on earth, which could fructify his desire. The man's wounds had healed, less the scars. His vital organs were normal, but the terrorist was slumbered into a deep coma since 03rd March.

What an ironical situation.

Three months of blissful sleep for the traitor and worst kind of deepest anxiety for the country's protector. That rodent of a traitor snores, silent, uncaring and big fat ulcers he, the esteemed saviour, reaps. But why blame him. It was the classic case of putting your own shit-steeped foot in your mouth. A good material for a moralistic story, to be published later, on what all is not to be done while commanding a unit.

But this was the least of his worries.

The idiot could sleep for a decade more as if he cared or die sleeping or be induced to die sleeping so he could go quietly to his unmarked grave. The timing had gone wrong and they overslept. The trouble lay in that the main body of his relieving unit, 14 Rajputana Rifles, was already in location. Those 'Raj-ruffians' had surprised everyone in reaching his location, ten days earlier. In the same location the issue could not be safely hidden. Within the next two weeks, his unit was to move out. Should he or should not he confide in the relieving units Commanding Officer. On looks, Colonel PP Singh looked a very positive man, but he was not sure that he could trust him. Anyhow, no one was sure of anyone. That was the problem of the Indian Army. There were many legendary tales of woe, on handing and taking over, he contemplated. Already the over-zealous junior staff officers of both the units were trading blows on the state of equipment, when only twenty five per cent of it had been handed over. God only knew what would happen when they reach the desired objective of total turnover.

Despite that, his heart told him otherwise.

A proud second-generation officer, Colonel Vishamber Singh Thapa, lifted his field telephone set, to invite his slim and tall counterpart.

Gund Machar, Lolab Valley (2000h, 11 Jun)

The meeting was in the order of things.

Both willingly met for the fourth time.

Nazir with a cocked 7.62 mm Chinese pistol tucked inside his loose shirt and Yadav with his snipers aiming at his perceived friend's back.

Both still lacked trust.

Both hated each other.

Both spoke to each other.

Both smiled at each other.

Both shook outstretched clasping hands as long lost friends.

The one uniformed could not love an anti-national, the other, the son of an ardent *jamaiti,* nothing un-Islamic. Something Indian was very opposite in meaning for the both of the interpolators.

They met again for not more than two minutes. Beyond that there was no trust.

Two days later, Major Yadav's Rashtriya Rifles Battalion conducted a spectacular raid, killing five Pakistanis, owing allegiance to *Harkat-ul-Ansar*. The hideout, their home, for the last one year, deep inside the jungles was not known to many.

Same night seventy thousand rupees astounded Farida, the wife of the dreaded Hizbul terrorist Nazir.

Sixty for the five heads and ten just to buy more trust.

Both hated each other. Both did not trust each other. But both loved something, Yadav the information and Nazir the money. Both had nothing more to give.

Nothing happens in Kashmir without profit.

Srinagar
(1250h, 10 Jun)

He had gone crazy. It was visible on his face.

His Nafisa had gone missing after her picnic trip. No one was telling anything. Her friends gave dumb blank stares. Thought he saw fear registered on some. Worst was that most denied knowing her in any way? Even her best friend, the one she endlessly chirped about, was not forthcoming. That woman's gaze scorched him, as he was a thief. The University Dean was not at all helpful. He said that she might have gone home. But why, he could not answer. The local police did not want to register the case. The University staff, or her relatives or her friends had not made any statement. His statement was not valid, as he was a mere acquaintance and that too from outside the state. He would have gone mad if his old unit officer, posted in staff, at 302 Sub Area in Srinagar had not helped him in running about and retain his sanity.

He was certain, that she was in acute problem and he was also certain that it was due to him.

8
Ambush

"Slay quick, sudden violence in death.
On thy earth, thy time, violent death.
Slay silent, slay his sane serene mind."

— Jesse

Km Stone 235,
Jammu-Srinagar Highway
(1345h, 15 Jun)

What a waste of muscle power.

Brain, by any standards of a civilized society, the army was excused in its rightful application, he forcefully reasoned with his inner conviction of six years service. God forbid if you mentioned it in any civilian forum. They brazenly will flake apart laughing. Goons, all of them plus sheer wastage of time and effort.

Scrawny Major Ashutosh Gupta, sitting under the shade of an apple tree, was quiet reflective. Lying on his bony bums, staring up at the green budding leaves on top, smoothened his tense nerves. From his grassy den, he could see the entire stretch of the winding road, a seven km stretch, which formed the part of his daily, seven times a week, road opening duties and responsibility.

He thanked the good man, who had painstakingly created such a lovely and an exclusive orchard, on such a strategic height. The furnace-hot May sun was directly atop them. Standing out in the open, was heat wilting and heart stopping. Personally, he loved the months of September and October, when the apples were ripe and he would shamelessly scrump on them. Munching as much as his heart willed was good for his cholesterol filled heart. He had become a burning chimney and one could smelt steel in his burning lungs. His saner senses rebelled at this nicotine dependence but excuses as always labelled the tensions floating here with his job to think rationally. This apple orchard was the pick of an area. That ever-pleasing Mir was always ready to oblige.

Gunpowder power? Maybe.

He remembered the days, when innocent tourists lured by enchanting orchards plucked, an apple. " *Oye Allah, katil-katil. Buchus Amri marakh. Khudda tala buchus un kon.* (Oh God you murderer. My Amri apple has been killed. God turn me blind.) Oh! my God, did you pluck the apple straight down? Oh! God, what a ruination (as if there were other ways of plucking an apple). That poor branch will not bear any fruit for the next five years. Oh! *Allah,* you have ruined me. You must pay rupees five hundred, for compensating this evil loss," they would lament. The poor tourist, five hundred rupees lighter, would tread back, considering himself lucky, to escape the rampaging mobs, who would materialise magically.

Wily enterprising people.

He had also witnessed chickens magically appear under the tyres of running cars and the confused tourists getting overawed by the resultant threatening village. Same mammoth breast beating lamentations, about their golden goose, would start. Tears, actual big tears, on their red rosy cheeks, were a dream twenty yards basketball three pointer. The conniving *taxicab* operator would also screech to a perfect skidding halt, in a wide-open lonely road and beg forgiveness, palms open, pleading the furious mob to let his poor tourists go. He would collect his share of the loot on the way back.

Rupees five hundred for an apple and double that for a chicken. It was a well-oiled extortion racket.

But now, no tourists to cheat; sad, very sad, very very sad indeed.

Of late, mundane lackluster life. No zest to live, no abetting con artists, no cunning excitement, lest of course, when the terrorists came knocking by.

Poor, flea-infected, scrotum-scratching, goat odour like, ankle thought bound, pitiable terrorists.

Give rupees five hundred per lay for a dirty village belle and rupees two hundred for a grassy meal.

On this, he remembered some Major Jesse's law that the price of a strumpet was directly proportional to her English speaking abilities. Good business sense, fleecing *Jihadis* – no the terrorists, no-no foreign terrorists, no, not terrorists but pure Islamic tourists.

Notwithstanding a bagful of endless noxious cribs, a Kashmiri always on top.

He chuckled at this glorious situation.

Road piqueting was one of the most boring, repetitive and tiring operations. It was difficult to stimulate men, again and again, come hail, storm or snow, to do their tasks, effectively. Heavens would plummet and he will face annoying music, if anything happened on his part of the responsibility. His boss had developed piles, just watching the convoys pass safely through his battalion boundary. Bums in air, unit doctor was having a torrid time, staring endlessly up the malodorous ass of the old man.

Today the up-convoy was half an hour late. It would further complicate his operations, planned for the night. There was no let up and no respite. Wish they could post in some humanoid robots, to do this task. Tell any commander that the troops were tired; they will stare back accusingly, as if you have raped an innocent idea. Motivate your command, was their advice, wrapped in silver foils of their age-old wisdom, a facade behind which everyone seemed to hide, like an ostrich.

Abruptly, a slow hum of noise built up into a large crescendo, as he sighted the convoy of fifty trucks, meandering towards his area. Almost instantly his radio operator informed him of the same and as a drill he passed this information to various parties scattered along the road. He watched the serpentine lumbering move of vehicles towards him with a jaded expression.

He had seen the identical scene a hundred times earlier.

He took a quick puff on his Charminar cigarette and concurrently lifted his ass to one side and let out a huge fart. You couldn't fart with both bums on the ground. You just cannot, however hard you try, he thought and he was ready to place an undisclosed amount of wager on anyone who could do so. These *puris* and *alus*, his daily cold stale food, would be the death of his digestive system. He unconsciously started counting each vehicle of the cavalcade as they blurred past him, one, two, three, four...

So did Gul and Captain Ahmad, hiding on the upper loft of a mud walled house, fifty metres from the road.

So did Jalal Omar, dragging hay-filled bullock cart, on the road.

So did Rasool Bhat, hidden behind a huge bush, on left flank of Gul's party.

So did Mehmood Usman, under a culvert, on the main highway.

So did Tahir, sipping on overtly sweet *kawa* at a tea stall, bang on the road.

So did the three other parties of three men each, very ingeniously placed, between the Indian stops guarding the road axis.

Ashutosh espied the third leading vehicle lift clean into the air. He had been saved the drudgery of counting beyond four.

The shattering blast hit his ears much later. Intoxicating cancer smoke choked on his collapsing windpipe.

The airborne vehicle in a slow motion sailed down and on hitting the mother earth it majestically rolled over. Did he also see men flying like birds? Yes, he was sure. Then his peripheral vision, captured a huge ball of fire, hundred metres down the road, engulf another vehicle. Permeating acoustics of firing defied any stereophonic Dolby music system with those beat enhancing Bose speakers.

Rasool Bhat, tapped a little man to his left, his best sniper. "I don't have to tell you to what to do," he whispered. His slayer nodded silently lifting his weapon to aim. The single whip like cracks got suppressed in general mayhem. He then slipped sideways about ten metres to his Rocket Launcher detachment to supervise its death like effects. A similar caution and a similar reaction later, the big executioner started selling his strong points fast.

Bloody shit, a jolly good show screamed the dazed brain of Major Ashutosh.

Yes, like a real war movie, on hundred and five millimetre screen. Yes, it was vile, fascinating magic. He had the best seat in this amphitheatre. Bewildered, he stood up in sheer confused admiration. Short of clapping and cheering for the home run, he was stunned. A bullet, grazing his thigh, snapped him out of his enjoyable dream. He turned back for his radio operator. Krishan Kumar was lying on the ground facedown; his back decorated by a spray of red paint. The fire was coming from a hillock above. The terrorists had sneaked behind his position.

Where were his men?

He heard a distant earth splitting thunderclap.

Bravo.

Some good soldier had fired a rocket launcher at the terrorist location. Bravo and to boot a direct hit. Again in repetitive cine-vision, he saw two terrorists, firing at him a little earlier, tumble. "Fire, fire, fire," was all he could recollect, yelling later.

Jalal laughed maniacally as flames ate up the vehicle and its occupants inside. He got up to fire at the vehicles, halted a little away, from which soldiers were jumping out like rats. He slumped suddenly, maintaining that silly despicable smile. There was a gaping hole, bang in the middle on his forehead.

The convoy had come to a grinding halt. Befuddled drivers finding the road blocked with no latitude to manoeuver screeched to halt wherever they could. Few dumb ones sat inert awaiting orders to roast inside their driver cabins, while a few smarter ones ditched the entire sundry in tune with the confused mayhem of the situation to survive unscratched. Vehicles piled up, bumper to bumper haphazardly along the road, an ejaculatory target for anyone.

Initial shock over, men from the inside vehicles, over the vehicles, under the vehicles, along the road culverts, in the open fields, of road opening party, not of road opening party, specific protection parties, just tagging reaction teams, anyone with a weapon, started firing back.

On whom or which target, they were not very astute in their vision, nor had they the silliest inclination to find out such useless details.

First magazine fired was just to kick start the right amount of adrenaline into your veins.

It had no target.

The second magazine brought your spasmodic breathing under control.

It also had no specific target.

The third magazine allowed aimed fire provided the phantom enemy presented a target. He seldom did. Elusive foresights aimed elusively, firing pointlessly.

Any knoll, any bush, any house, any window, any nook, any defile, was being raked with fire by six hundred and seventy eight souls which constituted the rolling armada. Commotion, disorder and total confusion prevailed. Officers zipped, party hopping, trying to maximize the fire-effect and control the madness? Any management tip in confining madness was welcome, when faceless men, not their men, when overawed men lose basics of piss-control. Men did not recognize the officers. Even if they did, they refused to acknowledge their existence. More than elusive fictitious rank, the bonds of blood ran stronger. Men in self-formed, self-serving hordes were seeing and directing fire. Some in panic had poofed authorized quota of ammunition and were scrambling or yelling for more, robbing the dead for bullets. Some in terror had faces struck inside the earth, their big round bottoms protruding out in air. Heart rendering shrieks erupted from those alit or catching lead.

Blood, fire, smoke, sobs, shouts, bullets, rockets, grenades, this was definitely madness. Still a few brave men, gallant but foolish men, ran exposing their soft permeate skin to evacuate and provide firstaid to the injured.

Abruptly, Gul's temporary abode caught a direct rocket launcher hit. It shook its mud foundations. There was a big gaping hole. One whole sidewall disappeared along with his two *Paki* bodyguards. How come these mother-fuckers could home on to him so fast, not even two minutes into the ambush, he furiously thought. The top floor started creaking and listing to one side dangerously. Dazed, he jumped below, onto the haystack, stockpiled for this specific purpose. "Abandon, abandon," he kept shouting on his set, as he ran to safety, quiet perplexed at this peripeteia.

Tahir mysteriously patented unbearable stomach cramps. Not that he was ill by any figment of imagination earlier. It definitely had to do with those awful sounds coming from the front. He had taken his weapon out, to fire, but just couldn't. He fitfully froze in horror. For millions of seconds, he kept on fiddling with the safety catch of his Klashnikov. This was acutely different from aspects of delivering a fiery oration. Oh *Allah*, all the fire was directed towards him. Forgetting, his own group hidden behind the tea stall, waiting for him to open fire, he dashed to the side alley where his getaway car was parked. He had no time to call his comrades in arms. He quickly started his 800cc Maruti car and abandoned his point even before he received Gul's message to "abandon". Despite the fresh air clean blasting on his face, through the open windows, he was drenched in his personal perspiration up to his underpants. It was not only irritating, but also mind-meandering, at this crucial juncture of his escape. Somehow, he could not fathom why his car was also stinking with a very strong irritating aroma of human crap.

"Run, run," exhorted Rasool to his men, as bullets raked the bushy mound, where they were hiding. Oh my God, one Indian stop party was also closing towards them. They were advancing in an extended line, firing from their hips. His four men were panting like dogs, running along a small rivulet. He looked left. There was a steep precipice forty feet down. Without thinking, he jumped. While half way down, in the air, his twisted head could register four of his men, also hanging in air against the backdrop of the azure blue sky.

To stop their wild useless and aimless firing, later, much-much later, many tender butts had to be whacked ruthlessly, into military loving submissive control.

Awantipura (1845h, 16 Jun)

"How's Ashutosh?" Colonel Tejinder asked his unit RMO.

"Still in a state of acute shock. His wound is more superficial, than life threatening," replied harried Captain Bhola, who had been treating casualties nonstop. Few doctors from Srinagar had just flown in by helicopter to assist.

The Colonel reflected on recent tidings, sitting on a campstool, watching the casualties being treated. In this hour of adversity he lay shattered, totally a broken man. All the awesome and professional reputation built over last two years, washed down in one stroke. All those days he had dedicated and even sold his soul to the Army, all lost. All the days he had neglected his family over mundane military matters, all gone. Staff College, crucial key appointments, and foreign postings, all written off in one disaster.

This uniform was too unforgiving. He had been the part of a diabolical decision-making process once. There were too many waiting in the wings, to take over. There were too many to start, a sad, rueful, whispering campaign. "Poor old chap," they will say, "He always flew too high. No, you don't know the inner story," and some fables would be born.

He can't blame them. He too had been so shortsighted, once.

Now suddenly he wished that he should have spent more time with his lovely caring wife and two cute doll-like daughters, than his boss's intentions.

Bad fate.

But you can't blame fate, for terrorists infiltrating eight parties, into his road-opening piquets.

It had been a massacre.

One officer and eighteen soldiers killed, including twenty wounded, in critical state and not to mention five vehicles written off. Saving grace was that eight bodies of militants had also been recovered. Despite the loss, the stops and all his men seemed to have reacted very fast and professionally. Otherwise, these *jihadis* wouldn't have broken contact, in just a few minutes. Initial success could be attributed to sheer surprise and detonation of two Improvised Explosive Devices. After that, man-to-man battle was taken to equal terms. Eight *jihadis* wouldn't have been dead, just like that. Officers on spot had confirmed this and admitted that had it not been for one rocket launcher detachment, they all would have been dead. Which was that elusive detachment, which had knocked out two terrorist positions, within first few minutes? Must be Ashutosh's detachment. But he couldn't ask anyone, as all his team of six persons lay dead. But all the circumstantial evidence, pointed towards the execution of a brave deed, on their part. He must ensure they were adequately compensated.

He got up looking aloof and beaten. That confident gait was gone. His shoulders slumped and chest awkwardly shrunk inwards. He felt like an extremely old man. Still, he had his battalion to run. It was time to exercise his brains, to try and snatch something positive, from the jaws of this shocking defeat.

He also had this sudden, strange, but definitely an alien desire, to be in the comforting arms of his wife.

Badami Bagh, Srinagar (2100h, 16 Jun)

There was a hushed silence.

No one dared to speak. Infact, no one wanted to speak.

Even silently eying each other was painful. Speaking about own casualties was heart-breaking and very demoralizing.

"Have you found out exactly how the ambush was perpetuated," inquired glum General Dass staring at somber and affliction-ridden faces of his staff sitting opposite.

"Yes, sir," spoke his not-so-thin looking Brigadier General Staff, expecting expectantly, a gutter-gush of words to flood the small confines of the briefing room, any second.

He slowly walked up to the newly displayed enlargement and explained its various annotations to his boss. "The terrorists had planned it very well and without a detailed recce it could not have been done. The ambush was very professionally executed, a hallmark of military planning. They escaped the road opening area clearance parties by some clever maneouver and innovation. They had dug three feet deep pits near the road, in which they had hid and escaped detection. They knew precise areas, which are not swept by mine detectors. Five of such have been discovered till now, sir. Fields of fire were clear, fire zones effective and overlapping. The ingenuity in placing explosives was quiet remarkable," he paused to catch his breath.

The General violently interjected, "I am not here to hear the superhuman capabilities of these worthless scums and stop bloody glorifying these terrorists. These rats will be dealt like any lowly vermin that they are. Your work is to find out what went wrong and how it can be ensured that such a shameful act and a military disgrace is not repeated again. Please also constitute a full-fledged inquiry. Timeframe its completion in next forty-eight hours. Pin point the responsibility and onus. No individual can be a bystander in this episode. The inquiry should logically scar all the idiots sitting and accumulating fat around their ass-lips in all the headquarters along the lines of communications," he thundered, leaving no room for doubt of his intentions as he got up to leave his raped audience.

At his departure, microseconds later, orally raped soldiers ran in fitful circles to heed to the summons of their teamster.

In his room later, all alone, he cried. He lamented at his gross military neglect.

The loss was personally his. It was his wrong assessment, of not warning the troops, despite inputs to the contrary. On Gods' forgiveness mode he wished that he had sounded the general alarm at the first instance and may be this massacre could have been averted. He sat glum faced for a long time staring endlessly at his graying reflection in the massive mirror capturing his whole double bed frame. He got up slowly and dragged himself to his walnut writing table. He took out a sheet of his demi-official letter pad decorated by his Corps insignia, a parrot green Chinar leaf, and started writing of his failure, in this regard, to his boss at Udhampur.

It was his first step to his contemplated resignation.

Sedau
(0930h, 20 Jun)

The journey, or more exactly, the runback had been swift, uneventful, but tiring.

The safe house organized, in the residence of the local member of the Legislature Assembly of Jammu and Kashmir was not unexpected. *Maulana* from Srinagar had personally arranged it.

Mr Lone, a very reputable member of the Indian Government machinery, had been subverted, a long time back. Obviously few threats and one consummate killing, a year back, had made this suave politician, talking big in meets organized in the name of Kashmir, with complete anti-Pakistan bias, help them with open arms, in his backyard.

"*Allah* be praised," said Gul, after all the commanders and their cronies had assembled. "You have just tasted blood. See, what I was telling you all along. If we combine our might, then nothing can stop us. This was the result of only five men each from you all. Imagine, if there were fifteen each. We will storm the *kafir's* headquarters in Srinagar. This bloody Hindu *fauj* will scamper out of Kashmir with tails under their legs," he paused for effect and again continued, "Indian casualty figures must be at least four times of what they have published. They are known liars. I salute you all and the martyrdoms of our brothers. It was a great ambush."

But Gul was shocked by his other colleague's reactions. It was not what he had expected. There was general murmur of disagreement, especially from those who had lost their cadres.

"If ambush was so successful, how come we lost eight men," cried Mehmood.

"Yes, he is right," butted in Rasool. "My wise one let us not underestimate our adversary. It would be our greatest folly," he further advised.

"Then how come within only two minutes, if surprise was with us, the operation was abandoned. Just because the place you were in, got hit. Before that, I lost my two men. My boys killed the entire enemy lot in the apple orchards. We did not request to abandon positions. Blood and danger must be equal to all," thundered the Lashkar Commander.

"Stop bickering," thundered the Pakistani Captain in *jihadi* fatigues. "No operation, I repeat no operation, goes as planned. We had reconnoitered the place. We had rehearsed known issues. Bilal's sacrifice was not in vain. Yes, we were surprised by the Indian reaction. Next time, we will cater for it. We are fighters and soldiers. I lost my two men and I am not crying like a little baby. If you are a warrior, death will come your way. So let's not spoil the success of our first mission. Let us see what we have achieved and what is to be done next," he forcefully reasoned giving none any counter.

"Yes, spoken like a true believer," carried on Gul from where the cocky Army man had left. He couldn't let the cause slip into the hands of a war green rookie. "Now, we will begin phase two of the operation. Select fifteen men each. We meet at same old RV, say within four weeks from now. Remember, training now will be for a month. We will plan operations in between. Time, method and mode same as last time. Any question?"

"But that site cannot hold so many men," observed Rasool.

"Don't worry, we are blessed by *Allah*. We will be going to *Allah*'s Rock, our new camp site," replied Gul. "One question. All have been accounted for, except for Commander Tahir."

"We are sure, he got separated due to the nature of events. You will get confirmation through the normal channels," replied a feminish-looking man.

Srinagar
(2100h, 21 Jun)

Such an illustrious success, wonderful, he pondered reading of it in the newspaper. Had he participated, it would have been more wonderful. But these were trifle matters.

More importantly he had been in perfect hiding, since his dramatic escape. All his aunts and cousins had gathered around to facilitate his grand success, of course only after he had made himself presentable. Now the key issue was how to contact his group.

University was dangerous and most obvious place to be searched in a general crackdown, which had been started by agitated Security Forces in full animosity. It was expected. More the people will get troubled, more would join our cause willingly, he reflected. For now that place must be avoided. But more vexing was how to explain his sudden desertion from the battle-scene. Knowing the men under him, he was sure they would believe what he utters. Wasn't he the one with a magical tongue?

He, as an area commander of Muslim *Janbaz* Force, had more vital tasks at hand, as to increase his mass base, recheck funds supply, collect intelligence and supervise justice to traitors. Commanders overwhelm the enemy by their strategic thinking. Bloody, but necessary fighting should be left to foot soldiers, who were obtainable in plenty. Perceptive commanders, like him, were few. He should remind himself, not to partake in such childish activities, again.

On intelligence feedback check, Usman had told him of the interesting tale of Nafisa. In the camp, he had received a message from his organization that she had been safely interned. If the allegations were true, she will make great headlines. He will organize it in a way, so that the military officer, will hang and hang long.

It will also fix that bitch.

She had refused to bed with him. Now he will ensure that she begs him to romp her dry, Tahir pictured, excitedly. Oh *Allah*, the very thought was intoxicating.

His groins creaked.

The feeling was good enough to rub off the guilt and humiliation of his earlier deeds. It was time to contact his best lay till date, kissing Khushbu. She did things with her lips, he could never imagine existed. Why women in general are so gullible? He prayed hurriedly to God to keep them in that natural stupid state or otherwise how will he reach his personal target, he had so modestly set for himself of a century. Till date, his magnificent Tahir junior had pinned down, seventy-six. Not bad for a man who had lost his virginity, only three years back.

Good, God evoking *jihad*.

Rajauri
(0930h, 22 Jun)

"*Kulche garam kulche*," echoed the voice, behind a makeshift stall, from which delicious aroma was emanating.

Sardar Ranjit Singh, peeped out of his Public Call Office and saw a thin man with a flowing beard and supporting an out-of-proportion thick nose, set about his stall. This man had suddenly appeared one day, a fortnight back. Despite the man's ugliness, his eatables had been an instantaneous success. Not that it bothered him in any way, as crowds around the stall gave him more business. He had contacted Inspector Pathania thrice, as he had sighted the same *bakarwal*, in the bus stand. Could he be a terrorist planning some bomb blasts? Must be, otherwise Pathania would not have given him rupees 5000 for nothing. He had warned his fellow Sikh brethren. The only instruction Pathania had given was to instantaneously glue a red square paper, on his window.

How odd.

Wouldn't it have been better to contact him on a telephone? But today he will have to shut his calling booth. He had work to do in local district courts, basically to attest through bribe-infected lower courts that his son was a state subject, so he could buy some agriculture land near Jammu. It was a wise strategic thinking, to move out from this Muslim-besieged place.

As he turned inside the main gates of a ramshackle barrack-type building of local administration, a few minutes later, he saw him again. Call it luck, providence or sheer intervention of his Guru. He was destined to catch that terrorist. He pressed along the throng of people to be positioned unobtrusively, just behind that lanky tall *bakarwal* criminal.

Reshab went straight into grazing land-permit section. The lower divisional clerk Shammi Khan, jumped up in joy on seeing Reshab. The mother-fucker wouldn't have leapt so high, if he had not got his fat retainer, thought Reshab. Earlier, the clerk had barely moved his corpulent ass from his chair, during his first visit.

"*Salam-e-lekum,* Reshab *bhai*. What a pleasure in seeing you," he cajoled Reshab, clutching his hands.

"Permit," said Reshab without wasting any effort.

"Oh, here it is. I have been waiting for the last one week for you to collect it. Why the sudden departure from your old haven," Shammi inquired smilingly.

"The lands have been overgrazed. By the way, thanks," replied Reshab.

He shook hands and hugged the obliging man. Shammi's clasp was ' please-more-dollops' entreating.

Ranjit saw an envelope being slipped into Shammi's pocket.

After that Ranjit ran.

Sprint back; a replication of his clan's famous son, *Milkha's* unforgettable Roman Olympic medal-less run, was life-dependent. He did not repeat the legendary Roman medal-costing mistake. He ran straight, eyes fixed ahead, never looking back even once.

He huffed and puffed and on reaching his shop he quickly pasted a red square patch onto its glass window. Before he sat down on his padded chair, the thin ugly looking eatable stall owner was on him and asked, "Where is he?"

Sardar Ranjit Singh was taken aback, each beard-frayed barnacle sending 'save my sanity' SOS signals, jamming him to his leather cushion seat.

He stared stupidly, till Inspector Pathania removed his false beard, spectacles and a false nose projection. Ranjit Singh started staring more in awe, mouth opening and closing like an oxygen-starved fish. However, he managed to croak, "He is heading towards the bus stand."

Without much ado, Pathania shut his stall, to the total surprise of his clients and ran towards the destination, with a bulky tall *Khalsa* in tow.

Forty-five minutes later, Inspector Narendra Singh Pathania was seated in the last row of the bus, heading for Kalakot, with the *bakarwal* in a black *salwar kameez*, firmly in his sights.

Bn HQ14 Raj Rif
(1130h, 23 Jun)

Major PK Singh stood very still. His cute ever smiling baby doll face showed no protest, mind though rebelling to the contrary. He listened to his boss.

"PK, you will be self-contained for four weeks. Route is marked. Your task, as already reiterated by commander, is to conduct surveillance of rear zones with an aim to identify likely terrorist concentration areas. Your modus operandi will be, to move at night and observe during the day. Any question?" said Colonel PP Singh, authoritatively.

"No problem sir, I will fix RV for relieving the party later. However, administrative replenishment will be needed after fourteen days, basically the replacement for batteries for the radio sets," replied Major PK.

"Negative. No transmission except once each in morning and evening or in crisis. We cannot compromise your exposure by sending another party. I am sure that after four to five days, loads will become manageable. Please carry extra batteries and take that solar battery charger. One more thing, don't leave this captured guide. He is weak, but keep him covered and bound always," he further instructed.

"Anything else sir," inquired PK pensively. Hell, the load was becoming unmanageable. It will be a backbreaking exercise and it was no use cribbing to the boss who would surely quote a similar patrol he had undertaken in more battering circumstances a centuary before.

"Yes, when can I hear your briefing?" the Colonel asked flipping through the office mail, placed in a flat red folder in front of him.

"Patrol Blue Thunder, will be ready for the briefing at 1630h today, sir," PK saluted and cursing his luck, on now giving a formal briefing. That too was manageable. How the hell was he to lug loads for four weeks. Ammunition, rations, control stores and personal clothing were touching well above thirty-five kg per man.

Before the briefing in the evening, Risal, sitting amongst the group of soldiers, had mixed feelings. Less bedsores he was fine. He was amazed to be alive. Till now he had been treated very well, almost like a friend. Stories on which he had graduated, of torture and inhuman treatment seemed a distant distorted memory.

He was their enemy. By all logic, they should have killed him. But you can never trust this Hindu *fauj*. Fundamentally, you can never trust a Hindu.

Wily merchandisers, all of them.

They all were out to convert his community by all available guile. If conversion was not possible, massacre all the Muslims. That's what the Hindu *fauj* was doing in Kashmir. Why Kashmir, in entire India they were mixing population control medicine and administrating it to our children in name of Polio drops. It was a known established fact found out by a few true devoted Muslim doctors and *maulvis*. They want to make our whole generation impotent.

Being a Muslim, he could only trust his fellow Muslims. Hindus were unworthy of trust.

But why such a nice treatment.

It was confusing.

There had to be an ulterior motive.

Any one of their soldiers in any Pakistani piquet or in their hands would have been systematically mutilated by now. Still, he had to do their biddings, till the time was ripe, to organize his escape.

Srinagar (2300h, 26 Jun)

Tahir peeped from the sidewall of the girls hostel.

In the neon light below, a fat cow, the lady *chowkidar* was snoring, her head awkwardly hidden between her two mammoth breasts. It had taken him better part of two hours, to slowly make his way unobtrusively, into the Kashmir University campus, from where he had been in hiding for last few days. Almost a week hidden in his safe house, he had mustered adequate courage to move out.

He threw a small pebble, which struck Jan Bibi's nose. She woke up with a start and stifled her scream as she saw a gorgeous familiar face beam at her. He nodded at her. She smiled back naughtily and walked upstairs to knock on Tahir's latest girlfriends door.

Behind the hibiscus hedge, surrounding a small garden, hugging the sidewalls of the girls hostel periphery, Khushbu was finding it difficult to breath under the barrage of kisses and very intimate fondling. The first fifteen minutes passed erotically, without a word, desperately catching up with almost a month of separation and most importantly, of intimate, sexual physical contact. Only after Tahir's spasmodic grunts and a blissful moan did he untangle himself and asked, "How is my moon. Missed you terribly."

"So did I, very much," blushed Khushbu, trying to work on her lover's fingers, struck lazily, inside her wet legs. As usual, she was left high and dry, before she reached the magical moment of an orgasm.

Ignoring her desperate hip movements, he pulled out his wet slippery hand and asked in serious authority, "What is the information. Update me, now." It's better to keep them panting always, making them linger more desperately for more, he silently opined.

It took Khushbu, a few seconds to realize her lost cause. Catching her breath, she spoke incessantly, for the next ten minutes.

Unmarried, devoid of known physical pleasures due to her sheer massive frightening size and ugliness, Jan Bibi always had managed a peep on sly onto Tahirs activities, from her very own secret spy hole in the bushes.

It gave her excitement she was always denied of.

Though she loved her brood and fussed over them, but could not stop that handsome local *jihadi,* the pleasure of romping her girls. He was a bidder of *Allah's* cause. To help him was her solemn spiritual duty. Suddenly, the passionate voices grew harsher and she heard Nafisa's name, repeatedly being mentioned animatedly, by both the lovers. Her dear Nafisa, one of her own blood, first time in a University. Herself being a daughter of a wandering gypsy, her non-*bakarwal* community mother had died lusting for her handsome father, who made appearances once a year. Nafisa had become her secret icon. A flame to be nurtured and to make her the first modern educated teacher of her clan. Her Nafisa was missing and ominous silence of everyone was too heart rendering.

She had seen pain in the eyes of that young man, who had come inquiring. She was helpless in helping. But what about Nafisa did they know, which was unknown to others. Everyone had said that she had left for home, very hurriedly. She had not believed it at least. Nafisa would have surely told her.

What? Did she hear it right?

A prisoner, a *mukhbir.*

No, no it could not be, something was terribly wrong. To be executed and made an example of.

For what?

She could not trust what she was hearing. She must investigate further. No one steals her girls, not Nafisa, her only bloodline, studying for the greatness of her tribe.

Later, when Khushbu was walking up the stairs to her room, she no longer felt the wetness between her legs. Her lips below felt dry, as dry as the arid Sahara desert. The tingling pleasure had been replaced by whiplashes on her inner most soul. She felt broken, terribly beaten. Her each bone creaked and protested in pain. She felt cheated of her cause. She felt used by her cause. Wet eyed, in incomprehensible state of mind she entered her room. She did not notice Jan Bibi following her with a fierce, purposeful look on her big black massive face. It looked ominous.

Nor did both of them notice, canteen contractors' small working hand, wide-eyed, awake, under the staircase loft.

Batmalu, Srinagar (1030h, 27 Jun)

He strode around with a sense of purpose, heels on back burner combustion.

He had a lot of catching up to do. Since yesterday evening, he had been frequenting his old haunts to obtain intelligence. He could fathom that events were moving very fast. Next month would be crucial, in stepping up violence against Indian Security Forces. Many major and minor issues had to be attended. He had been out of circulation since the last four weeks, enough, time-wise to lose one's intelligence base and enough for other people to wreck his organization, he alone had created. He had loved his work. He had painstakingly, observed, selected, cajoled and trained his people. The cause was too great. Kashmir was at stake. There was no other better or bigger cause worth dying for.

He moved on unobtrusively and entered the vegetaɒle market. Swarms of small, big and bigger flies, stray dogs, goats, cattle, men, women and children, ran in circles hiding behind each other. A nice place to meet people innocently. A very nice place to bargain for food and information. A very very nice place to meet his various little monkeys. Most selected had to be here to bid for daily needs of their rich, innocent masters. Still none knew each other. He moved from one vendor to another critically inspecting vegetables. At each hidden kiosk a small hand would slip into his *firan*. Bits of papers, received from faceless informants, fattened his pockets. He would be a very enlightened man by the end of the day. From terrorists, whoring and other escapades, he would be the information king of Srinagar by midnight.

It was a very tired man, who opened his green wooden gate by late evening. He had approximately fifty-two slips to go through. At 2030 hours when he was browsing through the twenty-fourth one, he bit his lips. Not that it was serious, but definitely the actions were not in conformity with his own ideology, certainly defaming Islam and belying the already tottering remnants of Kashmiriyat.

He went to his kitchen, where his food tiffin was prepared and kept by the widow of a slain Hizbul Commander. The aroma was delicious as always. She was a fantastic cook. For her services, he paid her handsomely. She did not mind her eccentric houseguest. Herself with one daughter, without any support, she had welcomed the stranger. Worst still, she could not go back to her parents as she was a Hindu Brahmin girl, who had fallen in disgrace in the eyes of her community, by eloping with, then a dashing young Muslim computer engineer. A South Indian girl of seventeen could not comprehend her emotions when studying at Bangalore. He was an orphan, self-made man. She had fallen for his ideals first and body later. He had provided her well. Only seven months pregnant she had learnt of her husband's real work. She had cried and begged. He had been adamant. She loved him too much. Her daughter was seven months old when he was killed in a military encounter. The *tanzeem* men sometimes came calling on her. All wanted to marry her on the rebound. She was their showcase, a Hindu woman extolling a Muslim *jihad.* Very rich and influential Muslim men had proposed to her. But once was enough. Superficially Muslim, at heart Hindu, she continued to live in the heart of Srinagar, till this stranger had proposed an arrangement.

It was too good financially to refuse.

The tiffin was at the same place. Not an inch left or right. A small plate with napkin adorned the plastic table, ahead of a majestically carved, walnut-wood chair. Strange decor for a make shift dining table, but adequate.

He bent forward and dragged the heavy walnut, his very own food eating and buttock-resting chair, three feet back. Bending down, he rolled up a small drugget and with his penknife removed a small eight-inch square wooden plank from the floor. It was well meshed and the opening was very innocent.

From the small hollow below, he removed a telephone set with an aerial jutting out. Quickly plugging on the device to an electrical source he made a call and spoke quickly into the phone. His voice routed through the actual device, two hundred metres away, from the house of a retired High Court judge, was relayed to its destination. It was also an identical setup as that of tea stall owner, but here he let the terrorised judge make the payment. Judge *sahib* knew better than to tap the conversation or his ex-militant son, he had so painstakingly re-employed as a court clerk in Mumbai, would be behind the bars and he would have to miss his yearly sojourn with his loving grandchildren, an event which prolonged his otherwise miserable life.

Patrol Blue Thunder (1800h, 28 Jun)

Cool breeze, slapping Major Pankaj Kumar's face, sent an involuntary shiver down his spine. He quickly tightened the bulky army issue windcheater, around his shoulder. He had planned to rest here for the daybreak and move out on the last light, which was definitely after two hours. Under his Second-in-Command, Subedar Bahadur Singh, he had sent that *bakarwal* guide just on top of his native place, to gauge the activity below in the village. His acceding to that mumbling terrorist guide could jeopardize the entire mission. If his risk worked, at least he will have the loyalty of that terrorist toward him. At worst, if not loyalty, then an overburdening obligation will bind that chap to him. Loyalty, was a very serious word, as a person working against his country, could not be loyal to people working for that state.

It was give and take.

He had given something and taking part was yet to be seen.

"*Sahib,* that is my house. Look at those lands below and on to your left, the green ones, yes, and those goats. They are all mine," pointed Risal proudly towards a lone house, nestled innocently between three huge black rocks. A small brook flowed quietly near it. A photogenic scene out of a picture book, reflected his captor.

Subedar Bahadur just grunted, acknowledging the fact. His party of eight men was hidden inside thick shrubs, on a slope overlooking this small vale, only forty metres away, for the last half an hour. Bahadur, despite spitting out pure hate, could see gleam of excitement in Risal's eyes.

One should never trust these traitors, the patrol leader reflected, but PK *sahib* was too humane.

"Sister-fucker, with such a big house, so many cattle, goats and land holding, what are you doing hobnobbing with militants?" Bahadur asked after observing the house for few more minutes.

Risal had no words. His eyes looked down in shame.

"You mother-fucker's are of no one. You can sell your father in a second. So what is a nation for your emotions? Basically, all of you are *namak haram. Jis thali pe khate ho, usme me ched karte ho.* (Unfaithful. In the plate you eat, you are drilling a hole) Had I all this property, I wouldn't have ever joined *fauj. Bhainchod, kutta,"* added Bahadur venting out hot disgust. "You have another forty minutes, before we move back," he added a little later with a deadpan expression supporting his face.

The next twenty minutes shook Risal's life.

He almost jumped in joy, as Bijli moved out to clean some utensils. Barrel of the gun, nudging his back, made him slink down again, into the bushes.

"Bhainchod, agar awaj nikli, tere ko bhun dunga," (Sister-fucker, if you utter a sound, I wil fry you) threatened Phool Singh.

Quietly he lay not even daring to breathe harder. But from within the maze of leaves, he observed her every move. His heart was in his mouth, pounding furiously. She was so graceful, ever so beautiful.

His Bijli, his love, his *zannat.*

But why was she wearing such colourful clothes, looking almost like a newly wedded bride. May be, she was expecting him back. Suddenly his chest doubled up in pride. Yes, his beautiful, dutiful, faithful wife. But how would she know that he was coming back today?

He almost again jumped out with joy, when he observed his beloved, handsome, half-brother, Reshab walk out of the house towards Bijli. He was calling her and she seeing him approach, suddenly washed her hands and got up, facing him smiling.

How odd?

Then his vision froze and seconds later also his already threatened breath.

Why was he holding his wife's hand?

No dammit hugging her.

No, no caressing her back.

Did he also see gyration of Reshab's hips on back of his pure Bijli? No, no, you fucker, it is banned. She is my wife, and your sister-in-law. You have to be her protector. Its evil, forbidden and not Islamic, he screamed in voiceless anguish.

Now of one thing he was certain, Reshab, was about to receive a resounding whack from his spirited woman. She won't stand or allow for such silly games. His woman was a pure Islamic wife, a daughter of an esteemed village cleric from land of the pure, Pakistan.

He choked airless on his rising vomit. His tongue, moving inside his windpipe started playing silly asphyxial games.

Bijli sensuously smiled back, bouncing her big breasts almost upto his half-brothers chin, offered her hand willingly allowing Reshab to drag her. Drag her effortlessly to his evil chest, exchanging vile heartbeats of lust. Then both moved, moved towards him, smiling, mocking him, with deliberate sway of hips, and nearing him. You bitch, you whore. How can you? How can you, you insect? A small gentle nudge from his loved half-brother, Bijli, willingly moved inside a nook in the rocks, hidden by green shrubs. Little seconds later, her marble white legs were visible, rising to meet the sky above. Thin male hips were pumping the flesh below. The pumped adulteress below moaned in appreciation of positive force being applied from above.

He watched all this from a mere twenty metres away.

So did Subedar Bahadur and his boys, spellbound and speechless, not at least minding a free pornographic erotica. Guiltily, Subedar looked to his left. He could not understand why Risal was jerking around, in an epileptic fit. Big, burly, Naik Phool Singh had clamped Risal's mouth, to prevent him from screaming.

Brain deceased, he was silently weeping. Weeping silently, like a small lost child he swallowed his bitter bile. He wanted to die, he wanted to kill, he wanted to shout but shame suppressed his emotions. He could not think coherently. Confused and dazed he slumped onto the ground, listless. Something he had heard before, kept on resonating inside the confines of his brain, *"Jis thali mein khate ho, usme ched karte ho. Namak haram, namak haram, namak haram."*

Allah's Rock
(2000h, 29 Jun)

She had fallen in love with the place instantly.

It was a citadel, befitting a queen.

Beautiful, calm, serene, with gentle cool breeze blowing inside the carven, the feeling was wonderful. Across her, on other side of the pine wood log fire, her love sat cross-legged. He looked so gorgeous, so tall and so full of life. The face was long, sharp cut of the nose, and healthy outcrop of beard and fair skin gave him an aura of a movie star. She could dig her heart for him, on his gentle command. Man, such a good and great man, she never knew existed. A gentle smile spread across her face, as she stirred the pot hanging above the fire. Stew of mutton and vegetables seasoned with herbs was brewing.

A very special dish for her special man and none else.

Others could eat, what others cooked for themselves. She had refused to do general cooking for others, much to the annoyance of that young *angrezi babu*. Gul, her beloved Gul had put a stop to it, in no uncertain terms. Though that *angrezi babu* was also some sort of a *khudda.* His few people ran in circles around him. But ultimately her *khudda* was a bigger *khudda,* as that *angrez* always bided to what Gul said. This made her feel very proud and privileged.

In an effort to look busy, she went deeper inside the cave lit by oil lamps. Then she quickly adjusted the straw lying on the ground and the cotton mattress.

Her *khudda's* bed.

No Gul's bed.

No her bed.

She blushed and ran out to serve him piping hot food.

Captain Ahmed Khan watched with disdain the movements of the *bakarwal* girl. She was a cute little thing and surprisingly beautiful. Jeans and a halter-top will convert her to an outright city girl, he thought. But he was not here to admire her strategic assets. The whole idea was loathsome, unmilitary-like and totally unprofessional. It was not good for the morale and discipline of his men, whose eyes had been following her tight ass. There was an unmistakable lump in their *salwars* and heavy breathing of rapine lust. Only his iron discipline had reined in a certain mutiny. He had tried to reason it out with Gul. But he was adamant and behaved like a spoilt child. Gul had ranted and raved and even threatened to call the whole thing off.

That was unacceptable.

Despite his officer status, the whole mechanics of operation had been explained to him, in which Gul played the pivotal role. He was the operational planner and executioner. Gul was the control. He had to lump his ego, dignity and self-esteem, to subjugate to Gul, to accomplish the mission. He knew this woman was trouble. He would deal with this problem later. For now, he had to organize this place to work like a respectable unit. But he had to grant this rustic, the power to persuade and move things. He had already set few missions in motion, just by selling an idea. It would be a wonderful achievement without even training the *jihad* is as they had planned to do here. After this camp churns out its corrected personnel, then havoc thrown on the Indian Army would be worth gloating on.

What his father's generation could not do in half a century, their band of dedicated men will accomplish in few months—the destruction of India.

9

Fires of Hell

"The fire of hell, is fiercer in heat"

— Verse 81, Surah 9

Srinagar
(2330h, 24 May)

In the dead of night, suppressed sobs were very noticeable and within the confines of the four walls they were ear-splitting in harshness. Just beyond them, the silence was total.

Nafisa had no knowledge of it.

She had stopped comprehending the situation around her long time back. She had cried, wailed, shouted and pleaded to the bare walls. No one, no one came to speak to her. The only welcome sounds were metallic screech of a food plate, along with a plastic water bottle, being pushed in twice a day and the dirty bucket of her ablutions being dragged out, once in cycle of twenty-four hours. But were they twenty-four hours, a day or half of it? She was not sure. She had gone insane, rambling on like a lunatic. Only daily incantations of her love, made her retain little sanity. No one cared. Who would care for her?

Those pointed nail tips of accusing fingers.

Her own best friend, turning on her.

It was too much. Where was Khushbu? If she could not find her, then no one could. Without her knowledge, she could not have been dragged and kept here. Khushbu was a woman completely immersed in her *jihadi* ideology. She would not change. If she could rebel against her family, then she was just a mere acquaintance and now not even a friend. And now her status was of a *mukhbir,* a clitoris snapped useless bitch.

Her present predicament had strengthened her pain bearing capabilities and her sentiments seasoned in present turmoil allowed a deed peep into her inner-self. Her small cell gave her the isolation and the time, to reflect on her soul, her beliefs, her wants and desires. She played and toyed with them in plenty. With a newfound conviction she knew, she would never be a *jihadi.* She could never ever trust people with that innate ideology. She knew, she would free herself of her rigid bindings. She would soar in skies to fly with birds. She would reach heavens to hold and stare into the face of her loving *abbu,* who had shown her the right path. She would never walk with this pack of animals. She would teach. Teach love, teach happiness, teach how to achieve goals and most of all be a dutiful loving wife to Imran.

Suddenly, the bolts made a jarring din and the door opened. Sheer abundance of light hit her. She shielded her eyes; the brilliance of it was hurting her eyes.

They immediately watered.

Through the haze of her wet eyes and the glimmer of the light, she saw a feminish man leering at her.

The same finger painted eunuch, who had accused her.

"Out, you bitch. Today, we will show you what is life. You will enjoy tonight. We will enjoy tonight. We will see what your lover has taught you. If his efforts are found not noteworthy, then we surely will teach you very expertly. Our sexual class instructor is knowledgeable, charming, with massive long dick. You will be impressed. It's the beginning of a new life, so enjoy you bloody *mukhbir,"* he very calmly hissed.

He and one more boy dragged her out. Her heels could not dig in.

"She is smelling like a pig," said the smaller boy, twitching his nose.

They kept on dragging her till she was enclosed in a modern tiled bathroom. Before she realized, they were tearing her clothes away. She screamed uselessly. She put up a determined but a losing fight. She had no strength left. More sadly, she had no will to resist. She lay on the cold tiles and let the victors have their way. They peeled her like an onion, their eyes watering with lust; they peeled on her till she was in her raw form. Totally nude, she stared back, her arms crossing her breasts to cover her dignity.

The little boy was jumping up and down, like a little toad. "Take a bath little woman. Shampoo and soaps are here. Bath well and smell well in right nooks," he giggled like a little girl further.

She didn't mind this part a bit.

Month-old layers of dirt had accumulated on her. She could feel those yucky scabs. She indeed, herself felt like a dirty pig. She had lived like an animal, in her own filth.

Post her much-required bath, she was unceremoniously picked up. Giddy and in total gloom she allowed herself to be dragged to her new altar, a feather soft bed, in the adjoining room.

"Bye, bye love. Behave well, little darling. Move your ass well dear darling," smirked the girlish man, as he moved out of the room, swaying his hips suggestively.

She guessed the outcome of such a predictable largesse. The stark fact seemed inevitable, but she was helpless. Again, suddenly an adjoining door opened. She gasped in horror, covering the big surprised 'O' of her mouth with her both hands.

Khushbu's defender of faith, was staring at her.

He was standing stark naked.

Engaging her with a crooked menacing smile, he approached her. His hands were indulging unashamedly with his semi-erect maleness. The fist was moving to and fro, along its entire length, but with deliberate slowness. He looked very amused, with desperation reflected in her face. She stared helplessly at the neon light shining at the end of his stub. He intercepted the flight path of her looks and laughed maniacally. He liked what he saw, shocked fear.

"So, the wheel comes a full circle, dear darling. I had asked you once to sleep with me. You had the nerve to humiliate me by rejecting, such a wonderful offer. Now little girl, what will you do? Scream and cry to your heart's content. Do that to drown your fears. Today, I will bed you. A befitting tribute of your treachery and your loving friendship with Khushbu. You don't know, what your lovely friend does with her mouth. By end of the day or lets say a week, you will enjoy performing them," he grunted excitedly, continuing, "And if you don't, I will definitely kill your lover, that cute Indian Army Officer."

"No, no, please don't kill him," a totally nude wet-eyed girl opposite him begged.

He moved forward laughing, his hard dark brown penis, rock steady, straight and erect, shining, advancing before him. Left-right, left-right, Tahir marched forward, nude in his rippling muscles, his satanic manhood-tuber danced and spasmodically lanced in a life-threatening posture ahead of him.

A sharp noise diverted his attention.

It was most irritating.

Not when he was ready to do the prick penetrating rites.

Something again crashed and brushed heavily against the closed wooden door. He rotated his handsome face to inquire and in anger shouted, "You mother-fuckers, dare you peep. I will kill you. You will get your humping chance later. Learn the virtues of patience you imbeciles and join the queue like good citizens."

The door still had the audacity to open, despite his warning.

Usman and little Altaf fell inside the room, their faces bloody and quivering with fear.

"I wouldn't do that," said a firm voice, from the darkness behind his fallen men.

He stared at a pistol, its round bullet-pushing hole, staring shamelessly at his crotch.

His egoistic swelled penis, finding no succour, quickly swallowed its manly pride and fell, instantaneously limp.

Who were these silly, fun-killing, terrible people?

What, how, why, when, by whom, all questions flooded his muddled senses. By the time they had secured his feet, his mouth, he had started shaking violently, white with fear and his famous loving cunt pampered Tahir junior displayed the consistency of swaying in the wind, like a withered 'fenugreek' shrub.

Events flashed past Nafisa's confused mind to comprehend exactly, what was happening. Oh my God, so many men, all to rape her. Oh *Allah,* what have I done to deserve such a punishment, she sobbed and pleaded. She could not bear to see all this. She quickly pressed palms of her hands, over her already shut-eyes, to doubly ensure she did not witness this unholy drama. Expecting the deadly assault to begin any second, she kept on murmuring incoherently, lying on the bed. Constant fear, pecking and inability to live the way she wanted, angered her.

It was now or never.

Her ire against her state, slowly rose from her heart, subverted her fear pumped mind and she shouted opening her eyes, "You rascals, kill me now. Be and done with it. May you all rot in hell. You scum, you worst form of worldly conception." Then she screamed and screamed and screamed insanely.

Unexpectedly, in-between her ground shaking wails, she saw the stunned inquisitive face of her Imran. Her own beloved Imran. Totally nude, this time in sheer shame, she blissfully fainted again.

Arampur Op Base
(2114h, 01 Jul)

Single strand of rusted concertina coil, separated the lush green countryside, from the military area. The wire had been very lazily put, not for any protection, but basically to keep the flea-infected cows at bay. The termites had weakened the wooden supports. The wire mostly lay on ground than in air.

The fence was actually pathetic in its stated purpose and purely symbolic in nature.

Naik Hamid Bhai, was feeling good.

The night was pleasantly cool. Life was not bad. It was definitely better than in his parent unit. Rashtriya Rifles tenure was not turning out as scary as his counterparts had told him. Good administration, good food, timely duty, no favouritism and best was leave when you asked for. Shit, he could plan his stint at home once in three or four months, not bad at all, for planning leave had become almost a managing exercise, by getting false letters and telegrams, in his previous unit. One did not mind operations. There were hordes of volunteers to go out, than be cooped inside the base. Do your operation, come back and be pampered. Yes, the boys were not familiar, faces changed very fast, but basic goodness and caring was there. Officers ensured this. In his own pleasant thoughts, he moved to complete his beat of twenty yards, peeping into grey darkness, which had just set in, one hour back. He could not see anything beyond twenty metres. The moon was yet to come out.

It was one of the God's good omens. An omen, a soldier prays for throughout his life.

He died instantaneously.

Before Naik Bhai hit the ground his mind was frozen to his happy inebriated state. The burst of four bullets from Klashnikov model 56, fired from fifteen metres, had caught him squarely in his chest just below his twenty-seven year old heart.

Abu Hilal smiled, as his hated target fell. He had been stalking and observing them, for the last two hours. Working as a farm hand, with the family who were sowing rice, along the camp's fence, had been easy. When girls came in evening to deliver tea and food, they had got his weapons hidden inside their *firans*, along with his second Baluchi friend. Baluchi was a good man. Motivated, pure Islamic and had passion to kill, like him.

It had been easy to seduce the sickening Kashmiri family of Rashid Pandit, to help them in this venture. Though the above became possible only after using expected death threats, for non-cooperation.

Bloody half-cast.

The chap had converted maybe a few generations back. Not of uncontaminated Muslim blood. No wonder he was shaking in terror for aiding them. A true *Musalman* should wage *jihad* and assist them with their chest open. Must be his old scared shitless earlier Hindu side. It will take them a few more generations, to make them more solid, dependable Muslims, he thought.

The plan hatched by Gul, had been daring. A first of its kind in this valley. It would shake these revolting Hindu soldiers. They will run in panic. What a plan.

A *fidayeen* in their camp.

They will be terrorised out of their wits.

Baluchi was already inside the wires, slithering like a cobra. Baluchi will sure create mayhem tonight, Hilal reflected contentedly. Dose of opium had killed his friend's all known sum-of-fears. He let out another burst at the adjoining post, where the second sentry should have been. His plan was just to create diversion to effect an entry inside the encampment.

His other Lashkar friends, hidden fifty yards away in the forest fringes, in two separate groups on hearing the sweet clear sound of bullets being fired, in unison, let loose five rocket launchers and three PIKA machine guns. They were part of even bigger diversion. Confuse these Indian dogs totally. Make them run around in circles, like a rabid dog chasing his flea-infected tail. Not only it will divert their attention but reaction as well. In this generated-panic, they planned to kill all in their sleep.

The brave dope-laced Baluchi will spit venom tonight.

Sepoy Karuna Shankar, the number-two sentry, fifteen days old into his new tenure, was gazing towards his buddy, when he was whacked by the gunfire. He was frozen in panic. His bladder suddenly let loose. Warm liquid trickled down from the side of his trousers in a hurried rush. Suddenly, a loud explosion around him further rocked his vanished confidence. In sheer horror, his fingers clamped tightly on his already cocked LMG. Bullets flew haphazardly towards the direction, he had seen the initial fire come from. Engrossed in tracer chasing, he did not notice a grenade lobbed into his post from his behind. He could not comprehend, why suddenly his otherwise sturdy legs refused to support him. His weapon kept on firing in an upward arc towards the sky, as his weight dragged his weapon down.

Last few rounds went through the tin roof above, just where his previously alive head had been as he slumped dead.

Major Vikrant Dutt, the post commander was staring wide-eyed, mouth agape at the TV screen in front of him, engrossed in a blue movie he was sneakingly watching and at the same time browsing through an unabridged manuscript of some Major Jesses' laws stating that the virility of a bachelor is directly proportional to the ability of a virgin getting pregnant doing yoga on his semen stained carpet. He nodded intelligently at the quote and shifted his concentration to the screen in front, engrossed in capturing timeless details of sexual gymnastics on display. After three days of jungle bashing, he was entitled to his only entertainment. It was cleaner than trying to nose at the smelly local hussies around. He grunted, as the white blond haired woman riding a black man, screamed on the brink of her orgasm. Major Dutt, mimicking the passionate scream silently, now screamed back full throatily, as his room fell on him, after a huge earth-shaking blast.

Lance Naik Cook Himant Kumar, ran out of his kitchen in chest erupting panic, clutching his AK-47 rifle. His heart was pounding like a hammer and steam like breath chiseling his chest. Cold sweat broke from his brow. In fear, the only reason he could think for dashing out was to hit his protected bunker, to safety against the bursting bombs. Just outside, while running and fiddling with not so intimate parts of his personal weapon, clutched in iron grasp for first time in last three months, his shaky feet slipped on the cookhouse sullage. His feet flew straight backwards as he fell smack on his stomach, arms extended forward holding his rifle.

The sudden jerk initiated his weapon. Fire raked the tall Baluchi, as he got up to throw another grenade.

Dumbstruck Subedar Shakti Singh, of high caste warrior clan, from behind his room's window, crouched in sheer self-preservation posture, witnessed the brave deed, executed by the lowly low caste man, which stopped this suicidal attack.

Kot Buddhal
(1630h, 03 Jul)

He was bushed, brain weary and very tired.

Big blisters on his feet were a reality check of his lovely physical condition and it was not inspiring. Sitting on the chair in the office had taken its toll. He had trudged, to almost all the places, where his target in the black *salwar kameez* had boarded the bus, a week back. But he was happy and immensely satisfied, despite the painful exhaustion.

He had not been detected.

He would do his pompous instructor at Criminal Bureau of Investigations proud. He had spent three useful months at their academy at Delhi, trying to master this art. Though initially sent on deputation from state police, to learn about criminal investigation procedure, he had got around his temporary boss and attended a course on population surveillance and monitoring, as an additional study. He would never be caught napping again or put his family in danger. He had strong reasons to keep an eye on all suspects.

He, as a teenager, had picked up subtle behavioural changes of his neighbours, in Batmalu Srinagar, more than a decade back. He had warned his father, a retired forest officer, of his fears, but the old man had dismissed it, with an irritated wave of his hand. His father had loved his friends, had placed total faith in them, despite the religious divide. He loved them, despite the political turmoil brewing around them. He loved them, blind to the ugliness erupting around them. He had burned in his house with his wife, in total shock and confusion, still calling for help of his best Muslim friends, who had conveniently disappeared on that fateful hour. Strangely, he had not seen any hate registered in his father's eyes, when he himself had jumped out of the first floor window to escape those screaming flames.

His father was a sage, but he was not. He did not want to show it, for it would compromise his career, in an already militant-infected police force of his state. His present boss, Gulam Dar, Superintendent of Police, was a known Hizbul sympathizer. His esteemed elder brother was a Hizbul commander in Baramula. An army unit in valley even had his voice on tape attending one such meeting. He had been removed, but largesse bestowed by an equally tainted home minister from Shopian, had reinstated him. It was an open secret, but what could he do. He was sure of one thing that his fat corrupt boss would by now be hopping mad, as he had not reported his movements, since the last week.

In any case, reporting to him would have to be modified. A few facts spiced with lot of lies. If he told him what he was up to, he was sure that somehow the terrorists would be forewarned and he will be dispatched on a wild goose chase, in a dramatically opposite direction. Many of his colleagues had suffered this fate. For now, he must find a way to contact the nearest army unit for actual drama and create a meaningful diversion for his boss.

Inspector Pathania, sipped on his *nunchai,* slowly munching on the baked *kulcha,* as he plotted his next move. His efforts till now were brewing the right ingredients. The resultant aroma was invigorating. He had another twenty minutes to kill, before he boarded the dilapidated state transport bus back to Rajauri and to his routine boredom.

Pattan
(1146h, 05 Jul)

The medical camp seemed to be a run-away success.

Tired doctors had already treated or attended over four hundred patients, but instead of lines diminishing, throngs of crowd kept on swelling. It would be good news coverage. The TV anchor had said that it would be aired on the national news tonight. No wonder he had massaged and oiled his sleek moustache and twirled them with his fingers, into stunning ice picks. With his square determined jaw, blue eyes and this 'Bhagat Singh' like moustache, he definitely looked handsome. He knew it and prided himself in it. In animated zeal, he was shuffling from one leg to another, congratulating himself for the good show organized. His boss was just ten minutes away, coming to see this event and have sumptuous *wazwan* he had prepared for him and his bubbly wife.

Waiting impatiently, with nothing purposeful to do, he lit a cigarette, his favourite, Wills Navy Cut. After a deep inhale, he remembered he had vowed to give it up, a promise to his lovely daughter. He stared at the nicotine stained butt, but an alien interloper subverted his mind, the body, and his furiously sucking lips. He puffed on. It was not very intricate to his mind that he had in fact, very little will to give up this habit. As he exhaled a long column of intoxicant smoke, lazily through his nose, he thought, no, his mind registered, a huge rock being thrown from amongst the crowd towards the row, where harassed doctors sat. He instantly got up, in anger to shout at the offender, when a rippling blast knocked him down.

He woke up amongst sirens. He was confused. Why was he sleeping in the first place? Numerous jeeps along with array of escorts of his boss, pulled inside the driveway. He quickly got up and walked smartly ahead to receive him.

Commandant Y S Gaur of 46 Border Security Force Battalion could not comprehend, why abruptly the place was tomblike quiet, with three of his doctors covered in white bed sheets and he, bleeding from his face, copiously.

Reminiscent, the forty-nine-year-old officer smiled in his hospital bed, on the only goodness that had emerged out of that fateful day. He had stuck that dirty cigarette butt between his lips, for the last time, in so many days.

Kupwara
(1100h, 08 Jul)

The events had left him astounded.

He felt like a blustering slapstick comedian explaining it to his boss. His superior's retort also had left no room for misinterpreting that infinitesimal observation.

Three groups of three *burka* clad supposedly women tagging three unkempt children each had approached three of his different units at the same time spread twenty leagues apart. All three had engaged the sentries on the duty as children had dutifully lobbed grenades at the bewildered recipients. They were further stunned into silence as those three manly women magically produced automatic weapons, raking other sundry to oblivion. In the melee, they also escaped.

Four soldiers fatal and six with serious injuries was a foolish enough feeling.

Badami Bagh Srinagar (0930h, 10 Jul)

The underground operational room of 15 Corps HQ, was very very solicitous.

Officers from the operational and intelligence branch, nominated for its upkeep, ensured this. Running tapes around the maps they earned the same hazardous pay as their counterparts facing terrorist bullets in the jungles. Their jungle was their map. Their terrorist was their big-big boss and his insatiable yen for information. Not that it was in anyway less informative, during the last incumbent in the office, but this short, energetic, white haired boss had penchant for inventing work and more work. Of late, they had realized information in any form could be gleaned, tabulated and presented. It would not at least surprise them, if ordered to find out how many farts, smelly or odourless, a soldier would oblige the environment with, hour per hour, when fed with fresh food, stale food, rice, *puree* etc-etc. It was information. It could be obtained. Period. The lists were endless, but it was their job and millions of charts, annotations, markings, supported their untiring endeavours.

Collected inside was a bedlam of unruly jumble of officers, backslapping, exchanging serious notes, chest beating on terrorist killed, and cracking tainted jokes. It all rose to a deafening din. All commanding officers had been called for this sudden extravaganza. Like long lost women friends, they babbled not wanting to miss any chance to babble, jet releasing their pent up tensions invested firmly in their own minds. The Commanding Officer was the loneliest person on the galaxy, rarest of the atypical species, found only West of the planet Mars. With only himself to brood in trouble or happiness and latter a minus commodity in the valley, they made hay while they could. Few such meetings were as rare in chronology of a witnessed blue moon and rarely would they not pamper themselves, to indulge in such shameless babble.

But the hullabaloo of the general babble died down, twice.

Once, when all the other minor generals, entered the sacred podium, then the little forty-five year old plus youngsters i.e. the old men of their units rose quietly, in marked respect. These minor generals merely commanded a division, had only three to four brigadiers to boot and at best ten colonels to slay.

Then the real general-babble of minor generals rose, to sidelong smirks and acknowledgements of all other sundry present. They were even worse than young colonels, for their digs were well below the decency of their ill-fitting belts. Maybe, old age made them do that.

Hush the second time descended when Lieutenant General Rocky Dass, SM, VSM, and newly bestowed AVSM, strode, purposefully into the room. He was neither a minor general, nor a major general and was not to be confused with the lower status of minor major general.

He was a general man-eater.

He did not boot officers. It was not his stated or makeup of his constitution. He only clubbed inefficient to death and drove not so efficient to insanity and the efficient the ones just luckily survived.

His face was grim.

Muscles of his forehead were vibrating in anger.

The fury emitting radiations were evidently comprehensible.

But when was he not that, thought the young major, the grade two operations. In any case by trait, Rocky was inexpiable. General's eyebrows cocked up and his mouth rounded in a sarcastic scowl, as he began his monologue, "I am most dissatisfied with the present state of affairs———," and it went on uninterrupted for the next seventy-seven minutes, covering the entire spectrum of officers' useless pathetic existence and inert professional incompetence. President had done a sinful sin in granting them stupid commissions. The castigations were also liberal in character and content. Words like command responsibility, command failure, onus, fixing the responsibility, Court Martial etc were also uttered repeatedly and in ample measure. When all of them got up for a short tea break, none felt hungry, being well fed on diet of nonstop ineffable tirade.

Grade two could not help but notice that the backsides of the entire sundry looked, badly crumpled, deflated and ruthlessly whipped. The earlier camaraderie of unbridled babble was noticeably pregnant in pause.

Old Airport, Srinagar (0130h, 10 Jul)

Exactly after seven days, did someone speak to him?

He was thankful for that.

Living in his misery alone, with his fellow mates tied like dogs, in the cell opposite had been a nightmare of satanic proportions. He had broken down and howled to be shown mercy. His friends even howled louder. Less him, Usman and Altaf had been taken out of their cells. They had come back bloody and whimpering. They had even started shouting in fear, at shadows, or on just hearing the approach of their tormentors. After each such occasion when their eyes met, they howled in unison, even louder. But the captors only stared back, stone cold, sometimes smiling.

He was sitting on a single metallic chair, hands tied to his back and legs to the chair's steel leg support. Worst, he was almost naked, his decency covered by his soiled underwear. Despite summer heat, he was shivering. The chair danced to the tune of his terror.

"Who are you?" asked the faceless man. His eyes bored into him.

"Tarik, third year student of law at Kashmir University," he rasped back, looking down and surprised at the gentleness of the questioner's voice.

"You look me in the eye when answering, son. Do you understand," his expressionless face instructed.

"Yes," he looked up.

"What's your profession?" asked the faceless man, again.

"I am a student?" he rasped back a little confidently, but eyes still shy of looking up.

One stunning slap across his face made him reel back in pain. His eyes watered and he hissed continuously in pain. The chair sang to loud metallic notes of total fear.

"I will ask each question again, normally. Please reply back truthfully or you will learn that lies will become more painful with each wrong answer," said the faceless impassionate tormentor. "Did you understand what I said," the smiling face reiterated to now desperately nodding Tahir. "Look up, I said look up, and dare you not look me in my eyes," he further threateningly shouted.

"Yes, yes, please don't beat me. I will do what you say. Please don't beat me," quivered the young man on the chair. "I will tell the whole truth and nothing but the truth, I swear by the holy Quran," he said again, straining to stare back.

"Said like a true patriot and a good law student," smirked the interrogator. "Now tell me again, who are you?" he crooned softly.

"I am Tahir Yusuf, s/o Abdullah Yusuf, r/o Batmalu. I am District Commander of Muslim *Janbaz* Force of Srinagar district. I operate from Kashmir University, where I study Law," he howled back, not taking his eyes off his interrogator.

"But friend, tell me something that we don't know. Here is your resume..." and he rattled out all the known details.

At each truth, his testes sank a millimetre into his scrotum. His heart beat raced into limits of heart attack zone. It seemed he was sinking into a quicksand, quick time and nothing could save him. The plain truth of his life heard from an alien mouth was indeed shocking and disheartening. When that pig narrated his participation in the recent raid, he saw thorny gallows, his testicles had disappeared totally, and he, the *hijra* in making was running high fever.

Seeing the sweating dejected man in front, the expressionless man opposite, Srivastva let out a bellowing laughter. For a change, his demonic eyes smiled.

Tahir looked up through his feverish eyes, confused. What worse could be awaiting him?

The interrogator came up and opened a small green familiar looking dairy. Yes it was his handwriting. He recognised it as it was shoved into his face.

He turned white.

Oh no, not this, screamed Tahir not so silently.

The bad man laughingly carried on, "But this is the real cake, my boy. Your first step into the world of Noble prize. A first Noble laureate, in literature, of Islamic world. No need for cleansing your soul by Hajj. A real beauty. A gem unlike written after Omar Khayam. Ahm, let's see, Zarina's vagina is too tight... nice, Doctor Yusuf's wife is like humping a mattress.... very nice, Mariam wants simultaneous multiple orifice's blocked...good, Gulbadan's boobs are perfect and suckable... very good, Jan bibi loves it only in the backside... excellent, Khushbu uses her deep mouth perfectly.... fantastic, my boy, you are just too good. What an endless summation, for eager public consumption. We must surely make it public, all your legendry escapades of *jihad*. For one page of your private diary, you surely will be hanged, balls first, by your own loving *tanzeem*. Good, now you can keep quiet, act dumb or come out clean. I will see how best I can help you, to save your wretched rotten hide."

The fever turned into a delirious inferno.

The shrinking feat of his cute balls, was now vigorously repeating on his magnificent junior. The fenugreek shrub was wilting in heat at an endangered species pace. His parched throat was making strange noises, quality of it not even decipherable to his own ears. He slumped down in total defeat. Even his chair had stopped making those courageous protesting metallic tunes. His body, his brain, his heart, all were chilled to a deathly silence.

The door opposite jerked open.

Khushbu and Nafisa came inside the cell holding big mutton chopping knives.

They looked very onerous.

Without much ado they stripped him and placed his junior on a wooden block. He screamed, as they raised their arms, to strike a cutting blow.

He must escape.

He kicked his feet in sheer horror and tumbled down in his chair. In mindless haze, he was propped up again. They again roughly dragged out his junior and displayed it on the chopping block. He pleaded and pleaded for mercy, but the blow still came and his manhood lay twitching at their feet.

The bitches were smiling. No, laughing animatedly.

He opened his eyes in terror. He could see nothing but darkness. He was in total agony, but strangely felt no pain. He was totally ball-less and cock-less. Now, he was a perfect *hijra.* Tied, bound and at other's mercy, he did what he could best do. He cried and wailed out aloud like a little baby first time circumcised.

Watching the raving lunatic from ten feet away, the interrogator was more than happy. He let out a satisfied grunt, sipping his overtly sweet coffee. He had worked on the subject psychologically. He was completely broken. Those two police girls were magnificent with that dummy rubber imitation and goat blood. Shit, they should be in the movies. They had played their part, befitting an Oscar nomination. The plan had worked in clockwork precision. Now the quality of truth will be crystal pure. By evening next day, he knew he would have more information than he wished. Despite his boss pressing for immediate results, he will play it slowly and deliberately. His experience had shown, that this was the best method; otherwise most of the subjects, to avoid immediate pain, lied and lied more imaginatively and comprehensively, to avoid more pain.

Humming an old melody, "*Hasina Man Jayegi,*" he sauntered out of the room, with his clean hands in the pocket.

Patrol Blue Thunder (0500h, 11 Jul)

It was almost twilight.

The halo around the peaks of Pir Panjal were glowing fiercer every second. Major PK, having been woken up fifteen minutes back, with a cup of piping hot aniseed flavoured tea, was ready to go for his morning oblutions. He absent-mindedly scratched his chin, supporting a two week old beard to kill furious itching. Devoid of luxuries bathing, it was taking a furious toll on his soft skin.

He was very irritated.

Now as per latest instructions, he was to move more east, along the Pir Panjal ridge. He had been following orders to the last letter and spirit. Move by night and rest by day. But the biological clock was never in consonance with military needs and orders. For once breaking them, he had struck camp for one night rest, near a small brook, where his soldiers could take a much-needed bath, during the day including washing their dirty clothes. Left to his boss, he would be walking another twenty km in wilderness. Major Jesse's relieving party, now was being inducted through a different route, by vehicles, where they will relieve him after two weeks. Thus the return trip had been extended to their optimum forward march. The whole issue till now had gone off splendidly. Loads had reduced to bearable levels. Only worry was his guide, Altaf. Since his last visit to his house, he had been howling silently. Altaf had gone into a complete shell. God only knew for what. He must now cosy up to him to find the problem but before that he must remind Major Jesse to bring along his private mail. He missed his wife's daily one letter a day routine.

Jesse Sir was an enigma.

A contradiction, which defied logic in his otherwise simple life.

He was a tall, handsome, carefree, pukka *Thakur*, whose smile could melt a chocolate, ten metres away. The face was a bit oval, cheeks spouting, big bushy manly moustache and big beholding eyes, gave him an arresting face. He had seen many women glance back at him a second time. Worst was that Jesse knew it, and to irk them, he totally ignored them to irk them more. If he was a teetotaller, sir adored whiskey, if he was pure vegetarian, Jesse sir savoured meats, if he was perfectionist to a detail, the *Thakur sahib* called it *babugiri* and pure rubbish, if he was in awe of his superiors, he fought them tooth and nail, if he studied hard in courses and barely passed, *sahib* would gallivant and top it, if he prayed daily, his six months senior remarked "spirituality at this age, one had to be completely mad," if the girls flocked to him due to his gentle loveable disposition, Jesse sir ridiculed all of them to bed. And all those idiotic women outdid each other to be violated, despite his subtle warnings.

Unlucky him and lucky Jesse Sir.

He was stark opposite to his beliefs and revered covenants of his faith, but he still loved him. Jesse was a perfect human being, with no malice and infinite love for the organization, he earned his *namak* from. It would be great to be with him, even if it were for just a day.

Surankot
(1626h, 11 Jul)

Mehboob was ecstatic.

It was a golden chance to redeem of his self-perpetuated friends' treachery, the dreams of which had eaten his innards. For once, he was amongst the most trusted. With affable pride, he now knew what it would have been to be in the inner circle of the 'Messenger of *Allah*'.

A unique honour, a rare holy privilege.

But what Gul had instructed him to undertake was next to impossible. To organize almost a tonne of medicines. But he must do it, for he was one of the gentle Gabriel's angels. In fact, he was an angel. It was his blind duty to deliver. He must serve, he must treat the less fortunate.

Time was desperately short to organize such massive medical aid. He must do it and also not arouse any suspicion. He knew the gravity of his endeavours. Alone in small driblets, he must meet the target in the next three weeks. He was thankful that movement of the stores was to be coordinated by Reshab, by his own means.

First things first, he must put in an application for long leave. Yes, a long indefinite leave. Yes, a leave to escape the clutches of his evil employers. Gul wanted him at the camp. Gul wanted him to run the camp's infirmary, when established. Who could refuse Gul.

Gul was life.

Gul was reason to live.

Gul was his daily breath.

Gul was his blood.

Gul was the brother he never had.

Gul was the friend, he had lost.

Gul was redemption of his earlier sins.

Gul was the magic he had been seeking so furtively till now.

Allah's Rock
(0930h, 12 Jul)

Across him, sitting in semicircle, sat his faithfuls.

Each man apart, each man a Gaznavi.

He brimmed with pride for he knew of each man's capability. They were the best Muslim soldiers in the entire world. None could match their skills and dedication. Even Americans vouched their professionalism and had used their capabilities impudently. They wouldn't have won the war in Afghanistan otherwise, left only to their Rambo imaged but punk-less men. They were the pure, of true religion and his trusted hands, to destroy the worshipers of *Mannat*.

He saw the young *angrez* officer walk in.

Half infidel and not an ardent *namazi*.

He had been visibly peeved in Murree where he had seen him going through satanic magazines, picturing Indian film girls and to boot sipping ungodly alcohol. On the plus side, he planned operations very well and lead fearlessly from the front.

"So, *Kaptan Sahib*. How are the preparations for establishment for the camp coming up," he inquired.

His eyes only looked up.

Gul's indolent tone did not please him a bit.

"Slow, too slow for my liking. Everyone moves like a lumbering Indian elephant. Even the fearsome *jihadis* are lazy, their vigour, fervour to work is missing. Money, money, and more money.

Without money, they don't even talk to you sweetly. I don't know whether they are here to earn money or wage *jihad,*" Ahmad uttered contemptuously.

"Leave the motivation to me. I am the sword of God. I am the chosen one. I will make them see light and reason. But now specifically, how many more days for camp's readiness," Gul beamed.

"Another four weeks at this pace. If I can get them running, then may be in two. Only then can training start in the real sense," said the Captain.

"Ahm, I see," Gul replied, nodding his head, contemplating the outcome of the news.

"We have to reschedule everyone's arrival. Temporary camp was no problem. It was near a village, accessible, but here even a needle has to be planned and procured. Reshab is too sluggish. Always struck up for want of money. Rascal wishes for three months running advance. The chap is a swindler. In spite of abundance of money in our account, full stocking of food has not been done till now, leave aside arms, ammunition and other things which have to be dumped," he further complained.

"Ahm, I see. I will pass necessary instructions," Gul said strolling away.

Only if the idiot thought more from his head, than from the sticky maleness, pumping that *bakarwal* woman, half the issues would have been resolved amicably by now, Captain of the Pakistani Special Forces reflected. Strangely unlike his known dossier he had memorised earlier, Gul was acting out of character. His earlier reasoning had failed. He did not want to jeopardize the whole operation, for want of a *jihadi's* desire of humping a local woman.

10

Hangman's Noose

'The rope be short or long.
The dread is in its loop.'

— Jesse

New Delhi
(1230h, 14 Jul)

She was ecstatic, on top of the world.

Rashmi Srivastava smartly walked down twenty-six Italian marble steps of the Escorts Heart Institute. Nana's heart-valve rectification operation had been a runaway success. The girl had braved it and was recuperating so well, that the little witch had literally commandeered the nurses, to perform an hourly Russian circus.

She happily ran into the arms of Grover, waiting patiently at the bottom of the steps. Her instantaneous hug surprised him and it showed on his amused face.

"Wish you would do that more often," he remarked jokingly.

"Yes, you old fat, farting married man. Rashmi's one lovely hug should be enough to last you a lifetime – for she never obliges, but today she is so happy, that you can ask her to do anything," she smiled and replied.

Running back comically and then resting his fat bums on his car's front bonnet, he spread his chubby arms wide and said in a low husky voice, "Then kiss this incredible hulk silly baby," and after a seconds pause he added with a wink, "passionately."

Rashmi's eyes narrowed.

Her lips seductively smiled and swaying her incredible hips, she cat-walked five yards separating them. Placing one hand on Grover's shoulder and caressing his lips with her red painted fingernails of the other, she sweetly cooed lazily, "Sweet love, why a hug cannot suffice. Darling I meant anything professional and not hot lucid sex, as you are desperately drooling for."

"You all sexy haute females are the same. With wanton lust, lead a handsome guy like me all alone on the top a mountain, hand-in-hand behind a bush, take off the first peel of five knickers you are wearing and when you have him ogled on to your curves, sneak behind him and then kick him down without even batting an eyelid," Grover replied smilingly.

Both laughed, as they entered Grover's new Indica car. "Sexy automobile," remarked Rashmi lighting up a cigarette and then added, "When do I go."

"Day after, by the morning flight. Will Nana adjust?" he delicately inquired.

"Nana," she sighed and giggled further adding, "She has taken well to your girl. Twenty-four hours with her, you would desperately want me to personally whip you. Be assured, it would be less painful. She has agreed to stay with your family and without her satanic oppressive mom happily, as she puts it."

"You love her too much. It shows on you," Grover observed.

"Quote me another reason to live," she replied somberly, as the car meandered through mad traffic of Delhi.

Srinagar
(1310h, 15 Jul)

He was trying to look like a lone loony when he was not one.

Colonel Mushtaq was strolling lazily along the high school avenue, running parallel to once majestic, but now assuredly slimy-shit-clogged Jhelum River. The sweet clean air with its blue waters was an old grandmother's tale, which, at least, for now could not be believed in. Walking in ease he was slowly munching on salted peanuts.

It was difficult to pass as a local, when you certainly were not one.

After one's crisp hugging uniform, loose *salwar kameez* and *firan,* felt very alien to his body. His own security detail, similarly dressed, was following few metres behind. Two pistols amongst them three, did not amount to any positive safety. But he was not here to raid a terrorist hideout, but pick an urgent message from 'Falcon' at one of the dead-letter drops. Literally, it was not dead, but alive and kicking. Never had his asset ever made such an attempt. An innocuous blast at the already abandoned Nishat movie theatre and its subsequent news had made him jump about throughout the morning. Cancelling all his appointments, much to the annoyance of other staff, he had quietly sauntered out of his office and Badami Bagh cantonment. Wish by some magic, he could do more of this work, than silly paper pushing, he reflected.

As he turned right, into another lane, he squarely confronted the famous Adoo Bakery. The legend had it tickling Shahjahan's appetite, since the Mughal's sojourn in this vale of paradise. Right across it sat a small frail woman with a red shawl, selling lotus buds. Remarkable, thought Mushtaq. A detail worked out a year back, was in location, at the right time. He had tried earlier to pry on such impromptu dead-drops, but the key elements had always been missing.

He casually approached the footpath vendor lady and said, "*Bibi,* how much for a dozen."

Without looking up she replied, "I sell only in kilograms."

"But I want specifically only a dozen."

"OK, it will be twenty rupees," she said and started counting exact twelve, putting each bud one by one in a polythene bag. With slight movement of her hand, amidst her loud counting, she put a small packet along with the lotus buds. Smiling she held the full bag up for Mushtaq to inspect. Mushtaq quickly gave rupees hundred and did not bother for the change.

Mushtaq quietly walked along clutching the precious items in his right hand.

One hour later in his office, he almost tore open the small green packet. It contained a few letters, some instructions and three photographs. He glanced at the photographs first, reading the captions inserted in the rear. He smiled; the proof of tainted men in a group of armed terrorists was at last in his hands. But goons will claim abduction, if this evidence is produced and get away clean like all other money-minting traitorous scum. It would be interesting to obtain a data on politicians convicted in last fifty years on charges of treason. Surely none. Indian political entity was above board at least statistically. Then he read through each letter, each word and his throat quickly parched on the information provided. Falcon was too good to be true. He had appeared five years earlier out of the blue. Work done by him had been most instrumental, in nabbing the elite of the elites, helping Indian efforts, to stop this Pakistan-sponsored madness. Today's bonanza would require only the highest sanction of the country. Before that he must keep the old man at his HQ, adequately occupied. The basic information was more political in development, but one or two had a shred of contact-intelligence, which could be worked upon.

Old Air Port, Srinagar
(2130h, 16 Jul)

His eyelids opened.

A naked electric bulb, perched on high ceiling, stared down on him.

Today was somehow different.

He felt odd.

Yes, there were no tears in his eyes.

His metamorphosis into a normal human being was complete. *Jihadi* ideology looked like a very distorted past, an association he could not fathom why it had been part of his life, in the first place. The Major had been kind, in fact too kind, for men of violence like him. The Major was a very good man. He had saved him from certain butchery. He was vacantly staring across the bars of his cell, when his vision was filled of his saviour.

"How are you feeling today, my son?" his earlier tormentor inquired.

He scampered across the cell, poking his hands out of the opening of steel bars, kneeling down touching the Major's shining polished shoes he spoke in a melodious tune, "I am your servant, *Allah* has sent you to help me, for no sinner deserves what have you done for me. You are the *Khudda.*"

"Don't be so melodramatic," his saviour smiled as he spoke boring his eyes deeper into his subject now referred as terrorist-X in his being finalised case study for Military Intelligence School.

"You are giver of my maleness. I the sinner, thank you. You were bestowed on me to show the true light through *Allah,*" the supine man supplicated.

"In any case making you Sallaludin, the famous crusader was never in my mind. We want you to live in peace, like any good citizen," replied the Major.

"*Allah* knows that I am the most derogatory sinner. You are my saviour and please give me a chance to repent. Give me a chance to wash the feet of women I have despoiled. Please bring them to me or let me undertake a pilgrimage to their homes. Give me a chance to earn everyone's forgiveness," he spoke in sad monotone.

Major Akhilesh Srivastava quietly withdrew to the next room. He peeped through the one-way looking glass. The idiot was still murmuring, his brow resting on the floor, arms out, in total devotion.

The chap had lost his sanity.

Either it was too good a show to escape dungeons, or he was off his rocker. He firmly believed in the latter. The asshole's condition instead of bringing expectant kudos had him running around doing damage control. Thank God, that in little bouts of sanity and with his other two terrified conspirators, he had been able to get some actionable information. But this case had his acute professional curiosity aroused. He must quickly complete the detailed dissertation for a presentation to the School of Intelligence. He was sure, it would make a fantastic case study and earn him some brownie points in his otherwise dull carrier.

Back in the cell, Usman and Altaf saw their beloved leader clutch his penis in both hands and sing-songed, "Thank you Major, thank you father, thank you God, thank you *Allah* ..."

Both stared stupidly at each other.

Their tearful eyes did the talking.

Bn HQ, 14 RAJ RIF
(0930h, 20 Jul)

"How much faith you repose in me sir is upto you. I have a mission in life — to track and kill terrorists. Why, it's a long story. But what I have told you is the result of my two months plus of relentless efforts, mind you all alone – that too I have told you why. I can only trust the army on this and as the area was yours, here I am," said a frail looking man with sunken cheeks, but surprisingly bountiful energy.

Colonel PP Singh bored deep into the man's grey eyes.

He could not fathom any malice.

He studied the whole frame once again, objectively. He could not detect any abnormality associated with fear, apprehension or sliminess. He only could not digest the man's desire to work outside his organization. That was not loyalty, a trait he felt was essential for good work ethos. May be, his stated compulsions were many and being privy to few such anecdotes of local police, he could sympathise with this man.

He was burning in dilemma.

A dilemma twice, in the last three months.

He hated dilemmas.

He loved black and white cases.

They were clean, pure and uncomplicated. One did not have to exercise and allocate much of human reasoning to those. No energy-sapping thinking and no worrying. He had aged in seeing that handed-over terrorist come alive, even when the problem was not his and imported. But such delicate situations forced you to operate only in shades of greys.

He also hated greys.

To change with the ever-fluctuating events was beyond his mental mathematics. They hobnobbed from each colour and invaiably ended in red. Situations like these were never in control.

He also abhorred no control.

Army was run with total control, issues must be managed, always in control. Otherwise he could be in a happy civilian government department, floating always out of control. It looked bad, not in sync with his emotions.

Should he trust and act on this recluse policeman's story or not. Last bout of trust had brought white hairs in abundance. The man opposite looked unflappable, prepared for the consequences of his actions, again a trait he revered. He, on other hand, could not let someone down, someone who had placed so much faith in his organization.

Act he must.

There was something in this story, otherwise out of the blue, Patrol Blue Thunder wouldn't have been diverted that far East, much, much beyond his effective beat, that too on personal orders of the GOC of his Division. Intelligence summaries had stated concentration of terrorists on Pir Panjal, but these ranges were a mere hundred km long. Who will tell that to the boss's boss – not he, surely? But on this, he should cash on available information. As it is, he had no intelligence worth the name, at present.

He looked up and said, "I believe you. But there are also some connected issues, which we must be crystal clear on. They are my ground rules for people working for my battalion. First, no resolving personal enmity, no payment for information till the mission is successful, third, you will act in total consonance with the operational party commander," he said boring into the Inspector, trying to detect any disagreement. Picking up the phone he spoke, "Call Jesse immediately," and then again staring back at the man opposite, he added, "I will be introducing you to one of my officers. He will be in charge of the operation. Lucky for you, he is to operate in the same general area. Work out the mechanics with him and let me know the details."

Colonel PP Singh was now getting very irritated.

It has been more than thirty-six hours and Major Jesse had not made reappearance, despite two reminders. His Adjutant had informed him that the Inspector and Major Jesse had been closeted in his room, where continuous supply of liquor, snacks and food throughout the night, had prompted the exhausted mess staff to complain to the Second-in-Command. Both on consultation had let the matter rest. When Jesse sauntered in at noon on 21st July, he had a smirk smug look on his face.

"This Inspector is incredible, Sir. Not a dodo, but a Bohemian to the core. Devilish mind with acute sense of observation makes him a perfect intelligence operator," Jesse gushed, adding after a second's pause, "and he is a bit peeved at you, for the remuneration offered for the services to be rendered. It has wounded his nationalistic zeal, but don't fret sir, I have put adequate balm on his wounded soul."

Colonel PP Singh groaned inwardly.

Only if this chap across, would speak in simple English.

He bellowed, anger reflecting on his face, "I am not here to listen to inspector's qualifications as a social being. Tell me of any actionable information you may have gleamed after a day long orgy."

"An orgy sir? Wish Roman one could take place. The party was quiet innate. I was only loosening up the inspector a little bit.

That chap has some tanking capacity. He guzzles up liquor like a true policeman," gushed in Jesse.

"Information," half-screamed his boss, tapping irritably with his thin long fingers the massive Mahogany desk placed in front of him and observant Jesse instantly appreciated the divide between them due to it.

"Sir, there is too much to be told in one go, but here are certain salient aspects. Firstly, based on the information provided by a certain Sikh PCO owner, on his payroll, he followed a *bakarwal* who made calls to Thailand. Imagine Thailand. He then discovered that the *bakarwal* was organizing his yearly migration camp away from his original site, where he followed him and found him buying rations much in access of his family's requirement. He knows the general area and route on which he had travelled, but not the exact destination. Most probably it will lead us to a terrorist hideout. The *bakarwal* then led him to a doctor, who, he discovered, was a terrorist sympathiser. All indications point to a hideout being made," Major Jesse informed confidently and then added, "Lastly, he has now found that the doctor *sahib* is making regular purchases of medicines from Jammu to Udhampur, which he believes is being stocked for transportation later."

"Go slowly. Hope you have listed this raw information in sequence. If not, do it and leave a copy with me," said the Colonel now visibly more interested and nodding his head vigorously, as if he had been grasping these mundane minor details since the beginning. He also smiled to show appreciation.

Jesse was happily stumped.

"Sir, the plan is that after he leaves us at the exact site on the route, he falls back to tail the doctor and that *bakarwal*. We have tied up the communication part. The operation goes on as planned for relief of PK. It unbelievably fits into the relief organized perfectly. I may have to move about thirty km more eastwards on the old Pir Panjal Mughal route, to be in location, for which the Inspector will accompany," said Jesse.

"You want to hide on the route. I see. Not bad, hope you get that chap, but take care," Colonel reflected, "and also keep the unit informed of your movement plans and check out plans in detail, and also I will see the whole preparation-cum-briefing a day prior to your moving out," he spoke, burrowing in his files, implying instant dismissal of Jesse from the office.

Dal Lake
(1015h, 21 Jul)

On its first looks nothing looked great.

'Great Britannia', the houseboat was as old as the cliché, which had ceased to exist in its original meaning.

The frayed grandeur, chipped decks and faded paint stared back at you, painfully. It was a stark reminder of happier days it had seen and the present truth of sudden disappearance of its prosperous visitors was visible. Not made available even at ten thousand rupees per day, ten years back, now the proprietor was begging to sully her honour, for a meager two hundred rupees. The terrorism had gulped the tourists and his income. In the shallow gentle waves, the old British memorabilia creaked, a little too furiously. Notwithstanding her dilapidated looks, her two-room set still retained homely comfort. The cake was her surprisingly clean western toilet. She would have died without that, despite fulfilling her childhood dreams to lounge around in a boat. Moreover, as always, her journalistic instincts had proved her right. Local *jihadis* had flocked her from the lake route, in small skiffs, at odd hours at night. They preferred it, as unlike the roads that had massive security presence at each nook and corner, the lake's vast open expanse was a perfect cameo for terrorists to use.

Today, she was nervous and at the same time terribly excited.

She was two cigarette packets of Marlboro Lights down, in the last four hours. She was to meet one of the local leaders. Her anti-Indian credentials had been checked very thoroughly by local *tanzeems*, through ISI office in Muzaffarabad, who had given a green signal to allow her to propagate her biased coverage. She was sure, frantic work by ISI operators at their embassy at Colombo, who would have gone on a sudden overdrive, had clinched the deal. No wonder it had taken four days to reconfirm her meeting with terrorist leader after the initial contact. It was also a perfect backdrop, to develop further contacts in their organization, back home. Grover will surely be estatic on this development. All had been arranged by her endless nightly contacts and of course some *falus* had exchanged hands.

After *falus,* as always, came the terrorists.

She had seen their likes before.

Young fed on ideological crap, which defied any sanely explanation.

Young, full of life, ready to die for perceived cause.

Young, she had seen perish in her native country.

Young, who thought they alone, could conquer the world.

Young, who had no care and displayed nothing to lose attitude.

Young, who were entrapped in their own gloating.

Young, senseless, menace to themselves and society.

Young, who thought, any lonely women was a game – much to their dismay.

Young, who were foolish, boasted, overstated their capabilities to wage wars across the continents.

In the dead of the night, she heard unmistakable scraping against the houseboat's woodwork.

A few young had arrived.

Before she could stuff out her cigarette, an adolescent man made an eerie appearance and gestured her to follow. No words were exchanged or needed. She just followed. The subsequent boat ride was scary. Oars were being worked very deliberately and with marked silence. The man would row and observe, again row and observe. Tension was palpable and reflective in their actions. Suddenly, they docked amongst tall weed. A small wooden plank crazily zigzagging across the muddy slush, supported by single wooden beams, expertly hidden in grass, led her to a small street on land. They meandered into various by-lanes till they approached an illuminated crossing. All froze and lay observing the darkness beyond for any presence of security forces. When the leading guide was convinced of military void across, he quickly got up, keeping into the shadows, circumvented the crossing. She hurriedly followed suit. Before turning into another side alley, she could not help noticing a big board stating 'Zahir Silk Factory'. In the next couple of steps, she was roughly ushered inside, along with her five armed companions.

"Welcome to our poor abode, Madam," said a deep voice continuing, "We are terribly sorry for the inconvenience caused."

She quickly scanned around.

Taking stock, she found herself staring at a tall, white bearded man, with huge buffalo eyes. She smiled and clutched the man's hand. "I am here. These little problems are expected and nothing new in my line of work," she sweetly said. The place definitely did not look poor. Furnishings were of an acquired taste, of a well-to-do man. She could not see anything poor in *Maulana's* poor abode. Certainly plusher than her own apartment in Colombo, she reflected.

"From where would you like me to begin," *Maulana* whispered softly.

Surprised at his perfect English she replied, "From wherever you feel comfortable."

Taking the cue and adjusting his white *toosh* shawl on his shoulders, he first beckoned her closer to sit in a chair opposite and started, "The story is long, very long and in middle of it lies this evil Hindu country. It's a war and a world against Muslims. You scan your horizons across the face of the earth. Since centuries Jews are subjugating Palestinians. In Central Asia, Muslims subjected into disbelieving *Allah*, have found freedom. In Philippines, Muslim islands are being denied development, unlike their Christian counterparts. Here in the subcontinent, these infidels cleverly broke a Muslim nation and engineered a fight between two blood brothers."

"Who gained?" He thundered vigorously.

"Hindu India," he thundered more purposefully after a microsecond pause.

"In India, they destroy our mosques and expect Muslims to forgive. There too they ridicule our existence. Their pseudo secularism is for all to see. They want laws that are anti-Muslim. Their political corruption has not given anything to the only Muslim majority state in Hindu Union. We want to unite with our brothers in Pakistan. A Muslim will never let another Muslim down. Look in Kashmir, they soil our mosques, burnt the shrine of Charare Sharif, rape our women in thousands, kill innocent people in millions and you ask me to start from where I feel comfortable. I do not feel comfortable when Muslims are not allowed to offer *namaz* in mosques, when their traditions are being butchered and when they are being divided," *Maulana* said vehemently. He was breathing hard and efforts of the speech had sweat trickling down his forehead.

Ice broken and she accepted, she moulded into her act fast. Stream of questions, innocently poised between her anti-Indian position, about the fate of other Indian Muslims, their loyalty, better educational facilities, no discrimination in government services, unlike Pakistan, had *Maulana* shifting his uncomfortable pink ass. He could not answer what would happen to millions of other Muslims in India, if Kashmir broke in the name of religion.

Through endless tea cups and six hours later, she was sure that he was no trained *Maulvi*, but a perfect deep undercover mole. More probably, a high level ISI coordinator.

When she left this time by land route, with her now unarmed escorts, the sun was trying to make a desperate appearance through the early morning fog.

Murree, Pakistan
(2130h, 25 Jul)

"Brigadier, you may proceed with status of operation Gaznavi Tir," ordered General Lodhi loudly and at the same time patronizing others seated with a toothy smile.

Altaf stared back at the crammed table.

Numbers gave him courage.

All seats were taken and a few men were left standing.

It had become a ritual for the shit-head Lodhi, to descend almost fortnightly to personally oversee the panorama unfolding in front of him. He had seen the General's mood alternating between total dejection and unbridled euphoria, depending on the quality of the news. Somehow the General had survived a sure heart attack when the fiasco at *Khuni Nallah* had unfolded. His pride, happiness and will to live slowly rekindled, as news of each small success, started filtering in. Like all good seniors, the general was now labeling it as his plan. A vision he had acquired years back but being implemented only now. A plan he had nurtured since his heroic capture in Bangladesh. With each bout of boasting at the whiskey peg circuit in Islamabad, he increased his clout and demonstrated it by herding them all here at Murree. Good place anyway, away from the blistering heat of Islamabad. Gloating idiot, mused the brigadier.

Brigadier smiled.

His smile instantaneously captivated his audience.

There was a hushed silence when he broke into endless dialogue. Animated body swirls, hand gestures, video projections and facial contractions glued the listeners even more solidly onto their chairs. None wanted to waste a body-movement lest they miss anything trivial, sound so pleasing, or music so enchanting or words stimulating their souls, which was nothing but destruction of their arch rival, India. India should be destroyed, beaten, weakened, brought to its knees, by hook or crook. It was reason of their existence and enigma of Pakistanis security concern.

The drama continued for over thirty-five minutes non-stop.

"So to sum it up statistically, for twelve *jihadis* lost we have killed, six Indian officers, thirty-six men, destroyed ten vehicles and injured thrice as many. A small price, gentlemen to defeat India, no, in fact, an insignificant price, if I may add. So my ardent request to you all is to see how few motivated men, can bring down a lumbering elephant. Please support the cause. Any laxity on our part will make us miss this wonderful opportunity provided by India, to bring about its own downfall. Thank You, I have finished, sir," and he sat down flushed.

All got up, thumping the tables in front.

It was his pristine hour of glory and surely many more in his pocket as future investments, if he kept finding people like Gul and idiots like Lodhi to serve under.

They had their Messiah.

Surankot
(1315h, 28 Jul)

An old frail looking man maintaining a perfect kyphotic stance was lumbering across the street, aided by an equally ancient rosewood walking stick.

At each step his body trembled in mechanical jerks, egging his tottering bent-body to move on. His long white beard, vacillated like a perfect pendulum. After a few steps, he would stop, to wipe his dripping nose, with the cuff of white stained *kurta*. The comic had been pestering the entire sundry at this dispensary to admit him. His tales of problems, perceived illnesses had irritated the senior resident doctor. Doctor Mehboob had also been asked for a referral opinion, despite him being on leave, in the station. Both the doctors had agreed after several tests that he was suffering from a paranoid syndrome. It generally happened to old people. They craved for attention, when denied by loved ones. Despite politely shooing him off, that idiot would still come back. He had given dozen of calcium tablets and numerous coloured multivitamins to just get that old faggot off his back. But may be, that abandoned recluse found too much love here, so he always came back. He had staked a permanent corner, outside his small dispensary. Every time he looked out, he saw the pathetic old man, his fragile body swaying with the wind. For last couple of days, he had become an inescapable entity of this small medical community.

Mehboob was relishing the first arrivals of *dusheri* mangoes, in his two room government flat, when he heard the bell ringing. It rang with persistent irritation. Cursing he stopped, never wanting to end this lovable action of squeezing and sucking the sweet honey-like pulp. Washing his hands, he opened the door.

Reshab was pacing up and down in the small verandah. He looked at Mehboob accusingly and said, "You can't keep me waiting in front of everyone. Brush up your reactions."

"I am sorry. I was having mangoes," the doctor replied.

"What, sucking on mangoes, when a war is on. If we lose this war what will you say? I was sucking the *madarchod* mangoes. It's disgusting. By the way, have you collected everything," he angrily hissed.

"Yes, a week back and stop shouting at me. You are the one who is late. I only know, how I have made all these purchases alone. There was so much checking and indescribable tension. My boss is hopping mad for not joining the dispensary, while I am farting in this house, guarding the medicines. I can trust nobody. I even fired my servants, so they could not pry," angel thundered back.

"I know the problems you are facing. You think I have been getting my ass humped in the jungles. All rations had to be moved up, including arms and ammunition. Only your load is left. I will start and work tonight. I have got a government truck with papers to deliver food to government godowns. Will use it to transport medicines and then use my mule chain," Reshab said.

They went into a huddled discussion, focusing on the quantity of stores to be moved from different locations. Reshab was astounded when he learnt all two tonnes worth of medicines were hidden around this house. Good, at least, it eased his transportation problems a bit.

Muffled tap on the door may have been happening for some time. It was Reshab who noticed it first. Both stared at each other. In a silent gesture Reshab inquired if Mehboob was expecting someone. Mehboob shook his head in negative. Reshab quickly took out his pistol and cocking it went to open the door.

The door creaked, half ajar. Reshab peeped out and saw an old man shifting on his feet, staring expectantly.

"Doctor *sahib,*" he croaked.

Mehboob appeared on the scene, already feeling nervous at the sight of half-hidden pistol, and on seeing the old man, he groaned.

"*Baba,* what do you want now," he asked impatiently.

"I am not well, please admit me in the hospital," the old man faintly whispered.

"Nothing is wrong with you, shoo off. Go away. Go to your home. You cannot be admitted and stop wasting my time," Mehboob said irritably.

"Doctor *sahib,* you are my *khudda.* Please listen to my *fariad.* I am dying, please admit me in the hospital," the old man again lamented.

"Fuck off, you old cow. Can't you hear me," screamed Mehboob, shutting the door on the old man's face. The next minute he spent explaining the situation to Reshab. Reshab after sometime again peeped out of the side window. The idiotic old man was now sitting on the stairs leading to the verandah. The accumulated tension swept the dam of patience, a personal virtue not bestowed in plenty.

He rushed out, losing his cool and shouting "*kutta, kamina, phut, bhag.*" He kicked the old man to his feet.

With every shower of expletive and each slap or kick, whatever came his way first, the old man retreated out of the house compound. In all the fury directed towards him, the old man's eyes never wavered.

They were rock-still.

Not that excited Reshab noticed.

LAYOUT OF TERRORIST CAMP

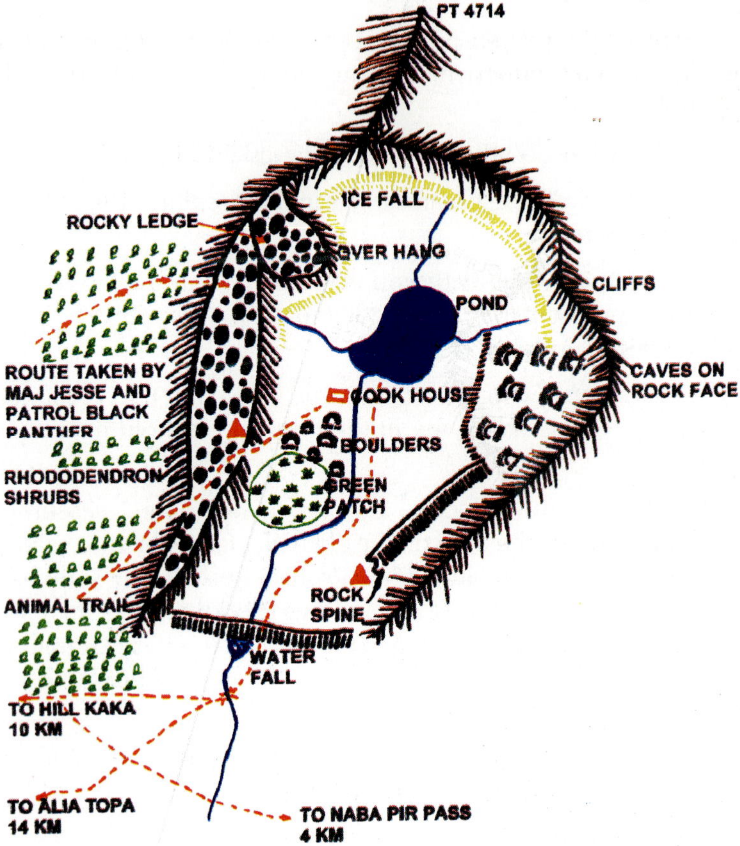

LEGEND

SENTRY POST: ▲

CLIFFS / VERTICAL ROCK FACE: ||||||||||||

Map not to scale

11
Crimson Red Blood

They gently flow in with the wind.
Happiness, eases in slowly.
Love, at even more sullied pace.
Surety is only in one swiftness.
The gallop of death.

— Jesse

Patrol Black Panther,
Alia Topa
(1630h, 01 Aug)

His nose had been two inches above the mother earth for last forty-eight hours.

He had never realized that the rustic smell of gravel was so invigorating. He had never realized that the soil could smell wonderfully, in so many different ways. He would have never contemplated the earthly difference in odour, in the morning, or evening, with or without grass cover, of tree sodden humus, dry rocky earth or wet mud, each so distinct, yet so intoxicating, like a goblet of rare wine, being presented by nature, at each step. Hugged to the earth's surface, Jesse reflected that given a few more opportunities, he would be able to decipher the secret language of crickets, ants, spiders, birds, etc. It was enchanting and equally fascinating.

"Stop," he ridiculed himself. It was no time to be a nature-lover or muse like Shakespeare. He had very serious work to do.

Hiding his party in this small thicket, atop this rugged mountain had been a task in itself, specially, when they had been hiding for the last four days. Soldiers were beginning to protest and his 2IC had also mumbled in a complaint. He had stoically charmed them into silence.

Seven days earlier, they had debussed in the middle of the night, at Samkot Town of Bajliaz area. Two days of forced march by night, Major Jesse had contacted PK's party and had rendezvoused, just short of Marat village. PK had been ecstatic. To welcome his party, he had raked up a decent meal magically from their depleted resources. Later, PK was in total confusion, seeing six civilians in his own party of twenty-four.

"Who are they, sir?" He had inquired.

"My luggage train. We all have chipped in, to hire help and help ourselves, when our organization refuses to help us," retorted Major Jesse.

"Bloody hell. *Hum to chutia nikle, sir. Peeth tut gayee, saman uthate,"*(We were cunts. Our backs broke lifting the loads) complained PK.

Major Jesse had a vigorous laugh.

"But sir, won't your operation be compromised," he inquired seriously.

"PK, my chap, do you think I am infiltrating into Pakistan, to do this operation. I am in India my friend. Merge with locals, look like locals, move during day or night, behave like locals. I will be damned if I move by night and observe by day. I will move, when I want to move or feel the situation is right to move. Haven't I moved in the last two nights, when I had to. Wake up. Use your grey matter more adroitly," Jesse patted PK teasingly.

"I should have blindly followed your law on comfort, it being inversely proportional to one's motivation and directly proportional to the hard working idiots like us around," he had ruefully replied.

"Who told to neglect the sayings of a military sage? Do so at your peril," he had guffawed.

That had been a week ago.

He had not felt the inclination to move, as his inspector had warned him, not to move from this very spot, till he contacted him, but patience was a virtue which came to very few. Luckily he had it in abundance.

His buttocks and his cute paunch, had gained an inch, waiting since last week, working on sumptuous food prepared by his civilian staff.

Weight, and more body weight, another bugbear of his life.

But this is how the Mughal Army used to move, he mused. Less the dancing nautch girls and an extended harem, he felt so very comfortable.

At present, he felt a shade less than a Mughal King himself, maybe for the absence of the nautch girls.

Allah's Rock (0700h, 02 Aug)

Roaring shouts of "one, two, one, two" irritably woke him up, from his nonchalant slumber.

He peered out of the quilt.

It was still icy cold.

He snuggled more close to and pressed harder against Nurie for warmth. Abusing her firm breasts as a soft pillow, he talked inwardly.

This was life.

A woman, a weapon, a camp, an army and an enemy.

What more can one wish for from the all-merciful *Allah.*

He had been an idiot, depriving himself from such natural pleasures of life. In the name of *Allah,* his youth had been squandered, living a life of a pure zealot. May be that was what *Allah* had desired of him at that precise moment. To be just that selfless, to have that determination and to exist in that exact form, to defeat the communist infidels. It was *Allah's* way of being pleased with him. But wasn't he doing the same now, despite living with Nurie. At least he enjoyed his work now. Was he, soiling *Allah* or watering down his convictions, now? No, I don't think so. Even the great true Mohammad was happily married. He had waged wars for *Allah.* He sure loved his wife. Why can't I love Nurie and still wage a successful war against the Hindu infidels.

Abruptly, a draft of cold air hit him like a whiplash.

He turned back to protest. Nurie had scampered out of bed and teasingly said, "Get up my king. The sun is about to set. Birds have started flying home. Get out and fight your enemy. I have a very small task, preparing food, befitting my Lord."

He hated un-clutching his Nurie.

But the woman was right. He had more important work to do than just hug her. She was clouding his desire for what he had been born for, *jihad.* But shockingly he did not protest this impasse with his beliefs. He, of late; had started liking it more than his cause. Was this the evil *Allah* had advocated, falling to the bewitchery of a woman?

When he emerged out of his cavern 20 minutes later, properly fed and adequately clothed, the toughening up routine of *jihadis,* under an iron fist discipline of captain, was almost one hour into start. All *jihadis* were panting, puffing, cribbing and moving around like raped whores.

Seeing him, someone from the crowd of 146 leered. "*Emir sahib,* exercise in the open with us also sometimes. We know your bed is very comfortable." All others laughed clutching their bellies.

Wrath whipped his wisdom for a second. He was routed to the spot in frustration. Red faced, he started trotting after them. Ten minutes into it, he himself, was moving like a raped virgin.

Captain seeing the situation, intervened, calling the physical training off and requested Gul for an operational meeting. Gul readily obliged.

Sitting on a stone ledge, Captain Ahmad said, "You will have to bear such remarks. I had told you, no woman."

"I will kill that man with my bare hands," fumed a very agitated Gul.

"No use aggravating the situation. I will handle it. Just forget it and let us plan some impending operations," said the Captain.

"OK, what are they," Gul asked.

The discussion went into huddle mode, "So, what should the target be, Police, BSF or the Army," asked the Pakistani officer, later.

"Why Police, as it is most of them are with us. Other security organizations have been adequately terrorized. Destroy the Indian Army. If it breaks, everything else breaks," reasoned Gul.

"My sentiments exactly," remarked Ahmad.

Gul's eye fell distantly on Reshab, sitting and warming his hands on the makeshift kitchen fire. He hailed for him. They hugged on meeting.

"When did you come in?" Gul inquired.

"Yesterday night. All stores are in, except one load of medicines and your precious doctor. Though medicines have moved to a makeshift house next to a road, it will take a few days to shift the stores here. I only came ahead to organize the mule train and dump more rations," he replied.

"Then don't waste your valuable time sitting on your dirty asshole here. Collect the list of latest requirements from *Kaptan sahib* and come back quick. Because of you, we are already late, by two weeks," Gul accused.

Reshab did not like the accusation and let a frown show his displeasure, not that he had any more guts to shout back, that too, at Gul. And now if he moved fast, it would take him little over two days to meet the doctor guarding his medicines at the base of his village Nusur.

But he was sure of one very basic thing, the camp ran, if he ran.

Patrol Black Panther,
Alia Topa
(1630h, 08 Aug)

Dark brown, chestnut colour *Hangul* had been feeding on the green grass, at the base of the spring, with his other three mates, two hundred metres away. Though his pedigreed ancestors came from the great Zanskar Mountain Ranges, he, the lesser genetic mortal lived avidly in the heights of Pir Panjal.

Jesse, from his hideout in the bushes, had been tracking his prey through the telescope of a 7.62 sniper rifle for the past two hours, with thoughts of its sumptuous mutton already gladdening his Mughal civilian retainers. He knew it was an endangered specie. But the legendry taste of its venison as urged by his cook, had thrown caution to winds. His Second-in-Command also did not approve of his lunatic act and no wonder he was still in a moral quandary, to slay or not to slay, two hours later.

Before he could gather courage, to press the trigger for a clear headshot, a similarly coloured predator, the Himalayan Snow Leopard, broke the ground from broken rocks to the East and in a silence of a second, snapped the poor *Hangul's* neck, dead. Growling excitedly, with blood and saliva dripping from his mouth, he dragged his dead prey, a mere 20 yards and sat to devour his meal. Other *Hanguls* just scampered another 50 metres away and again got busy munching their lively green sprouting grass nervously, lucky to be alive.

Jesse put down his weapon in admiration.

A true vicious act of nature and he the fated audience. That beast required the real meat, more desperately than himself. It was his inescapable bread. He could live without it and better make do with his *alu* and *pyaz sabji* for now.

That Inspector Pathania was overdue for more than five days. It was a marvel that his team of 24 soldiers excluding civilians and one terrorist prisoner had not been detected till date, despite the movement of locals. They were getting quiet restless, in fact anyone will, cooped in a small bushy hole. Not that all abhorred it. That slothful Limbu Ram, one of his brainless riflemen, had been sleeping non-stop for the last ten days. The idiot only got up to eat to heart's content and shit, and complain to go on his turn of duty. Even that evil *Ravana's* brother would be insanely jealous of him. Wish he had that such vigour to just lounge around and sleep so compellingly. Bored and in sheer frustration, he put his rifle up and peered through the telescope to scan the countryside. Little later, he focused on a *bakarwal* slowly making his way up the beaten mud path, goading two frail goats in front of him, with the help of a willow stick.

He smiled as he saw a red cap supporting a very thin man in black dress.

He had his man but more importantly he had his mutton.

Allah's Rock (2245h, 08 Aug)

The magnitude of the camp had captivated him.

He had been in this business for the last seven years and he had yet to come to a camp so well organized and being run with the sole aim of demolishing anything Indian. Sentries alert, in pairs, as per the duty roster. Qualified instructors for physical training and imparting all aspects of war. A smart young nameless man he had met earlier, but now referred as *Kaptan sahib* covered tactical aspects. He taught well, displayed an acute sense of enemy reaction to a particular action. Basic weapon handling, making bombs, creating booby traps was left to his muscular loonies. But it was Gul who always held the centrestage. In rhetoric, passion and sheer *jihadi* propaganda, none could match Gul. He was the indoctrinator. All listened to him in agape fascination. He could give the famous Indian politician 'Lalu ji' from Bihar the run for money. Good food churned out from a proper cookhouse. A medical room to boot but without a doctor and medicines though. General talk had indicated that he too would be reporting soon. A proper ammunition dump, minimum 18 mule loads had been dumped. Arsenal adequate for a conventional battalion attack. A like of a *Jehadi* camp he had never spied before.

He was impressed and so were the 15 men of his organization.

The only problem facing him was, when, where and in what manner his men would be employed. What should he do? The timing of the mission and enormity of what he had undertaken racked Rasool Bhat's weary mind, throughout the night. Kashmir was at stake.

His men were quartered inside one nook of a half open cave. Thankfully his smarter Second-in-Command, on reaching the camp site had reconnoitered the living accommodation first and had stoically plonked himself in a place, which could only house his 15 men. It was nice to be together and alone. One could discuss many issues without raising any suspicion and they had discussed in detail numerous contingencies. They were all unanimous to a decision, to watch and wait and in no way compromise their advantage in the camp.

With nothing better to do and take his mind off the complex situation confronting him, he switched on a small Phillips radio, a dear gift from a dear friend. At least he will listen to a few melodious Hindi songs and make someone slog at night.

Patrol Black Panther (0900h, 09 Aug)

"And no dogs. For God's sake kill them. They always compromise your move and ambush. Last man will carry a silencer carbine. Shoot to eliminate and I will skin anyone who dithers on this," he instructed his party again. Menaka Gandhi, the Animal activist Madam could shriek due to this indignity towards her favourite animals for all he cared. Too many Indians were dying in more squalid conditions to ever find time for displaying psuedo-love for the animals.

Either the dog died or he died.

He would rather prefer the dead dog.

He then moved around in circles within the confines of the shrubs, to think of any more instructions he may have missed. His agitated walk displayed hidden tension immediately picked by observant policeman.

"Keep little more patience, Major *sahib*. In an hour or so the head of the column will be visible," said Inspector Pathania and little later further added, "Smart chap that *bakarwal* organizer. Last time he had moved up via Samhot route. I farted for two days there, before I realized something was amiss. Thank God, I went back to Thanamandi and picked up their scent. The general melee of unloading and loading their stuff gave me an adequate headstart. Had I missed the boat I am sure you would have slit my throat."

"Yes absolutely," replied Jessie. "But why didn't you contact us on radio as discussed," he again inquired.

"You will now definitely kill me. I accidentally sat on your radio set and it became as flat as a *chappati* when I was musing over where to head. I am sure you will excuse this small fault of mine," the inspector sheepishly said.

Jesse groaned. It was not the loss of it he feared, but stacks of paperwork he was sure to do alone, to regularize the loss. "Could you pick up that famous doctor of yours," he further asked.

"Yes, yes. Doctor *sahib* is in great mood. He is singing, swinging and with that big rucksack on his back, it seems he is planning on going for an extended picnic, straight to the gates of *zannat*," said Pathania and laughed at the thought.

Jesse turned back, to brief his stalking group, minimum sixth time in the last 12 hours. All soldiers looked very somber. Tension was emanating abundantly from their sweating faces. Only non-committal face was that of Risal, his recently freed prisoner. About him, PK had filled him with certain details. He thanked his intuition to work on him for the last two weeks or so, when they were in hiding. The Pakistan-trained *jihadi* border-crossing guide slowly had opened up and had broken down only three days back narrating the treacherous tale of his cousin brother and his once-loved wife. His instantaneous hug and sharing the burden of Risal's grief had broken the deadlock of low trust, not before he also had cooked up lamenting tale of his ditching chain-smoking beloved. An attractive manipulating woman who manipulated a millionaire now. It was the tale that bonded.

They had to wait for another agonizing six hours when the terrorist administrative mule train was first sighted.

Dugrian
(0930h, 09 Aug)

They had decamped and made the start before the first ray hit the peaks above him. His clan's four little urchins had done a remarkable job. Including him, four mules to a person, 20 mules had been fed, harnessed and cajoled into moving, in time, was indeed a feat in itself. He had to make up for the loss of 24 hours, of initial confusion and esteemed angel's physical inability to cope up with prolonged rigors. He should have been here yesterday. The doctor had slowed them to a point where he was forced to halt at base and on the banks of Parnai River. Imagine a halt after only six hours of walk. The situation was ridiculous and he helpless. On marches, one camps just below the higher crest line or passes, lest they have to trudge upslope early in the morning when your body is not warm. It's disheartening even for animals. Then how can humans be any different? But who will say this to the learned doctor *sahib*, thought Reshab.

Badami Bagh, Srinagar
(1200h, 09 Aug)

They had been picking them up since last two days.

The ingenuity of fixing an emitter signal in Phillips radio had worked.

All monitoring stations of 56 Direction Finding Unit had listened to them in various decibel levels of signal strength. By normal standards a bit faint, not regular in emitting, but adequate in time lag to generate a precise fix. A similar sister unit stationed South of Pir Panjal ranges had been tasked on specific request from the valley.

Both monitoring units had reached the same conclusion.

The beeps were being emitted from around Point 4712, South of Naba Pir pass on Pir Panjal ranges. With fixed accuracy of 300 metres, they had an approximate area of one square km to home down too.

Colonel Mushtaq again studied the map. So now he had his camp. Now what? Attack or a raid was a good option but time permitting. To induct troops even by helicopters to that desolate corner of Pir Panjal ranges would take three to four days, not an acceptable time frame, especially with the ulcer causing information available to him. It was already 10th August. Something very sinister was to happen before the Independence Day. But what? Wish he knew more. He knew this much that it was hovered around that bleep. Thanks to Srivastava, and those two helpful police girls that raving mad lunatic terrorist that something tangible had emerged. But still the intelligence was hazy in content and more importantly, not ripe in time, to act decisively in Srinagar.

He was only sure of one thing. If those bleeps disappeared or moved, all would be lost.

He picked up the phone and dialed the office number of the Corps Commander. He requested for an immediate audience.

Alia Topa
(1530h, 09 Aug)

Something to observe at last, his now less-tensed mind reflected.

From a little rat hole they had been hiding, Jesse and Pathania watched the slow progress of the mule train. At the fag end of the day, the mules seemed oblivious to the goading and sometimes brutal egging administered by stout bamboo sticks in the hands of their young masters. Sighting water, they lingered hurriedly over to the stream, where a day earlier, *Hanguls* had danced and died. They drank water in huge gulps, braying excitedly. Then they gorged on the lush green grass. Few kicked in air trying to dislodge the misery of loads, strapped to their backs.

Reshab looked around. The place was a natural haven. Good grass and fresh water for animals to feed on throughout the night. Though it was a bit early, but he must camp here and wait for the doctor to show up. He had instructed the doctor not to leave this prominent trail, three hours back, as he had surged forward to catch up with his young cohorts. In their excitement, they would have driven the mules dead throughout the night. Wisdom would dawn on them how to take best and maximum from an animal, as they would gain experience over the years.

"We will camp here tonight," said Reshab assertively.

Mules brayed in unison, in total appreciation. All the urchins immediately ran over to unload their baggage.

It was another five hours into the day, when the tired bedraggled doctor trudged into the camp, shouting profanities.

"You bunch of morons, you all left me alone. I could have got lost. There are dangerous animals around. I could have died alone of sheer exhaustion. Gul will definitely not like it. Now open that box. I have to treat my feet. They are full of blisters and a few of them have burst..." he kept on whining.

One small boy handed over a mug of salted tea, along with some baked bread. Forgetting everything, the doctor ate in acute hunger reflected avidly by his gobbling-up process.

Reshab strode in and said, "Doctor *sahib*, Gul may cry on your death, but he will surely kill us all if these precious items do not reach on time. Stop whining like a little puppy. *Jihad* is not easy to wage. Difficulties are many and you cry over blisters. Have your food and rest. We leave again early in the morning."

Two hundred metres up, Reshab instantly recognized, his half-brother's voice midst the cacophony of other noises. He had physically recognized him when he had sauntered in with the last of the mules. He had been in vile agony since. Now again hearing his tone his hands clutched in absolute frustration. He could participate in a willful murder, in the next one second. Jesse anticipating the response, held Risal's hand, patting them slowly, "Wait, wait, have tolerance, you will get your retribution, keep faith in divinity, and above all me," he slowly murmured.

"No," pierced a shout through the still of the night. "I will not leave at daybreak. You go if you have to. I can't walk or you give me a mule to ride on," an echo screamed out of the black obscurity.

"Ok, I will carry your rucksack but I cannot give you a mule for your comfort. You can start late. The camp is only four to five hours walk from here. Do not leave the track. After about two hours the jungle will suddenly disappear. There the two tracks bifurcate. Take one going to left, over a black face of the mountain. You will surely meet someone two hours up. Now keep quiet and sleep," shouted back Risal walking off.

Before the daybreak, Reshab moved out as promised.

Six men, including Jesse and Risal slinked out, few minutes behind them.

It was much beyond the routine throes of the morning, when sudden colic cramps, induced Dr Mehboob Shah, MBBS, to limp behind a nearest bush for ablutions. The pleasing relieving sensation suddenly disappeared, when five uniformed Indian Army soldiers got up from the neighbouring thicket, pointing their guns, menacingly at him.

Fighter Base, Awantipur (0800h, 10 Aug)

The request was quiet queer.

At least to him it seemed so. It was too explosive in intent that at first glance he had the right to shout back, "Drop dead pal." However on better sense, he routed the Army's requirement to his Western Air Command at New Delhi.

Wing Commander PV Rao was incredulously stunned on being instructed by a return signal message within two hours of the requests dispatch.

OPERATION HUNTER (.) MISSION GREEN (.) STATUS GO (.) COORDINATE DETAILS WITH 15 CORPS (.) KEEP HQ WESTERN AIR COMMAND INFORMED AT SIX HOUR INTERVALS (.)

Now no wonder, the Pongo Air Surveillance Unit, co-located at his base had their unmanned probes flying for the last one day.

He felt like an out-of-information loop idiot.

Patrol Black Panther, Tiger's Party (1600h, 10 Aug)

Skinned knees and bleeding elbows left an impressionable trail on the vertical rock face, which Major Jesse was negotiating since the better part of the day. It was pure harakiri without specialized mountain climbing gear, he reasoned. But time did not consent to indulge in such niceties of life. More he saw Risal operate, more he admired the man's skills. He could beat anyone in his unit in basic field craft. Without him, they could not have shadowed the mule train and without him they could not have found their way up the slope, hidden from the progress of the muleteers just below and beyond his patrols 'fart-jet-stream-feel-distance'.

As he heaved himself on to a big rock, Risal urgently gestured him down. Major Jesse quickly crawled towards Risal, who was peering at a small hollow below. He caught the sight of mules lingering. From four hundred feet above, they looked like small dogs, on an animated stroll. Feverish activity of few men below caught his attention and imagination, as he desperately grappled to focus his binoculars.

It hit him a few seconds later.

Sister-fucking holy cow! My God, beholding Krishna, he was sitting on top of a terrorist camp. It shook his military sanity.

Suddenly he felt extremely lonely and vulnerable, atop this chilling cold ridge.

Some seconds later, after regaining his composure, he again peered down the slope and through his binoculars he studied each nook and corner in detail. From the entry point, its sentry, the training area, the cookhouse, the thunder box location and unending maze of caves, each distinctive detail registered in his microcomputer of the brain. Dragging Risal back, after about 15 minutes, behind the rock, he took out his notebook and started drawing lines across it. He had almost finished when a distant thunderclap distracted his attention. He looked up due South, a red streak of lightening tore through the sky striking somewhere on the Kalidhar mountain ranges. Dark clouds beyond them looked even more ominous, than the terrorists below.

There was also this faint mechanical whir he had been hearing since yesterday evening, but he could not place his finger upon. He had far more worrying things at hand than to fret about some vague distant noise.

Fighter Base, Awantipur (1630h, 10 Aug)

He had it on his visual.

Eureka!

They had done it.

It was that terrorist camp which his unmanned drones had been searching for the last one day. The intercepted location fix was more than a km off. It was nestled amongst a break in two massive ridges. No wonder it had made them look like novices in their earlier endeavours.

A first operational success, promptly logged in his unit war diary.

Colonel Vikram Singh quickly walked over to his Air Force counterpart to give him the good news.

Patrol Black Panther/Patrol Base (2000h, 10 Aug)

They had scampered to the patrol base, half an hour back. The whole patrol was huddled around Major Jesse. Other men of Tiger's party who were in the earlier foray were whispering excitedly. Even Limbu Ram for a change was not sleeping and listening to the general gossip with his ears flaring up like a baby elephant. A small campfire hidden from immediate surroundings, by making an improvised shrub wall, emanated adequate light and warmth. Since his taking the seat near the warmest nook, Jesse had not spoken. He hid his nervousness-cum-fear by involuntary fiddling the red-hot wooden embers in front. Being a leader, he could not allow it to reflect in his body language. It would be a sacrilege. If he did so, the operation would be a non-starter from the beginning.

Angst and fear was his baby alone to reason and surmount.

Stark reality of the situation had snapped his earlier childlike fascination of seeing a terrorist or a soldier's professional dream of bursting their hideout. But by swift estimates he had counted more than 120 terrorists at the camp. Thank God, none of his men had seen them. Otherwise, they would have been very, very reluctant to even move from this base, leave alone going back to kill them.

What could he do with his 24 soldiers?

With surprise totally factored in, any stratagem thrown in, he could take on equal, twice, and at best, thrice the terrorist numbers, but anything beyond seemed militarily suicidal. In any case surprise was as stupefying as the first shot and only lasted till the next millisecond. God also would not be able to help him or his unit. They were too far out and waiting for a general build-up will give the game away. But such opportunities came rarely in one's lifetime. He also could not seek solace in his one-liner laws. Surprise was inversely proportional to your desire to seek contact. Don't go, retain ample surprise, go and screw with it. The thought was not very refreshing.

It was now or never.

Again the faint rumblings of clouds far away kicked him into activity. The weather was most likely to deteriorate further in the next 24 hours. He could use this to his advantage, but shivering cold and damp clothes would impede his move. He must act fast. He summoned Subedar Lekh Ram, his Second-in-Command, and spoke decisively, "*Sahib*, we will strike at the terrorist camp tomorrow."

Everyone looked up expectantly. The earlier childlike gibberish excitement vanished. There was curious concern on their faces.

"Plan, is like this. We will form four basic parties. One led by me, consisting of six soldiers and Risal, second party of six men with LMG and Rocket Launcher detachment will be headed by you *sahib*, the third party will consist of eight men under Havaldar Ram Prakash, with 51 inch Mortar and LMG detachment and fourth will be headed by Inspector Pathania, with four men with him and other civilians," he said and then added, "Now look at the deployment on the map."

All inched closer to see minor details, on a tiny makeshift map.

Limbu Ram almost snatched major's diary as if his life depended upon it. Havaldar Ram Prakash nudged him back, taking Limbu's anxious neck-protruding place. Limbu gave a rueful look back. He had to be in the midst of an all-important briefing. His ex-serviceman father had told him, one of the basic principles to rise high amongst ranks was to look interested at all times, specially at important times. This was a very critical time and dare this Havaldar take his strategic briefing position and before he could protest loudly, loud voice of *sahibs'* brought stillness to his shifting ass.

"I will lead the party to the Rock Ledge. Havaldar Ram Prakash's party will take position, at the place where my party hits the ledge. Your party will guard that terrorist doctor also. Then my party will move south and silence the sentry on the animal trail. Subedar *sahib's* party, will move north and occupy overhang. Order of march, myself in lead, followed by Ram Prakash and Subedar Lekh Ram. Pathania, you will fetch the rearguard and will hold the meadow one hour up and prepare it for helicopter landing. If the operation is aborted then we all will marry up with you at that meadow. Now Sunil, pass this coded message to battalion headquarters immediately. Now we will discuss specific tasks, equipment and contingencies ..." instructed Major Jesse, carrying on till the better half of the night.

It was at 2350 hours when Jesse said, "OK, all can rest now. We leave at 0330 hours." He scanned around expecting any queries.

There were none.

Pin drop silence was punctured by musical snores of inert Limbu Ram. Snores had a typical tenor of a flute, interrupted constantly. Too tired to check or even protest Jesse turned back. Exhausted, he slumped into his mattress, stone dead.

Few yards away, trussed like an animal destined for the slaughterhouse, Angel overheard that he too will be visiting Gul, but under changed circumstances, along with someone called Ram Prakash.

He instantly did not like the idea.

He wetted his pants to show his absolute disapproval.

Pir Panjal Ranges, 14 Raj Rif Bn HQ (0345h, 11 Aug)

It broke his blissful sleep.

Irritating, persistent knocks at his door woke him up in abrupt rudeness. It took him some time to realize that he was snugly cuddled in his warm sleeping bag. The knocking had an urgency associated with unpleasantness. Flutter of worry hit his brow. Quickly putting on his woollen light brown nightgown, he opened the door. He saw his adjutant, in the dim light, shivering in the cold. He saluted at the movement of the door and said, "Sorry to wake you up at this hour sir, but an important message has come in from Patrol Black Panther."

Before adjutant could utter anything further, he cut him off asking, "Hope everything is OK."

"Yes, sir, all is fine till now, but they want urgent assistance. The message will make it clear. I have also informed the Brigade Major, tentatively," he said, handing over the accusing piece of paper.

Colonel PP Singh took the paper tenderly in his hands and put on his Gandhian spectacles, to read. Each line made his heart beat faster. His testosterone levels reduced dramatically.

PATROL BLACK PANTHER STOP TERRORIST CAMP SIGHTED AT GRID REFERENCE 562279 STOP RECONNAISSANCE COMPLETED STOP OVER HUNDRED TERRORISTS SIGHTED STOP PLAN TO STRIKE THE CAMP BY 1000 HOURS ELEVENTH STOP TEMPORARY HELIPAD AT GRID REFERENCE 555270 AVAILABLE FOR LANDING STOP REQUEST HELICOPTER REINFORCEMENT BY MINIMUM THIRTY TROOPS STOP ADDITIONAL AMMUNITION BE ARRANGED STOP IDENTIFICATION OF FRIEND OR FOE AT HELIPAD COMMA

SMOKE ON WEST FOLLOWED BY RED OVER RED FLARE STOP REINFORCEMENTS NOT BEFORE 1030 HOURS STOP.

As he comprehended the full message, he snatched the phone and passed a flurry of instructions, to wake up his bosses. His signalers too were desperately trying to raise leader of Patrol Black Panther, for last so many minutes. He banged down the phone in frustration, as he got the patent reply, "*Sahib*, Patrol Black Panther is not responding."

He did not know that Major Jesse and his patrol were already trudging up the dark steep slopes, in complete radio silence.

Allah's Rock (0530h, 11 Aug)

Nurie was a wonderful girl, reflected Reshab, as he sat by the makeshift fire in the cookhouse, sipping tea made by her. She could make anyone proud. Spirited girl that she was. She had even nudged Gul, as he was lambasting her uncle, over the episode of missing doctor. Loyal and faithful, what more could one ask for in a woman. Unlike her useless sister, who was no good to her clan? Why waste money on education and, that too, on a woman. But his uncle, to whom they all owed everything, was adamant in wasting his precious money. For the same sum, they could have brought over hundred goats and what had she given in return, big nothing. Imagine learning useless satanic teachings. Here Nurie seemed happy with Gul and he with her. *Allah* had destined their match, who was he to revoke it. Earlier, the whole brood including her had been expectantly waiting for the doctor to show up. But the worries multiplied each second as by the evening, the doctor had failed to make an appearance. Gul had dispatched him along with two other armed *jihadis,* to look for him, at the base of the cliffs. He even had gone down, much further along the track, but was forced to return, as darkness crept upon them.

Gul had been lunacy-induced irked.

He had promised he would leave in the morning to check on him, with his returning, now empty mule train. It was time to go and search for that stupid city pig. He got up, hugged his niece and moved out. As earlier, youngsters had the mules ready to move.

He had to make a clean getaway in darkness, lest someone could back trail him to the camp. The movement was slow and treacherous down the spine of the cliff. Small waterfall made it more non-negotiable, as fine spray of water wetting the path had crystallized into fine slippery ice. One false step, one could tumble at least 200 feet down to the base. Definitely a quicker way to go down and assured of instant death. The column cautiously serpentined down at the base and they later picked up speed. Reshab quickened his steps cursing the doctor, amongst melodious chimes of tiny bells clanging and hung around the necks of his donkeys. He should have foreseen the outcome after seeing the doctor's pitiable physical condition yesterday.

But then he was known for his acute foresight. He missed his dead brother terribly in such situations who had this ability in seeing through the haze.

Air Space, above Kashmir Valley
Operational Room 15 Corps
(0645h, 11 Aug)

"Falcon one, I have the visual," informed Squadron Commander Nirmal Singh, flying his upgraded MIG-21.

"Falcon one, weather deteriorating. Wind speed increasing to 20 knots. Direction South to North. Rain likely in the next four. Good luck, out," said Nirmal's weather-God from his mother base.

"Falcon one, weather update roger."

"Team leader Falcon one, mission hunter is a go. Repeat mission hunter is a go. Good hunting out," instructed Tactical Air Control (TAC) Commander, seated in a hushed 15 Corps operational room.

Lieutenant General Rocky, watched transfixed at the visual of the camp, in the activated screen in front, a direct relay from a drone above. A technological wonder he could not have contemplated two years back.

A jarring shrill on the hotline interrupted engrossed Rocky. He reluctantly picked up its phone. Operation was in execution phase and he could do without interruptions. On the other end Major General RV Singh, his GOC in whose sector the strike was to go, was on the line. Shit, I had not informed him, thought Dass, but then where was the time.

"Falcon one, climbing to thirty eight thousand feet, turning, one eight two degrees and lined for the final run," static radio replied.

"Yes," the Corps Commander asked impatiently.

Nirmal glanced out of his cockpit. His other two wingmen were abreast. Target nestled in the midst of the rocks below.

"Sir received a message from one of my patrols near Naba Pir pass. They have a fix on a terrorist camp. The leader has sent this message received by us at 0430 hours. He is alone and is going in for a raid," General Officer Commanding 19 Mountain Division replied.

"Grid reference," asked suddenly alarmed Dass.

"Sir, 562279," he replied. It matched with the target to be obliterated.

Shit, shit.

"Abort, abort," the General screamed at his TAC commander.

Nirmal had the target in his sights. He flipped the protective cover, freeing the red firing knob. His thumb was sensuously caressing its flat projection, ready to squeeze it at the exact moment. The earth was rushing at him in terrifying rapidity.

"Abort, Falcon one, abort. Mission hunter is red. Abort," Nirmal heard a scream in his ears.

Instinctively he pulled on his joystick. His MIG strained to pull out of the dive. He was not to reason why.

"Falcon one, mission aborted," informed the team leader. In the first place the whole issue was too far fetched, fancy and too good to be true. It could just have been a local *bakarwal* camp. One couldn't make out the weapons to be sure. His objections had been shot down and now he felt relief.

"Falcon one, return to base," told the deflated TAC commander.

Dass nestled his shaking head in his hands. The telephone had fallen at his feet. RV Singh, still on the line, could not fathom the ruckus he had overheard. After repeated "hellos" and getting no reply he went off line.

Respective Locations (0647h, 11 Aug)

In a blink, they shook the earth. Three MIG-21's, screamed past, their round visible rears on fire.

Inside the rhododendron thickets, well short of the crest, Jesse saw the earth shaking fly-past. Shit, what the hell were these Air Force buggers doing here, he screamed. They will wake his den of snakes.

Reshab, moving down the mule track looking for the doctor, dived for cover as if he had been attacked. He also sighted the aircraft fly over in a blink of an eye. Fearfully he kept hidden for the next five minutes and later it took him three times more than his hiding time, to regroup his panicked mules.

Gul jumped out of his Nurie warm bed in alarm. So did all the other *jihadis.* Seeing the threat-less fly-past, they quickly fell back to their normal camp routine. In any case the camp was too well hidden from above, nothing to waste one's brain upon.

Only one person, Rasool Bhat, commander of *Freedom Fighters,* could not stop thinking. He hurriedly switched off his Phillips radio, giving the latest BBC news.

Patrol Black Panther (0700h, 11 Aug)

So far so good.

Everything was going as per the plan.

All parties were in position and he crawling amongst the broken rocks, to the place he thought he had seen someone last evening. He had assumed it to be a sentry, an appropriate place for one seeing the layout of the camp.

He was not taking any chances.

The only glitch had been in the morning, when they had heard some movement while moving up and that din later created by those Air Force guys. All had frozen to their positions. Even the doctor was grabbed and more purposefully gagged. It was the mule train. Surely, emptied at the terrorist camp and returning back. They had passed the muleteers about fifty metres up the slope clinging like spiders on the naked face of the rock. Half an hour delay in his time plan, they would have surely banged into each other, as none could have avoided the sole path, squeezed and gasping for space. Definitely God sent luck. It was a commodity he would require in abundance today, he thought.

Risal without any orders, took the lead.

Jesse didn't mind it a bit. Better to have a confident pointsman, than a nervous trusted soldier in front. Using small breaks in the ground, afforded by huge crumbling rocks, they both crawled ahead. Rest slithered behind. Over razor sharp rock edges, none dared to cry in agony, as rocks cut into their ice numb elbows and knees. They stared, step-by-step, into unknown void in front and inched another yard, behind another rock.

The visibility was poor if not totally bad. It helped their cause.

The swirls of mist from the valley below rose in concentrated, clusters, giving him more and much needed cover from a chanced observation. At such occasions, Jesse dared a few yards extra, with less precaution. He would beckon others to hurry along to avail such small advantages offered by unpredictable weather. But the game could be dangerous, if he was left stranded naked in the middle of a barren expanse, due to whiff of a cleaner wind. They kept on crawling, towards the suspected sentry position, in such spurts and pauses.

To his right and below, in the Bafliaz valley below, the approaching vortex of black thundering mass pleased him. He occasionally sighted crimson flashes streak out in the sky. The angry murmur of their advance was music to his ears.

This further, furthered his cause.

Rumble of thundering clouds, muffed his parties approach over tumbling stones. They had been at it for more than one and a half hours, when Risal raised his hand, signalling danger. All froze. Jesse slowly moved up to Risal and his hand inquired in gestures.

"Fire ahead. I can smell smoke," Risal whispered, funneling words through both his hands, straight into his ears.

Jesse inhaled deeply. His canine genes could not detect anything.

He stared at the fat, flat doggish nose, six inches ahead of his perfect vision. Smiling Risal held Major's shoulders reassuringly and said "*Sahib,* trust a *bakarwal* on this. It's my bread and butter."

The impending danger ahead and its unknown contents was quickly passed down the line. Jesse summoned the second silencer carbine ahead. The first one was firmly held in his hand. Its weight, if not its awkward sight, was comforting. He clutched on his weapon more purposefully. It was his only key, for successful culmination of the task intended. In spite of this armament's notorious malfunctioning ability, it was the weapon in Indian Army's arsenal. A British Tommy would have died laughing, at the sight of this old vintage Word War II technological wonder. In armouries all over India, it was caressed, massaged, cleaned with hot water, applied minimum hundred strokes to its barrel, oiled and then kept safely for next bout of cleaning, next month.

Bloody marvelous, reflected Jesse.

He gestured to his soldier to hand over the weapon to Risal.

Limbu Ram looked at Jesse, as if a snake had bitten him. Idiotic rascal trusts this evil, raged Limbu. How bloody mad? He was about to turn back, flouting orders of his impudent, senseless officer. However, his menacing officer's eyes stopped him. He obeyed when Jesse nodded yes again.

Jesse inched closer to Risal, to show how the weapon worked. Wish he could have foreseen this, groaned Jesse. Risal astounded him, in the next 15 seconds, telling him he could fire the weapon. The only question he had asked was how to disengage the safety catch. Risal grinned, and gave a knowing full hand pat to incredulous Jesse. With renewed confidence, both shoulder to shoulder started moving up again.

Jesse sighted them first.

Hand signals flew desperately to warn others and Risal to stop and observe.

There were two of them, sitting on the base of the rock, staring down at the animal trail disappearing into the rhododendron bushes about 75 metres below. The same bushes, which had provided them a covered approach earlier, the same track Risal had vehemently refused to tread upon yesterday, stating it was the best method of getting detected. The smaller one was tending fire with his palms spread out to absorb maximum warmth, while the taller one, warming his lean muscular backside, was supposedly on watch, facing outside. He seemed too engrossed watching the incoming rain-bearing dancing clouds emitting angry crimson red flashes.

They were not very far, about 20 metres to his right and little below. Good, it gave him a dominating position to observe and also if needed, fire. The standing one, like all over-confident sentries had his AK 47-slung cross-arm. Excellent, reasoned Jesse. Will give him those few extra seconds to react, if sighted and be engaged by that man. He could not see the weapon of the sitting man.

It was a small rock pebble hitting his side, which distracted him from the evil dread in front.

Risal, 20 metres to his left, was excitedly pointing to his watch.

He spied at his watch. It was 0745 hours. That he understood. Risal then opened his right palm thrice. Fifteen minutes. This too, he understood. Then without much ado, Risal supporting a huge grin started crawling forward again. This, he did not understand. In helpless frustration, he saw Risal dip behind a rock and disappear. It was only then it struck him that Risal was outflanking the sentries from their rear and above.

He quickly brought his carbine to aim, keeping the torso of the militant in his foresight. They were the longest 15 minutes his biceps had encountered.

At 0750 hours, he remembered the torturous, buttock splitting, two days of forced mountain hopping march in the Indian Military Academy, to find that stupid Queen's lost golden ring. His training platoon of fat buffoons had come last, only to be raped more intimately by its ape-brained furious instructor.

By 0755 hours, the memory switched to endless ruffians, who desperately tried bettering his limp military bearing, since his days at Khadakwasla, without much success.

At 0759 hours, he was cursing his commando instructor, for goading him and his blood-stained back to finish that last 400-metre lap, a small last slice of 40 km run.

At 0800 hours, the sitting man suddenly got up in panicked alarm, grabbing his weapon. It seemed that Mister Risal loved and reveled in military punctuality.

Jesse fired. The bullets flew true.

The silent burst tore sentries back, just a little right and below the heart. The standing man clutching his chest sat down.

The sudden flurry of muffled puffs brought the sitting guard, to his feet. He managed to stand erect and then with incredulous surprised facial reflection he lazily fell, smack in the middle of the fire. Without comprehending anything more loathsome or burdensome, Jesse charged the fallen sentries. Five metres short, he stopped and pumped two shots, one each in each head, to ensure the sentry's slumberous state.

By the time he could catch his breath, sickly burning smell of human flesh entered his nostrils. He bent down quickly to drag the dead man, sizzling in fire. Despite *jihadi's* small frame, he could not drag him out. Eventually he gave a push. The body overturned, slain terrorists charred black face was placid and reeking of ugliness.

Risal tumbled down from a small ledge above, supporting an infantile smile. Jesse instantaneously clasped him.

He was truly spiritually ecstatic.

Jesse quickly opened his pouch and took out his hand held Radio Set and spoke, "All stations Black Panther, stage three complete, out." Before he finished his transmission, his balance party sprinted to join them. Maniacal looking faces, weapons ready, they could have fired at anything that moved. Luckily they didn't spot a target to engage or pulverise. Their intentions precisely were meat mincing in appearance. Jesse thanked God for small mercies. He cooled them with a disarming smile. Seeing the dead bodies at their officer's feet, instant jubilation on their faces, displayed immediate relief. Immediately his earlier worried party Second-in-Command started deploying his six men, to meet unknown dangers, from minimum six different directions.

Rifleman Limbu Ram took few hesitating steps towards Risal. He smiled and bear clamped stunned Risal. Strangely both had tears in their eyes. The senseless dodo of a soldier has emotions, observed Jesse and was God testing human sanity through him? Please, no, oh God, no, he prayed liberally, to object.

They hugged each other for a long time.

Pir Panjal Ranges (0830h, 11 Aug)

Where the hell was that city pig, that illegitimate cock-less male prostitute.

His throat had gone sore, shouting for the doctor. His other nephews had also been fruitfully engaged in this hide-and-seek game. Bloody city-bred doctor. They had been at it since daybreak. They had formed an extended line and worked slowly downwards, but with no success. It was about eight in the morning, that his nostrils too, tasted smoke. He quickly localised the search to about 100 metres, dispatching his ever-eager youngsters, all around. After few minutes, an excited shout beckoned him to pine grove, a little distant, off the track.

On reaching the spot, he saw smoke rising through clump of moss and sand, hastily thrown on burning logs, to wipe out its existence. Amateur idiots, trying to obliterate the existence by doing a very shoddy job, reflected Reshab. But why would someone try to hide its trace. No *bakarwal* did it. Who was hiding from whom?

He scanned for more details.

He went down on his four limbs sniffing like his favourite dog Shera. Sniff-sniff, sniff-sniff, he sniffed, nosing around and then lifted a stone with great fondness. He spied on some paper wrappers. Ah-ha, even an uneducated fool could tell that they were outer covers of earlier food inside. Any idiot could tell that it was not anything civilian and had the stamp of something more organized. Now on his stomach, he confirmed his thesis, with few footprints near the site. Crisscross impressions on ground, was definitely reflecting movement of soldiers, earlier. Yes, he had seen that pattern few times earlier; of rubber canvas shoes they wore. He then caressed the broken branches, constituting the bed, a spread to take in about 20 men. Later about 50 metres out he spied on their shit mound again not very expertly hid. Yes surely about a score or a little more men judging by the quantum and rise of it. To his best of knowledge no *jihadi* outfit had passed through this area. So they must be soldiers, Indian soldiers

Soldiers were OK, it was not that disturbing, but where was the doctor.

Sudden arrival of Indian soldiers or *jihadis* for that matter had become almost a routine nose digging exercise in these hills. Dig the nose and the results could equally shared by *Jehadi's* or *Fauji's.* The frequency of such visits had increased and so had the soldier's humiliating, aggressive behaviour. Earlier, soldiers paid and decently requested for milk or food, but now they demanded it. "Rascals you feed the terrorists, feed us also," was their patent reply. On that sole logic, he could not fault them, as all known *bakarwals,* did provide food to the *jihadis.* They had to survive in these hostile conditions.

Only a fool would not give food to a man holding a gun. So much for any dose of nationalism or any other belief.

But where was the doctor, he bemoaned.

He would have come up along the same path, visible from this hideout.

His throat instantaneously parched on the thought.

They must have captured the Doctor.

It was a possibility he could not refute, seeing the location of this small hide and the path coming up. Doctor could have been spotted 15 minutes down, enough time to affect his capture. No wonder that city shit hole had not reached the camp.

But why had the soldiers left, so quickly?

The fire was still warm, indicating it was well lit till early morning. Their foot trails moved upwards. To the camp, may be. Yes, he was sure soldiers were headed towards the camp. That city piglet was too soft, to withhold anything from the cruel Indian soldiers. They would have manipulated his soft muscles and in minutes he would have squealed. But why blame the doctor, anyone would have. Their torturing methods were legendary. Ask anyone in a camp in Pakistan. Few who had escaped their clutches had come and given long talks on methods applied, along with visual display of their naked mutilated bodies.

Oh, *Allah,* please save the poor doctor. But what all could he have squealed. The doctor only knew the approximate route, that too, short of the actual camp. The knowledge was heartening.

He sat down for a moment, head held firmly between his both palms, to reflect sanely. Gul must be warned immediately. He was devoid of a radio set so all the excuses of not trudging back were a closed option. Exploring the options part a little more, he correctly reasoned that going back along the same route would be longer. As the doctor did not know the exact location of the camp, the soldiers will surely keep this prominent track under observation. He knew a shorter, but more difficult route, across the small mountain crests. He will hit another track going to Hill Kaka and from their follow a small animal trail to the camp. It will save an hour and if he moved faster may be, another 30 minutes. He will also avoid the track most likely under observation. He quickly summoned his imps and instructed them to go down the track, back to Nusur, while he himself turned back, climbing the black rock face, above the track.

Allah's Rock
(0845h, 11 Aug)

Gul was having a field day. So was his Pakistani Captain.

It was his audacious plan, being eulogised by Gul.

It was shocking.

It was fascinating Gul enough and the effect on others was stunning. If *Allah* willed, there would be chaos in Srinagar. Its rippling effect would shake the valley.

Beauty of it lay in its simplicity.

In phase one, by 0900 hours peace procession lead by women cadres of *Dukhtarane Millat,* will suddenly congregate at Badami Bagh cantonment's Batwara gate. They initially will come and infiltrate in ones or twos, mothers, sisters, friends, minimum 2000 in all. Mixed amongst them will be Gul, and his balance of elite commandos.

In phase two, by 0915 hours the local police will surely arrive, summoned by helpless army guards to disperse them. *Lashkar-e-Toiba* men suitably dressed, would form part of three such vehicles, posing as police personnel.

In another five minutes the phase three will commence. Now two ambulances will appear, with all *jihadis* of *Al Badar,* posing as doctors. Two seriously wounded women and one in last stages of labor (already identified) will beg to be treated in the name of humanity at the Military Hospital, a mere hundred metres inside. *Faujis,* women and samaritan work are a sure recipe for an entry. Once at the hospital, weapons concealed inside panelling will be removed and mayhem will proceed.

In phase four, four other major groups, men of *Harkat-ul-Ansar,* posing as tourists at the Shankracharya temple to the East, *Hizbul Mujahidin* shepherds on bare mountain tops in due West, *Jammat-ul-Mujahidin* men posing as vegetable supply contractors at Second Badami Bagh gate and *Freedom Fighters,* working as labourers on the road opposite the golf grounds, will go in and join the fray, as the fire-fight starts.

In the last phase, other groups i.e., *Tarique-e-Jihad* and *Muslim Janbaz Force* will pose as fishermen on river Jhelum and sneak into the transit camp from the rear.

The fight will be for finish.

No retreat, no run backs, no trying to save oneself. Before attaining *shahadat*, kill maximum *kafirs*, thundered Gul. Spare no one, not even women or children, for *kafir* women breed snakes and their children cannot be allowed to grow to take revenge.

So best was to leave none, hack all.

Aghast and shocked, all stared at each other and when they got tired of that, they looked at the beautiful mock-up of the Badami Bagh cantonment. The person, who had modelled it, had done a remarkable job. It looked so live and so real. On its precise details, blood, lots of blood will be shed. No one could question the workability of the plan. It was ingenious, clever and ambitious. None could muster any courage to say no. It was the pride of all involved. The stakes were enormous. The plan looked so attainable.

Bhat nervously got up. His group was to play labourers. He said haltingly, "We all are indeed lucky to be the chosen one for such a task. The plan is explicit and work of *Allah's* ingenuity. But can we clarify certain issues."

Captain stared at him stoically and Gul nodded.

"What about thousands of women at the gate. They will surely be massacred by Indian troops returning fire and that probability is definite in occurrence," asked Bhat.

"Yes, yes, what about poor women," asked others in general murmur of consent.

"Yes, they will be massacred. There should be a massacre. I bank on such a massacre and have it war-gamed in our plans. If the Indian Army does not perpetuate it, then I will initiate a massacre. I want a filmed massacre, for no battle is won without shedding blood. Imagine the international repercussions, that too, on India's Independence Day. Shock of such an atrocity will move the people in the entire Muslim world, White House, Kremlin and Beijing, to brand India as a naked, cruel aggressor. In West Asia, the Indians will be butchered and driven out in hordes. Who the hell benefits? We Muslims. We, our brothers, our people will get all those lucrative jobs now in the hands of Hindus. More importantly, mass uprisings across the valley will be very violent for them to control. Our men will mingle in the crowds and make the rioting more unmanageable. They will have to leave this vale, run like sick dogs, to save their miserable lives. So what are a few thousand women in sacrifice and some dedicated *jihadis.* It is not a price even worth mentioning to drive infidels away," shot back Gul.

Bhat sat down speechless. He looked around for support. All eyes on the ground, none met his.

"What about the escape plan? If we run out of ammunition, that we sure will, we must have a viable escape option. It's no use dying without fighting. Fight we will, reach our objectives we will, but we must not waste our valuable fighters, uselessly," butted in *Laskhar-e-Toiba* Commander, now a little confident, after Bhat's first rebuttal.

"Yes, yes, we all agree with him," all others nodded in synchronisation, but still not all dared to look up.

Gul did not like the idea. Sitting in a circular fashion, on a small green patch in the valley, their makeshift training squad post, he surveyed them all. Standing amidst them, in his black dress, he felt like an emperor.

"No, no, no," he screamed. "Without our sacrifices popular uprising cannot be sustained. Why sustained, it will not take place. The Kashmiri has never revolted. History is witness to that. He has to be shocked while his conscience has to be butchered into revolting. You have to become idols for others to look up to and take arms. Youth have to emulate you. You are the *jihadis, Allah*'s chosen ones. So why are you afraid of *shahadat*? After death, you all will live amongst thousands of virgins, in heaven. *Allah* has promised that, he and I cannot be wrong. We have to die to show the true cause."

"No, certainly no. I don't agree with you, nor do I want to live amongst virgins, at least not as yet," spoke the *Hizbul Mujahidin*

Commander. "Of what we know of you and your exploits in Afghanistan, you came back successful, after each and every raid. Even alive, people idolised you. They worshipped the ground you walked on. Let us live and be idolised," he sat down with vestige of happy veneer masking his fear. A few started looking up.

There was a sudden rush of general agreement.

The Captain abruptly got up. The situation seemed to be going out of hand. Immediate nipping in the bud, of this cankerous and emotionally charged issue was required and before Gul could interject, he said, "OK, I see merit in your arguments. We must conserve strength for our subsequent plans. We will modify the plans accordingly. But let me remind you, if anyone, I repeat anyone does not execute the basic plan of going in, then all the might of Pakistan and its controlled *tanzeems*, will target to eliminate that rascal, that blot in the name of Islam, in an exemplary manner. Let there be no mistake on this."

All nodded. This still seemed reasonable enough. Gul stamped around in total frustration. Semen-less whoring cockroaches. All of them, he screamed to himself.

"Now, all can break up and discuss within yourself for the next 10 minutes. If anything additional is required, let me know. We leave tonight. By 12th, ,we will be in Srinagar. We conduct reconnaissance on 13th. All other arrangements have been made, including your dresses and other materials. Finer details will be tied upon on the 14th. Go, may *Allah* be with you," the Captain again quietly added.

Everyone broke in animated crescendo. Small clusters, generally at the same place, fingers jabbing, all were shrieking to understand their specific roles. Bhat collected his men and moved a little distance away, near the small rivulet. Grave faces, were ashen, in acute worry. Now what? Before he could mutter anything, he heard a shout, shout of a woman, in agonising distress.

Nurie was running out of the caves, approximately 250 metres away, shouting, "Gul, Gul, Gul."

All stopped at their tracks, to watch her slow progress, through the rock-strewn surface.

Nurie had just gone back from the makeshift cookhouse, just above where her beloved was marshalling his troops after preparing Gul's favourite baked Afghani *Nans.* Inside her one-room-cavern-cum-home she busied herself in finishing Gul's important personal chores. His soiled clothes had to be washed but more urgent was the removal of semen-stained bed sheet. Hurriedly with a damp cloth as she was blushingly massaging the blots of her lusty sexual interludes sitting on the floor by her bed, suddenly the small radio set crackled to life. Gul must have accidentally left it there and that too switched on, she reasoned. As she held it in her hands, it spoke strange words. Wish like her educated intelligent elder sister, she could comprehend this weird language.

"Black Panther three, in position. Target visible, over."

"Black Panther two, in position. Target visible, over."

"Black Panther for all stations, wait for orders to fire, out."

"Black Panther three, *isse accha mauka nahi milega. Unka leader kali dress mein baat kar raha hai. Sabhi ikkate ek jagah par baithe hai, over."* (Will not get a better opportunity. All are sitting together in one place. Their leader in black dress is talking to them)

But this bit did not require her esteemed sister's help. There was nothing queer in it. This was her very own tongue. This part she digested in a flash. From her position inside the room, she saw her Gul dressed in black, addressing his men.

Oh my God!

Someone was spying on her Gul.

He was visible and vulnerable from hidden men. Unacceptable was that someone wanted to fire and kill her Gul. Must be the *faujis* of the Indian Army. Who else on this earth could dare otherwise? She had saved Gul from their earlier evil inflicted wounds.

She will not let it happen again, the second time.

She screamed and ran out.

Tiger's Party (0855h, 11 Aug)

On the animal trail, Jesse profusely cursed at his ever-jumping Second-in-Command of his transgression of radio control. As he radioed him out, in even stricter terms, he heard Risal scream, "You mother-fucker, you stole my life, you stole my *izzat,* you stole my wife and now you are begging for mercy."

When problems arrive, they do not come in ones or twos. As the famous story of his life, they gravitate towards him in bomb-let clusters. They come in hordes, Jesse's mind flashed, confirming his another universal laws that a problem appears suddenly and more problems multiply in Power Square to suddenness in time, with their resolution totally inverse in time.

Jesse sprinted towards the screaming noise, trying to beat the inverse time.

Basically he ran towards Risal, where he was on sentry duty, guarding the approach and performing the task of earlier killed guards. Suddenly more trusted, armed now with a weapon of those dead terrorists, and Jesse engrossed in other affairs, all had lost track of Risal.

As he approached, he saw another *bakarwal* kneeling on his knees pleading. "No Risal, please no. My brother, it was a mistake. Please forgive me. I thought you were dead. On your honour. On *Allah's* honour, I left you as dead. How come you are with these *kafirs*? We must warn Gul. We swore to *Allah*. We took oath on the holy Quran. Forgive me, my brother. Please see the reason. I will make up," he kept mumbling.

"No, Risal, no," also shouted desperate Jesse, from 20-metre away, sensing his intentions. It must be his other brother, who had broken his home and his cute dreams. "No," he shouted even more loudly, this time.

Risal in a trance, negative sway of his head in monotonous motion, conveyed his resolve.

Risal looked at his newfound friend, his beseeching eyes pleading no. But no, he could not forgive. His clan had lived with that genetic defect since ages. It was not going to change now. "Dog, vermin, sister-fucker, you have no right to live. Brothers like you have no right to exist. You protect your dead brother's wife or hump her. You bastard..." he screamed, pumping a burst of AK-47, from 10-metres away, straight into the chest of his brother.

Jesse realized his stupidity now of arming unstable Risal. The game was lost. Echo of bullets was too loud to be hidden. He shouted into his radio set. "All stations Black Panther, fire, fire. I repeat fire." This factored situation, in any case on surprise being compromised, as per earlier envisaged contingency, all were to fire, at any available target without awaiting orders.

Jesse ran up to Risal and let his impatient palms fly in a blurring arc. It culminated in a resounding slap right across the left cheek of ex-terrorist. Stunned, Risal dropped his weapon.

"You nincompoop, you have given the game away. I will skin you alive. Now pick up that weapon and come with me to the edge of the cutting," he shouted, dragging wet eyed, sobbing Risal with him. Even if the forgiveness gene was defective or missing, the gene manifesting guilt was alive and active. Risal, limping and whimpering closely behind Jesse, felt awfully guilty in slaying his once trusted and beloved cousin brother.

Terrorist Camp
(Same Time)

Gul was a bit muddled at seeing Nurie dashing towards him.

What could have happened?

Had someone fiddled with her honour?

Ire-laced blood pumped into his veins immediately. God, let that not be the case. Today heads will roll. To be ridiculed once was unpardonable and the second time was honour-avenging time. He will personally emasculate that man he fumed to himself.

The second sound was crystal clear in its announcement and arrival.

The sharp retort of gunfire, filtering down from sentry position atop the southern rock face, muddled him, even further.

What could that be?

Initially concerned he and all equally amused *jihadis* forgot innocent Nurie running towards them and looked towards the source of this ominous sound in apprehension.

It was not so sweet sound of an automatic weapon discharge.

It had an unmistakable tenor of Klashnikov family of weapons.

It was the sound they had heard so many times earlier and one does not forget it in a hurry. It was the sound of a warning. It was the sound, which is never echoed for peaceful overtones. It was the sound which harbours along with it death. The sound was of a killing. It was a sound indicative of one's life saved and one ebbed into oblivion. But who eventually lived. They could not tell now. In any case, it was not a pleasant sound. It was sinister in intent, content and its stated purpose. It was dreadful, fear evoking and courting evil.

It was a bark none loved; its universal dislike was total. Civilians hated it, *jihadi's* hated it and so did their enemies, the *fauji's* hated it.

Bhat, in a flash, comprehended the sound's sinister implications. He had trained very extensively for that. Somehow since the morning, he was expecting that and had even had warned his alarmed comrades. It was ingrained in his psyche. His ears had been grilled into submission by such sounds. What they dispassionately heard seldom was wrong. The sentries had engaged someone, on the rocks to the south. Someone was an assuredly Indian soldier. Soldiers seemed to be approaching from that direction. As the sentries on the rock spine had the best view of the waterfall and the base below and had not opened fire, that area seemed safer. Any moron strategist would not have launched a suicidal bare-naked cliff assault and let be picked in ones by guards above. By magic reconnaissance seemed to have been done or they compromised by a traitor amongst them. Whatever be the circumstances, this hollow bowl was not the right place to stay.

"To the sentry post on the rock spine. Go, go, go," he screamed at his men. Without blinking, all jumped across the rivulet, racing along with him.

Captain Ahmad of Pakistan Third Special Services Group saw Rasool Bhat and his spineless men making the escape. "Come back you sister-fuckers, come back," he thundered, running after them. Chasing them with the weapon in his hand, he rushed across to stop them. The toe of his left foot, got entangled in a small split in the rocks. He lost his balance, as he grimaced in pain, falling down. A huge boulder impacted his left temple. He immediately lost consciousness, becoming oblivious to issues around. Not that in the events that followed thereafter, any one missed him or wanted his divine presence.

Death this day, did not come in small spurts.

It made an impressive announcement.

It arrived with a huge ear splitting bang, a muted thud a micro second earlier, followed by a ferocious blast. It was stunning in cruelty and earth shaking in its perpetuated effect. The 84 millimetre rocket launcher fired from the overhang across, burst smack in the middle of men in green patch, with sickening accuracy. High explosive shells and its millions of shrapnel, flew in all directions, inviting death.

It had the 'Midas touch', instantaneous golden death.

Gul, shielded by a few of his trusted cronies, was knocked down by the shock wave. He lay stunned on his back, with mass of human flesh and their slimy blood and bile coating his face. For those millions of seconds, he lay dead, amongst the dead. Before falling down, like a camera flash capturing the endless moments of time, he saw a huge fireball engulf his men.

He saw the earth spew up the sacred dust.

He saw no *zannat.*

He saw fear.

He saw death.

Atop the overhang, brave Subedar Lekh Ram jumped in joy. "Well done, *shabash* Khumba, *laga rehe,*" he shouted excitedly. Naik Khumba gingerly peeped out from his telescope sight, surveying his work.

He liked what he saw.

Lasting artful impressions of dead terrorists on the canvas of valley's landscape. Report of "ready" followed by a hard pat on his back, told his drilled mind that his rocket launcher had been adequately rearmed by his number two. He, being the number one, had the privilege of squeezing the trigger, again. The second round also zoomed off, this time a wee to the left of the last one. The impressions of his second masterpiece were identical in nature. An excellent work of a seasoned, old, master forger. Dead men, in another cluster, on the same canvas. "*Shabash, shabash,*" rung in his dizzy ears as he got busy in replicating such appreciated master copies.

Then the death came in all its other glorious forms.

It was mysterious and cunning in its appearance.

The dreaded poisonous lead was paving its way through labyrinth of one body carcass to another then laughing off through three more, entering from the mouth and disgustingly peering from stained rectum or vice versa as it pleased its devilish intent. The blood starved 'general lead' was taking a full-fledged military salute, moving in tuneful slow march, reviewing its death parade with minute deliberateness. Chatter of bullets, whining of ricochets, report of single shots, crunching sound of bursting 51 millimetre mortar bombs, blazing tracer rounds, all arrived around that identifiable green patch on the valley floor.

Each impact, thwack of bullet entering the human flesh, crunching of crushing bones, brought blood-curling screams to the throats of those dying men. Lucky were a few, who died without blinking, in abruptness of vanishing life, blessed by a heavenly swift silver bullet, straight through the heart or head. Unlucky were those condemned humans, unblessed, maimed, crawling like crushed maggots, pleading for a speedier deliverance from life.

Gul, frozen in fear, willfully struck amidst the dead, saw pensively this lively dance of death. These *kafirs* inhuman destroyer dancing God in his magical destructive *tandav* dance was becoming a sickening reality. How come his dear God seemed to be so pronounced in his absence? A headless man ran past him, with blood sprouting from his neck like a fountain in the mystical Garden of Eden. His numb mind again registered a legless sprinting man ironically hollering, "Run, run, run."

Initial shock over, an armed *Lashkar* commander was firing his weapon in hapless frustration towards the perceived threat. Through the edifice of dead around him, he saw the huge rock boulders ahead. Summoning courage, amidst chaos, melee and riotous noise, that brave commander screamed, "To the rocks in front, to the rocks in front. Take covers behind them. Run."

More than five-dozen of surviving men ran. It made more sense than to be on this open death plain. All ran except Gul. He was too shocked to move. Immobilized by terror, his mind could not reason an excuse good enough to speculate or venture.

He felt safe in the company of his beloved dead.

Oblivious to the horror which dramatically unfolded in front of her eyes, Nurie kept on running towards her lover, her voice hoarse screaming his name. Amidst chaos, jostling by other *jihadis* scampering to find haven from sure death, she ran for her lover. Her gait never faltered, her resolve never diminished. Oh *Allah*, the pure one, please save my Gul, she prayed at each bounding step. Gul, she must save and save she will. He was her life. Nothing else mattered. Protected by hallow of an angel, bullets whizzing past her, steel fragments caressing her sensuous body, she reached the green patch, where she had last sighted her love. Mangled mass of dead horrified her. Her Gul, no her Gul cannot die, she lamented, at the same time scanning the dead.

Screaming insane, blabbering mutterings to her *God*, she ran in circles, looking for her love.

She shrieked, as a blood dripping gory hand grabbed her wrists, dragging her into the pile of dead. She screamed in horror, at the dead ghost, punctured with a bullet-ridden chest, pinkish cream bile oozing out of his split open stomach pulled her towards him. She screamed in fear and her bladder burst in sheer terror. Warm trickle below strangely gave comfort but was very oblivious to the difference between her own personal wetness and blood dripping in abundance, seeping into her *salwar*. God help, help her from this beast. She screamed incoherently for her true God, in fear, eyes closed. No help came. Whimpering like a little baby, innate, helpless, she allowed herself to be pulled into darkness of unknown.

A dead man, beyond a dead man, spoke. A dead man, masked with paint of human blood, spoke, "It's me Gul."

She screamed at the face. It was not her Gul.

The magician of dead ghost again spoke, "Nurie, its me Gul. Come to me love. Hide here."

Yes, it was his voice, if not the face. It was her very own Gul's voice. It was her lover's deep resounding voice. It was her Gul. Giving into her excited exhausted state, she quietly melted amongst the dead, clinging to her Gul.

Tiger's Party (0905h, 11 Aug)

"Black Panther two for Black Panther, message over."

"Pass, over."

"Black Panther, ammunition level below fifty per cent, over," reported harried Havaldar Ram Prakash.

"Black Panther three for one, similar situation here, over," butted in equally harried Subedar Lekh Ram.

Shit.

Not even three minutes had passed, their ammunition was already running out. Not that they were wasting it. From his position, on the edge of the animal trail, overlooking the small terrorist infected vale, a ledge he had occupied after the fire had been kick started by a chain reaction, on part of Risal's foolishness, he had witnessed a fine carnage.

An unbelievable drama in death.

Clear, concise and conclusive in argument.

Bullet always wins pal. It yet again confirmed another of his self-coined universal law thesis that the life expectancy of a soldier is constant to the accuracy of a bullet and is in direct proportion to your ability to outrun it.

Despite the military excitement of things going good and savage precision-butchery of these national traitors, the wastage of good human life saddened him. Oh God, take pity on those poor souls struck below, he quickly prayed.

Stunning echo of munitions discharge, resonating and amplified by the narrow confines of the ravine, helped him to reasonably measure the rate of expenditure of the most precious commodity of a soldier – ammunition.

It had him worried and stupidly cursing on again another of his coined laws that in war the rate of ammunition expenditure is in inverse to actual enemy threat and is in direct proportion to the total sum of the fear of the each constituent of the sub-unit. But on this he was ready to bite dust, as he indeed had been a witness to a fine killing, each bullet well shot and excellently delivered. At this rate, his main firing parties would fall silent in another three minutes. Ammunition expenditure had to be restricted, though his own party had its ammunition intact, having not joined in his executioner's fray, in any measure.

Much against his desire but on saner thoughts he gave the order. He rapidly spoke into his radio set, "Black Panther for all stations Black Panther. Switch to aimed single shot fire. I repeat, switch to aimed single shot fire, out." He sat down and again stared below, as two other parties acknowledged his call.

All soldiers, promptly switched to single shot aimed fire, and momentarily for those few magical seconds, quiescent calm descended on the basin below.

Terrorist Camp
(A Few Seconds Later)

Freedom fighters of Bhat's miniscule organization had managed a safe dash across the valley floor and were lying behind a small rock spine projection, adequately guarded from direct fire. Through the small fissure in the rocks, he graphically witnessed an unbelievable holocaust unfolding before him. Two excited sentries of *Al Badar* from Multan Pakistan, who were on duty at rock spine, were also watching wide eyed the pulverisation of their dreams.

They were dumbstruck into total submission.

After initial welcome of Bhat, much to their relief and pointing out at places from where the hostile fire was being sprayed, they had gone totally innate. Bhat for himself thanked his intuition and subsequent correct decision in running away for the cover. It was God's divine intervention. It had taken a lot of load from his shoulders. Despite morose and skeptic thoughts he felt like dipping his head into a sweet goblet of wine. As swiftly as the acoustics of the one-sided conflagration had started some minutes earlier, it vanished. Silence seemed eerily out of place. It left a strange drone in his ears.

Alarmed, he peeped out again to witness silence.

It was the moment *jihadis* had been searching till now.

Earlier, broken in spirit by sheer magnitude of surprise and fire, now sheltered behind these huge rock boulders, they had been screaming at each other, in making some retaliatory plan. Havaldar Aminullah Khan, the second-in-command of unconscious Captain Ahmad of Third Special Services group, had assumed total command in such a tiring and hopeless situation. Earlier, he had been in a few in Afġhanistan, fighting the Russians first and other oppressors later. He knew what to do. But where was his officer. Always missing at crucial hours. Only, if he could lift his head up.

Rage in one of the finest commandos of Muslim world, pinned down like a dog, was immense and tearing his wide chest open. The slippery *Hindu* vermin *fauj*, had crept on them, with their predictable guile. Man to man, Indians will not come out in the open to face his wrath. As the enemy fire ebbed, he sprang up in a flash with a rocket launcher on his shoulder and let loose its round, towards the overhang in front. Similarly the other *jihadis* followed suit, in retaliating at the places identified by them earlier, spouting fire.

Till now, happy, smiling and smug Subedar Lekh Ram, watched in mock horror, as a streak of smoke rushed uninvited towards him. He ducked instinctively, as a huge shockwave caused by the exploding rocket just below his position, threw him back and pressure ruptured his nearest eardrum. He shrieked in pain. All immediately went behind the ledge, an action aped by the Black Panther three, as two similar rounds burst near them.

Bloody shit, they were under fire.

A hurray of exclamation rippled through *jihadi* ranks. Now even exposing themselves, they let out all the weapons in their inventory.

Jesse disbelievingly saw the rapid change in fortunes.

Patrol Black Panther positions were too stunned to be at the receiving end and shocked to effect effective retaliatory response. The initiative till now so firmly imprisoned under their fat bums had wriggled out and was galloping away to the tune of cheering *jihadis*'. He withheld his own fire. At least, one party should retain ammunition for personal safety. It was a minor setback, nothing that could not be restored by purposeful sniping. At least those rascals were cornered and confined to a few rocks in an area of 50 metre square.

Jihadis by now had almost started a *Bhangra* jig. Revenge was around the corner.

Along with each volley of shots, abuses hurled across the space became a motivating factor. Importantly it hid fear. Their crescendo of curses increased proportionally with fire. They had adequate ammunition at present and a few without had dashed back to the green patch, to snatch more from their fallen comrades.

Gul, huddled along with Nurie under the pile of dead, was quick to grasp the reversal turning to a favorable tide. He crawled out from under the pile of his dead colleagues and scanned the landscape to evaluate his escape options. Through the tunnel of dead carcass he saw boisterous jumping gleeful *Jihadis* engaging the enemy. Situation despite his men's sudden elated shouts was grim.

Indians were on top and they below.

Whoever dominates the higher ground, is a winner.

It was the basic principle of war, which defied any more deft reasoning. It would be stupid to join them, in this suicidal mission. Useless brave bravadoes will not alter the ground advantage and wounds inflicted by the surprise attack. Indians would surely have covered the entrance of this hideout, if they had surprised them from the rear. He had fleetingly glimpsed the firing positions in north of this bowl, just above that massive overhang. The route on which his sentries had first engaged the Indians, just below the small trail seemed a safer option. He firmly clasped Nurie's hand and dragged her slowly out of the blood soaked green patch.

He made slow deliberate moves, hiding, posing amidst his slayed men, and slowly crawling to the base of the cliff face, above which the trail started.

Bhat from his escaped to safe position quickly digested the situation. Any dithering now may elude such a golden opportunity and he be ruing to his grandchildren if he ever had them. The battle could be lost given any more twists of fortune. His two earlier downcast *Al Badar* colleagues had also jumped up in joy and started engaging hopelessly out of range Indian positions, far above in the horizon.

He must act now.

Extracting his Beretta 9 millimeter pistol wedged in his belt, he cocked it and fired without thinking at the target, two metres to his right. The big head of one earlier *Al Badar* sentry hid under the mask of blood. The pumpkin atop the shoulders burst in a noisy 'pop'. The other sentry in reflex looked towards new origin of fire. Before he could register anything more alarming, a bullet ruptured his heart. Both died without knowing why. He then hastily nodded to his men and said, "now."

All brought their weapons to aim and on his command, "fire," simultaneously all let loose their volleys, into the exposed backs of jubilant *jihadis.*

It took Aminullah Khan some time to realize, that something was terribly amiss.

When his fellowmen flanking him slumped forward quiet dead, did he realize something was definitely wrong. It was not the earlier and known direction of death. The fire now was being raked, very mysteriously from his rear. Most of his men died facing the wrong way. He cautiously peeped back, lying on his stomach in confused apprehension.

Latest death threat had emerged from the area of rock spine. It was the place he had personally chosen for the sentry position. No one, even an Army division could have bypassed that strategically placed sentry. The sentries could pick up one by one, any one who dared to climb the steep rock face along the waterfall. Despite that these infidels had managed that. How, his seizure filled brain tried to reconcile? But what he beheld from his now exposed position intrigued him further. The men firing were not wearing any standard uniforms, identifying an army. They were his pattern of clothes. What they all generally wore. They were their own brothers, firing at their own brothers.

Traitors.

Betrayed by shitless hordes of trusted *jihadis*. Plotting, money swapping, faithless brothers, pests, rascals and may they all rot in hell. He screamed in fury, as he now let loose already loaded rocket launcher round, towards the betrayers of the true cause.

The Khan delivered round lifted Bhat's two men, clean off their feet. Before Havaldar Khan could reload his launcher again, alone this time, five bullets pierced his stomach. The punctured intestines emptied its contents at Havaldars wobbling feet. He fell down dead. Along with him died the last remnants of resistance. Totally perplexed, few remaining *jihadis* ran helter-skelter, to be easily picked, one by one deliberately, by the now recharged Indians.

"Disengage," ordered Bhat.

Men quickly again stole behind the cover of the rock spine. He gathered his men. He gave a few, precise and curt instructions. It was time to escape from the scene. Tears flew down his cheeks as he saluted his two men lying dead at his feet. They hurried in imparting some decency points to the twisted mangled mass of their comrades. They had been together in many a battle.

But a soldier must die when he has to die.

They were brave good men. He, with tear-dripping eyes, saluted and turned back.

As he turned, the jerk freed a small silver amulet, his most precious possession, and a gift that blossomed the soul of his existence. It hung across his neck secured to a thick black thread. He quickly grabbed at it, kissing three horizontal golden lines running across it, he asked for blessings of his departed father and tucked it in the safety of his shirt. His entire party crawled though a small cutting in the rock face, his team had reconnoitered earlier, away from the vista of battlefield behind.

Tiger's Party (0915h, 11 Aug)

Jesse, watching from the rockhang above, was totally stumped.

It had been too quick in execution to comprehend its exact implications. Who was firing at whom, God only knew. But of one thing he was certain, that *jihadis* had been totally decimated.

Raped in death from left, right, above and now their rear.

A few running around were a good mobile target practise for his men. It was now time to deliver the coup de grace. He quickly assembled his men in an extended line and radioed to his other positions, "Black Panther for all stations Black Panther. Time now 0915 hours. Stop firing by 0920 hours. I repeat stop firing by 0920 hours. My party will commence search at 0921 hours. Keep our backs and flanks covered, out."

Six minutes later, in an extended line, eight persons including him and Risal looked like a complete mockery of an assault line. It was worse than a skirmish line of American civil wars. Not that he was charging on to an enemy held objective, but rolling down very steadily, weapons at their shoulders, ready to engage anything moving. He shied going down the prominent animal trail, as it was a sure expected direction of approach. Any fool, half-dead or willing to die, in extracting some revenge, could cover it. He kept the track to his left, planning to hit the base below, from South Eastern direction.

They cautiously strode down a very steep rock face. After sometime, it was more rappelling down on all fours, than maintaining a semblance of an assault position. Despite the destruction in front of them, his heart quivered. They were totally exposed on this naked un-vegetated rock. But fear he could not show, or any hesitation. He had to lead, go over the area before clearing it off. Mopping up was difficult but necessary and was the most insipid part of any operation.

It was Risal again who spotted the movement first.

Just below them, a shadow had moved, in between the rocks. An arm of caution froze everyone in their tracks. Yes, they were two of them, slowly lumbering up the slope. After a few moments, it became evident the one leading, was a man and other surprisingly a woman and in things befitting of male chivalry, he was gently goading her up, with the support of his outstretched hand. It took them another two minutes, to just come twenty metres below them, on a flat parapet.

Gul turned after putting Nurie up on the small ledge, just enough for both of them to stand. He slowly faced up the slope to find the route his heart skipped a beat, at the sight confronting him. That bitch of his oesophagus refused to obey his breathing commands.

As one, eight men rose, pointing their weapons at the chest of the man-target.

"Stop," shouted Jesse, "and raise your hand," he further added, breaking the tranquility of the surroundings. He was staring at a multi-coloured fool, painted in various shades of reds and dark browns.

Quivering in abject terror, mind comprehending nothing, his hands went up in the air. Gul knew he looked quiet silly in this pose. A famous commander, hands in air, subjugating, begging for mercy, begging for his life, he must look like an ass-swollen pansy. For once in his lifetime, he seemed defeated. Faceless entity of moribund reality stared at his face.

It was yet again that Risal distracted the developing events by shrieking out profanities. "You, Gul. You rogue. Ha-ha, you pig-eater. Running away, like a true warrior. Coward, why aren't you with your dying men. They died for you and yours truly, ran. That death defying rhetoric was only good in Pakistan and for those now dead poor scoundrels. Had enough after getting all killed and darting away to save your miserable skin. Can't stomach the pain of a penetrating bullet. You used all others and me like pigs. You half-mad *jihadi,* Afghani cockroach, I will kill you now," he belched jumping up and down in ardent aped animation of the 'Toady King'.

He gleefully started taking aim at the middle of Gul's upper frame, the end-target. His bestial eyes deadlocked, breath stilled for a fraction, imparting stability to his wavering weapon and taking stock of the rapidly paling prey across, when a woman shielded behind Gul till now yelled, "No brother, No. No dear brother Risal, spare us. You are making a big mistake. Please don't kill Gul."

Briefly taken aback, he lowered his weapon reducing his threatening posture signatures. He had a vague inkling having recognized the voice at the first instant, but the bloodstained face when reflected against the sky, shocked him in totality. Suspicion does not bestow visibility behind a mask.

"Nurie, is that you Nurie," He mumbled.

"Yes," came back a faint reply.

"What are you doing here Nurie? What the hell are you doing with slime like him in the first place or has this scalawag kidnapped you? Dear sister say something. These people boast at camps in Pakistan how they use our women. Tell me Nurie, what is it?" he questioned across the expanse.

Nurie by now had come ahead of Gul, shielding his body with her instead. She persisted her invocation, "Brother please, spare us. Let Gul go, take my life instead. I am his, given in by my own choice, by your brother Reshab. On your clan's honour, you cannot harm your brother-in-law." Pink tears were flooding her rosy red cheeks.

Jesse again was totally dumbfounded. Predictability of it was becoming sickening.

Twice in the last half an hour, no, the third time in the last one. Dumbfounded and stumped.

It was a situation he never liked to thrive on.

Of all coincidences, a brother meeting his sister, that too, at this desolate God forsaken place. That too in a death orgy raid, in the midst of a battle, was remarkable.

Godly fate?

What a typical *Bollywood* Hindi movie finale, with melodramatics thrown in full measure, a heart-stopping gasping story worth lakhs, if he could market one. And, had he heard the name being repeated correctly Risal addressing Gul? Was he the same Gul whom Risal had escorted across to India? The same famous Gul, on whose name the Russians in Jalalabad would shiver as per earlier braggart Risal. The chap already on the executioners' block had something he could not immediately pin on. Yes, fatalistic arrogance.

Maniac laugh bellowed by Risal chilled the air to minus zone. There was this strange eerie shrillness in his voice.

"Clan honour, my dear sister. Did Reshab arrange the union? That ass-eating pig can count the money he must have made in hell. He is dead and I killed him. Clan honour is as deep as your shit hole. It's repugnant and dirty. What happened to my wife? The bitch is remarried and I am here breathing alive. Did you marry him or like a common *randi* you were attached to him? Boys of our clan are not good enough for you and you have to dream, legs spread apart for a smelly Afghani cur. You *bhainchod,* I thank my clan for delivering me from the yokes of these evil men. But this evil, I must definitely kill, including you," he quipped again, raising his death delivery instrument more purposefully this time now.

Gul transfixed in fear, feared his end.

It was Jesse's flying tackle of his good old football playing days that Risal was knocked over. Lying on his butt, Risal looked up and complained, "That man is a monster, he must be killed including that brazen women. Let me do it. I beg you, *sahib.*"

"You take another step, I will kill you now, and by God that is a promise," he thundered. "Firing only on my orders," he barked his orders to everyone. "It will be on my dead body; if anyone injures that woman. Now you," he again shouted pointing towards Gul, "You step aside."

What Gul heard immensely pleased his ears.

By now millions of options had been generated in his scheming mind.

That softly speaking man seemed like an officer of the Indian Army, thought Gul, a complete idiot.

Placing such importance over a woman, over a commander like him. Thousand of women would have died to save him, back home. He couldn't have cared any less. They were good in fact very good for pleasure and that he had learnt here, in plentiful measure. But, bullshit, never over a worth of a man. But these sentiments are exactly what will help me to escape, from this fat, mellow, Hindu officer, he quickly reasoned.

Shitless clan, shitless people, shitless religion and shitless country.

Which honourable religion allows worshipping of females?

These women were perpetually dirty, leaking every month, weak in body and mind, always to be protected or otherwise the true one would have found some use for them. He knew disobeying the Hindu officer would mean a sure death in the immediate future. These military men had withheld their fire because Nurie was with him. Few *jihadis* came back to narrate stories. They kill all mercilessly. *Allah* willing, he will surely utilise her armor shielding services in full measure, to make good his escape. There was no time to remove the AK-47 slung across his back. Any such provocative gesture would invite sure fire and sure death. It was the inevitable that he had to postpone by hook or crook. He sat on his haunches, behind swaying and protecting Nurie and in a flash took out his steel knife, hidden on one side of his boots. Before anyone could comprehend anything further, his arms were firmly across Nurie's chest and steel blade wedged stoutly below her Adam's apple.

"You, sister-fuckers, you think you have got Gul. You rascals. I will kill her if you do not let me go," he thundered, staring in equal measure to all eight around. "You Hindu officer," pointing to Jesse now, "I tell you, I will kill her. She is expendable like a worthless crap. A woman is worthless in relation to a man. By God, I will kill her, I will kill her slowly and you can enjoy the joys of an ebbing life. You go back now," he hastily screamed.

"Gul you are surrounded, and don't be foolish, let that woman go. I give you my word, you will not be harmed," Jesse said calmly.

"Believe a *kafir's* word. Like cowards you crept from behind and killed my men and you will let their commander go? No I don't believe you. Now turn back before I start killing this Kashmiri bitch," Gul shouted.

Nurie could not comprehend her changed status, so instantaneously. From a saviour, she came to be slaughtered like a lamenting goat. She quirked, "Gul, what are you doing? Gul no, I tell you, they will let you go. Trust me on this."

"Keep quiet you wanton woman," he hissed and added, "That's what you are and will remain in my eyes. You think I will take you back to my native Afghanistan and let my people mock me. There you get women of better constitution. They do not whore for one or uncover their bodies for all to see like you. Your foolish brother is right for a change. I had paid more than fifty thousand for your services to your now I believe dead brother. I brought you for simple whoring and keep quiet you bitch. Now you go before I slay her like a pig. Officer *sahib,* I am telling you with the finality of *Allah's* resolve that I will not hesitate a moment to kill her. I will count only once till ten. Then you can kill me but this cheap girl would be dead. One, two, three," he started saying each count, with paused deliberation.

"Satisfied you Afghani male flesh salivating whore," Risal could not help taunting his sister and at the same time disgustingly looked at the officer.

"Two," came a harsh shout.

Jesse turned back.

"Three," Gul shouted louder.

To Risal and all his men's innate horror, their officer turned back. He turned back and gave them a general wave of his hands, instructing them to move backwards.

"No," screamed anguished Risal

"Four," Gul shriek-shouted more louder.

"Yes," happily screamed beaming Nurie.

"Five," he continued.

They were saved, in spite of Gul's out of character earlier shocking behavior. It had her worried for a moment. She tried to strain her neck backwards to smile at her Gul. Deathlike grip across her slim neck defeated her.

A soft smile crept on Gul's face.

"Six," the voice echoed a relaxed tone.

His tense body also eased in elation.

"Seven," the tone jarred in Jesse's ears.

He will again escape.

"Eight," the shout hit Jesse's brain.

It was the will of *Allah.*

"Nine," the screech was defeaning.

In that madness of violence, *Allah* had let Nurie reach him safely, to save him. Save him she will. Stupid devoted woman. He surely will miss her lively body when he finally abandons her. Sad, but cannot be helped. Having tasted the fleshy fruits, he could acquire them in abundance. The markets of Pakistan were full of them. In every situation, people must be manipulated to serve the cause. Escape today and fight another day seemed a very just cause. What are people, nothing, but a replaceable commodity? No use crying over them.

"Ten," the cresendo of evil commands culminated.

Jesse had taken two steps backwards, his hands mysteriously invisible, working at some sinister plot, when he whirled around.

In that longest billionth of a second, he registered the smirking face of Gul. If Gul had tricked everyone in producing a knife, Jesse like a magician had a pistol extended out of his arm.

Chanting the warriors' prayers and evoking the blessings of his Lord Krishna, he willed himself to register and focus on one target, the four-inch square forehead of that merciless terrorist. Unlike Krishna's master disciple Arjuna, he knew he did not have the ability to pierce the 'fishes' eye, that too, without looking up. But he had to try at least. Before the echo of the pistol report died down, Gul's forehead had a red spot directly between his eyes. Like a Hindu women's coloured *bindi* extolling the beauty of their foreheads, Gul now supported one.

Gul rocked back, under the impact of a nine-millimetre caliber round cracking the thick bony sheet of his cranium. The force took him off the rock cutting. His sinister smiling face had not even registered a mild shock. Instinctively his hand clutched closer and tighter on petite confused Nurie. As he fell, the long sharp ribbed American commando knife, a gift from his previous CIA and Special Forces instructors, whom he had given ample opportunities to be proud of, in missions inside Afghanistan, sank deeper into the soft muscular tissues precariously supporting the gentle neck of shrieking Nurie.

Like her beloved forehead, her neck now oozed spurts of crimson red blood.

They had come from a very long way.

They had traveled over a thousand miles a few times over.

Gathered over the Indian Ocean, they had pushed their way up the Indian sub-continent, egged on by the force of Southern winds. They rose to cross the tall imposing Himalayan crest line. The meeting was as ever violent, as witnessed for millions of year. The thundering of the anger-laden clouds had an arrogance of invincibility, the purposeful stride of roaming cheetah. Their subsequent fight and protest had been registered by cheering millions in the form of thunder and lightening. Cooler atmosphere encountered by moist laden air mass culminated into a boring predictable physics experiment: fine rain. As the first raindrops of monsoon for the year 1997, fell on the face of Gul, blown by the Southern winds, he lay quiet dead.

Quiet dead, still supporting that silly grin across his crimson red stained face.

For Jesse, there was no remorse.

The task seemed to have been executed to perfection, belying Professor Murphy's law that if the attack is going without a hitch, beware, you are getting into a perfect ambush. He wasted a second on Mr. Murphy, smiling at his superior knowledge of constituents of a successful ambush. He walked over the granite platform and looked below. Gul lay inert below him, his body crumpled into millions of unbelievable distorted angles.

Suddenly feeling very tired, his injured back and knees flared in a knowing pain. A pain he had the right to lug alone since his mischievous childhood. He sighed and heavily sat down on the rough stony inclined gravel slope. The needling tiny rocks upping the ante up his soft bums didn't feel very uncomfortable strangely. He had given it his best shot and let the chips fall in as they may.

Men around him were tending to the injured woman. His radio operator was summoning for that civilian doctor he had interned a day earlier. He had no further zest in balance to do anything more purposeful. By an executive order on his radio set, he postponed the mopping up a little later, on recall of an advice of a dear friend Major Shamsher who had just finished his tenure in the same location: never ever chase an injured militant. In any case let them evoke their natural deaths by unbridled bleeding, hollering in pain without proper medical facilities. A good shrieking motivational movie for other terrorist suckers struck helplessly in a hide.

Jesse took out a cigarette, lighting it, took in a deep nicotine deficiency restoring lungful of smoke. It got him thinking. It cleared some of the cobwebs imbedded deep in his brain. It also evoked some of his patent beliefs.

Like this one, that 'a good terrorist is a dead terrorist'.

12

Fatherly Tales

The encounter ultimately and its subsequent mopping up took another 48 hours to complete. Colonel PP Singh, with his Quick Reaction Team, could manage to land by the morning of 12th August, when the rain Gods showed a little mercy in relenting. His tension evaporated when terrorist body counts climbed above hundred. Later, he was quiet cheesed off when an order not to carry out mass burial was received. How would he lug all those dead men to the civilization? The order was immediately revoked once a Colonel flew in from Udhampur, handpicked two dead bodies and flew back. The whole episode looked odd, but who was he to crib. It was celebration time.

Inspector Pathania was promoted instantaneously by over-glowing Jammu and Kashmir, Inspector General of Police, for great role played by his police force. He is now a Deputy Superintendent of Police (Operations) at Kupwara, where his ingenious ways is proving beneficial to all Army units deployed to fight this Pakistan-sponsored proxy war.

When the news of encounter broke at Corps Headquarters, Colonel Imtiaz, shepherd all his persuasive powers, to convince the GOC to meet the Chief Minister and the Governor of the State in the evening. Before midnight, the tainted Minister from Shopiyan was arrested and the Zahir Silk factory in downtown Lal Chowk area of Srinagar raided. The raid was a botch up, as few excited Special Operation Group men, opened fire, as soon as the front gate opened. *Maulana* caught the burst in the middle of his chest and his six-year-old daughter standing behind him was also hit and died instantaneously. With that also died any worthwhile information, to keep likes of Major Srivastava in business and write more astounding research papers. Police had much more at their hands to do, then to make further arrests, in quelling down a violent mob, next day morning. Colonel Imtiaz later caught a rumor that execution had been ordered by someone in the state cabinet. Life in Kashmir was not as simple as it seemed.

Rasool Bhat is back living with the Hindu widow of the slain Muslim terrorist in the heart of Srinagar. He has a new mission in life, to appendage himself into the services of a promising tainted *Maulvi.* The '*inpa*' in him is still shimmering. The escape of his group was uneventful and not comprehended by a few other lucky escapees. His groups of young monkeys are still in business.

Doctor Meehboob Shah was imprisoned for two years for his complication in the matter, though he was out in eight months, due to his exemplary behavior. His *jihadi* fervor much to the relief of his now toothless mother has dimmed considerably. Out of the Government job, he now runs a small clinic in shantytown of Bijebera, Srinagar. He now speaks only of Pakistani exploitation of the Kashmiri people – again a dangerous situation to live by, in the valley.

Nurie, despite everyone's efforts and frantic prayers to the God's of one's faiths, she could not be saved. Her slit throat had spilt too much precious blood, despite angel's frantic outdoor operation on her. The cut had been too deep. She died by the time the first chopper landed with reinforcements. She died chanting Gul's name, but in a sense negative, disbelieving betrayal. When she died on that rain soaked afternoon, Angel unashamedly cried. One of the few bodies flown out, her autopsy report showed that she was five months pregnant on the day she died. No one came forward to claim her body.

Nafisa finally eloped with her beloved Captain Imran. As his parents never relented, Imran's unit organized the wedding, which could have put his ICS parents to shame. Second-in-Command and his wife gave away the bride from their house while Commanding Officer of that Grenadier unit led a boisterous *barat* all the way from the unit's Officers Mess to claim her. The entire unit other ranks, joined the wedding without showing preference to any particular side. The Subedar Major, had acted as the facilitator between both the warring factions, as *baratis* demanded dowry, more dowry, better food and more importantly, more whiskey. Mischievously totally sozzled, *baratis* temporarily forgot about the bride. As she was produced before them Nafisa's heavenly beauty radiating out of her bridal costume, stunned and goaded them into frenzied activity to take her back safely. Nafisa now is the pampered bride of the regiment. They also have a son named 'Kash Khan'.

Tahir, along with his sideling Usman, charged for waging war against the Indian State, are presently serving sentence in all male Jodhpur Central Jail, where now the terrorist's former boss, is believed to be a very famous pansy fairy queen. His total sentence has been reduced due to the services he later provided in identifying and eliminating the entire terrorist *Muslim Janbaz Force* organization in the Valley.

Risal never went back to his village. He could not forgive his household for treachery. For the help he had rendered, he was quietly relocated at Ramban. He now has a new wife and thousands of goats to brood over. Yes, his dead cousin brother had judged him perfectly. Risal was smart. In fact he was one of a few intelligent ex-terrorists who had utilised their award money sensibly.

Sardar Ranjit Singh, the PCO owner, still has no clue of crucial role played by him, in the whole affair. He sometimes in good humor still muses over that incredible inspector Pathania and his famous masquerade.

High flying and hot shot Colonel Tejinder Singh now supervises reservation of army personnel traveling on trains, at some obscure station in Central India. Army never forgets nor forgives.

Rashmi is back doing what she loved doing most, the investigative journalism, but not at Colombo. With her daughter totally cured, she now heads SE Asian Bureau from Hong Kong, of an Australian owned TV News Channel. Not that her friends have forgotten her or are willing to forget her. She is their hottest property to ever let her go. They are still very good friends.

It was supposed to be their fourteenth meeting. However, it did not take place. The seeker learnt automatically by the evening why? Throat slit body of Nazir Lone, Battalion Commander of *Hizbul Mujahidin* Lolab Valley alias Gazi, was found in the nearby jungles. It did not prick the seeker's heart nor he felt any remorse. The terrorist had been more than adequately compensated. The greed had got better of his terrorist acquaintance and so he had died. He had atoned for the betrayal of his fellow terrorists but not before relocating his family in Srinagar and ensuring his son got admitted in an engineering college in Manipal, Karnataka. For Farida, whether Nazir went to hell or heaven, it did not matter. Farida had adequate money to buy her and her sons' future. Nothing moves in Kashmir without profit. Seeker is already seeking another profitable venture. He has only some convincing to do.

Beautiful, educated, with highly appreciated thesis on social philosophy from the Delhi University, Karina could not take the humiliation of her earlier abuses from a rustic murderer and a rapist. The hurt was heart deep and her soul etched constantly by venom of *jihadi* acid, the scar that refuses to heal. She became uncommunicative; a dead recluse in her household, a fate bestowed by terrorism to many others such ill-fated women. Her father also could never forgive himself for suggesting to one of his poor relative in a remote village confronted with a similar situation, 'so what if some *Safed Chamri* was gifted to a beloved *jihadi* who had come to die for our cause.' God had rightly slapped him so, wet eyed he mourned, at the soiled *Safed Chamri* of his house. Her economics gold medallist father died in guilt and shame. Some say, he willed himself to die.

When various hues of gallantry awards were read out on 15th August 1998, all those who had been in action, were awarded. Rifleman Gobar bagged Kirti Chakra, Havaldar Pun and his ambush party commander got Shaurya Chakra and all others in the group got Sena Medals (Gallantry). Major Thapa was conferred with Sena Medal (Distinguished Service) for planning the operation, while his whiskey loving Commanding Officer, bagged the Vishist Seva

Medal, for even better planning. Of Major Jesse's party, the battalion won two Kirti Chakras, two Shaurya Chakras, four Sena Medals, but strangely Jesse's name was not amongst them. As usual, they had botched it up by recommending him for a wrong medal. Not to forget, Cook Hemant Kumar also received a Sena Medal (Gallantry) for having beaten back the *fidayeen* attack. Major Ashutosh was not awarded. One of his killed Rocket Launcher detachment commander got a minor award. One doesn't bestow largesse on failed botched up military operations. Of Major Yadav's unit, it bagged many awards, one of the highest numbers in the valley. Somehow his name also got left out in the long list of citations. He was too well decorated to cry foul for more. Only mystery surrounded the awards of two posthumous Shaurya Chakras to jawans and one Kirti Chakra, to an officer of Alpha Team of Nine Parachute Commando Battalion. People had never heard their names in their unit, except may be their Commanding Officer.

Khushbu has shockingly mellowed down. She knows that she has been used like thousand others. She along with Jan Bibi attended Nafisa's marriage. She was taken aback by the Hindu soldiers love for their Muslim officer. May be that tilted the balance.

Ah, yes of General Rocky. On that crucial day he could not witness his terrorist fight on the TV display mode due to subsequent bad weather and then it was so discovered by the duped Indian Army that the friendly manufacturers to please some more friendly countries had deliberately tampered with its thermal toy, so promised. His resignation was not accepted. Army needed people who had faced adversities. Believe the baton of this strategic corps has changed to an even more puny looking red beret creature. Don't be fooled by his size, his other staff cautioned. He is more terror-some than the terrorist. An easiest thing to do in the army and that's a last thing a soldier needs in the terrorized valley.

Captain Ahmad Khan, of Third Special Services Group of Pakistan Army that day, died an un-soldierly death. It was not the way a warrior is supposed to die. Knocked unconscious by rocking of his head on a rock, he drowned in six inches of running water stream. Retired Colonel Nazir Khan, his father when informed of his son's sad demise in extreme courageous conditions, requested for his body, to pay befitting tribute to his brave dead son. He was a bit peeved when he was informed that the body could not be handed over, in the interest of National Security. A soldier never questions, if it's for National Security. Poor next of kin of other killed soldiers didn't even know any channel to make this strange request. *Sarhad par shaheed* (on the border martyred) was all they were told or knew.

Despite they being identified as Pak Special Forces soldiers, the proud Islamic nation did not accept their bodies. They were buried in some corner of Udampur cantonment. As always, sensitive shy Indians did not attempt an international publicity coup.

At Gul's old *Madarsa* at Peshawar, a special *Namaz* was held, to honour his death for the just cause of Islam. He was a legion, a holy warrior, only a step lower than worshipping God. It was a sequel to a spectacular funeral procession, which had intertwined along various pathways of Peshawar, cheered by thousands upon thousands of frenzied spectators. Speaker' over speaker vied to outdo each other, in glorifying Gul's actions and extolling his life. Each speech terminated with one central aim, *jihad,* to destroy *kafirs* in India. Little children, aged six to twelve, their target-audience, clapped and clapped till their palms went red. A few got up screaming, "Take me, take me."

Brigadier Altaf Ghaur had been at his lunatic best, for the last so many months. To hide his disappointment, he buried his head deeper into his anti-India master files. On one such night, when he got up suddenly in frustration, he accidentally rocked his desk. The most prized photograph, of his handsome father in a Pakistan Army uniform, now in a golden photo frame, fell off the table. It fell directly atop some scattered marked maps of Indian dispositions, lying haphazardly on the floor. He picked up the photograph and was caressing the glass above with his gentle hands and misty eyes, when his eyes fell on Indian dispositions on the LoC. He bent down on his knees and gave it a second and a closer look. Oh my God, why had I never seen it before? How could he be so blind, an anklet bound dodo of unidentified magnitude. It was in front of him for so many days and it was not decipherable to his acute anti-India brain. Was it his dear father's way of bestowing on him light? Yes, the more he studied the map, the more he got convinced with the idea. He burnt the midnight oil, much to the annoyance of his waiting clerks, runners and other staff officers. By the morning, he knew he could cut off the whole of Ladakh from the rest of India, with the help of one irregular battalion. Oh no, the cost, Indians would have to pay. He smiled after so many forlorn days. The *'inpa'* in him was complete, up to the brim of his inflated chest. He stared at his father's photograph. Smiling, he saluted and said, "Thanks Dad." However there was one little prick in the whole scheme, but nothing that could not be surmounted. It was at the tip of the Mushkosh Valley on the Indian side of LoC. It was the Indian picket at Pt 4202.

And Jesse happily serves on in his chosen arm, infantry.